THE DARK-HA
WOMAN WHO
THE MOSAIC T
FEET RAISED
LOOKED UP AT HIM WITH
UNFATHOMABLE EXPRESSION IN
HER HUGE, LUMINOUS
EYES.

She was not exactly pretty. Her nose was too big and she had a wilful mouth, but her figure left nothing to be desired ... He swallowed hard and felt a flush of heat about his neck and shoulders. Yet she still hadn't answered his questions.

'Who are you and what do you want?' he repeated.

Instead of replying, she gave him a long, piercing look and then flattened herself on the ground ... prostrating herself before him as Egyptians always did to their god Kings and Queens. Worshipping him. Him? Gaius Julius Caesar! As if he were a god. He felt dizzy with exhilaration at the thought ...

'Who are you?' he breathed again. 'What do you want?'

A strange smile curved her lips. 'I'm Cleopatra Ptolemy, Queen of Egypt,' she replied. 'And I want my throne back.'

ABOUT THE AUTHOR

Angela Devine grew up in Tasmania, which gave her a taste for places off the beaten track. Later as a post-graduate student in Rome she developed a passion for mossy crumbling ruins, the golden light in the Alban hills and the *dolce vita*. After obtaining her Ph.D. in Classics, she became a university lecturer before rashly deserting the academic life to be a writer. The gamble paid off and she has published numerous romances with Mills & Boon, as well as a children's novel.

She loves travelling (her most exciting destination so far being Antarctica) and enjoys lurking in secluded nooks of libraries, preferably among leather-bound volumes. Her other hobbies are gardening, drinking tea and neglecting the housework. She lives in Australia with her husband, an American marine biologist, and her four children.

ANGELA DEVINE

FOR DESTINY OR DESIRE

A SIGNET BOOK

SIGNET

Published by the Penguin Group
Penguin Books Ltd, 27 Wrights Lane, London W8 5TZ, England
Penguin Books USA Inc., 375 Hudson Street, New York, New York 10014, USA
Penguin Books Australia Ltd, Ringwood, Victoria, Australia
Penguin Books Canada Ltd, 10 Alcorn Avenue, Toronto, Ontario, Canada M4V 3B2
Penguin Books (NZ) Ltd, 182–190 Wairau Road, Auckland 10, New Zealand

Penguin Books Ltd, Registered Offices: Harmondsworth, Middlesex, England

First published 1995
1 3 5 7 9 10 8 6 4 2

Acknowledgement

Thanks are due to my editor, Luigi Bonomi, for his unfailing tact, encouragement and critical insight, to my agents, Anita Diamant and Michael Thomas, for their support, to my daughter and son for endless hours of typing and to my mother for baby-sitting. Above all, I am grateful to my husband, Roger, for many patient hours of proofreading, cooking, trouble-shooting the computer and holding me together whenever I threatened to fall to pieces. *In angustis amici boni apparent.*

*The action of the whole book covers the period
55–30 BC*

CHAPTER ONE

What do you do when you see your father about to cut off your sister's head?

For a moment Cleopatra could do nothing. She lay mesmerized on her dining couch like a sparrow before a rearing cobra, unable to believe that the menace was real. All around her a sudden hush was falling on the crowd of people gathered to celebrate the King's return from exile. Only the seed-filled gourd gripped by one of the African dancers gave a last, convulsive rattle and then fell silent. Everyone held his breath and watched in mounting disbelief as the King staggered towards his eldest daughter, lying prostrate on the floor, and repeated his threat.

'Seize my throne, would you, bitch? Take my crown and my rightful rulership of Egypt? And then beg my pardon when the Romans restore me to power? Pardon? Pardon? You'll get no pardon from me, you scheming little whore! I'll cut your head off your shoulders! Give me a sword, give me a sword!'

Berenice uttered a low whimper and raised her head from the mosaic tiles, gazing wild-eyed and terrified at her father as he lurched into the surrounding crowd. In the guttering light of a hundred oil lamps his shadow flailed wildly across the carved cedar walls of the banqueting hall and his courtiers cowered shamelessly at his approach. Sober, Ptolemy Auletes was an unimpressive figure. Graceful, mild-mannered, even charming. Drunk, it was another matter entirely. He had been known to impale a slave with a Macedonian sarissa, spilling blood and guts all over the floor and remembering nothing the following morning. But surely he wouldn't harm his own daughter? If only someone could persuade him to dance or play a tune on the flute, wouldn't the crisis soon be over?

'A sword!' he bellowed, slamming his hand down on one of the three-legged tables and almost losing his balance as it tipped. 'Are you all deaf? I want a fucking sword! Pothinus, see to it!'

Cleopatra's throat went dry as she saw the massive, shaven-headed eunuch smile blandly and heave himself to his feet. In a moment he would reach the row of Macedonian guardsmen who stood impassively along one wall of the room, each with a short sword hanging in a scabbard at his belt. Armed with one of those, her father would be immeasurably more dangerous. And yet nobody seemed to be doing anything, nobody seemed to be taking any action to restrain him. It was as if time had slowed down and was creeping forward as slowly as a cat stalking a pigeon so that Cleopatra had leisure to notice a swarm of irrelevant details. The King's magnificent gold and purple robes, the serpent crown rearing above his forehead, the suffocating scents of rose and cinnamon and myrrh that wafted from the tables, the lamplight gleaming off the double axes hanging crossed on the panelled wall, the hairs on the King's wrist glowing in the torchlight as he reached for an axe . . .

'No!'

She was unconscious of any decision to speak, but heard the cry ripped from her own throat as she tumbled off the dining couch and ran to her sister. Her legs were shaking so badly that it was like trying to run underwater and the room blurred about her, lightness and dark and a roaring like a cataract in her ears. Then her hands dug frenziedly into Berenice's armpits.

'Get up! Run! Save yourself!'

She had heard cries like that before from women in the final throes of childbirth. A deep, animal yelping so frenzied that it was barely human. At first she thought it was Berenice and only when she felt the rawness of her own throat did she know it was her. Berenice was simply intent on escaping. Picking up her skirts, she was running full tilt down the centre of the banqueting hall towards the huge bronze doors at the far end. And she was going to make it! Please, Isis, she was going to make it, if only those gawping fools would get out of her way!

'Think you can save yourself, do you?'

The King's voice rang out, rich, triumphant, gloating. How had he got there? How had he cut off her sister's retreat? In those precious moments while Cleopatra was dragging Berenice to her feet, he must have crashed through the crowd and turned back to block her escape. Now he stood swinging the axe about his head with a manic light in his eyes and a cruel smile playing about his lips. Berenice uttered a faint moan of terror and bolted back the way she had come. Auletes lurched after her, rotating the axe and laughing uproariously.

'Cleopatra, save me! The door to the kitchen – '

Berenice blundered into her arms like a terrified quail caught in a net. Her skin felt clammy, her eyes were dilated and her heart was beating so frantically that her gold silk gown was palpitating with its movement. And suddenly Cleopatra felt a rage so intense that it banished all fear. Wouldn't anyone help her? Were two hundred people so servile that none of them would lift a finger to save her from her drunken

3

father? Flinging her arms around her sister, she turned to face the oncoming madman.

'You crazy, murderous bastard!' she shrieked. 'This isn't some slave who's broken a wine cup. This is your daughter! And it's not her fault they made her Queen when you were gone. She was only fourteen years old! What choice did she have?'

'Stay out of this, slut! Or you're next!'

His hand closed on her head, wrenching her scalp so hard that she felt the hairs being torn out by the roots. A crashing blow made her ears ring and sent her reeling to the floor. The impact winded her and while she was still clambering dizzily to her feet she saw the sight she had feared most of all. Berenice with her arms upraised and the axe gleaming, whistling, slicing through the air towards her.

'No!' shrieked Cleopatra.

There was a terrible grinding thud as the blade struck skin and muscle and bone. Berenice's head shot through the air like a medicine ball and struck the floor. The trunk stood upright, twitching for a moment, as a great fountain of scarlet came spurting forth. Cleopatra screamed again as the stickiness sprayed her face and hair and clothing. It was a horror too great to be borne. Her ears roared. Through the hot, drizzling fluid that glued her eyelashes together she saw her crazed father coming at her with his bloodied axe. She shrieked and backed away, but there was nowhere to run. A row of dining couches and small tables blocked her way, with their occupants twittering and fleeing for safety like a flock of startled sparrows. The terror that gripped her was inconceivable. Her heart beat so wildly that she thought it would burst from her chest and her breath came in tiny, fluttering gasps as he advanced on her with that manic smile still pinned to his lips. Then he roared and charged.

'No!' she screamed again.

In that instant she tasted death. Ducking and weaving and flinging herself full length, she expected the blade to slice through her neck at any instant. Her nerves and sinews clamoured with the expectation of appalling agony. Instead she heard the crash of a dining couch, the rattle of an overturned table and the tinkle of breaking glass. She staggered breathlessly to her feet to find an unexpected miracle. Auletes had slipped and was lying baffled and shaken amid a welter of blood and broken furniture.

'Catch her!' he howled at the milling crowd.

Cleopatra took a single, sobbing breath and launched herself at the mess of broken furniture with the Macedonian guards coming at her like wolves. She wrenched an ankle and tore her dress, but hurtled on, scrambling and whimpering and stepping on warm, squashy bodies until she burst free. Scanning the threatening dark mass of panelled wall in front of her, she heard a squeal of hinges and a rectangle of light appeared. A black woman stood in the doorway with a torch upraised.

'Cleopatra?'

'Iras!' she moaned gratefully, hurling herself at her serving woman.

Iras thrust the blazing torch into the face of the foremost guard, grabbed Cleopatra's arm and ran. Fortunately the quadrangle outside was filled with horses belonging to the guests and Iras simply snatched a bridle from a startled groom and hoisted Cleopatra on to a snorting bay mare.

'Ride to the Roman camp,' she ordered. 'Tell them what's happened and place yourself under the protection of Mark Antony. Not the commanding officer, Aulus Gabinius, he's an arsehole! Mark Antony, the Master of the Horse. Have you got that?'

Cleopatra nodded, felt Iras clasp her hand.

'Then ride! Ride like the wind!'

The black woman slapped the horse vigorously on its hindquarters so that it snorted and shot forward over the cobbles.

It seemed incredible that the moon could still be shining with such serene radiance, illuminating the façades of the palace buildings and turning the sea to a sheet of hammered silver. The uproar behind her died away and there was no sound but the drum of the horse's hooves and the rustle of a faint breeze in the palm trees that fringed the road. The palace gardens were vast and she had no clear idea of where the Romans had pitched their camp, but sent the horse hurtling towards the barracks of the Macedonian guard with a vague feeling that it should be somewhere nearby. Dark branches whipped at her hair, a group of drunken soldiers carrying torches and bellowing an obscene song scattered at her approach and then the horse turned of its own accord on to a sandy track near the Zoo. Cleopatra gasped and clutched at its mane for support as her eyes widened in surprise. She knew this area well. It was a park outside the entrance to the Zoo. Or it had been. Now, although the Roman army had only arrived in Alexandria that very morning, the whole place was transformed. The rose bushes and cypress trees had been cut down and in their place a huge stockade loomed in front of her. A deep ditch had been dug in the sandy ground and the earth taken from it had been piled up into a rampart topped by a wooden palisade of cruelly sharpened stakes. There was a drawbridge across the ditch, but the massive wooden gates above it were shut fast. Sliding off her horse, she ran to them and pounded on the wood, skinning her knuckles.

'Open up, for the love of Jupiter, open up!'

A bored legionary appeared on the rampart and looked down at her.

'Password?' he demanded.

'I don't know!' she shrieked. 'But if you don't let me in to see the Master of the Horse immediately, I'll have your prick cut off and shoved in your mouth, you misbegotten son of a whore! Now open the gates.'

The legionary blinked, sighed and scratched his backside. Bitch. Covered in blood too, so there must have been trouble in the city. Well, Mark Antony should be able to handle a lone woman without any danger.

'Open the gates,' he shouted to his comrades below.

The woman who stumbled into the guttering circle of torchlight inside the Porta Decumana looked half crazed. Blood spattered her from head to foot, her hair was hanging in wild, black shreds and her dress was half torn off. Yet the quality of that ruined silk gown and the gold and amethyst snake bracelet on her arm suggested that she was of high rank. It might be wise to find out what she wanted, even if she was a poxy foreigner.

'Yes. What can I do for you?' drawled one of the sentries, letting his gaze trail down over her tits and belly.

Cleopatra had been accustomed to seeing even the highest ranked courtiers falling on their faces at her approach since she had first toddled across her nursery and the insolence of this slimy little Roman toad infuriated her.

'I wish to see Mark Antony immediately,' she hissed.

'And you will kindly behave with more respect in my presence, you pariah dog. Tell your Master of the Horse that Cleopatra Ptolemy, princess of the royal house, wishes to speak to him. No, better still, take me to his quarters.'

'Yes, domina.'

More impressed than he cared to admit, the soldier summoned a groom to take her horse and led her through the forum, then off to the right where Antony's leather tent stood at the end of a long row of makeshift quarters.

'That's his tent there, the big one at the end. Wait here and I'll just ask him – Stop, you can't go in there!'

But Cleopatra had already broken free of his restraining grip and with a frustrated cry, scrabbled at the tent flap and launched herself into the darkness inside.

'Mark Antony?' she wailed. 'I must find Mark Antony.'

She became aware of a steady, rhythmic squeaking noise which stopped abruptly and was followed by a muffled oath and the scraping sound of a flintstone. An oil lamp hanging from the far wall of the tent guttered into life and Cleopatra had an impression of too many arms and legs as the figure in the camp bed reared up. No, two figures. A woman with hennaed hair, heavily made-up eyes and big, pouting lips, and a man built like a statue of Hercules, with massive shoulders, a bull neck, a nose that twisted to one side and patches of bronze-coloured curls that coiled all over his body. His head, his chin, his chest and even – Cleopatra averted her gaze – his groin. His hazel eyes, which had been wide with a mixture of amusement and exasperation, suddenly narrowed as he took in the details of her appearance.

'You're covered in blood! What happened to you? Has one of my soldiers harmed you?'

Cleopatra shook her head.

'No,' she gasped. 'It's not my blood, it's my sister's. My father, the King, has killed Berenice.'

Antony sprang to his feet, hauling his companion after him. He gave the girl a resounding slap on her fat buttocks. 'Go on, clear out of here! Take your dress.'

A flimsy, scarlet robe of Coan silk flew through the air and the girl fielded it and hauled it sulkily over her head. A moment later her sulks turned to smiles as a purse full of coins came chinking after it. Blowing Antony a kiss, she undulated out of the tent. Pausing only to knot a towel around his waist for decency's sake, Antony strode across the leather groundsheet and seized Cleopatra by the shoulders.

'Now, tell me what happened,' he instructed roughly but with an undertone of warmth. 'You say you're Berenice's sister?'

His kindness was too much for her. With a low groan, she dropped her face in her hands and burst into tears.

'What has he done?' persisted Antony. 'Has he really killed his own daughter?'

'Yes,' she choked. 'He cut her head off!'

Antony swore and slammed his hand down on his hairy, muscular thigh.

'The bastard! I should have guessed something like this would happen. Why didn't I set a guard on him?'

Even in the midst of her grief, her sense of justice was too strong to let that pass.

'How could you possibly have known?' she protested.

Antony strode back and forth in the tiny space,

running his hands through his hair and grinding his teeth.

'Because he behaved like such a madman when we crossed the frontier at Pelusium a few days ago! He had scores of unarmed people massacred before I found out what was going on and put a stop to it. But I never imagined he'd do such a thing to his own family ... Look, where is he now? Has somebody placed him under restraint?'

Cleopatra shrugged, shook her head, dashed the back of her wrist across her eyes.

'I d-don't know,' she stammered. 'I only just escaped with my own life. You see, I tried to help her. But nobody else was doing anything to stop him when I left. Cowards! I hate them!'

'Oh, shit,' breathed Antony. Releasing his hold on her, he opened the tent flap and bellowed an order in Latin, then came back to her. His face was as grey and drawn as if his own sister had been the victim instead of hers. 'I've given orders for a detachment of my soldiers to go and place him under guard. I'm sorry I couldn't save Berenice, but I swear that nobody else will die tonight.'

Cleopatra looked up at him through a blur of incredulous tears. All her life she had been taught to hate the Romans, to believe that they were little more than monsters in human form. And yet this man was sheltering her, helping her, intervening to stop the slaughter.

'Th-thank you,' she breathed wonderingly. 'You're a good man.'

He reached out and ruffled her hair, then winced as his hand came away covered in blood.

'You poor little sod,' he murmured. 'We'd better get you cleaned up. Do you want me to send for a woman to help you or can you manage yourself?'

'I can manage myself.'

'Well, just sit on the bed and I'll find you some water.'

The realization that she was safe now assaulted her so abruptly that her legs buckled beneath her and she had to sit on the truckle bed and drop her head between her knees to control the sick, shaky feeling that whirled inside her.

'Are you all right?'

His voice seemed to come from far away, against a background of roaring. When the roaring at last subsided and she raised her head, she saw that he was crouched at her feet with a bronze basin of warm water and a sponge in his hands. There was a concerned expression on his weatherbeaten face.

'I think you'd better let me help you,' he said with a wry smile. 'You've had a nasty shock.'

She sat, passive and grateful, while he used the warm sponge to wipe away the hot, sticky fluid that was gluing her eyelashes together. A shudder went through her as she saw the water in the bowl turn red and smelled the odd, metallic odour that rose from it. But Antony simply continued sponging her, whistling softly to himself under his breath, as if he were grooming a frightened horse. Before long, her face was clean and her hair restored to some kind of order, but her torn and bloodstained gown defeated him.

'You'd better take that off,' he ordered. 'I'll find you a clean cloak.'

He turned his back and rummaged in a carved chest on the ground. She tried to obey, but when she hauled the ruined garment over her head and saw that even her breastbands and loincloth were splashed with gruesome stains, horror overtook her again. With as much urgency as if they were soaked in poison, she tore them off her body and flung them to the ground. Then without warning she began to choke and crow for breath like an asthmatic in the midst of an attack.

'What's wrong?' demanded Antony sharply, swinging round. 'No, don't fight it. Put your hands over your face and breathe your own air again. You're suffering from shock, I've often seen recruits go down with it in battle. Do you feel cold? Here, let me wrap you in this cloak, that will warm you. And you must try and drink some wine.'

Her lungs were on the point of bursting as if she had dived too deep in the baths, then suddenly she managed to take a gulp of air. She was cold, so cold, utterly frozen and sick and shaken. She wanted to erupt into tears again or batter something with her fists, but her body seemed paralysed. Then she felt the rough warmth of Antony's woollen cloak, the reassuring pressure of his hands on her shoulders.

'Take this,' he ordered.

Her hands closed around the pottery drinking cup and her teeth chattered on the rim. She spilt half the wine, but the rest ran into her veins like liquid fire.

'Are you feeling better now?'

She thrust the empty cup at him, hugged the cloak around her and nodded, but another fit of violent shivering overtook her.

'Can you hold me?' she whispered. 'Can you just hold me?'

He made no reply, but crouched on the floor and took her in his arms. It was like being hugged by a wild bear. He was so huge, so strong, so warm. She had never felt such a sense of safety in her life. Burying her head in his massive shoulder, she began to sob. Yet this time the tears were healing. They fell like hot, soft rain and he did not rebuke her, but simply held her tightly. How long she remained like that she did not know, although at last she became aware not just of herself, but of him. Of the dense, masculine odour of his body, compounded of leather and sweat and campfire smoke, of the rough, bristly beard which was pressed against her cheek, of the immense power of his arms around her. She had never been held by a strange man before and the realization shocked her. Was this what it was like when men and women . . . when . . . Colour flooded into her cheeks as she realized suddenly that she was naked, apart from the haphazard covering of the cloak. She shifted uneasily to pull it closer about her and made another discovery. Antony was kneeling on one knee and as she moved she brushed against him. Beneath the rough towel that girt his loins she felt something stir and harden. Antony looked down in consternation.

'I'm sorry – ' he began and made as if to rise to his feet.

'Don't be!' she retorted, putting her hands on his shoulders and stopping him. 'Don't be.'

An impulse she didn't understand and couldn't control surged through her with all the impetuous frenzy of a flash flood. She knew only that it was something to do with Berenice being dead and her feeling that the whole world was being turned upside down and nothing mattered any more. That, and a blind, primitive affirmation of her own need to survive, to continue, to choose life over death. Winding her arms around his neck, she raised her open mouth to his and kissed him with a savagery that shocked and delighted him.

For an instant he hesitated, then his arms tightened around her and he crushed her against him. She could feel the blood drumming through her entire body in hot, coursing waves and his weight and power and size intoxicated her. Her eyelids fluttered and she swayed against him, feeling as if she would drown with pleasure from the way his tongue was thrusting hotly into her mouth. And not only his tongue. With a muffled oath, Antony suddenly tore away the towel that constrained him and stood looming above her. Through half-closed eyes she saw him as massive and burly as a wrestler with his legs planted wide apart and his male organ swollen and scarlet like a statue of Priapus. His eyes were dark and strange with desire and his breath came in shallow gulps as he gazed down at her. Yet something in his face, some half-formed question told her that he would stop even now if she asked him. Instead she lay back on the camp bed and held out her arms to him. He uttered a faint growl deep in his throat, straddled her with his suntanned, hairy thighs and then crushed her beneath him.

His body felt different from anything she had ever imagined. Not soft and covered with flesh like her own, but hard and tough and muscular. He threaded his fingers into her hair and an odd thrill sparked through her at the way his whole body seemed to tense and ripple with that slight movement. A strange, unfamiliar ache of desire began to throb through her and she felt her nipples tauten into tight buds against his chest. He kissed her with unexpected gentleness, light nibbling kisses that made her eyes flutter shut and her lips tremble as his mouth moved down over her face and throat. The kisses changed to licks – warm, moist rubbing movements like the washing of a cat so that she shuddered and giggled as her throat and ears and breasts were subjected to this extraordinary, delicious torment. Then lazily, deliberately, he squeezed one of her nipples, drawing it out between his finger and thumb, and popped it into his mouth. His deep, rhythmic sucking awoke an uncontrollable response in her groin. At first no more than a strange tingling. Then wave after wave of hot, urgent spasms so that she wanted him, wanted him now, deep and hard and thrusting inside her. Her body arched against him and she cried out, feeling her hips quiver in search of him.

A secretive smile lit Antony's face and he turned his attention to her other breast, reaching down as he did so to part the silken delta between her thighs and feel for the pleasure bud where all women love to be touched. She was already moist and shuddering, ready for him, but he wanted her more than ready. He wanted her so excited that she would whimper and moan and cling to him in a frenzy as she came. His fingers began to rub teasingly, expertly . . .

Cleopatra had never imagined that such frenzy was humanly possible. Her whole body seemed to melt and flow and throb so that she was no longer fully certain of where she ended and he began. They lay side by side, kissing and sighing and murmuring. When he took her hand and guided it down to grip his swollen organ, she felt a fresh surge of excitement. It felt unfamiliar, but wonderful, to stroke that hard, hot projection and she was eager to give him the same pleasure that he was giving her. A strange, slippery moisture began to seep into her palm and she caressed him faster and harder, feeling him grow slicker and more rigid with each stroke. Suddenly Antony uttered a savage oath and rolled over, crushing her beneath him. Groping with his hand, he lodged himself against her moist, willing opening, paused and then drove in.

There was a momentary feeling of tightness, of something resisting and then tearing. Cleopatra cried out at that brief, piercing pain. Then suddenly he was inside her, filling her with his hard, hot pole, thrusting away at her like a battering ram at a city's gates. It could have been painful, but by now she was so slick with the hot juices of desire that she felt only a deep, shuddering satisfaction at his invasion. Raising her legs instinctively, she locked them around his waist and let her head fall backwards, groaning and gasping as he besieged her. It seemed to go on for ever, but she could not get enough of his violent, thrusting masculine power. Until at last she had an indistinct sense of forces gathering, massing, building inside her and without warning something convulsed within her, catapulting her over an invisible edge. She soared, cried out, clung to Antony. For a long time they remained locked in that frantic embrace, slick with sweat, gasping for breath, their pulses hammering. Then he heaved a profound sigh, rolled off her and lay crowded beside her in the narrow bed. She found the silence companionable, drowsy and nestled into his shoulder, wanting only to drift into sleep with his warm, breathing body beside her. I'm a woman, she thought incredulously, I'm truly a woman now. I never thought it would happen like this. I thought I'd be married off to some squint-eyed bastard son of a Seleucid king and expected to bear cross-eyed children for reasons of state policy. Instead I've had . . . this. She was overwhelmed by affection and gratitude. Putting out her hand, she stroked the dense mat of hair on Antony's massive chest.

'Thank you,' she whispered huskily.

He jerked away from her as if he had been stung and sat bolt upright. His face now wore an expression of intense loathing and disgust.

'For what?' he snarled. 'For ruining you? Gods, I must have been mad to touch you!'

She stared at him in dismay.

'I thought you liked me,' she said with a tremor in her voice.

He made an exasperated sound low in his throat and slammed his open palm down on his upraised thigh.

'Don't look at me with that whipped puppy expression!' he snapped. 'It's not about liking you or not liking you. It's about your rank and status and mine. All right, I know you're only a foreigner and I'm a Roman, but it's not as though you're a street whore. You're a princess. What will your husband say if he ever learns of this?'

'I'm not married.'

He stared at her, aghast, taking in every detail of her heavy bosom and curving hips.

'Not married? But you must be at least sixteen?'

She shook her head, feeling a perverse pride that he should think her older and more sophisticated than she was.

'How old are you then?' he asked, his voice sinking a semitone.

'Fourteen.'

He stared at her, appalled. Of course, most girls were married at fourteen. His own wife Fadia had been no older than that when she moved into his apartment in Rome. And their union was only a common law arrangement like most Roman marriages. Yet a princess was another matter entirely. Antony had always liked women. In his twenty-seven years he had lost count of the number he had screwed up against walls in dark, Roman alleys or in haylofts in occupied territory, or in spacious senatorial bedrooms when their husbands were away on active service. But he had never yet deflowered a virgin of good family and it sickened him to think he was the kind of man to do so.

'I suppose you were a virgin –?' he began and then, looking more closely, saw the evidence of it with his own eyes. He shuddered. 'I can't tell you how sorry I am for this.'

Her eyes flashed. His apologies only infuriated her, making her feel hurt and unwanted.

'What's the matter? Wasn't I good enough for you?' she taunted bitterly. 'Didn't I excite you?'

'Excite me . . . ?' He gave a harsh laugh. 'If you hadn't excited me so much this would never have happened. That's not the point.'

'Well, what is the point?' she flared.

'The point is that you were a virgin of good family and I've shamed you. This incident could ruin your whole life.'

She stared at him incredulously.

'Good family? Good family?' she cried with a half-hysterical laugh. 'Oh, yes. A very good family! My mother's dead, my father's a raving lunatic and alcoholic who has just tried to carve me up and you're worried that I might be shamed by losing my virginity? That my life might be ruined? What does it matter? What in hell does any of it matter?'

His eyes followed her uneasily as she rose from the bed and began to pace restlessly about the tent, no longer seeming to care whether he saw her naked. Something about the controlled violence of her movements reminded him of the panther he had seen that very afternoon in the Zoo. Confined in a cage, the animal had prowled obsessively back and forth, back and forth with a murderous, desperate tension in its movements. This girl awoke the same helpless bewilderment and compassion in him.

'It does matter!' he insisted. 'Oh, you're young and you think the world has been turned upside down, but believe me, these troubles will pass. Life will settle down and become normal again faster than you think is possible. When that happens, your family will arrange a marriage for you. And I think it would be best if you keep this secret, what's happened between us tonight.'

Cleopatra's head jerked up and she gave him a burning look.

'Why? So that you won't get into trouble?' she sneered.

Antony shook his head.

'No, sweetheart. None of the Roman senators would give a stuff anyway, they'd just roar with laughter and tell each other what a stud I was. And your father is too dependent on Roman goodwill to utter a peep of protest about it. They can't do much to hurt me. You're the one I'm concerned about. I don't want to feel that I've caused you unhappiness, that your husband might beat you or divorce you because of what I've done tonight. You must think of your future.'

She was unwillingly touched by his concern, yet she blazed up angrily at his words.

'Future? What future? I'm not even sure there will be a future! You Romans have been creeping through the eastern kingdoms like a cancer ever since I was born. And now it's Egypt's turn. Oh, you've restored my father as King, but everybody knows that it's the Romans who will rule here from now on. And if you're really lucky, you might manage to get rid of us Ptolemies entirely. By the time I'm twenty I could be dead, or living in exile in some three-room apartment in Athens. Don't talk to me about the future!'

Antony looked uncomfortable.

'You shouldn't be like this,' he muttered. 'So angry, so full of hatred, so unhappy. You're young and attractive and you should be enjoying yourself. You ought to be going out to the theatre and dinner parties, going shopping, visiting your friends, being admired by men, enjoying a normal life.'

'Normal life?' echoed Cleopatra with a bitter laugh. 'Normal life? Do you seriously believe that a princess can ever have a normal life? I've never been shopping. I don't have any friends to visit. The only dinners I attend are state banquets and if I go to the theatre I have bodyguards to prevent the crowds from crushing me to death or maniacs from assassinating me. Tonight is probably the only time in my life I've ever been alone. Do you call that normal? It's like being a prisoner or a freak in a side show!'

Antony stared at her, appalled.

'You've never walked down the street alone? You've never been inside a fast-food shop or a bar? You've never laid a bet on a horse race or gone fishing?'

'No,' she said wistfully.

'It's cruel, really, like caging up a bird. What a pity you aren't just a house slave or an auctioneer's daughter. I could show you some times!'

She stared at him in hopeless longing, like a prisoner gripping the bars that confined her and sniffing at the tantalizingly sweet air outside. Then a crazy longing borne of the nightmare uncertainties of her situation swept over her.

'How long are you staying in Alexandria?' she asked.

Antony looked back at her with a bewildered frown.

'I don't know. A few months, probably, until affairs are stabilized here. Until I receive orders to move on.'

With a sudden movement she flung herself at his feet and seized his hands.

'Then do it!' she urged passionately. 'Show me what

normal life is like. You could manage it, I know you could. My serving women, Iras and Charmion are my friends, they could get me a disguise and pretend I was resting or having my hair done. I could sneak out to meet you and if I sold some of my jewels I could rent a little house where we could meet. Oh, please, please, it might be the only chance of freedom I ever have in my life!'

Antony stared at her in shock. All his preconceived notions about women were being turned upside down! This little eastern hussy wasn't behaving in the least like a modest, unmarried daughter of a good family. She reminded him more of various flute girls and barmaids and actresses who had shared his bed from time to time. Yet Antony himself had always enjoyed being outrageous, had loved shocking the old, traditional moralists with their noses stuck in the air like a herd of rhinoceroses. Looking down at her vivid, determined face, he felt a stir of sympathy and amusement.

'You'd get into awful trouble if your family found out,' he warned.

She tossed her head defiantly. What he was saying was true. They would all assume she was having a love affair with Antony and they would probably be right. In a private family such behaviour would be punished with lifelong disgrace. An unmarried girl who sneaked out to meet a lover would be shut up at home and never allowed out until the day she died. Never given in marriage to anybody else. Yet in a royal palace it might be different. Princesses were in short supply and useful for marriage alliances with other kingdoms. Amid the continual ferment of eastern politics, the simmering discontent against Roman rule, the loss of her maidenhead might be overlooked. I'll trade you forty triremes, five hundred talents of gold and one slightly used princess in return for access to ship building, timber lands and a guaranteed market for Egyptian trade goods. Would any princeling of Pontus or Syria hesitate for a moment? Her lips twisted.

'No, I won't,' she said. 'And even if I do, I don't care! It would be worth it to me, just to feel that I was really alive for a little while.'

Antony suddenly gave an explosive chuckle and slapped his knee.

'All right, I'll do it,' he vowed. 'Anyway, now that Berenice's dead, you're next in line to the throne, aren't you? Once you're Queen, I suppose you'll be able to change the rules and do exactly as you like.'

Queen? She hadn't thought of it until now. The idea was strange, frightening, oddly exhilarating. She had always assumed that Berenice would be Queen on her father's death and that she herself would remain absorbed in the Museum and Library until the time came for her to make a marriage alliance. Now everything was changed. She realized with a sickening lurch that they would expect her to marry her little brother Ptolemy. On the other hand, she wouldn't have to leave Egypt to marry some Seleucid prince and she would be the one who made the final decisions about everything. The Romans, the grain trade, the army, the endowment of research in the Museum and Library. An intoxicating sense of power began to shoot through her bloodstream.

'Queen,' she whispered. 'Yes, I'll be Queen. And I will change the rules to do exactly as I like.'

Chapter Two

A heavily muffled figure came striding forth from the commander's quarters of the Macedonian Guard, paused under the shelter of the colonnade and surveyed the dark and lowering sky. It was an appalling night. Driving rain came slanting in from the sea and even the fires of the huge lighthouse far out on the island were scarcely visible for the storm. At times like this Alexandria did not seem like part of Egypt at all. Instead it was just another Mediterranean city totally at the mercy of the elements.

Well, Achillas had more to worry about tonight than the weather. And, if all went well, he would soon be a very wealthy man. A gloating smile spread over his face at that thought, lending his thick and rather brutal features the look of fervour that is sometimes seen in the statues of triumphant generals. Yet it was not the expectation of the money that pleased him most. Nor the lure of promotion to the rank of supreme commander of all Egypt's armed forces if the plot was successful. No. It was the prospect of wiping out that meddlesome little bitch Cleopatra who had made his life a misery these past three years. Pulling forward the hood of his cloak, Achillas licked his lips and plunged into the storm.

Inside the palace two of the boy King's closest councillors were awaiting him with barely concealed impatience. Theodotus, a middle-aged rhetorician with a thin, sour face and a nervous manner, was pacing distractedly up and down the room which belonged to the eunuch Pothinus. Pothinus himself was too fat to pace anywhere. He only ever moved when it was strictly necessary and an assassination plot was not one of those occasions. Two couches had been pushed together to accommodate his massive bulk and with his bald head and jowly features, he looked rather like a huge caterpillar, drowsing in its cocoon. Nevertheless there was a latent tension in the way his plump, white fingers gripped his wine cup. Gazing out from beneath half-closed lids, he watched Theodotus's restless progress around the room. Theodotus had a vast knowledge of Egyptian politics and he was invaluable at winning the support of the Macedonian nobles for Pothinus's pet schemes, but he was inclined to panic under pressure. In the past there had been some regrettable and quite unnecessary murders when corruption inquiries had come too close to Theodotus. It would be a pity if Pothinus had to part company with such a long-standing associate.

'Do sit down, Theodotus,' said the eunuch in the pure, boyish treble which had been the reason for his original disfigurement. 'I'm sure Achillas will be here soon.'

Theodotus obeyed, but he sat tensed on the edge of a chair and darted nervous glances over his shoulder towards the door. The silence lengthened agonizingly.

'Something's gone wrong!' he burst out at last. 'Achillas has been caught, I know he has! And if that little slut finds out we're in it, she'll crucify us!'

Pothinus sighed. Really the fellow was becoming quite tedious, but he couldn't risk provoking him. The fool would be quite likely to go and confess, if he thought it would save his neck. Picking up a çup, the eunuch poured out a generous stream of the finest Falernian wine.

'My dear Theodotus,' he murmured, smiling tranquilly. 'You and I have run this country between us for the past thirty years and never a major disaster to show for it. Now why should this be any different?'

Theodotus took a swift gulp from the cup and, under the twin influences of the wine and the flattery, grew a little calmer.

'That's true,' he agreed, gulping again. 'Even when Ptolemy Auletes was King, we were the ones who really ruled this country, weren't we, Pothinus?'

'Indeed we were,' said Pothinus, surreptitiously re-filling his cup. 'And when Auletes was driven out and his daughter Berenice took over, we ruled for her. And when Auletes was restored by a Roman army, we were never blamed for the revolution. It was Berenice who paid with her life, not us. What's more, if Auletes had not drunk himself into his sarcophagus, we'd still be reclining beside him as his most trusted counsellors.'

'Yes, instead of being thwarted at every turn by his bitch of a daughter!' retorted Theodotus with some heat. 'Every time I spend a tetradrachm that girl wants to know about it!'

Pothinus sighed.

'It's a pity she couldn't realize that a Queen's func-tion is to dress up on state occasions, throw a lot of expensive parties and mind her own business the rest of the time,' he agreed. 'But she's so power crazed, she wants to rule the country herself. Well, she'll simply have to go and we'll see if her sister Arsinoë can do any better.'

'At least the King gives us no trouble,' observed Theodotus.

'Her brother?' said Pothinus. 'No, he's a complete dolt. No more brains than an ant. Of course, he's only thirteen, but I don't think we'll have any trouble with him.'

'So once Cleopatra is gone, you think we'll be safe?' urged his companion.

Pothinus shrugged.

'As safe as anybody can be with the Romans up in arms,' he said. 'This civil war of theirs must end sometime and, whether Pompey or Caesar wins, the victor is sure to set his sights on making Egypt a Roman province. It's too rich a prize to be left to the Ptolemies. But we'll cross that bridge when we come to it.'

At that moment there was a muffled knock on the door. Theodotus started and Pothinus smiled wolfishly.

'Come in!' he commanded.

Achillas came in, covered in rain.

'Is everything ready?' asked Pothinus, when the door was shut.

'Yes. I've bribed the guards. There can be no possible failure.'

'You won't let them cut her throat?' demanded Theodotus anxiously.

'Do you take me for a fool?' snapped Achillas. 'The people are so devoted to her that there will be riots in the streets if there's any sign of violence on the body. No. It must all look completely natural.'

In the scented warmth of the royal apartments Cleopatra lay brooding on a vast purple covered bed against a pile of Tyrian cushions. Her knees were drawn up and she was drumming impatiently on her silk clad thigh with her hand. On her small, vivid face was an expression of extreme discontent. Her dark eyes glinted dangerously, her hawk-like nose looked more aggressive than ever and her mouth was set in a stormy line. There was good reason for her to be worried and ill-tempered. She was no longer the naïve girl who had spoken so blithely of changing the rules to suit herself when she became Queen. Four years of waiting for her father to die and a further three years of struggling with the realities of power had made her realize how difficult it was to change anything. She was still impatient of conventions, but her eagerness and vitality had given way to scepticism. Where once she had expected to sweep everything before her, to convince others of the need for change, now she expected nothing. Unless it was stupidity, corruption and sheer bloody-minded obstinacy opposing her every step of the way. Her independence of thought had done little except to win her enemies. She had been forced to marry her brother and her defiance of convention in other ways had brought her nothing but trouble. Most of the nobles hated her; she knew perfectly well that there were moves afoot to depose her and put her half-sister Arsinoë on the throne in her place, and there had even been several attempts on her life in recent weeks. Small wonder that her household attendants, who were genuinely fond of her, had begun urging her to abdicate and go into retirement on a Greek island. She gave a mirthless snort of laughter. Good advice, probably. Except that she could more easily hack off her right arm at the elbow than give up her place as Queen and own herself beaten.

All the same, the tension of remaining constantly alert for danger was beginning to fray her nerves. Even here in her own apartments with her serving women Charmion and Iras, where she usually felt relaxed and happy, she was conscious of a mounting tension. Iras's little boy Timon had been sent to the kitchens to fetch their supper and was taking an alarmingly long time to return.

'Why does that wretched child have to dawdle so much?' demanded Cleopatra in an exasperated voice.

Iras looked offended. 'He'll be back any moment. Anyway, if you're so desperate for your supper, why don't you go and see what's happened to it?'

Her brother Ptolemy would have flogged any slave who used such an insolent tone to him, but Cleopatra merely shrugged. Her habit of treating her servants as intimate friends was considered scandalous by the rest of the Macedonian nobility and was another reason for their hostility towards her.

'Perhaps I will,' she said.

For some reason, she could not shake the chill feeling of dread that settled on her like a damp cloak as she went to the door and opened it. But everything outside was reassuringly normal. The two Macedonian guards on duty at the end of the corridor stood like twin statues with the lamplight winking off their long spears and polished helmets. And coming around the corner at the far end with a heavy tray in his hands and a frown of concentration on his face, was little Timon. All the same, Cleopatra felt a rush of relief as she ushered the child into the room and barred the door behind him.

'Put those on the table and we'll all have some supper,' she instructed.

There was a plate of honeycakes sprinkled with chopped nuts and a jug of the sleeping draught. Timon's eyes gleamed as he set out the cups. But just as he was gingerly lifting the jug to pour the drinks, Charmion gave a low cry of annoyance.

'Cleopatra, I forgot to show you the plans for the new astronomical observatory at the Museum!' she exclaimed. 'The architect brought them this afternoon and you were busy with the trade delegate from Arabia Petra. Do you want to see them now?'

'Yes, please,' agreed Cleopatra. 'Lay them out on the bed so we can have a good look at them.'

As she took the rolled papyrus that Charmion handed to her, she saw the disappointed look on Timon's face.

'Oh, don't start fussing, child,' she said impatiently. 'We'll come and have those drinks in just a moment and, while you're waiting for us, you can start your supper.'

In spite of her snappish tone she piled four or five of the choicest honeycakes on a small plate and handed it to the boy. His eyes lit up and he bit happily into the first one. The three women clustered around the bed and began poring over the details for the new observatory. Half the sand in the hour glass trickled away as they talked of celestial maps and the need for an accurate calendar to predict the flooding of the Nile. At first there was no sound but the hiss of coals in the brazier and the distant rattling of rain against the limestone walls of the palace. Timon finished his cakes, drank some honeyed water and began humming tunelessly to himself as he took an old piece of papyrus and scribbled on the back with a reed pen. He drew his mother Iras with a leather tunic and a long dagger and corkscrew curls all over her head. It was a beautiful picture and he was very proud of it. He was just colouring in the tunic when the first pain ripped through his belly.

'M-Mummy!' he faltered in bewilderment, half rising from his seat.

The three women turned their heads with one accord. As they did so, the boy gave a long, bubbling shriek and a jet of straw-coloured vomit shot out of his mouth and struck the floor. He slid off his chair and lay groaning and writhing on the mosaic tiles. Iras was across the floor in one cat-like leap.

'Those bastards! They've poisoned my boy!' she howled in anguish.

Seizing the child by his silk tunic, she hauled him into her arms and shook him frantically.

'Speak to me!' she begged.

His eyes rolled up into his head and his limbs contorted violently. For an instant he seemed to respond to his mother's voice and his wandering eyes met hers. He opened his mouth as if to speak, but then a fresh spasm shook him. There was another burst of vomiting followed by a fit of violent twitching, then the boy lay still.

'No!' cried Iras. 'No! No! No!'

She was on her feet now, cradling the dead child in her arms and, against all reason, trying to bring him back to life. Like a wounded animal she lunged about the room, shaking and cursing and pleading with the boy. But all in vain. When she peeled back his eyelids, his eyes were white and staring and when she put her face against his chest and listened for his heartbeat, there was no sound. Only the muted uproar of the wind and the horrified sobbing of Charmion, who stood rocking and trembling like a madwoman. Laying the child out on the bed, Iras crouched over him and lowered her head as if she meant to breathe life back into his body.

'No!' cried Cleopatra, running to her and gripping her by the shoulders. 'Iras, you mustn't! It's too late and you might swallow the poison yourself. Charmion, help me stop her!'

It took both of them wrestling furiously to drag the black woman away from her baby. Like some raving Gorgon, Iras whipped out her dagger and towered above them with the weapon upraised and her eyes flashing. For a moment she stared at them with hatred blazing in her face, then suddenly the fight went out of her. With a low moan, she collapsed on to the floor, covered her face with her hands and began to weep. Folding her arms around her friend's shoulders, Cleopatra crouched beside her, stroking her hair and murmuring to her.

'Oh, Iras, don't! Iras, I'm so sorry, so terribly, terribly sorry! They must have meant it for me and instead it's destroyed your poor little boy. Oh, how you must hate me . . . Iras, say something!'

But Iras could only choke out her grief with painful, inhuman cries.

'It's my fault too!' muttered Charmion, rubbing her tear-stained face. 'If I hadn't brought out those wretched plans, he might still be living.'

Cleopatra took a swift, shuddering breath and bit her lip.

'If you hadn't brought out those wretched plans, we would probably all be dead,' she pointed out. 'And we can't afford to sit here grieving any longer. We must decide what we're going to do.'

'I know what I'm going to do,' hissed Iras, rising to her feet and fingering the blade of her dagger. 'I'm going to find the bastards who killed my boy and cut their hearts out.'

'No!'

Cleopatra's voice cut through the air like a whiplash and she darted across the room to block the doorway with her own body.

'Iras, think!' she urged. 'Ten to one, the guards are in this plot too. If you go out there with a knife, they'll cut you down before you go twenty paces. And then they'll come in here and finish off Charmion and me for good measure. If you want to live long enough to have your revenge, you must use your brain.'

Iras was silent, breathing like a foundered racehorse.

But her narrowed dark eyes showed how intently she was listening.

'What do you want to do?' she demanded at last.

'Let me think, let me think,' muttered Cleopatra, pacing restlessly round the room. 'We can't trust the guards, so we'll have to use our wits to escape them. Wait, I have it!'

Both the other women looked at her expectantly.

'Charmion, you must run and fetch my doctor Olympus. Scream and cry out as you go and tell the guards that I am taken ill. That won't surprise them and I don't think they will try to stop you. And when Olympus comes we must throw ourselves on his mercy and beg his help. If I pretend I'm dead, perhaps he can carry me past the guards.'

'What if he's in the plot too?' demanded Iras suspiciously.

'Then you will have to draw your dagger and make him die with us,' retorted Cleopatra. 'Now go, Charmion, go!'

Within moments Charmion was racing out the door, tearing her hair and shrieking as she ran.

'The Queen, the Queen!' she screamed. 'Fetch a doctor, for the love of Isis! The Queen is dying! Let me pass, let me pass!'

Cleopatra beckoned to Iras and the two women took up their station behind the door. Iras was gripping her dagger, but her gaze kept straying to the still figure of her child and more than once a convulsive shudder ran through her athletic frame. Hesitantly Cleopatra reached out and squeezed the other woman's free hand. Her own mind was in a turmoil of shock, but her grief was not the acute suffering of a mother. Beneath her watchful exterior, her fertile brain was leaping over the obstacles that lay ahead. If Olympus could smuggle them safely out of the palace, they must find a safe refuge for the rest of the night. Perhaps one of the warehouses belonging to Charmion's father? And by dawn she must find out the extent of the uprising against her. Could it be put down or must she flee the country?

There was the sound of footsteps in the corridor outside. The anxious, scurrying movements of Charmion and a slower, more tranquil tread. Iras tensed into readiness and Cleopatra herself unbarred the door. A stocky, bearded man with crisp, grey curls and sky-blue eyes entered, followed by Charmion who barred the door, so that he was alone with the three women. His eyebrows shot up as he saw Iras's dagger and he gave Cleopatra a quizzical glance.

'You've made a rapid recovery,' he said with a dry chuckle. 'I was told you were on the point of death.'

'It's no laughing matter!' flared Cleopatra. 'Someone else has died in my place tonight. From that honeyed sleeping draught. Or the cakes.'

She stepped aside to reveal the pathetic sight of Timon's body.

'Dear gods!' breathed Olympus softly.

He crossed the room and knelt beside the boy, examined the staring eyes and rose slowly, shaking his head.

'Poor child!' he muttered. 'They're worse than wild beasts. But did they really intend to kill him?'

'No,' said Cleopatra through her teeth. 'It's me they want and, unless you can help me, Olympus, I won't live to see the dawn.'

'What can I do?' he asked.

Hastily she began to explain and Olympus suggested only one alteration to the plan. Cleopatra must pretend to be ill, but not yet dead. Otherwise the guards might demand possession of the body. Seizing a thick cloak, he wrapped her thoroughly in it and then signed to Charmion to open the door.

'And you,' he whispered to Cleopatra. 'Groan as loudly as you're able.'

Her performance was inspired. As they neared the door, she thrust a finger down her own throat and vomited violently all over the hunting mosaics in the hall.

'Aaaah!' she shrieked. 'It's like acid in my belly. Save me, you fool of a doctor. Do something! Urrrrgh!'

The guards came running, but Olympus waved them off.

'Can't you see that the Queen is dying?' he roared. 'Get away and let me find some cordial to soothe her passing.'

Through her half-closed eyelids Cleopatra glimpsed the look of triumph that passed between the two guards and rage boiled through her. I'll crucify you, you bastards! she vowed to herself as Olympus carried her through their cordon. Lowering his head, he made for the stairs at a stumbling run and then clattered down them.

Once inside his large dispensary on the ground floor of the palace, he dropped Cleopatra unceremoniously on her feet. Moments later Charmion and Iras rejoined them.

'I don't think they suspect anything!' gasped Charmion, still out of breath from the stairs.

'They soon will!' retorted Olympus, hauling down rough homespun cloaks from hooks on the wall. 'They'll be expecting me to produce a body within the next half hour, so we must be well away by then. Iras, go and check whether they have a guard around that outside door.'

But the assassins had been over-confident. Outside there was nothing but drenching rain and a chill wind blowing in from the sea. In their dark cloaks the four muffled figures were able to slip unseen through the palace gardens and find their way into the city. Within an hour, they were sheltering in a spice warehouse belonging to Charmion's father, Soranus. The slave foreman brewed hot wine with cinnamon for them and, after a hasty talk in his office with Cleopatra, woke two of his workers who slept on the premises and sent them out into the rain. One of them was back within the hour, accompanied by Soranus. The other did not return until nearly dawn and his news was not good.

'I've spoken to your spies within the palace, my lady,' he said. 'The place is swarming with soldiers, all bent on your destruction. They say that nearly half the palace guard is in Pothinus's pay, not to mention most of the Roman soldiers. If you try to regain your throne now, there will be a civil war and no great chance of success.'

Cleopatra gazed questioningly across at Soranus. The grizzled old sailor with the shrewd brown eyes was one of the most intelligent men she knew.

'Is that your judgement too, Soranus?' she asked.

He scowled fiercely and then nodded.

'Aye, it is, madam,' he agreed. 'We've talked of this day often, you and I, although I prayed to Castor and Pollux that it would never come to pass. It's time for you to leave Egypt.'

Cleopatra started to her feet and pressed her fist against her mouth. Rage swelled through her like a bubbling lava flow.

'No!' she protested. 'It's not fair! Why should Pothinus rule this land? Haven't I done my best for Egypt these past three years? Aren't I the true-born Queen of the line of the Ptolemies, close kin of Alexander the god? And am I to let some self-serving eunuch cast me out? I won't go, I tell you, I won't go!'

Iras who had been watching silently from her place in a corner of the room, rose to her feet. In the lamplight her shadow grew huge and threatening, as she crossed the floor and took Cleopatra by the shoulders. As she looked down at her friend, her face was distorted by something very close to hate.

'And if you don't, how many mothers must mourn their children tomorrow to satisfy your pride?' she demanded.

Cleopatra's eyes blazed.

'How dare you speak to your Queen like that?' she hissed.

But Iras's brown eyes still held hers unwaveringly and, after a moment, it was Cleopatra whose gaze faltered.

'All right,' she muttered bitterly. 'I'll go.'

It was shortly after dawn when the ship which was carrying them slid out of the harbour to the steady beat of its huge oars. The rain had tailed off, but the skies were still grey and threatening. More than one watcher on the shore marvelled to think that Soranus the merchant should care so little for the safety of his ships as to put to sea in the teeth of winter. Yet there was a pressing reason for it, had they but known. The life and safety of the young woman who sat huddled on the poop deck in a sailor's cloak, watching in a mute agony of rage as the ship carried her steadily away from all she had ever known. Alexandria, city of a thousand marvels, with its street lighting and its wonderful temples, its glorious palace, its works of art, its Museum and Library. Alexandria, the show place of the civilized world. As they reached the massive marble lighthouse that guarded the entrance to the twin harbours, she was overwhelmed by a sense of terror and exaltation, as if she were casting her destiny upon the grey waves that ran to meet them. Turning back, she took one last look at the vanishing city and swore a silent oath.

'I'll win my throne back, if it's the last thing I ever do. And I swear I'll take my revenge on those who drove me out.'

Several weeks later a caravan of camels made its way towards the valley where Petra, the royal city of the Nabataeans, lay tucked away from the world. It was almost sunset and, as the dying rays of light struck the red sandstone cliffs, the air seemed filled with an ethereal rose-coloured light. A narrow gorge with towering walls of stone loomed overhead, and here and there magnificent tombs with soaring columns and lavishly carved entablature stood hewn from the living rock. Yet the two women who clung to the swaying camels with sore knees and aching backs had little interest to spare for these architectural marvels. Charmion who was pregnant had remained in Alexandria in her father's care, but Iras had insisted on accompanying Cleopatra in her flight. The Nubian woman was still withdrawn and surly in her grief and even Cleopatra was too preoccupied to notice much. All her thoughts and hopes sped before her like arrows to the city that lay ahead.

When the caravan reached the central square and came to a halt under some waving date palms, she did not ask directions to the royal palace of King Obodas, as her companions expected. Instead she paid a guide to take them to the home of the ethnarch, Malchus. Here, after a note had been given to the hall porter, the two women were led to a pleasant suite of rooms, built in the Greek style looking out on to a shady colonnade and a courtyard garden. By now it had grown dark and the first stars were winking out against the dark blue backdrop of the sky. Several young slave girls appeared to help them bathe, before massaging them with scented oil and bringing them a choice of clothing. Upon careful reflection Cleopatra decided on a gown of transparent yellow Coan silk to be worn without underclothes and a necklace of violet amethysts around her throat. An hour later she was on her way to meet the master of the house.

Malchus was reclining on a divan with a gold cup in his hand when she was shown in to meet him. Everything about the room was luxurious from the scarlet embroidered wall hangings to the inlaid wooden tables, the carved ivory couches and the heady fragrance of myrrh that hung in the air. Only the ethnarch looked rather out of place, like a crocodile lurking in a placid backwater and trying hard to look harmless. His robes were made of the finest linen, but there was no disguising the tough, muscular body beneath them. The hand which held the golden cup was split by a white scar that ran all the way to his elbow and his limbs were covered with coarse, dark hair. Even his eyes had the intense, narrowed stare of a man who is accustomed to scanning long distances in fierce sunlight. His nose had been broken and looked like a clenched fist in the centre of his face and his temples were frosted with grey. And yet he was not completely repulsive. Indeed, when he smiled suddenly, showing white, even teeth above a sensual lower lip, there was a certain charm about him.

'Come in,' he growled. 'And tell me what you want.'

Cleopatra advanced into the room, eyeing its occupant warily. He showed no inclination to prostrate himself at her feet, as any courteous Egyptian would have done to a Queen, but perhaps customs were different here. Or perhaps this desert Arab with the ruined face and the bright, watchful eyes expected a similar courtesy from her. The thought sent a rush of indignation through her, but she was willing to endure any humiliation to regain her throne. With unconscious hauteur, she padded forward and kissed the ethnarch's feet.

'You do me too much honour,' said Malchus. 'Rise, Queen of Egypt, and tell me what you want from me.'

Never letting her eyes leave his face, Cleopatra rose like a ballet dancer, who has just completed a difficult solo.

'I want an army,' she replied boldly.

Malchus gave a startled gasp of laughter and the wine in the cup spilled over his embroidered robe.

'Why ask me for that?' he demanded. 'Am I King of Nabataea that I should give away armies?'

Their eyes met and held.

'Not yet,' murmured Cleopatra. 'But the day may come. In the meantime I have heard that you are the most powerful man in the country, Ethnarch. Also that you are closely related to Obodas the King, who is old and weak. Something may happen to him. An illness, perhaps. In that case, you would want friendly monarchs of neighbouring countries to recognize your right to rule, wouldn't you?'

Malchus gave her a long, assessing stare, then beckoned her towards him.

'Come, lie down at table and eat. Then you can tell me why I should give you an army.'

There were delicacies in plenty on the table, but as always in times of worry Cleopatra felt her stomach knot into a hard ball. She ate only the simplest food. Some succulent fried fish with a crisp skin and a dash of citron, green vegetables, a piece of crusty bread torn from a fresh loaf, a handful of sticky dates. And she quenched her thirst with plain water. Then she lay back watchfully and waited for Malchus to finish.

He ate sparingly enough, but his intake of wine was prodigious. Like a Scythian barbarian, he drank it unmixed with water and took it in long gulps. By the time the meal was finished, his face was flushed and there was a hint of belligerence in his voice.

'So what kind of an army do you want from me?' he barked, looking at Cleopatra from under heavy black eyebrows.

'Cavalry,' she replied. 'Archers. Foot soldiers. Enough of them to restore me to my throne. I'll need to make an attack on the land border at Pelusium and then march forward swiftly to take Alexandria by storm. It won't be easy, because the city is well fortified.'

He gave a rumble of laughter.

'You've a sound grasp of strategy for a woman,' he observed. 'And you're quite right. It won't be easy. Your brother has a competent army, most of it Roman trained.'

Cleopatra's eyebrows arched in surprise.

'Your spies keep you well informed,' she said.

'Better than yours did,' retorted Malchus. 'Or you wouldn't be here asking for my help. But why should I help you?'

They were into it now. The real cut and thrust of negotiation. And, as always, Cleopatra felt excitement rising in her veins. She might have been watching two well-matched wrestlers in the palaestra for the thrill it gave her.

'Because it's in your own interests,' she urged passionately. 'If you help restore me to my throne, I'll have access to the treasury of Egypt again. And Egypt is a very wealthy country. I'll pay you well for your support. I can offer you gold, precious stones, ivory from India.'

'Those would all be welcome,' he murmured. 'But I might want something else as well.'

His gaze travelled slowly down over her body, lingering on the swell of her breasts and hips under the transparent gown. Her lip curled contemptuously. It always came to this, didn't it? Did all men think that women were merely a nice, warm, comfortable way of masturbating? Not that she cared! She had long ago conquered her disgust at the unscrupulous way they deceived and wheedled and bullied for the sake of a few mindless moments of grunting release. And she had learnt that if only a woman could keep her head, never fall in love, never trust one of the bastards, she could make use of men's lust. They might think they were in control, but they were wrong. The one in control was the one who pouted and sighed and fluttered her eyelashes, as she did now. The one who cleared her throat and whispered huskily, 'I don't know what you mean.'

'I think you do,' growled Malchus, seizing her by the hair. Her gold hairnet fell off and her thick, dark tresses tumbled loose. He snatched at them and hauled her in, hand over hand, like a fish.

'How dare you?' she gasped.

Struggling just enough to lend spice to the encounter, she found herself pinned beneath his muscular, towering bulk. He was already breathing heavily and his face and neck were flushed with desire. Oh, well. Apart from the smell of unmixed wine on his breath and the broken nose, he wasn't unattractive. That massive, bull-like frame reminded her of Mark Antony. A pang went through her. No, better not to think of Antony! It only made her feel like crying. Better to think of how this lecherous Nabataean brigand could help her regain the Egyptian throne if only she satisfied his hunger. And she wanted her throne, wanted it with a fierce, angry passion that consumed her! Deliberately she let some of that raw, urgent longing flash in her eyes, knowing he would think it was for him. Fool! Fool! She almost laughed out loud when she saw the gleam of triumph in his gaze.

'You want me, don't you?' he demanded thickly. 'You want me hard up inside you, don't you?'

'No-o!' she breathed, twisting against his shoulder. She wrenched away from him, making sure that her groin jerked up against his male hardness, that her breasts rubbed his tunic. 'Oh, how can you? I'm a respectably married woman. Please! Let me go.'

'I'll let you go when I've screwed you senseless and not before!' he vowed threateningly and, without more ado, he hoisted up his robe and rammed into her.

Considering the circumstances, it was not bad. She had not intended to become involved, apart from an obligatory amount of stifled gasping and writhing and subdued cries of reluctant pleasure. But Malchus surprised her. What he lacked in finesse, he made up for in sheer animal gusto. To her astonishment, she experienced an involuntary thrill of intense sexual excitement at being crushed beneath that mountain of virile muscle and pounded like a batch of bread dough. Surrendering to the inevitable, she began to thrash and moan and cling to him. And when at last he roared like a rutting lion and drove deep inside her with a final, convulsive thrust, she gave a low groan of completely genuine delight. Not that it mattered. It was the effect the encounter had had on him that concerned her. She waited until he had heaved himself off her and his breathing had returned to normal before she propped herself on her elbows and rubbed her cheek down his arm like a cat inviting stroking.

'You're a wicked man,' she breathed admiringly.

His chest seemed to expand before her eyes and his flushed face beamed.

'And you're a scheming little siren,' he retorted, pinching her cheek.

She smiled at him, half shyly, half boldly.

'Will you give me an army?' she whispered.

His eyes shadowed.

'You'd do better to stay here out of harm's way,' he grumbled. 'I could marry you as a secondary wife, if you like.'

'I don't want to be a secondary wife, thank you. I want my own throne back.'

'Well, what's to say that if I help you back to your throne, the Romans won't come and take it from you?' he blustered. 'This civil war has to end sometime and Egypt would be a mighty rich prize for the victor. Don't forget how the Romans have gobbled up Bithynia and Cilicia, Judaea, Crete, Germania, Gaul. All independent nations a few years ago and now they're under the Roman heel!'

'I don't forget it!' Cleopatra said soberly. 'And nor should you. Nabataea has as much to fear from Rome as Egypt and you know the Romans' motto in war. Divide and conquer. But if Nabataea itself is ever threatened by Rome, you would be glad of a loyal ally in Egypt. Someone who could send you ships and corn and soldiers.'

Malchus was silent for a long time, brooding over her words. Then at last he slapped her decisively on the rump and gave a harsh laugh.

'All right, girl. You shall have your army and see if you can claw your way to power again. But I'll tell you this. If Pompey wins the war, you may reign a few years yet. But if Caesar is victorious, you had better pray to all the gods you know.'

'Why?' demanded Cleopatra.

'Because I know the old fox well. And he has only one ambition for Egypt. To seize and pillage it until all its wealth is his. Remember that.'

Chapter Three

It was high summer in Thessaly and warm enough to make it pleasant on the plain of Pharsalus even in the hour before dawn. By midday it promised to be a scorcher. Not that Gaius Julius Caesar cared. He was as indifferent to heat as he was to snow or hail or wind or obstacles of any kind. With his craggy, weather-beaten face and his tall, spare soldierly frame, it was obvious that he had spent much of his life in conditions of extreme hardship. Yet even at fifty-one, going bald and troubled by twinges of rheumatism, he still looked ready to tackle an army single-handed. And, if he ever succeeded in bringing his arch rival Pompey into a conclusive battle, the odds wouldn't be far off that! Pompey had seven thousand cavalry to a thousand of Caesar's and his infantry forces were larger too. But sooner or later the arrogant prick would make a bad strategic error and Caesar would crush him like an ant. It was in the hope of spotting such an error that he came out each morning to reconnoitre the enemy's movements. In his opinion, good preparation and a readiness to take advantage of the unexpected were the secrets of military success.

Treading soft-footed through the dew-soaked grass, he craned his neck to watch as the first pink flush of light crept over the distant mountain. The enemy were camped on those heights and each day Pompey sent them out to drill near the foot of the slope to display their superior numbers. That was typical of the man's determination to flaunt his power and invincibility at every opportunity. Antagonism burned through

Caesar's veins like neat wine at the mere thought of him. This time Pompey would not escape vengeance for the way he had deliberately thwarted Caesar's ambitions over the last three years! Even when Pompey was his son-in-law, Caesar had never liked the smarmy bastard and, now that his daughter Julia was dead, he would feel no remorse whatsoever about rubbing him out. He intended to capture Pompey alive, gloat over his humiliation, display him in a triumphal march through the streets of Rome, then release him and arrange for a conveniently fatal accident to afflict him.

Caesar's chiselled features relaxed into an expectant smile at the thought and his dark eyes glowed viciously. Any woman at Rome who had bathed in his charm would have been shaken and repelled by that smile. On the other hand there were many women of Gaul and Germania who had fled shrieking before his cavalry and seen that savage, exultant grin before they were hacked to pieces. Caesar sighed nostalgically. A pity he couldn't treat Pompey's troops in the same way as the barbarians, but there was a limit to what public opinion in Rome would stand for. If he wanted to keep his popularity, he would have to offer an amnesty to Pompey's troops after the battle.

Of course, there were a few soldiers up in that camp on the mountain whose safety concerned him as much as their treachery infuriated him. Brutus, for one. Servilia would never forgive him if he let her son die and Caesar didn't want to antagonize his favourite mistress. Yes, he must give special orders to his troops to spare Brutus if they captured him. But most of those who were in Pompey's army he hated like poison. Well, if anyone he specially detested was mutilated or killed in the battle, it shouldn't be too difficult to convince the citizens at home that the troops had simply been rather too boisterous to control. High spirits, that was it. After all, in spite of the thousands of Roman youths who had been left glassy-eyed and rotting from one side of the Mediterranean to the other in the last eighteen months, Caesar's reputation for mercy was largely undamaged. And he would need that glowing reputation in the time ahead, for with Pompey out of the way, there would be no other serious obstacles to establishing himself as the chief man in Rome.

A rapturous pang of excitement went through him at the realization that his dreams of power and glory were now so close to fulfilment. There had been times along the way when he had almost despaired of making it, but soon the whole world would be in the palm of his hand like a walnut for him to crush or feast on as he chose. He was proud of what he had achieved after such an unpromising start. His public career had been erratic to say the least, his progress maddeningly slow. In the past it had made him sick with jealousy to think how much men like Alexander the Great had achieved at an age when *he* was still plodding through dull provincial appointments. Yet he had achieved it in the end. Look at him now! In the finish he might even soar higher than Alexander himself, might conquer Parthia, march into India, go to the shore of the mighty River Ocean itself, where the water roars over the edge of the world into nothingness. Reluctantly, he reined in his dreams. First things first! What he must do was defeat Pompey and then look to his finances. Conquering the world would be expensive and he had already shelled out millions of sesterces on his progress thus far. The next step must be to seize Egypt, which was rich enough to supply the funds for his further expansion. It was a pity he had no son to succeed him as ruler of the world. Or no legitimate son, at any rate. But at fifty-one, he was surely still young and virile enough to beget one? Perhaps it would be wise on his return to Rome to divorce Calpurnia and marry a younger woman. A plump, fifteen-year-old virgin would be delectable. Preferably one with some brains so that he could talk to her after he had fucked her. Caesar liked intelligent women. Yes, a new wife might be just the thing . . .

Nodding thoughtfully, Caesar made his way back to the stockade and gave the order to strike camp and march for Scotussa, where they could hope to cut Pompey's communication lines. The tents had already been struck and the head of the column was passing through the camp gate when he suddenly noticed how far Pompey's troops had moved from their base. An incredulous smile of exultation split Caesar's face. The stupid cunt to let them stray so far from safety! This was the very moment he had been waiting for . . .

The battle of Pharsalus proved every bit as decisive as Caesar hoped. All over the sun-bleached grass of the plain men lay dying in their thousands in the sweltering afternoon heat. Pompey's camp had just been success-fully stormed and a messenger had brought back the news that Pompey himself had flung away his scarlet cloak and other badges of rank, mounted the first horse he could find and fled out the back gate with only three senators to accompany him. Caesar had immediately sent troops in pursuit, but was now making a brief pause to move among the wounded and dying. To his relief he saw no sign of Brutus among them, but he summoned a young recruit to his side and questioned him.

'Has there been any news yet of Marcus Iunius Brutus?'

'No, sir, not to my knowledge.'

'You're quite sure that everyone received the order that he was not to be killed in the battle?' he demanded. 'And if he was found afterwards he was to be treated kindly and sent to me?'

'Yes, sir!' insisted the youth. 'All the centurions told us that special only this morning. As far as I've heard, Brutus hasn't shown up yet, but if he does, we'll send him straight to you.'

'See that you do,' ordered Caesar, remounting his horse. Then he clapped the young man on the shoulder. 'You're brave fellows, all of you, and I'm proud of what you've done for me today.'

The young soldier gazed after his general as he watched him vanish through the gate of Pompey's camp and couldn't repress a quiet chuckle. The randy old satyr! If what they said in the taverns was true, Brutus's mother Servilia had been Caesar's mistress for twenty years or more. No doubt she was the one who had sweet-talked the dictator into sparing her precious son's life, even though he was fighting on the side of Pompey.

Once inside Pompey's camp, Caesar shook his head in amazement at the luxury he found there. Pompey's officers, not satisfied with tents, had had pavilions made out of wood with ivy trailed over them to keep out the rays of the sun. Dismounting and entering one of these, he found tables loaded with silver plates and pitchers of wine. Several soldiers were already there, looting the precious items as fast as they could go and cramming them into their rucksacks. With a few curt, well-chosen words, Caesar made them drop their booty and go about their business.

'Time enough for plunder later, lads,' he announced. 'What we have to do now is prevent the rest of the enemy from escaping.'

Before long he had rounded up the rest of his troops and set off in pursuit of the remnants of Pompey's army. It turned out to be a long night. The fugitives took refuge on a hill beneath which there was a stream. Although Caesar's troops had been fighting and marching since dawn, he called on them to make another effort and build an entrenchment between the hill and the stream, to prevent Pompey's men from reaching water. Then, tired though he was, he sat down with a smile of quiet anticipation to await the enemy's surrender. The first red streaks of a new day were showing in the sky and birds were beginning to whistle and chirp in the nearby woods when Pompey's men came down off the mountain, laid down their weapons and knelt with their arms outstretched to beg for their lives. It was a satisfying moment.

Even more satisfying were the emotions Caesar felt when he arrived back at Pompey's camp. He was met by Mucianus, one of his most trusted senior centurions, a veteran from Calabria whose face was so scarred after sixteen years in the legions that his own mother would hardly recognize him. One drooping eyelid hung over a milky and sightless eye, his poorly healed broken nose ran perpetually and his teeth were few and blackened. But he was a vicious and capable fighter and he understood Caesar's tastes.

'I've saved the best of everything for you, sir,' he leered. 'All in the back storerooms under guards who know how to keep silent.'

'Excellent,' murmured Caesar appreciatively. 'The captive soldiers first. Who do we have from my little list of most wanted Pompeians?'

'M. Valerius Scaurus, A. Pupius Silanus, P. Terentius Rufus and L. Terentius Rufus.'

Caesar's eyes kindled and he quickened his pace as he followed the centurion. The hut was dark and malodorous. Above the smell of pepper and grain and onions came the pungent stench of men who had lain chained for many hours in their own filth. Sweat, urine, faeces and the sharp odour of fear. As his eyes grew adjusted to the gloom, he saw them lying there, watching him, waiting like criminals being herded at spear point into the arena. He let the silence lengthen deliberately. Aulus Pupius Silanus broke first. Eighteen or nineteen years old with auburn hair and an aristocratic profile, he had written pamphlets attacking Caesar and given public readings of them.

'In the name of Jupiter, sir, be merciful!' he begged in a voice that verged on hysteria. 'My two brothers are already dead in this war and my mother is a widow. I beg you, take all my property, but unchain me and send me home to her.'

'Nothing simpler,' said Caesar genially. Raising his sword, he advanced and brought it down hard, cutting off the youth's right hand. The boy's screams of shock and agony had barely died away when Caesar repeated the act on the other wrist. 'Let him bleed to death, Mucianus, then have the body burnt and the ashes sent home in an urn to his mother with my compliments. Tell her he died bravely in battle and I mourn his passing.'

There was a babble of moans, pleas, agonized shrieks from the other prisoners. Their eyes leapt with terror as they realized that none of them would leave this place alive. Then Caesar began to pace the room, humming softly to himself as he pondered who should be next . . .

Ah, yes. The forty-year-old senator from Velitrae with the receding hair and the bulging frog's eyes who was shrinking back in the shadows trying not to show his mingled terror and loathing. Marcus Valerius Scaurus, who had already been pardoned once for fighting Caesar and had broken his sworn word never to fight him again.

Ignoring Scaurus's moans and shrieks, Caesar hummed softly to himself as he tied a leather thong into a noose and slipped it over the victim's head. Then deftly he inserted the sturdy green oak stick through the loop and began to tighten it. Scaurus bellowed and choked, his frog eyes bulged, his cheeks turned purple and his mouth gaped open in a hopeless fight for air. It was the moment Caesar had been waiting for.

'Hold this,' he instructed Mucianus, offering him the stick. Then he drew his dagger and hacked out Scaurus's tongue. 'I do hate a liar.'

Tossing away the warm, quivering lump of flesh, he resumed his place and began tightening the thong still further. Scaurus gurgled and bubbled obscenely, his body twitched and then slackened. It was all over. Slightly disappointed that the entertainment hadn't lasted longer, Caesar sighed and turned to the remaining pair.

'How touching,' he murmured. 'Father and son, am I right?'

Although they were chained and could not embrace each other, they were huddled together as if for mutual comfort and support. Caesar felt a flare of jealous rage at the intimacy of that tableau. Terrified, helpless, knowing that they faced certain death, the pair still seemed to extract some mysterious strength from each other's nearness. The young man who was about twenty-four, curly haired and probably handsome when his face wasn't distorted by terror, was gazing beseechingly at his father. And, in defiance of all logic, the older man's eyes were sending messages of reassurance, hope, high courage. Fools! Didn't they know they were about to die?

'And you, Publius Terentius Rufus, you who benefited from my generosity to act as a tax collector in Spain, what excuse do you have for bearing arms against me?'

The grey-haired man bowed his head.

'None, domine. But have pity. Spare my son, who only acted in obedience to me.'

'Oh, so he's an obedient lad, is he? Order him to cut your throat then.'

Smiling brilliantly, Caesar unchained the youth's right wrist, withdrew out of range and tossed a dagger at the young man's feet. He could move far enough to kill himself or his father. No further. As if he were watching an absorbing scene at the theatre, Caesar saw the pair exchange appalled glances.

'If you don't order him to do it, you'll have to watch me cut his throat instead,' added Caesar.

'Do it, Lucius,' urged the father. 'Strike swiftly before he thinks of worse. Me, then you. All over in a moment, lad, and no more pain or fear.'

The young man raised the dagger, paused irresolute and groaned.

'I can't. Forgive me, father!' he choked and plunged it into his own breast.

The elder Rufus bellowed like an enraged bull as his son toppled, dying on the dirt floor. Unable even to cradle the younger man in his arms, he rattled his chains and roared.

'Curse you, Caesar, you black-hearted monster! May

you die the filthiest death the gods can devise! May those who love you turn against you and slaughter you! May you – '

His words stopped abruptly as Caesar stepped closer and precisely, almost delicately, drove his sword into Rufus's breast. An irritating end to the little father and son drama. It always annoyed him unreasonably when affection triumphed over even a faint hope of survival. In similar circumstances, he would slit his own father's throat unhesitatingly.

More than an hour had passed by the time all his little scores were settled and the next post-battle ritual began. The checking of the plunder. There were some beautiful silver dinner services which would fetch a good price in Rome and some exquisite sardonyx cameo rings, some still with a bloodstained finger attached. Best of all was the decorative silver bowl with a figured bust of Pompey in the centre which had been used to pour libations of wine to the gods. Caesar decided to keep that as a chamberpot. It would amuse him to piss on Pompey's upturned face every morning.

Last of all was the examination of the women captives. Not the whores and camp followers, but the daughters of farmers who had supplied grain to Pompey's troops. Virgins, every one, personally inspected by Mucianus. Caesar chose the prettiest, a girl of about thirteen with widely dilated eyes and heaving breasts, quite attractive in spite of her disordered hair and torn gown. She didn't scream at first but whimpered like a beaten puppy as he led her quite kindly into one of the empty officers' tents and raped her. Only when he burst through her membrane did she begin to shriek frantically, threshing from side to side and sobbing for the Virgin Goddess Artemis to protect her. Dear me, he thought, Artemis seems to be on holiday today. Perhaps the girl would do better to pray to Eileithyia, goddess of childbirth?

When he had finished with her, Caesar generously ordered Mucianus and the men who had served him best to take their pick of the plunder and the rest of the girls. He came back to watch for a while as they began screwing the virgins. There was a lot of screaming and drunken laughter and one girl managed to stab a soldier in the throat before his outraged companions killed her. Still, on the whole he thought the men enjoyed themselves. Caesar liked to see his lads have a good time . . .

While Caesar was thus occupied, Brutus himself passed an uncomfortable and frightening night. He had escaped from Pompey's camp only moments before the Caesarean forces broke in, and crashing down the hillside, had taken refuge in a swamp, where he lay concealed among the mud and the reeds until Caesar's troops had all dispersed. Then, once night fell, trying to ignore the torment of the clouds of mosquitoes, he splashed through the muddy shallows towards the nearby town of Larissa. Arriving there at dawn, soaked, smelly and with one eyelid almost swollen shut with mosquito bites, he learnt to his dismay that the town was already in the hands of Caesar's forces. Bribing his way into a peasant's farmhouse, Brutus sank exhausted on to a rickety old couch and took stock of his situation. His horse was gone, he had only a few coins left in the pouch around his neck, and the surrounding countryside was now swarming with enemy troops. The mere thought of attempting an escape seemed like a recipe for instant death. With a faint groan, Brutus scrabbled once more inside his tunic and drew out the crushed history book which he had been reading the night before the battle. Tearing off a jagged fragment of it, he looked gloomily at the peasant.

'Have you got a duck's quill I can use for a pen?' he asked.

It was late that evening before the mud-spattered letter was delivered to Julius Caesar in the house which he had commandeered as his headquarters in the centre of Larissa. The brief scrawl was terse, ungracious, typical of the man who had written it, but Caesar read it with an expression of dawning relief.

Marcus Iunius Brutus to Gaius Julius Caesar wishes very great health.
Sir,
    I have the honour to offer you my surrender.

'Praise be to Jupiter,' breathed Caesar, then nodded to the messenger. 'Go and find the man who gave you this and bring him to me.'

Half an hour later Brutus was shown into the room where Caesar sat writing. In spite of the late hour, the heat had not abated and the atmosphere of the room was made even more stifling by half a dozen smoky oil lamps. Moths fluttered around these, occasionally blundering too close and singeing their wings so that they fell and died writhing at Caesar's feet. He sat, oblivious to both heat and insects, writing furiously on a small three-legged table, his face thrown into strange light and shadow by the guttering flames. But at the sound of Brutus's footsteps, he dropped his pen and rose to his feet with a glad cry. In three strides, he was across the room and embracing the younger man fervently, in spite of the mud and sweat and stink that clung to him. With a flash of resentment, Brutus noticed that Caesar had already found time to bathe and change his clothes, although he must have spent most of the day dealing with prisoners of war.

'Your mother will be greatly relieved to know that you're safe,' said Caesar, drawing forward a chair for Brutus. 'I gave orders that nobody was to kill you in the battle, but it's always hard to be sure that a tragedy won't happen by mistake.'

'You had no right to do such a thing,' protested Brutus hotly. 'I didn't expect any special treatment.'

Caesar resumed his own seat and gazed at the younger man with a sardonic lift of his eyebrows. In spite of the stubble growing on his chin and the flecks of grey that were already beginning to show in his dark hair, Brutus still reminded him of the surly adolescent who had glowered at him so sulkily twenty years before.

'There's no need to be so touchy, Marcus,' he reproved him. 'I'm only concerned about your welfare and it's hardly polite of you to speak to me in that tone of voice when you've come to offer me your surrender. I presume you *are* offering your surrender?'

'Yes,' growled Brutus.

Caesar picked up the note which had been delivered to him earlier, turned it over and read the back aloud.

'"The dictator has absolute authority,"' he read aloud. '"When he is appointed, all other officials in Rome lose their power, except for the Tribunes." Polybius, isn't it? Good gods! Am I to suppose that you sat reading Roman history before a battle, my dear Marcus? How very learned! Most of my soldiers, if they're able to read at all, peruse handbills of forthcoming gladiatorial attractions or plod through pornographic novels before they go into battle. Still, your tastes may change with experience. You haven't spent a lot of time in actual fighting, have you?'

'No,' muttered Brutus.

He began to have the uneasy feeling he had often suffered in his youth that Caesar was systematically humiliating him by mocking his weaknesses. Before he could be sure that he was being teased, Caesar rose to his feet, picked up an earthenware jug and moved towards him with a hospitable smile.

'Will you take some wine? It's well watered. I know your tastes are abstemious, unlike those of your recent leader. You know, I've always thought it odd that you've supported Pompey in this civil war. I would have expected you to hold a grudge against him.'

'Because he killed my father, you mean?' blurted out Brutus.

There was an odd, defiant intonation in his voice, but Caesar simply smiled mildly at his words.

'Yes,' he agreed. 'If you choose to put it that way. Tell me, isn't it a little odd that you should support him in this war against me, when I've always been on such friendly terms with your family?'

'I suppose so,' said Brutus and was enraged to hear a tremor in his voice as if he were a belligerent adolescent. 'But I thought Pompey had better reasons than you for going to war and I don't much like the friendly terms you've been on with my family.'

'Don't be petulant, Marcus,' warned Caesar. 'It doesn't suit you. And if you're referring to your mother, I must remind you that she's a grown woman, quite capable of deciding for herself where her affections lie. What's more, while I don't wish to rub it in, I think you ought to be rather glad of the attachment that exists between us, seeing you owe your life to it.'

Brutus smarted silently, scowling at his tormentor.

'Still,' continued Caesar in a warmer tone. 'I didn't

send for you just so that I could rake over past griev-ances. Tell me, how old are you now?'

'Thirty-seven,' replied Brutus warily.

'H'm. It's really time you were further advanced in your career than you've been so far. How would you feel about taking a post in my administration?'

'What do you mean?' asked Brutus. 'I don't want to do anything disloyal to Pompey.'

Caesar smiled, that unusually sweet smile which had made women fall helplessly in love with him since he was two years old and had often led men, too, to act against their better judgement.

'Pompey's hardly been very loyal to you, has he?' he pointed out gently. 'Running off with only three sena-tors and leaving the rest of you to fend for yourselves. In any case, Marcus, I think you can safely assume that Pompey's day is now well and truly over. You may not realize it yet, but his defeat at Pharsalus will undoubtedly be the last important engagement of this civil war. And if it makes you feel bad to think of accepting favours from me, console yourself with the thought that there will soon be plenty of others in the same boat. Now that the war is finally over I'll need all the intelligent, capable men I can muster to rebuild Rome's shattered institutions.'

Brutus raised one eyebrow wearily at this blatant flattery, but he was more interested than he wanted Caesar to guess. Like any Roman noble he had em-barked on a career in the public service, but so far he had not distinguished himself dramatically. It was ten years now since he had joined his uncle Cato in wrest-ing Cyprus from Egyptian control and shipping its treasures to Rome. Even his stint as quaestor in Cilicia under Appius Claudius was five years in the past and his only notable achievement there had been to marry the boss's daughter. Much as he loathed the thought of accepting favours from Caesar, the prospect of a comfortable, well-paid administrative job dangled before him like a juicy plum.

'What sort of post did you have in mind?' he asked, keeping his voice deliberately indifferent.

'Probably the governorship of one of the provinces as soon as it can be arranged.'

'That's generous of you,' said Brutus, unable to hide the flare of excitement in his eyes.

'Yes, it is,' murmured Caesar. 'Of course, I shall want something in return.'

'What?'

Caesar leaned forward confidentially as if they were simply two friends chatting over a cup of wine. 'I believe you know where Pompey's fled to. I'd like you to tell me.'

'Why?' demanded Brutus. 'What are you going to do to him?'

'Marcus, Marcus,' chided Caesar. 'I've just accepted the surrender of many thousands of Pompey's soldiers, yourself included, and given them all an honourable discharge so that they can return to their homes. Most of them were men with no claim on me whatsoever, whereas Pompey was once my son-in-law. What do you think I'll do to him?'

Brutus frowned. An uneasy expression flickered across his face. Should he divulge what he knew? But, after all, Caesar could soon find it out from other sources and what he said about Pompey's disloyalty was all too true. Besides, a provincial governorship wasn't on offer every day. Brutus made his choice.

'He's fled to Egypt,' he said.

It was the twenty-fourth of September, a day after

Octavian's fifteenth birthday, and even by the third hour it was stinking hot. Once again the calendar had fallen out of phase with the seasons so that instead of being autumn, it was mid summer. Yet in spite of the heat, Octavian's hands were cold and clammy with excitement as he dressed. Not in the fine woollen tunic embroidered with purple which his family's senatorial rank entitled him to wear, nor even in the white toga of manhood which he had hoped in vain that his stepfather Philippus would give him for his birthday. But Philippus had said he wasn't mature enough yet for the manly toga. No. Octavian was getting dressed in a patched and threadbare tunic which he had stolen from one of the house slaves to use as a disguise. For Octavian was planning a secret adventure to celebrate his birthday. His lip curled scornfully as he remembered the official celebration of the day before, with the birthday cake and the incense offered to the household gods and all his relatives clustered around drinking his health. That had been deadly boring, but Octavian was planning something far more exciting. He was going to get laid.

He had already made one hesitant attempt at losing his virginity, but that had been a humiliating failure. The blood rushed to his soft-skinned cheeks as he remembered how he had cornered Phyllis, his mother's maid, in a spare back bedroom and with his heart pounding had reached out and squeezed her breast. Phyllis had simply stared at him incredulously and then burst out laughing. Even now it set his teeth on edge to remember it although he had had his revenge a few days later by having her stripped and flogged for breaking a glass jug. Well, nobody would be given the chance to laugh at Octavian today. By loitering and snooping in the slaves' quarters, he had discovered the whereabouts and prices of several brothels in the Subura, an unsavoury district where nobody was likely to recognize him and where his money would be as good as anyone else's. All he had to do first was slip out of the house unseen by his mother or his stepfather or his elder sister Octavia. If Octavia saw him, she would start fussing about wrapping up his chest so that he didn't have an asthma attack, or sending a slave to protect him wherever he was going.

Impatiently Octavian sucked in breath through his teeth and glared at himself in the bronze hand mirror that he was holding up to his face. If only Octavia would stop treating him like a puny baby. It infuriated him the way everyone fussed over him and under-estimated him. Just because he wasn't good at riding or swordplay and because he had had those frightening asthma attacks from infancy onwards, nobody thought he could do anything. Well, he would show them! One of these days he would show them that he was a force to be reckoned with. Critically he ran a comb through his blond, curly hair and peered more closely at him-self. Really he was remarkably handsome with his unusual blue eyes and the sweet, serene expression of his face. It was a pity that his eyebrows grew together over his nose and that he was so short and slightly built for his age. Perhaps he ought to get platform shoes to make himself look a little taller? He filed the thought away for future reference and took his neatly folded cloak out of his clothes chest. It would just about suffocate him in this heat, but he needed some-thing to cover his rags while he slipped past the hall porter. He could always leave it in a clothes locker at the nearest public baths and collect it on his way home.

Feeling breathless with excitement, Octavian made

good his escape into the street outside. On the far wall of the apartment block opposite, he saw some gigantic graffiti scrawled in red chalk. JULIUS CAESAR, MURDERER! CAESAR, WHERE ARE OUR BOYS? A mingled surge of resentment and pride rose in his breast. Julius Caesar was his great-uncle and, while it enraged him to see people criticizing him so openly, he felt a thrill at this evidence of Caesar's importance. Not that he had anything but the haziest memories of his great-uncle, for he had only been four years old when Caesar left for his nine-year killing spree among the Gauls. Yet when he had heard of Caesar's defiant crossing of the Rubicon and his march into Italy the previous year, he had been alight with enthusiasm and envy. Of course, his stepfather Philippus had launched into his usual gloomy muttering about the wicked, vile inhumanity of any civil war, but Octavian had taken no notice. His biggest secret ambition was to be introduced to his great-uncle Julius, who would shake him by the hand and instinctively recognize his fine qualities which had lain hidden for so long. Perhaps he would even adopt him?

Smiling pleasurably at this fantasy, Octavian strode down the uneven footpath and headed for the nearest public baths. These were located in a vast, brick building off the Vicus Sabinus. Apart from its massive size, there was nothing impressive about the exterior, but once inside it was a different matter. The huge quadrilateral exterior walls enclosed thirty-two acres of porticoes full of shops, gardens and promenades, gymnasiums, massage rooms, snack bars and libraries. Octavian made his way down an echoing public hall which was often used for literary readings but was at present empty, to the entrance to the main baths. Here the noise was deafening. The shouting and splashing of boys hurling themselves into the hot and cold pools, the volley of sound from a handball court next door, the patter of masseurs touting for customers. But Octavian barely paused to observe the marble dolphins squirting jets of water or the scented, steamy air that drifted in a haze above the main pool. He was too anxious to be on his way. Snatching off his cloak, he handed it across the counter along with a quarter as coin to a bored-looking attendant. The attendant blinked as he glanced from Octavian's expensive cloak to his threadbare tunic, then his lips curved into a sardonic smile. He probably thinks I stole that cloak! thought Octavian indignantly, yet there was no reason why he should explain himself to a bath house slave. So he simply accepted the bone tile with the number on it which the attendant pushed across the counter to him and spitefully retreated without offering a tip.

Well, now the big moment was approaching and all he had to do was find his way to the Subura. At the thought of what might follow, his stomach contracted suddenly and began to churn. To his embarrassment, he realized that he urgently needed to go to the lavatory. Octavian always avoided the public latrines if he possibly could, because although they were warm, scented and properly drained, he detested having to uncover himself and take a crap in full view of dozens of other people. Yet when he sidled uneasily into one of the semicircular cubicles with its twelve circular holes set above a channel of continuously flowing water, nobody took the slightest notice of him. He gripped the sculptured dolphin arm rests and strained quietly in an agony of embarrassment. How could they sit there laughing and joking and inviting each other to dinner and discussing the horse races and be so unaware of the vulgarity of what they were doing? It was indecent! If I ever build a public lavatory, there will be separate cubicles for everyone, vowed Octavian.

At last, after a judicious use of water and scented oils and a towel which cost him half an as, Octavian was on his way again. The Subura was the gully between the Viminal and Esquiline hills, opening out of the Argiletum, and its squalor was extreme even for Rome. Hundreds of dark alleys twisted away in the shadows of densely packed, towering, ramshackle apartment blocks. Naked children played amid the filth of carelessly emptied chamberpots, rotting cabbage leaves and foraging rats. Once Octavian took a wrong turning and found himself in a cul-de-sac with a stinking cesspool at the end. The stench was overpowering, a dank, earthy pungent smell that made him choke for breath. A dead baby was bobbing face downwards among the floating turds and filth and another lay red and screaming at the edge of the pool. Holding his nose, Octavian advanced a few steps and peered at it. Newborn, obviously, from the cord and placenta that were still attached. No doubt some impoverished family couldn't afford to raise it and it was probably just another worthless girl anyway. He took another step closer, peered at the child's sex and was pleased to find his guess confirmed. Turning to go, Octavian saw a mongrel dog slink out from a gap between two buildings, lope across to the pool's edge and begin tearing at the placenta, swallowing it down in hungry gulps. He grinned unpleasantly. No doubt the baby would soon follow. Well, one more of Rome's little social problems tidied up . . .

It took him another half hour to find a brothel that looked clean enough to appeal to his fastidious tastes. Even so, it was rather squalid. A huge, leering black man stood outside with his arms folded and smirked as he watched Octavian's hesitant approach.

'You want a girl?' he asked. 'Good value. Hand massage twenty sesterces, full screw thirty sesterces, blow jobs on special this month, only thirty-five sesterces. Payment in advance.'

Octavian recoiled. He hadn't expected something quite so . . . quite so . . . blatant. But, after all, this was what he had come for. He swallowed hard.

'Who would you recommend?' he croaked. 'For a screw.'

The black man held out his hand and counted Octavian's thirty sesterces.

'Lupa,' he said in a friendly voice. 'She'll make your cock so hot you'll think it's going to explode. And if it's your first time she'll show you the ropes.'

Octavian's face flamed.

'It's not my first time!' he denied hotly.

The black man's grin widened.

'If you say so,' he agreed amiably, slipping Octavian's coins into a pouch at his belt. 'Go on, upstairs. Third floor. Second door on the right.'

Having handed over his money, Octavian was left with little choice but to obey. His legs felt shaky and his mouth was dry as he climbed the dark, stone stairs. The air was as hot as an oven, filled with the stifling smells of garlic and rancid oil and some foreign spices. His hand trembled as he knocked on the door marked LVPA. The door swung open, revealing a room filled with blinding sunlight and containing nothing except a black haired woman naked to the waist, with the largest boobs he had ever seen in his life, and a narrow bed. But at least the place looked clean. He gazed at her.

'A-are you Lupa?' he stammered.

Her eyebrows rose wearily as she took in every detail of him. Well, at least she didn't laugh.

'Yes, I'm Lupa,' she said in a resigned voice. 'What'll it be, love? Massage, screw, or blow job? Or the lot?'

Octavian's eyes widened. Was there anyone so virile that he was capable of enduring the lot?

'Just the screw, thanks,' he said hastily.

Lupa picked up an hourglass with enough sand in it to last about a quarter of an hour and tipped it upside down.

'You've got until that runs out,' she said.

Whether it was the pressure of listening to those softly hissing grains of sand, or the huge, intimidating warmth of the woman beside him, or just the strangeness of the whole situation, Octavian didn't know. But to his intense humiliation, he could do nothing. Whatever Lupa tried, his prick still dangled uselessly like a pathetic white worm. He was almost in tears by the time the last grain of sand ran out and he had still achieved nothing.

'Never mind, love,' she said briskly, rising to her feet and hitching down her skirt. 'Come back in a year or so when you're a bit bigger and we'll give it another try.'

Octavian's fury erupted. Clenching his fist, he smashed her in the mouth so hard that she gave a startled gasp and a tooth shot forward, followed by a jet of blood.

'You bitch!' he shrieked hysterically. 'You filthy, disgusting bitch! This is all your fault. How could any decent man possibly want you when you've given yourself to hundreds? Slut! Whore!'

She stared at him incredulously for an instant, then uttered a long, primal scream, hooked her fingers into talons and sprang for his eyes. If the Negro hadn't come pounding up the stairs and separated them, Octavian wondered whether he would have survived that nightmare onslaught. In less time than it would have taken half an inch of sand to trickle through the glass, he found himself outside on the street, with his face stinging, his wallet missing and every bone in his body feeling as if it were broken. He ran until he was out of breath and finally sank down in a doorway, unable to hold back his sobs any longer.

'Bitch,' he moaned to himself, rocking backwards and forwards. 'Slut. Whore.'

He didn't realize that he was sitting outside a similar establishment to the one he had just left, so he was surprised when a tall, handsome man of about forty came to a stop in front of him, put a hand on his shoulders and spoke to him in a cultured voice.

'Dear me! What's this? A pretty little boy crying in the streets? Whatever has happened to you, my lad? Were you set upon by cutpurses?'

'Yes,' sobbed Octavian, taking refuge in the welcome lie. He raised his eyes to his companion's face and stiffened in shock and dismay. It was Publius Valerius Cotta, one of his stepfather's closest friends whom Octavian had met at least a dozen times at receptions and dinner parties. Yet to his relief and faint resentment, Cotta showed no sign of recognizing him. But what on earth was such a man doing here? A rich, handsome senator, married to a woman of good family, with children of Octavian's own age? His question was soon answered as Cotta's hands grew more caressing on his shoulder.

'Why don't you slip upstairs with me, dear boy?' he suggested in honeyed tones. 'There's a room I often rent there and you're far prettier than any of the boys who usually accompany me. I'll pay you a good price, you know.'

Half revolted, half excited by that lingering, caressing touch, Octavian allowed himself to be led inside in a daze. What followed both thrilled and disgusted him. It was not the way he had expected to lose his virginity, but it was a violent, sensual experience for all that. Cotta led him up the stairs to a room very similar to the one he had just left. Barring the door securely behind them, the senator drew Octavian into his arms and smiled down at him.

'What smooth skin you have,' he murmured. 'And such fresh little pink lips. I'm sure they must taste as tender as a girl's.'

The muscular arms tightened around him and Octavian felt a tremor of confusion and panic as he realized the older man was about to kiss him. He opened his mouth to gasp a protest, to plead for release, to say that he had changed his mind, but it was too late. Cotta's mouth came down teasingly on his and the sensation, though strange, was unexpectedly exciting. This was not the soft, melting texture of a girl's mouth that he had dreamed of. It was harsher, rougher, indefinably threatening. Cotta's chin brushed against his and he felt the bristle of shaven skin. A strange, tingling sensation spread through him and there was a stirring in his groin. Instinctively he put his arms around the older man's waist. With a groan of pleasure Cotta pulled him closer and darted his tongue into the warm interior of Octavian's mouth. Octavian shuddered at that intimate exploration. Then, hesitantly and because he thought it was expected of him, he moved his own tongue in the same way.

'Oh, such sweet, shy little kisses,' murmured Cotta, nibbling his way across Octavian's cheek and up to his ear. 'One would think you had never done this before in your life.'

'I –' began Octavian and broke off with a gasp as the senator reached down to the growing bulge in his tunic and began rubbing it playfully.

'Naughty little thing. You enjoy this, don't you? Pretending you're so innocent and yet here's your cock as hot and hard as a sausage. Well, I'm going to have a taste of your sausage, lad. Stand still, there's a good boy.'

Octavian couldn't have moved if his life depended on it. He felt as if he were frozen to the spot with shock and embarrassment as Cotta dropped to his knees before him, lifted the tattered tunic and brought his warm, demanding mouth down on to Octavian's male organ. A startled quiver went through him so that he jerked against the older man's teeth.

'Little tease,' murmured Cotta and began to suck.

To his intense shame and delight Octavian discovered that it did not need a woman's mouth and hands to stimulate him. Indeed his whole body seemed to be on fire, as if he were suffering from a fever and he found that his breath was coming in short, shuddering bursts through his nostrils. Cotta paused in his work and looked up at him, letting the tip of his tongue trail lazily just below the sensitive glans of Octavian's cock.

'I'm sure you'd like to do a little sausage tasting too, wouldn't you, sweetheart?' he murmured. 'Come over on to the bed and we'll get cosy so that we can enjoy ourselves together.'

Never in his wildest moments had Octavian expected to find himself with his head thrust into the fiercely bucking groin of one of his stepfather's friends. In a way it was disgusting. The hair, the rank masculine smell, the swollen red organ, the deep, animal groans that Cotta kept uttering. And yet shamefully, in some inner part of his soul, he had to admit that he was enjoying it himself. Not only the exquisite, sensual torment that the older man was rousing, not only the way his cock was throbbing and oozing as if it were ready to explode, but also the sense of power that it gave him. The overwhelming, red-hot, triumphant surge of exultation that he felt when at last he convulsed and shot arrogantly straight down the senator's throat.

'Mm. Wonderful, sweetheart. So passionate,' murmured Cotta, indistinctly. 'Now, my turn for a little fun, I think.'

Octavian was still shaken and gasping, his pulses hammering, so that he scarcely realized what Cotta was doing until it was too late. With a series of swift, expert movements like a spider bundling his prey, the older man hoisted him up, swung him over on all fours and uncovered his backside as if he were about to beat him. He didn't beat him. What he did was worse.

'Such a pretty little bum,' he whispered and, positioning himself against it, drove shamelessly in.

Octavian cried aloud as a shaft of pain stabbed through him like a red hot lance. He tried to twist away, to gasp his indignation, but Cotta was utterly ruthless. Clapping one hard, powerful hand over Octavian's mouth, he continued to thrust violently in and out of him with no thought for his pain or indignity. Octavian felt a flush of sweat break out all over his chest and face. His arms and legs trembled and tears pricked in his eyes. He wondered desperately whether he was going to shit himself. Half suffocated by Cotta's grip, he longed to break free, but realized with a leaden sense of panic that struggling would probably be useless. What if he told Cotta who he was? No, he dared not! The humiliation would be too great. All he could do was to endure this agony. But I'll pay him back for this one of these days! he vowed silently. The bastard, the bastard! Doesn't he know how much he's hurting me? It went on and on until at last, mercifully, Cotta stiffened and cried out.

Octavian felt a revolting sense of something slimy bursting inside him. Then Cotta slid free and dismounted him. Gritting his teeth, Octavian kept his eyes downcast to hide the murderous rage in them. Somehow he had the feeling that, in spite of Cotta's compliments and caresses, he might be a dangerous man to cross. But one day I'll have the power, Octavian vowed. I won't be the one who gets fucked over any more! I'll be the one who does it to other people. Something sticky was running down his buttocks and thighs. He reached for the dirty bed cover and rubbed at himself fastidiously, feeling a dreadful sense of revulsion as if all the water and towels in Rome would never cleanse him. Turning his face to the wall, he closed his eyes and wished he had the courage to kill himself. It was an agony too deep for tears.

'Everything all right?' asked Cotta lightly, rising to his feet and pulling on his tunic.

'Yes.'

'Well, I must be away then, dear boy,' Cotta said, tossing a purse full of coins on to the bed. 'Duty calls, you know, and these are busy times for men of rank like me. I don't expect a boy of your class to understand it, but word has just come through that Julius Caesar has won a decisive battle at Pharsalus. The civil war is over.'

CHAPTER FOUR

Inside the limestone palace of the Ptolemies Caesar sat drumming his fingers angrily on a finely carved citrus wood table studded with rubies. Even the fact that he had now been moved into the most magnificent guest chambers at his own insistence did little to quell his ill-humour. He was far too preoccupied to notice the gold-leafed pillars, the delicately painted landscape frescos on the walls, the gilt couches covered with lavish scarlet cushions. All he could think about was his own fury at being thwarted. His arrival in Alexandria had been marred by the shock of Pompey's death and he was still trying to grasp what had happened. The news had been brought by an eager messenger who rowed out to his fleet of warships as they came to rest in the eastern harbour. A greasy little jackal of a man who was exultant at the message he bore. On the orders of the King, he announced importantly, Caesar's enemy Pompey had been assassinated as he came ashore in Egypt. Would Caesar care to inspect the severed head for himself? Infuriated at this Egyptian interference, Caesar had thrust the fellow aside and ordered his own sailors to ferry him ashore. Now he sat in the finest guest suite of the palace, trying to sort out his feelings and intentions.

Uppermost in his response was a sense of acute disappointment. For months he had looked forward gloatingly to the moment when Pompey would be in his power. He had even intended to spare his adversary's life, at least for a brief time. It would have been worth it to see the exquisite humiliation in Pompey's noble features as he knelt and begged for mercy. Now that pleasure had been snatched away from him and he was furious at being robbed of it. Ptolemy and his advisers would pay for their blunder and they would pay in the most painful way possible. By watching Egypt become a Roman province. A feral smile crept over Caesar's rugged features.

It was seventeen years since he had first put the proposal to the Roman Senate that they should annex Egypt and all that time the country had tugged at him like a lodestone. The crippling debts of military and political life had always made it shine like some fabulous jewel held tantalizingly out of reach. Well, now he meant to have it, whether the Senate liked it or not. With Pompey out of the way there would be nobody of sufficient stature to deny him anything he wanted. The realization sent a surge of exultancy jolting through him. He heard the ringing in his ears that usually preceded one of his epileptic fits and clapped both hands to his head in dismay.

'Careful. Careful, Gaius,' he admonished himself.

Rising to his feet, he strolled around the room, taking deep, calming breaths. When the roaring in his ears subsided, he sat down again and stared at the litter of documents that had been brought to him from Pompey's possessions. Egypt must be his, but how was he to do it? Caution dictated that he should wait until he had adequate troops to take over the country without risking his own annihilation. But Julius Caesar had never been cautious when it came to setting his goals. Nothing made him feel so vividly, gloatingly alive as the scent of danger. He enjoyed taking risks in much the same way as other men enjoyed watching chariot racing. And the fact that he might be the one to graze too close to the turning post and come screaming to a halt in a welter of blood and dust only added to the thrill.

He toyed with the reckless urge to announce the annexation of Egypt immediately and then watch the fur fly. The temptation was almost irresistible, especially since it would offer the chance to pay off a few scores. There were senators in Rome who would die of envy if he pulled off such a diplomatic coup. Not only that, but there were people here in Egypt who deserved to see what Roman anger could really mean. That fat slug of a eunuch Pothinus, for a start. The fellow seemed to think he ruled the country single handed. And he was so stingy that he would pick a quadrans out of the dirt with his teeth! In fact, he had actually had the audacity to serve Caesar and his troops mouldy grain and refuse them funds from the royal treasury. Well, let him see how he liked tasting Roman revenge. For some reason Caesar had a sudden vivid memory of a gladiatorial contest in Rome, where one of the competitors had slit the other one open, spilling his guts into the arena like sausages. What a pleasure it would be to do that to Pothinus! Impossible unfortunately, but perhaps a similar agony could be achieved by diplomatic means. And, while he was at it, he would bring those arrogant Ptolemies to their knees.

Of course it might be easier to leave them to scratch each other's eyes out. According to his scouts they were already doing their best to achieve exactly that. From what he heard the boy King and his sister/wife Cleopatra were camped on opposite sides of the Syrian border, using their respective armies to try and annihilate each other. Yet the hostilities so far had been inconclusive and Caesar was in no mood to wait any longer. Better to depose them both from their thrones and seize Egypt for Rome once they had been safely induced to commit suicide. By then he should also have adequate troops to ensure that the transition to Roman rule went smoothly. The matter must be handled carefully to avoid the least suggestion of illegality or impropriety, of course. Caesar had always prided himself on that. Both Ptolemy and Cleopatra must be given a chance to appear before him and plead their causes. After that he would produce a fresh will from their father Auletes, which . . . er . . . had just come to light in Rome and which showed conclusively that he had bequeathed Egypt to Rome, not to his children. It would be sad, but understandable, if they both slit their wrists on learning of that. Neat. Very neat.

Opening the door of the room, Caesar shouted for fresh papyrus to be brought to him. With a sour smile, he sat down and began to write. He would begin with the girl and settle the boy later. The first step was to issue a legal summons for both monarchs to appear before him to plead their causes. The boy King would find no difficulty in that, since his forces held the road from Alexandria to Pelusium. But for Cleopatra it would be no easy matter, with an army barring her way. How tragic if she were to be killed on the way . . .

Nobody had ever seen anything like the rage of the Queen when Caesar's message was delivered to her. At first she was taken aback by his blandly worded summons. It said simply that he wished her to appear before him and plead her right to the throne. This sent a lightning bolt of pure, unadulterated fury through her.

'By what right does Caesar set himself up to judge who shall hold the throne of Egypt?' she snapped at the messenger.

The man shrugged with barely concealed insolence.

'He is master of the whole Mediterranean now, madam,' he reminded her. 'He can judge anything he pleases.'

She glared at him, outlined as he was against the bright, hurtful blue of the sea and the searing radiance of the sand. Curbing her anger, she dismissed the man with a wave of her hand. When he had left, she turned fiercely to Iras.

'What do you think this means?' she burst out.

'I think it's a trap,' growled Iras. 'If you're fool enough to try and go to Egypt he's hoping you'll be killed by Ptolemy's troops on the way. After that he can poison Ptolemy and take Egypt as a province for Rome.'

Cleopatra ground her teeth.

'That's what I think it means, too. But what else can I do? If I don't go, he'll seize my throne anyway.'

'You could just give up and go into exile somewhere,' suggested Iras, stepping back out of range of any possible missiles.

A wave of rage and humiliation swept through Cleopatra at the mere words. Give up? Own herself beaten? Let that fat, smug-faced, smirking eunuch oil his way into the Roman's good graces and be appointed chief treasury official after the takeover?

'Never!' she shouted. 'There must be some other way. Iras, when Mark Antony was in Egypt years ago, he told me a lot about Caesar. He said his greatest weakness was for women. According to Antony, Caesar would squander fortunes on his mistresses, sometimes just in payment for a single night.'

Iras caught her drift at once, but rolled her eyes dubiously.

'And you think Caesar would squander Egypt on you for a single night?'

Cleopatra paced stormily around the tent, crossing her arms and flailing herself with her open hands.

'It's worth a try, isn't it?'

'Is it? Have you forgotten how the Romans stole the kingdom of Cyprus from your uncle Ptolemy a few years ago and forced him to slash his wrists?'

Cleopatra paused in her pacing and a spasm of hatred crossed her face.

'I've forgotten nothing,' she hissed. 'All the same, I'm going to try.'

The night sky was spangled with stars and a fresh breeze was blowing from the sea, sending the waves slapping against the stone walls of the palace, when a fisherman called Apollodorus stepped ashore with a bedroll slung casually over his left shoulder. Whistling idly, he lounged into line near the gate leading to the palace kitchens. As he had hoped, the Roman legionary waved him through without searching him. A quarter of an hour later as Caesar was taking a late supper in his rooms there was a sudden commotion outside the door. Hastily snatching up his sword, he set down a piece of bread and strode out to see what was happening.

'Is something wrong, centurion?'

The Roman soldier who was on duty in the corridor stood barring the way of a wiry, coarsely dressed man with a bundle over one shoulder. The fellow was unremarkable except for the determined expression on his face.

'It's this fisherman, sir,' replied the soldier. 'Says he wants to bring you his finest catch and won't take no for an answer.'

Caesar looked suspicious.

'What sort of a catch?' he demanded, his hand tightening on his sword hilt. It was as well to be cautious. Pompey's assassination was still fresh in his mind and there had been angry demonstrations in the street on his own arrival.

'J-just something special for you,' stammered the fisherman.

Caesar lost patience.

'Be off with you, man, and take it to the palace kitchens, whatever it is. I've no room here to gut fish.'

He poked at the bedroll with the tip of his sword to emphasize his order and was rewarded by a muffled gasp, instantly suppressed. Caesar's eyes narrowed and he stepped back a pace. Then, keeping his sword point trained on Apollodorus's breast, he groped for the door with his left hand.

'You'd better come inside,' he said. 'And no fancy tricks or you're the one I'll be gutting.'

He kicked the door shut behind him and motioned Apollodorus into the centre of the room.

'All right,' he rasped. 'Put the bedroll down and then leave.'

Slowly and respectfully Apollodorus set down his load.

'Be careful how you handle that, sir,' he warned.

'Why, is it dangerous?'

The fisherman gave an odd smile.

'Perhaps. Or precious, depending on how you look at it.'

When the fellow had left, Caesar circled the bedroll carefully. It was nothing but a coarsely woven cloth, cream with a border of scarlet and blue meander patterns and fringed edges, the kind of thing a peasant would wrap himself in to sleep. Yet he very much doubted that any peasant was inside it at the moment. Someone was, he felt sure of that. But who? Could it be an assassin? The man would be a fool, if that were so, since Caesar would have no trouble at all in stabbing him before he could even rise to his feet. Amused and intrigued, he gave the bundle an energetic prod with his foot and watched as it unrolled.

'By the Good Goddess!' he exclaimed. 'It's not a man at all, but a girl. Who are you and what do you want?'

The dark-haired young woman who lay sprawled on the mosaic tiles at his feet raised her head and looked up at him with an unfathomable expression in her huge, luminous eyes. She was not exactly pretty. Her nose was too big and she had a wilful mouth, but her figure left nothing to be desired. Through the transparent folds of a Chinese silk robe, the tantalizing curves of a shapely waist and luscious bum were invitingly displayed. Caesar wished she would raise her head further so he could see her tits. Obligingly she did so and he felt a pang of instantaneous excitement. Excellent. As big and swollen as melons with the nipples thrusting at her gown. He swallowed hard and felt a flush of heat about his neck and shoulders. Yet she still hadn't answered his questions.

'Who are you and what do you want?' he repeated.

Instead of replying, she gave him a long, piercing look and then flattened herself on the ground, burying her face. Was she mute? Then comprehension dawned on him as she began to slither across the floor towards him. She was prostrating herself before him as Egyptians always did to their god Kings and Queens. Worshipping him. Him! Gaius Julius Caesar! As if he were a god. He felt dizzy with exhilaration at the thought. When she reached his outstretched foot and kissed it, he could not hold back the exultant smile that spread over his face. All the same, it was just as well to be cautious. A woman could be an assassin as easily as a man. Not that this girl had anywhere much for her to conceal a weapon. Still, he had no objection to doing a complete body search.

'Take off your clothes,' he ordered hoarsely. 'All of them. And watch how you handle that gold brooch. If you try to stab me with the fibula I'll run you through with my sword.'

Gracefully she sat back on her rounded thighs, then rose to her feet and began to strip. Her hairnet came off first, sending her long, dark hair cascading in a whirling mass about her shoulders. It was followed by the gold brooch, which she held out to him obsequiously with just a touch of mockery. After that she kicked off her sandals. Then the moment he had been waiting for arrived, when she hauled her silk dress over her head and displayed herself to him. He caught his breath at that cornucopia of wonders. The creamy flesh, the pink nipples, the taut belly, the triangle of silky hair. And, above all, her expression. Elusive, mysterious, faintly taunting.

'Why don't you speak to me?' he demanded again. 'Can't you talk?'

She gave a slight shrug and the hint of a smile played around the corners of her provocative red lips.

'What are you doing here?' he persisted. 'Are you a whore sent to smooth the way for some favour?'

Something rippled in the depths of those dark eyes as if he had guessed right. Amused and fascinated, he set down his sword and beckoned to her.

'I'm right, aren't I? Someone has sent you here to pleasure me in the hope that I'll grant them a request. Isn't that true? Is that why you're here? Don't be frightened of me. Come closer and explain.'

She obeyed half of his command. Sinking to her

knees, she fell at his feet, yet instead of offering any explanations, she suddenly reached boldly up under his tunic and squeezed his cock. He gasped, feeling as if it were leaping into her hand with a life of its own. It was already hot and hard, but it swelled enormously in response to the sheer audacity of her touch. Bending her head, she took its full, thrusting length into her mouth and began to suck. Caesar groaned and shut his eyes, seizing her by the hair and ramming her against him. She knew her art, he would give her that. The warm, moist, teasing tightness of her lips, the way she used her tongue and teeth and hands drove him to the verge of insanity. It was years since he had been so violently excited by a woman. When at last he came, spurting into her in a series of savage, convulsive jerks, he cried out as if he had had a spear thrust in his vital parts.

For the space of several heartbeats they remained locked together in that peculiarly intimate situation. Then with a few deft, almost furtive gestures, she rearranged them both, he found his tunic hauled down and patted into place before she swallowed, dropped her eyes and turned away. A moment later with almost maidenly shyness, she pulled on her own garments and did her hair, still without saying anything. Then she faced him again, fully dressed and demure, as if nothing had happened. He felt mystified and fascinated by the extraordinary transformation, by the contrast between her former self, as abandoned as any whore who had ever sucked his private parts, and her present image as remote and aloof as the goddess Isis.

'Who are you?' he breathed again. 'What do you want?'

A strange smile curved her lips.

'I'm Cleopatra Ptolemy, Queen of Egypt,' she replied. 'And I want my throne back.'

Caesar was so shocked that he stood rooted to the spot. Whatever he had expected, it was not this. As the implication of her words sank in, a whirlpool of conflicting responses seethed inside him. Disbelief, incredulous admiration, amusement, a flash of resentment. Even now he could scarcely believe that she had made it safely through the cordon of guards, although the proof was before his very eyes. He had to give her credit for her cool nerve and ingenuity. And that trick with the bedroll had been a stroke of genius – obviously she understood the value of surprise as well as any army commander. It flattered his pride to think that a Queen had so recently been abasing herself and bestowing such lavish sexual gratification on him. Yet even while he was revelling in the memory, he felt a twinge of disapproval at her forwardness. It was not the first time he had enjoyed the favours of a high-born woman, but he preferred to be the one in control of the situation. He should have been laying siege to her and, like any decent woman, she should have protested and hesitated before her resistance finally crumbled. To find himself in thrall to such an assertive woman made him feel deeply uneasy. She had me right where she wanted me, he thought resentfully – between her teeth! Well, she needn't think that she'll be the master in this relationship. I'll tame her if it's the last thing I do!

Cleopatra, her own face carefully impassive, sat watching Caesar's features attentively and made a shrewd guess at the thoughts reflected there. She felt as keyed up as a gambler playing for very high stakes in a game of strategy that had become a war of nerves.

Her own feelings towards Caesar were essentially simple. She hated him. If she could have run him through with a sword as she stood there and seen him die in agony at her feet and by doing so have freed Egypt from Rome, she would have done it joyfully. But she knew that the mere attempt would be both rash and pointless. Even supposing that she could slip under his guard and achieve the deed, it would accomplish nothing. She would almost certainly die soon after the assassination and the Romans would appoint another general to annex Egypt. While Cleopatra might hate the Romans like poison, she was a realist at heart. She didn't want to die and she was prepared to parley, however unpalatable the task. Now she felt a brief thrill of satisfaction at the success of her opening move. She saw clearly that Caesar was intrigued by her and she vowed to follow up her advantage. There must be some way of persuading him that it would suit his own self-interest to give her back the throne. It wouldn't be easy, but she had never been able to resist a challenge.

'Queen of Egypt,' he said thoughtfully. 'And what are you doing here?'

Her eyes widened.

'You summoned me, domine.'

Was there a trace of irony in the way she used the word 'domine'? It was what a slave girl would call her master and he was both pleased and piqued by her use of the title. Was she secretly mocking him, or did those inscrutable dark eyes hold only respect? He wasn't sure and the uncertainty disturbed him. By the gods, she stimulated him with that serene face like a Vestal Virgin's and her wicked box of harlot's tricks beneath the maidenly manner! Suddenly he wanted to shake her, to rattle the truth from her. Instead he crossed to a side table and returned with two glasses of watered wine.

'Drink this,' he ordered, 'and we'll talk.'

She eyed the glass warily.

'Don't worry, it's not poisoned,' he growled. Although it might have been if I had known you were coming, he admitted to himself with sardonic amusement.

Seeing that she still hesitated, he took the glass from her fingers, sipped the pale, straw-coloured liquid and then restored it to her. As her lips touched the place where his had been, the ironic thought occurred to him that he had just performed a lover's gesture.

'What are you doing here?' he repeated.

'I've already told you.' It was not a whine or a reproach, as it might have been. Her voice was low, melodious, soft and it reminded him of doves cooing on a summer afternoon. 'I want my throne back.'

'And you think I'll give it to you?'

She nodded slowly, but he saw that a spark of mischievous amusement lit her dark eyes. Obviously she was conscious of the audacity of her request.

'Yes,' she agreed. 'You summoned me here to plead my cause. That's what I've come to do.'

He permitted himself a frosty smile. The girl was wasting her time, he had already made up his mind to annex Egypt as a Roman province the moment he had sufficient troops to do so. Yet the proprieties must be observed. He must make a show of impartiality. Besides, he wanted to listen to that low, warbling voice a little longer before he took her to bed and screwed her senseless. He was beginning to be charmed by the girl's impudence and wondered whether there was really any need to poison her or force her to slit her wrists once Egypt was taken over. Perhaps instead he

85

might buy her a nice little villa on a Greek island and visit her between campaigns.

'Go on, then,' he invited, in the indulgent tone of an adult urging a child to tell a rambling and pointless story. 'First tell me why you were driven out.'

'Because of the petty-minded obstructionism of some members of the Macedonian nobles,' she replied with a flash of anger in her dark eyes.

Caesar thought of his own long, weary, infuriating battles with the Roman nobles.

'I can well believe that,' he agreed drily. 'What did you do to upset them?'

'There was a low Nile three years running,' she explained. 'The harvests were terrible and the people were dying of starvation like flies. When I learnt that some of the nobles had hoarded grain and were selling it at outrageously high prices, I commandeered it forcibly at the pre-famine price and made a free distribution to the people.'

He looked at her with grudging respect. It had always been an important part of his own political principles to keep the common masses well fed.

'Anything else?' he demanded.

'Yes. The native Egyptians have never had any real political rights compared to the Macedonians. I wanted to make them all equal. It didn't seem right to me that talented people should be shut out of all opportunities just because of their birth and background, but the Macedonian nobles were outraged at the thought of sharing their privileges.'

This time Caesar gave a harsh bark of laughter.

'I can well believe that you antagonized them. So when they drove you out, you raised an army to try and get back in?'

She nodded, without any sign of bravado, as if it

had been the only possible action to take. In spite of his original intentions, he was taken aback by the sheer force of her will. She's a dangerous woman, he thought. Too shrewd, too full of inconvenient principles, too set on having her own way. If she were a man I'd have her killed this instant. But what harm can a woman do me? It might even be amusing to let her continue recounting her fantasies about how she would set up a Golden Age. Instead he brought her back to earth with a dry, practical question.

'Can you give me one good reason why I should restore you to your throne?'

Cleopatra caught her breath. This was it, the most nerve-racking moment of all. She felt like a tightrope dancer poised high above the crowd, preparing for death or glory. She was aware that Caesar only asked her in order to amuse himself as a cat might play with a mouse before devouring it. Yet there was a chance, a faint chance, that she might convince him.

'I'll give you two,' she replied staunchly. 'The first is that everybody in the east regards you as a second Alexander the Great. You've conquered the entire Mediterranean and we've all been wondering what you'll do next. Well, I'm sure I can guess. You'll go to Parthia or India or somewhere so far away that no other Roman will dare to attempt it. When that happens, you'll need an eastern city to use as a base and what better place than Alexandria? Don't you remember how Alexander sent back treasure and strange wonders of every kind to his tutor Aristotle in Macedonia? Well, you could do the same here. Our Museum and Library are already famous throughout the world for their knowledge. I could send teams of historians and scholars to accompany you on your expeditions, to write about your exploits. Imagine what they might do with you as their leader. Your name would live for a thousand years.'

Caesar felt a wild jolt of excitement, but held it in check.

'That could happen just as well if Alexandria were the capital of a Roman province,' he said in dampening tones.

'No!' She couldn't quite keep the edge of contempt out of her voice. 'I know you're a learned man, but you're exceptional among the Romans in that. What other Roman would have the wit to see how priceless the knowledge and skills of our scholars are? It would be like Archimedes and Syracuse all over again, with the Roman soldiers stabbing him as he drew his geometrical theorems on the ground. If you make this place a Roman province, all the men of learning will be scattered or killed before you finish putting up the first statue of Mars in the market place.'

Her criticism of Rome set his teeth on edge, although he realized that it was true. Scowling at her he crossed the room and then swung round.

'You said there was a second reason why I should give you back your throne,' he reminded her harshly. 'What's that?'

Her eyes seemed to glow like fire in the luminous pallor of her face.

'Your own self-interest,' she said. 'I'm sure you must have considered how dangerous it would be to you if you put a Roman governor in here to control Egypt.'

He had no idea what she was driving at, but tried to conceal his bewilderment.

'Tell me about it,' he invited in an off-hand tone.

'There's nobody you could trust. Alexandria controls nearly all the grain trade to Rome. Once a Roman proconsul was established in Egypt with a large army, he could cut off your corn supply and defy all your attempts to get rid of him. You'd have to fight another civil war all over again.'

It was so blindingly obvious and yet he, the master of strategy, had never seen it before. She was right, curse her! He had to have Egypt and its revenues, yet any Roman governor he installed there would be a perpetual threat to his own power. He clenched his fists in frustration as he paced back and forth, back and forth across the room. Cleopatra watched his narrowed eyes and gritted teeth and fought to subdue her smiles.

'But you could trust me,' she murmured.

On the following morning when King Ptolemy was summoned to Caesar's presence, he was stunned to find his sister Cleopatra lying smirking at the Roman general's side. He was even more stunned at the herald's formal announcement.

'By order of the Roman Dictator, Gaius Julius Caesar, Cleopatra the Seventh has been restored to her throne to rule on equal terms with her brother Ptolemy the Thirteenth. She will be under the protection of the Roman army from this day forward.'

Chapter Five

It was not to be expected that the Macedonian nobles would give in without a fight. Diplomatic protests were followed by outright hostilities and a month later on the ninth of November the Egyptian army finally reached Alexandria. Caesar had done his best to fortify the palace by erecting makeshift blockades of hewn stone forty feet high in the streets surrounding it. Moreover he insisted that Cleopatra remain safely inside under guard at all times, although fortunately both Olympus and Charmion had been allowed into the palace to join her. Yet by the time the crisis came, the Queen had other things on her mind apart from the approaching conflict. For several days now she had been suffering from an unfamiliar nausea and, when Charmion arrived with news that the army had been sighted, she gave only a wan smile.

'What is it?' demanded Charmion. 'Don't you care?'

An unaccustomed fatalism had taken hold of Cleopatra and she simply shrugged without replying. Casting her a worried glance, Charmion went out of the room and soon returned with her breakfast on a tray. Fresh bread rolls, honey, a bowl of raisins. Cleopatra ate ravenously, but half-way through her second roll, another wave of nausea seized her.

'Bring me a basin. Quickly!' she commanded.

Horrified, Charmion rushed to obey.

'It can't be poison!' she protested. 'I tasted those rolls myself.'

'No, not poison,' gasped Cleopatra, still heaving.

At last, grey-faced and spent, she leaned back on her pillows and did a hasty calculation on her fingers.

'I think I'm pregnant,' she muttered.

'Pregnant?' echoed Charmion at last. 'Cleopatra, that's dreadful! What on earth will you do?'

The notion was so new that Cleopatra herself had had little time to consider it. Now, snuggling under the covers, she did so. To her astonishment, she found her misery and discomfort were transcended by a sudden flash of pure joy. A slow smile spread over her face.

'I suppose I'll have a baby,' she said wonderingly.

'Don't be a fool!' snapped Charmion. 'You can't just sit there babbling about having a baby as if you were some new bride in a normal family. Don't you understand what this means?'

Cleopatra winced as she hauled herself further up on the pillows.

'I suppose it means trouble,' she admitted.

'Trouble! That's an understatement. This isn't trouble, this is catastrophe! Even if Caesar wins this war, what's to become of you now? Think of the scandal. Everyone will know the child can't possibly be Ptolemy's and they'll take the throne away from you. They may even decide to execute you for treason against the state.'

'I'd like to see them try!' retorted Cleopatra defiantly. 'With Caesar as my protector, the Macedonian nobles are totally powerless and they know it.'

'But what makes you so sure that Caesar will stand by you when he hears the news?' protested Charmion. 'What if he just abandons you? Men often do, you know, when they've got a woman into trouble.'

Cleopatra bit her lip and remained silent for a long moment. She knew perfectly well that Charmion was right and that Caesar might well deny paternity and leave her to deal with the problem alone. Even after several weeks of intimacy with him, she found herself unable to predict how he would react. After their initial encounter, he had always been affable and charming with her, yet she sensed a latent violence in his nature. When she was a child, she had been taken to see the sacred crocodiles at Crocodilopolis and much the same sense of uneasiness had gripped her as she watched the attendants stroking those reptilian snouts and dropping titbits of chicken into the gaping, pink jaws. At any moment she had expected a lunge, a flurry, a gnashing of cruel teeth and utter disaster. For some reason the thought came into her mind now of the Gallic town of Uxellodunum where Caesar was said to have cut off the right hand of every man in the place simply because they had tried to gain their freedom from Roman rule. There was always the chance that he might feel proud and overjoyed to learn that he was about to become a father, but she didn't feel at all certain of it. A worried frown puckered her forehead.

'Are you going to tell him?' asked Charmion.

'I don't know,' burst out Cleopatra irritably. 'As far as I'm concerned, I'd be perfectly happy to have his child on my own and never see him again. But I know there'll be trouble with the Macedonian nobles if I do that. My only chance is to try and get Caesar's protection. If he acknowledges the child as his, there's less risk that anyone will dare to murder it.'

'But will he acknowledge it?' persisted Charmion.

'I don't know!'

It was a question which troubled her for the rest of the morning and it was not until after lunch that she had the chance to put it to the test. By then rain was hurtling down outside the windows like a flurry of javelins and the air was damp and cold. Caesar had come fresh from the barricades; his rheumatism was troubling him and his temper was short. As long as these cursed storms kept up, there could be no hope of reinforcements reaching him by sea. Which meant that this troublesome war might drag on for several more months, leaving Gnaeus Pompeius, the son of his old adversary Pompey, free to raise fresh troops against him in the west. Caesar's view that his victory at Pharsalus had put an end to the civil war had not been shared by all his opponents and there were still ants' nests of resistance scattered around the Mediterranean, which he itched to destroy. Small wonder then that he was thoroughly out of patience with Egypt and half wished that he had simply waited another six months and declared it a province after all. He ignored Cleopatra's tentative smile and spoke curtly to her.

'I want you to command all the Macedonians of rank and influence to attend a dinner in the banqueting hall tonight.'

She gave him a startled glance.

'Why?' she demanded.

His eyebrows rose haughtily. He was not accustomed to having his orders questioned.

'Because there's a traitor in the palace,' he replied. 'Someone is leaking information to the enemy and I've uncovered a plot to assassinate the pair of us tonight and open the gates to the Egyptian army.'

She caught her breath on an anguished groan. More plots! Would she never be free of them? Yet somehow she managed to keep the tremor out her voice.

'What does the banquet have to do with it?' she asked.

'I want you to declare martial law, after which I intend to put the fear of the gods into those Macedonian nobles. Tell them that any communication with the besieging Egyptian army will be treated as high treason, punishable by death. And make it clear to them that the standard of proof will not be very exacting. The merest suspicion of treachery and I'll have their heads for it.'

A cold shiver ran down Cleopatra's spine at these words. What made it even worse was the fact that Caesar did not sound at all vindictive as he spoke. His tone was simply that of a bureaucrat insisting on administrative efficiency.

'All right,' she agreed uneasily.

'Good girl,' he said and bent to kiss her sleek, dark hair. 'Just leave things to me and the throne will soon be safe for you and your children. If the gods send you any.'

It was a meaningless phrase, but it cut her to the heart. A pang of alarm struck her and then she gambled recklessly.

'Th-they already have,' she stammered.

His whole body stiffened and he stared down at her with an appalled expression.

'What did you say?' he breathed.

'I'm pregnant, Gaius.'

After a single, horrified expletive, he turned and walked away from her. Absurdly, as if to underline his age and unfitness for fatherhood, his thigh muscles locked into a painful spasm, so that he had to come to a halt. Swearing and muttering, he kneaded the cramped tendons with his fingers. By the gods! With all the problems he was already facing, why did this have to tumble into his lap? Half turning, he became aware of her gaze resting on him. Her dark eyes were brimming with emotion and her face looked haunted.

'Why didn't you take precautions?' he snapped.

'I did! I used a sponge soaked in vinegar and tied with string. What more could I have done? It doesn't always work, you know.'

He let out his breath in a long sigh. What she said was true enough. The whole process was infuriatingly random. In more than thirty years of legal marriage he had only ever produced a single legitimate child and now Cleopatra confronted him with this. In the name of the Good Goddess, it was almost funny! He had probably impregnated her on their very first night together.

'Oh, never mind!' he said irritably. 'It's not the end of the world, you know. You'll simply have to have an abortion.'

The silence was so long that he could have run a two hundred yard dash in it. Cleopatra stood motionless, staring at him in dismay. Abortions were dangerous. Desperate women did resort to them, but they often died from them. A flame of rage scorched through her to think that he should care so little about her safety, or about his own child. How dare he stand there telling her what to do? And speaking as off-handedly as if this were some minor nuisance that would soon be over and forgotten? For him, perhaps! No doubt he had sown children all over the Mediterranean shores as recklessly as Cadmus with the dragon's teeth.

But it was a different matter for her. Whatever happened, she was bound to risk her own safety now for the sake of this tiny infant inside her and she would rather take the risk to bring it life than death. She had wanted a child for years now, ever since that passionate affair with Mark Antony. In fact, she could not believe her luck in falling pregnant, even in such awkward circumstances. Her arms ached to hold her own baby and her insides seemed to melt and flow at the thought of its tiny hand curled around her finger. It had always hurt her unbearably to see her attendants suckling their children while she was still barren long past the age when most women became mothers. And all she had had to hope for was that her brother might one day impregnate her! It was outrageous, unnatural. The Macedonian nobles might pay lip service to the incestuous Egyptian marriage customs, but there were always whispers, sniggers, a sense of pollution about it all. Well, now that she had found herself pregnant by an outsider, no power on earth would persuade her to kill the child. If she could win Caesar's continued protection, so much the better. If she couldn't, then she would manage without him somehow!

'I don't want an abortion,' she announced flatly.

'Don't be so stupid!' he stormed. 'What choice do you have? Everybody in Alexandria knows that you're married to Ptolemy and that the marriage has never been consummated. You haven't a hope in Hades of convincing them that this pregnancy is anything other than an act of treason against the succession. And I've no wish to have my honour embroiled in the matter, let me assure you! So either you abort that infant before anyone knows of its existence, or I swear by Jupiter I'll withdraw my troops from Egypt and leave you to face that pack of vultures on your own.'

Her face turned deathly pale.

'You wouldn't,' she breathed. 'You wouldn't do such a thing!'

'Wouldn't I?' he asked with a grim smile. 'If you've any sense at all you won't put it to the test. Now then, we've work to do, you and I. Just arrange this banquet for me and, as soon as it's over, I'll send for your doctor to perform a small, discreet operation.'

★

An hour later Cleopatra was lying on the bed with her eyes blotched and swollen from weeping when there was a knock at the outer door. Hastily she dashed away her tears, smoothed her ruffled hair and rose to her feet.

'Come in,' she said in a muffled voice.

The guard entered the outer room with an apologetic expression.

'It's the Princess Arsinoë,' he explained. 'She wants to see you, my lady. Shall I send her away?'

Cleopatra gulped.

'No. Ask her to wait,' she replied.

Darting back into the inner room, she washed her face hurriedly in a basin of cold water, combed her hair and tidied her dress before she went out to face Arsinoë. It wasn't a confrontation that she welcomed. The two sisters had always been as different as nature could make them. Not only in appearance, with Cleopatra small and dark and swift while Arsinoë was grotesquely fat, red haired and slow moving, but also in character. From childhood Cleopatra had always been rash, wilful, and full of fun. Always in trouble, but always forgiven since she was so adept at wheedling her way out of difficulties. Arsinoë, younger by two years, had been the goody goody, the obeyer of rules, the whiner, the telltale. Yet for all their childhood quarrels, they had always been fond of each other and Cleopatra had never suspected Arsinoë of playing any part in the moves to depose her. If Arsinoë had any ambitions beyond being a perfect housewife, Cleopatra would be very astonished. As she emerged from the inner room and saw her sister fussily dusting a perfume bottle on a low table, a rush of wry affection overtook her. It was all she could do not to fling herself into Arsinoë's arms and blurt out everything to her. The baby. Caesar. Her hopes. Her fears. If her sister had been different, she might have done. But Arsinoë was ... Arsinoë. So morally upright that she made the Virgin Goddess Diana look like a prostitute. If she did tell her, Arsinoë would probably spew out some Hebrew text about the stoning of women taken in adultery. Instead, Cleopatra kissed her on the cheek and smiled bleakly at her.

'Hello, Arsinoë. Can I do something for you?'

'This banquet. Why has Caesar commanded it?'

Cleopatra looked at her sister more closely. There was something odd about Arsinoë today. She was like a cat on hot bricks, fidgeting restlessly, her gaze darting over her shoulder. An appalling thought entered Cleopatra's mind as she remembered Caesar's revelations. Surely Arsinoë couldn't be involved in the assassination plot? No, it was too ridiculous. Too dangerous, too daring. Yet caution made her answer warily.

'Even in a siege we still have to eat. And Caesar wants us to keep up our morale.'

The relief in Arsinoë's face was unmistakable.

'Well, that's true,' she said. 'There's ... no other reason?'

'No.'

Still Arsinoë hesitated, her fingers playing with her gold necklet, patting her hair, smoothing her Coan silk dress. Then she seemed to make a decision.

'Cleopatra,' she said abruptly. 'Why don't you leave Caesar? Come over to our side? Put yourself under Ganymede's protection?'

'Ganymede?' echoed Cleopatra in shock.

'Yes. My tutor. Oh, I know you'll say he's only a slave and a eunuch, but they're often the most powerful people in the palace. You know that. And Caesar can't hold out for long under this siege, so you'd be wise to dissociate yourself from him. It's bad enough the way you've been playing the whore with him these past few weeks, but if you're still in his hands when the Egyptian army breaks through, the nobles will never forgive you.'

'Whereas if I hand myself over to you, it will save them having to fight to take me? No, thanks, Arsinoë. It would be too easy for you to betray me.'

'I didn't come to betray you!' exclaimed Arsinoë indignantly.

'Didn't you? I thought you believed I was playing the whore with Caesar.'

'I do. But you still happen to be my sister and the lawful Queen of Egypt, however much I disapprove of your morals. In God's name stop this collaboration with the Romans before it's too late. Stand up to Caesar and don't let him destroy you!'

Cleopatra smiled bitterly.

'It's already too late.'

After Arsinoë's departure, Cleopatra sat motionless for a long time, but if her body was as still as a statue, her thoughts whirled like a cloud of locusts. Her sister's words had been far too penetrating for comfort and she could not deny the attraction of simply giving in. It would be pleasant to be hailed as a beloved Queen, instead of being abused as a renegade and a traitor. It might even be pleasant to be on more affectionate terms with Arsinoë, however infuriating she was. Yet her sharp intelligence saw the consequences all too clearly. If she gave in and did what the nobles wanted, she would never have more than a ceremonial role to play as monarch, while all real power would be in other people's hands. Her only hope of ruling Egypt in truth was to remain loyal to Julius Caesar, the man who wanted to destroy her unborn child. A shudder of horror went through her at the thought and suddenly her sister's words rang loudly in her ears. 'Stand up to Caesar and don't let him destroy you.' But there was no way she could do that, was there? Unless ... A wild scheme began to form in her mind.

There were several shocks in store for the diners in the royal palace that evening. As always, it was an excellent meal and if it had not been for the distant uproar of fighting on the barricades to the south, it might have been one of those festive banquets of happier times. Flute girls played, the guests wore garlands of flowers and the young King Ptolemy was resplendent in a full-length purple tunic with a transparent yellow coat over it. Even so, the atmosphere of tension was unmistakable. At the outbreak of hostilities, many had found themselves trapped within the besieged quarter, whose sympathies lay with the attacking army outside. As the lyre players tuned their instruments and the slaves milled around setting the tables, Macedonian nobles gathered in worried groups. There was a low buzz of speculative conversation until Caesar arrived in full ceremonial uniform to take his place with the royal family at the far end of the room. Cleopatra, pale but composed in a gown of transparent Sidonian purple with a necklet of Red Sea pearls, lay on the central dining couch with Caesar on her right. To her left was her brother Ptolemy and, on the far side of him, Arsinoë. Their other brother had been considered too young to attend.

Throughout the meal Cleopatra's nerves were on edge as she awaited the declaration of martial law and the chance to put her plan into action. At last the moment arrived. When the second tables had been brought in and the nuts and raisins eaten, Caesar motioned a herald to come forward. Catching his eye, Cleopatra handed over the roll of papyrus that contained her proclamation. To her dismay she found that her breathing was coming in shallow gulps and her palms were sweating, although it was not the declaration of martial law that was upsetting her. On the contrary, she barely heard the herald's rich baritone as he read the proclamation. All her energy and courage were focused on what was to follow.

'. . . state of emergency . . . Cleopatra, Queen of Kings . . . therefore declare . . . treason punishable by death . . .'

The cries of outrage from the assembled guests brought her hurtling back to full alertness. Theodotus, one of the King's foremost advisers was on his feet, shaking his fist at Caesar and howling with rage.

'How dare you announce a death penalty in our country, foreigner?' he demanded. 'How dare you?'

Caesar smiled lazily and saluted Cleopatra with his drinking cup.

'It is not I who make the proclamation but your own Queen,' he replied.

'But the document is not signed by the King,' wheezed Pothinus from half way down the hall. 'Without the signature of both King and Queen it is invalid in Egyptian law.'

There were cries of approval. Cleopatra saw Caesar open his mouth to respond and, with a lurch of panic, realized that her moment had arrived. Rising to her feet, she held up one hand in a regal gesture for silence, took a long, agonizing breath and spoke.

'Citizens,' she said clearly. 'Pothinus is quite right. Without the signature of both King and Queen, no proclamation can have the effect of law in Egypt.'

There were cheers from the back of the hall.

'However,' she continued, 'the plain fact is that my brother Ptolemy is no longer King of Egypt.'

Roars of protest and disbelief broke out, but some in the audience hushed others.

'By right of conquest,' she added defiantly, 'the Roman general Gaius Julius Caesar is now the legitimate King of Egypt just as my ancestor Ptolemy was when he conquered Egypt two hundred and seventy years ago. It is therefore Caesar's signature which is required on this document, not Ptolemy's. Caesar, will you kindly sign here as Julius Rex?'

In the furore that followed she was dimly aware of Roman soldiers rushing into the centre of the room, to hold back the outraged crowds. She was aware also of Caesar's hastily smothered chuckle and the alacrity with which he seized the reed pen and added his signature to the document, saluting her with an ironical lift of his hand. But most of all, she was aware that her task was not yet finished. By now her whole body was shaking as if she had a fever, yet she kept going doggedly. The moment his signature was safe upon the papyrus she held up her hand again.

'There is one more announcement which it is proper for me to make tonight,' she said. 'As the de facto King of Egypt, it is also Julius Caesar's right and privilege to wed me as Queen. I therefore ask you to join us in celebrating our marriage which has just taken place in private and the forthcoming birth of our child, which is due in the month of Payni next year. If it is a boy, I will name him Ptolemy Caesar in honour of his father.'

Her legs would no longer hold her and she collapsed shakily on her dining couch. Caesar's face went dark with baffled fury and he half rose as if he would strangle her with his bare hands. But the awareness of the interested onlookers restrained him and, in any case, there was a sudden diversion. At the entrance doors half way down the hall, a Roman soldier appeared with a hound on a leash and asked to see his commander. With a face like thunder, Caesar strode down the hall and seized the animal's leash. It reared up at him, barking and snapping with a display of savage white teeth. Gripping its collar, Caesar controlled its murderous lunges and spoke above its ominous growling.

'The reason for the imposition of martial law is that we have a traitor in our midst,' he announced. 'Last night messengers were intercepted who were trying to smuggle documents to the enemy promising to assassinate the Queen and myself. This dog Cerberus has been taught to hunt and kill and he has an amazing sense of smell. His trainer has the documents in his hand. What I propose to do is to let Cerberus smell them and see whether he can sniff out the traitor in our midst.'

As Cleopatra sat watching the snarling black hound nosing the rolls of papyrus, she was suddenly conscious of a flurry of movement on the far side of her brother. A moment later her sister Arsinoë sank heavily next to her on her dining couch and stared at her, ashen faced.

'Cleopatra, you must help me,' she hissed. 'I am the one that creature seeks.'

Cleopatra's first reaction was disbelief. Still shaken from the ordeal of announcing her pregnancy, she could scarcely absorb her sister's confession. And, when she did, she felt little sympathy. Staring incredulously at Arsinoë's distraught face, she let out a low gasp.

'You treacherous bitch!' she breathed. 'Do you seriously mean to tell me you've been plotting to kill me?'

'Not you. Him! I swear I never meant you to be harmed.'

'Of course not!'

'Cleopatra, I beg you! You've got to get me out of here before that beast tears my throat open.'

'Let it!' seethed Cleopatra. 'It's no more than you deserve.'

At the far end of the dining hall, the hound had stopped nosing the papyrus and begun sniffing the air keenly. It gave a low, baying yelp and strained at its leash. Arsinoë's face was grey with fear, but she no longer begged. Instead she seemed to be trying to hold herself upright, to face death with a ghastly pretence of dignity. With a gloating look of expectation Caesar let the hound off the leash.

Cleopatra heard its snarling yelps of excitement, the clatter of its claws on the mosaic floor and saw its black, heavy body surge towards them in a terrifying leap. In that moment as she saw its slavering red mouth and wild eyes and smelled the foul odour of its breath, she acted without thought.

'No!' she screamed. And, moved by some mindless instinct, flung her arms around her sister and pushed her down.

It would have been useless if the hound had really been in pursuit of Arsinoë, but it was not. It leapt right over them and continued its hurtling flight down the banqueting hall until it reached the twin couches occupied by Pothinus. With a menacing growl it sprang at the eunuch and buried its sharp teeth in his silken robe, then crouched, awaiting instructions from its master.

'So we've found our culprit, it seems,' said Caesar, swaggering down the centre of the hall towards the hound's luckless victim. He snapped his fingers and gave the animal a single word of command.

'Kill.'

With a snarl of excitement the monstrous creature released Pothinus's robe and sprang for his throat. The eunuch gave a high-pitched squeal of terror, suddenly cut short as the animal's teeth ripped into his flesh. Pothinus's massive arms flailed in a frenzied attempt to get free, but it was useless. Blood shot forward in a scarlet fountain and he gave a couple of terrible, bubbling whimpers. The hound shook him like a rat, growling with pleasure as its huge jaws met through skin and fat and warm, palpitating tissue. The eunuch's eyes bulged, his face turned purple, his huge body threshed and stiffened as he fought for air. Then abruptly the struggle was over. His body went slack and his bowels, relaxed in death, suddenly evacuated their load. The pungent stench of shit was added to the smell of blood that hung in the air. The hound seemed unperturbed. Glancing smugly at Caesar, it wagged its tail, then settled comfortably to feed.

Cleopatra felt a rush of horror at the sight. She had hated Pothinus and prayed for his execution, yes, but she had expected it to be done decently, out of sight . . . Not this public butchery! And Arsinoë, what was to happen to Arsinoë, who was equally guilty? Half delirious with terror and disgust, she turned to reach for her sister. But Arsinoë was gone.

'Where can she be?' demanded Cleopatra half an hour later as she paced restlessly around her own rooms in the women's quarters. 'Do you think Caesar's soldiers arrested her?'

'No,' repeated Charmion patiently. 'I've already told you. I saw Ganymede, her tutor, hurry her out of the banqueting hall during the confusion. And one of the kitchen slaves swears she saw them going down the manhole that leads to the sewers. Ganymede knows those tunnels like the back of his hand. I'm quite certain they've crossed the line to join the besieging army.'

'I hope so! By all the gods, I hope so. I'll never forgive Arsinoë for taking part in that plot, but she is still my sister. I don't want to see her throat ripped out like . . . like . . .'

'Don't think about it. You've other worries to occupy you. What's Caesar going to do now that you've publicly announced your pregnancy?'

'I don't know and I don't care,' flared Cleopatra, fighting down the cold chill of fear that was rising inside her. 'I don't even know where he's gone!'

'Oh, Cleopatra, you're so rash,' lamented Charmion. 'I only hope he doesn't kill you for humiliating him in public.'

They were still gazing at each other anxiously when there was a frantic knocking at the door. A wildly excited Negro boy burst into the room, babbling that Caesar had left the palace, made a surprise attack on the harbour and was now burning the royal fleet to ashes. The two women exchanged disbelieving glances and ran to the window. As they wrestled open the heavy wooden shutters, they heard a distant roar like the blare of a trumpet or the noise from a sports stadium, but there was no way of knowing what was happening. Lights were visible near the causeway leading to the lighthouse, as if ships were deployed on the dark waters, but their movements were tantalizingly indistinct. Suddenly a full-throated roar of excitement burst from the dockyards as loudly as a thunderclap and a great wall of flame shot into the air.

'I think those are ships ablaze out there,' cried Cleopatra, hanging dangerously out of the window. 'And look, Charmion, isn't that a warehouse on fire?

Down there where they store the books for export?'

It seemed she was right, for soon the sky was full of the roar and crackle of flames and charred fragments of papyrus fluttered on the wind like a cloud of bats. The smoke became so thick that they could scarcely breathe and were forced to draw their heads inside and close the shutters.

'Perhaps Caesar is trying to clear his way through the harbour so that he can sail away and leave you,' suggested Charmion.

Cleopatra nodded bleakly. It seemed all too likely, but she would almost welcome it if she knew she never had to set eyes on him again. Yet if Caesar left and took his army with him, the nobles would soon be upon her like a pack of ravening wolves. Whatever happened, it seemed she was bound to suffer.

Hours passed and the sky remained red and filled with smoke, but Cleopatra scarcely noticed it. An unnatural calm had descended upon her and, leaving Charmion who had fallen asleep, she made her way back to Caesar's chambers like someone in a trance. If he did return to the palace, sooner or later there must come a reckoning for her defiance of his will, although for now she scarcely cared. My baby is safe, she thought, hugging the realization to her. Now the secret's out there is no point in making me have an abortion. And Arsinoë has at least a chance of survival. So I don't care what else he does to me. I simply don't care.

It was almost dawn when he entered the room. He stalked across to her and, as she rose to her feet, hit her twice across the face. His backhand was so violent that she spun against the wall and stood staring at him dizzily with a trickle of blood running from the corner of her mouth. Steadying herself, she straightened up and gave him a cold, glittering look. Anger surged through him at her insolence but he set aside his major grievance and confronted her with the minor one.

'What happened to your treacherous bitch of a sister?' he demanded curtly. 'Did she manage to escape?'

Her eyes widened and the fog of confusion that clung around her thinned for a moment.

'Y-you knew?' she faltered.

'Of course I knew! Her slaves confessed before they died. She was in the plot with Pothinus up to her neck.'

'Then why didn't you execute her?'

Caesar smiled thinly.

'It's bad public relations to execute royal princesses,' he retorted. 'I thought it better to let her escape and hope she gets killed crossing the barricades.'

'You're a ruthless bastard,' said Cleopatra through her teeth.

'And you're a conniving whore!' roared Caesar, sending her reeling with another backhand to her face. 'How dare you shame me before my own soldiers?'

Her mouth quirked into a parody of a smile, ruined by the lump that was fast swelling on her bottom lip.

'There is no shame involved,' she replied as steadily as if she were addressing her privy council. 'You are the de facto ruler of Egypt. It is your right to marry me and get children upon me.'

'Marry you! I'd as soon marry a Tuscan sow, you scheming little bitch!'

He clenched his fist and advanced on her again, but she regarded him as stubbornly as a punch drunk fighter. There was a brief spark of fear in her dark eyes, but it was overlaid by an obstinacy beyond belief. Incredible as it seemed, she was still determined to defy him. Enraged beyond measure, Caesar spun violently away from her and slammed his fist into the wall, sending lumps of fresco hurtling to the floor.

'What in the name of Jupiter possessed you to tell the entire world that you were pregnant?' he demanded at last.

She tried twice to speak and failed. Then, wrapping her arms defensively around her, she cast him a look of blind misery.

'You wanted me to kill my baby,' she muttered. 'It was the only way I could think of to stop you.'

He let out a hoarse, incredulous guffaw. She couldn't mean it! It was farcical, the sort of thing that characters gasped artistically in those comedies. The ones where actors ran around on stage with huge, red genitals dangling below their tunics and babbled about kidnapped babies and thieving slaves and hidden hoards of treasure. Yet she was standing here and telling him this with a completely straight face.

'Don't talk rubbish!'

'I-it's the tru-uth . . .' she wailed.

And, incredibly, she burst into tears. Her mouth crumpled ridiculously and she collapsed into an unbroken chair, sobbing like a child. This weeping unnerved Caesar as nothing else had done. Dimly he realized that he had begun to think of her as an adversary like any other. Formidable in her grasp of strategy, but essentially driven by the same laws as any man. To find her behaving like a woman appalled him. He felt as shocked and disconcerted as if his old Gallic adversary Vercingetorix, on being captured, had begun to bawl and beg for his dolly. Clumsily he reached out a hand and touched her on the shoulder. She shrugged him away and hid her face. Losing patience again, he seized a graceful klismos chair and hurled it against the damaged wall. Then he stood swaying like a drunken wrestler and ran his hands through his thinning hair.

'It may interest you to know that I've torched your warships and seized the lighthouse,' he hissed. 'The entire harbour is in my hands and I can sail away at any moment and leave you to face your loving citizens alone. Can you tell me one good reason why I shouldn't?'

For a moment her face looked white and horrified. Then she rallied, dashing away her tears and glaring at him defiantly.

'If you do, they'll say you fled because you were too frightened to stay and fight the Macedonian army,' she pointed out.

Caesar ground his teeth. His pride had always been his most vulnerable point. The voracious need to be first, best, smartest, bravest, most admired had eaten at him all his life. Now he was well aware that this sly chit of a girl was playing on it as shrewdly as a master angler, coaxing in a fish. And still he could not resist the tug of the line.

'So what do you want me to do?' he growled.

There was a gleam of triumph in her eyes. Swiftly hidden.

'Just what you've already begun to do,' she replied. 'Restore order in Egypt, place me securely on my throne. And support my story that we were privately married.'

'Don't be a fool! I'm already married.'

'That doesn't matter,' insisted Cleopatra hastily. 'I'm not asking for a genuine marriage. In any case, I know it wouldn't be recognized in Rome, since you're a senator and can't legally marry a foreigner. But it's Egypt I'm concerned about, not Rome. And it would be a help to me if my citizens believed I had been through a wedding ceremony with you. If you agree to that, I'll make you a god.'

'What do you mean – make me a god?'

'I'll set up a cult in your honour and have you worshipped as the god Zeus Amon,' she replied.

His senses reeled. To be worshipped as a god . . . ! Lights flickered in the air above him and he heard a sound of distant, unearthly music. For a moment he thought he was going to fall to the floor in a fit, but somehow he retained his balance. But his breathing was rapid and difficult.

'Are you all right?' she asked, putting out a hand to him.

A shudder went through his limbs and he sat down jerkily in a chair.

'Zeus Amon . . .' he whispered in a dazed voice.

'What's wrong?' she demanded. 'You look as if you've seen a daemon.'

'Perhaps I have,' he said thickly. 'Did you say . . . Zeus Amon?'

'Yes, why not? It's only fitting, after all. Alexander the Great came to Egypt and was hailed as the Son of Amon. You will be Amon himself.'

'So I will be worshipped as a mightier god than Alexander?' he muttered.

Aware that she was gaining ground, she watched him slyly.

'Why not?' she replied. 'There are many who believe you are greater than Alexander.'

He knew she was flattering him. Knew and didn't care. He was rapidly regaining his equilibrium and the blood which seemed to have frozen in his veins was beginning to flow again, filling him with a sense of energy and purpose. He rose to his feet and took a couple of turns around the room, exultant with the thought of temples erected in his honour, incense burnt before his image, revenue flowing into his coffers.

'And the income from my temples?' he barked.

Her misery evaporated like a morning mist from the Nile River. She gave him a small, secretive smile.

'Enormous. I'll have a scribe prepare estimates for you tomorrow, if you wish.'

'All right, I'll do it!' he agreed, slamming his fist into the open palm of his other hand. 'You make me a god, Egyptian, and I'll never deny your claim that I fathered your child.'

CHAPTER SIX

Caesar stood on the man-made lookout of the Sanctuary of Pan and gazed down on the city of Alexandria spread out below him. It was hard to believe that it was nearly six months since he had first landed here. An eventful six months in which he had more than once come close to losing everything in this ridiculous war. Arsinoë had proved a worthy opponent – he would give her that. Pumping sea water into the drinking supply of the besieged city had been a touch of brilliance. But in the end Caesar had won, as he always knew he would. Dramatically outnumbered, his army had clung grimly to survival until reinforcements arrived under the command of Mithridates of Pergamum. Joining up with his ally, Caesar had smashed the Egyptians within two days. Now that their army had officially surrendered, the country was his to do with as he pleased. A triumphant smile lit his face and he stretched out his arms, clenching and unclenching his fists as if he could seize the whole metropolis in his hands.

It was a beautiful city and from this vantage point all its most famous features could be seen. Gloating, he shaded his eyes and leaned far out to examine them in turn. There at the end of the harbour, blindingly white against the blue backdrop of the sea, was the Pharos, the huge lighthouse and the causeway where he had almost lost his life. To the left was the great Library and Museum smack on the intersection of the two wide boulevards that quartered the city, the Canopic Way and the Street of the Soma. Clustered around the same crossroads were the law courts and the tomb of Alexander the Great. And spread out in front of him was a jumble of brick and marble buildings, gleaming in the winter sun. Temples and houses and workshops, warehouses and shopping arcades and gymnasiums, every amenity a city could want. Beyond those, the palm trees and luxuriant greenery that marked the Zoological Gardens and the entrance to the palace. Mine, all mine, thought Caesar exultantly and smiled till his face ached. Yet, as always, victory brought responsibilities. There were still decisions to be made about the future of the country and about the two princesses in particular.

Caesar paused in his pacing and winced as a twinge of pain went through his right hip. All very well for him to be lingering here in Egypt for a few weeks, yes. No Roman in his right mind would expect him to put to sea while it was still winter. But when the spring came, what then? There would be a furore in Rome if it was known that he meant to cruise up the Nile with Cleopatra. The consuls would be in a ferment, there would be meetings in the Senate, urgent dispatches sent to demand his return and the recall of the troops under his command. Well, let them try! he thought, smiling grimly. I've been elected dictator, haven't I? That gives me the power to do whatever I want and they'll be fools if they try to oppose me!

The thought of thumbing his nose at the Roman Senate by brazenly handing the country over to his mistress made him feel amused and elated. By the gods, how they would squirm and fulminate in Rome! Servilia's brother Marcus Porcius Cato would have an apoplexy about it, red faced moralizing little hedgehog that he was. Or perhaps he was already in Africa trying to raise Pompeian forces for yet another battle against Caesar. Oh, there would be feathers ruffled and no mistake. Yet in many ways allowing Cleopatra to keep her throne was no more than simple good sense. However absurdly, the ordinary people did seem to have a fanatical devotion to the royal family so that she could rule with less trouble than a Roman governor. Besides, Caesar knew he could extract handsome revenues from her whenever he wished. Yes, it was much the best solution, particularly since it meant that this vast, rich country was one day likely to be ruled by Caesar's own offspring. Yet that still left the problem of what to do with her tiresome sister Arsinoë.

Sighing, Caesar made his way down the road that spiralled around the cone-shaped hill. Arsinoë was a cursed nuisance! He had hoped she would get an arrow through her fat guts as she crossed the lines to the besieging army, but no such luck. She had survived to take command of the army and had led it against him with a shrewdness that infuriated him. Caesar had won a reputation for mercy in his conduct of the civil wars, but the truth was that he never forgot an injury. While he had found it politic to spare the lives of many Roman nobles, he could see no point in sparing Arsinoë. If she lived, she could only provide a focus for rebellion, a rallying point for all those disaffected with Cleopatra's rule. No, better for her to die. Let her pay for the insolence of resisting Julius Caesar! Only this morning word had been brought of her capture and, by now, she was probably in the palace quaking in her sandals at the thought of confronting him. And well she might be! Not that Caesar would be fool enough to mistreat her here among her own people. But once aboard a slave ship for Rome she could be flogged and starved with impunity. With worse to follow. Yes, let her pay for her insolence and pay dearly . . .

'Have you heard the latest news from Egypt?'

Marcus Antonius, fighting his way up through a fog of drunken sleep, focused blurrily on his friend Publius Cornelius Dolabella. The crowing of a cock on the balcony of the apartment block across the alley and the reddish glow of the light filtering through the shutters confirmed his outraged suspicion that it was barely dawn. An hour when the most conscientious public servants in Rome were already stirring. But not Antony. He blinked twice at the red and white pattern of cubes on the bedroom wall and shuddered. At this hour of the morning they seemed to crawl like a mass of geometric worms.

'Oh, piss off!' he recommended, heaving his massive body over and burrowing into the pillows.

'No, this is serious,' insisted Dolabella and flung a cold, wet sponge at him.

A squeal of shock issued from the bedclothes next to Antony, startling him into action. He flung back the woollen blankets and blinked at the lush, naked figure of a blonde girl curled up beside him. An appalling thought struck him. Surely not the wife of that Cisalpine senator he was trying to nudge for a loan? The woman who kept making eyes at him?

'Who are you?' he demanded bluntly. 'And how did you get in here?'

She gave a shrill giggle.

'Don't you remember, sir?' she trilled. 'You invited me last night.'

Antony winced. No, definitely not a senator's wife, not with that accent. Then who? He yawned, scratched the hairs on his chest and squinted at her. She giggled again.

'You don't remember, do you? I'm Volumnia, the famous cabaret dancer and actress. I performed at your party last night. You said I did the most amazing act you'd ever seen since the North African rope dancer.'

Antony shuddered. Yes, it had been an amazing act. And not only at the party. Dim memories stirred in his brain. His wife Antonia had been safely away in the country and he had taken advantage of her absence to throw a wild party. After the revelry had ended and his friends had finally staggered away into the night, Antony had felt it his duty to escort Volumnia home. They hadn't got very far, though. Only to the Fountain of the Nymphs on the street corner, where Volumnia had decided to strip off and take a bath. Not wanting her to catch cold, Antony had plunged in after her to fetch her out. He distinctly remembered the fine, plump feel of her naked breasts in his hands, the nipples hard and erect from the cold water. It was a pity that he had lost his balance and fallen on top of her, sending a great tidal wave lurching out of the fountain to drench two elderly senators on their way home. And it was an even greater pity that when they had come huffing and blustering with their walking sticks to give him a sound thrashing, they had recognized him Mark Antony, the Master of the Horse, cavorting naked in a fountain with an actress! Not that he had cared at the time. He had been too drunk and too busy laughing uproariously at the discovery that he had landed with his face buried in Volumnia's wet, silky muff. An opportunity that seemed too good to waste, so that he had simply lurched genially to his feet, snapped the walking sticks over his thigh and hurled them at their owners before submerging to enjoy himself.

Volumnia had been splendid. While the two senators were still spluttering like antiquated volcanoes, she had dragged him out of the fountain, down a back alley and home so that she could dry him off. Drying him off had soon given way to sucking him off and, while the enraged senators hammered at the outer doors and threatened vengeance, Antony had returned the favour by fucking her on the stairs. It had been an ideal arrangement. By setting her two steps above him, he had compensated perfectly for her lack of height. And the wall of the stairwell had offered welcome support as he banged away at her. Volumnia had been most appreciative of his size and hardness and had given vent to her feelings by sighing and gasping and uttering loud, staccato shrieks during the best bits so that the hammering on the outer door had faltered to a halt. Perhaps the senators thought he was adding rape and torture to his other crimes? He had to admit that it was a plausible theory, especially when he remembered how abandoned Volumnia's screams of joy had been when he finally pinned her to the wall and shot his wad inside her. He grinned at the memory.

'You're right. You were magnificent,' he said, fondling her naked bum appreciatively.

The girl's face lit up. Watching these antics, Dolabella felt his lips curl resentfully. What was it about Antony that made women fall over themselves for the privilege of scrambling into his bed? he wondered. He was good looking, certainly, with that curly brown hair, thick beard and white teeth. And he had a powerful physique, which never failed to impress them. But there was nothing special about him, unless it was the way his hazel eyes roamed over women and then blazed up, making them feel unique, and urgently desired. Whatever the knack was, Dolabella wished that *he* had it in equal measure. Curtly he interrupted the scorching looks and low sighs which would soon have the bed rattling before he had even delivered his message.

'Send her off,' he said impatiently. 'I've got important matters to discuss with you.'

Antony sighed and tumbled the girl out of bed. He watched appreciatively as she pulled on a garish purple robe and stood pouting hopefully at him, then with a sudden growl of laughter he reached into a bedside chest, pulled out a leather purse and flung it to her. She caught it deftly with a faint clinking sound and ran back to kiss him. The kiss was a long, smacking one and followed by a slap on the rump which made her squeal and giggle before she loitered out of the room. Dolabella watched her departure with barely concealed irritation and then sat down on the bed.

'Wait till you hear this,' he announced importantly.

'I will wait,' retorted Antony. 'My bladder's bursting. Call that lazy hound of a slave lad to bring me a chamberpot.'

Once again Dolabella had to endure the irritation of waiting while a curly haired lout of fourteen tramped in with a silver chamber pot, a jug of hot water and a pair of towels. Inevitably he dropped the chamberpot with a loud clatter, making Antony wince and clutch his temples. The boy only grinned as he set it upright. All Antony's slaves were over-indulged, thought Dolabella sourly. He ought to give him a boot in the backside to make him take better care. A sudden loud splashing sound and a pungent odour showed that Antony was otherwise occupied. Dolabella retreated hastily to the other side of the room. At last Antony shook himself, splashed his face with warm water, cleaned his teeth with salt and pulled on the fine white woollen tunic and leather sandals that the boy had laid out for him.

'All right, clear off. You can bring us breakfast in half an hour. Hot rolls, honey and watered wine.'

The boy withdrew, loaded with damp towels and the chamber pot and Antony combed his fingers through his damp beard and darted a shrewd glance at Dolabella.

'Well, what's this news that's worth waking me at dawn for?' he demanded.

Satisfied that he had finally got his friend's full attention, Dolabella lounged back in a wicker chair and pressed his fingertips together. He had the fine-boned grace of a Gallic hound, wiry brown hair, long-lashed green eyes and rather sneering features. It gratified him to see Antony's honest bewilderment. Dolabella liked to be first with the news.

'Caesar's won the war in Alexandria.'

'Has he, by Jove? That's a damned clever bit of soldiering! How did he manage it?'

'Well, his reinforcements arrived and he did the usual stuff. Forced marches by night, surprise attacks. You know Caesar. But that's not the real news.'

Dolabella paused impressively.

'Well, go on!' urged Antony. 'Spit it out!'

'Caesar's staying on in Egypt.'

'What? That's ridiculous!'

'It's true,' insisted Dolabella.

'It's impossible! The bloody Pompeians are swarming round Africa and Spain like rats in a nest. If he doesn't get off his backside and crush them soon, we'll have the whole war to fight again.'

'I know that. But it's true. He's staying in Egypt.'

'Where did you hear this?' demanded Antony abruptly.

'My freedman Furcio arrived last night from Egypt. He says there was an official courier from Caesar on the same boat. You should hear from him some time today.'

Antony was silent, frowning and tugging his beard. Furcio? A trustworthy source, no doubt of that.

'But why would Caesar do such a thing?' he growled.

Dolabella shrugged.

'He's lost his balls over the Egyptian Queen Cleopatra, by all accounts. Now that the war is over, she's persuaded him to stay on for a little holiday.'

Antony's roar of startled laughter was as sudden and explosive as a thunderclap. He slapped his muscular thigh and sat down on his bed, grinning and shaking his head.

'The clever little bitch!' he marvelled. 'Got her ring through his nose, has she? Well, it doesn't surprise me. She always was too smart for any man's peace of mind. And sexy into the bargain. I'm not surprised Caesar's fallen for her.'

'He's done more than that. He's got her with child.'

'What?' echoed Antony incredulously.

'Hadn't you heard? She's five or six months gone now. And not only that. Caesar's sworn to acknowledge paternity.'

Antony whistled.

'How long is he staying?' he asked.

'Nobody knows for sure. My guess is he won't leave until the baby's born.'

'So another three or four months?' hazarded Antony. 'Gods! The west will be in chaos by then.'

'Oh, look on the bright side,' urged Dolabella.

'You'll still be Master of the Horse here in Rome with unlimited power to line your wallet. You could start by confiscating property from the Pompeians and sharing it out among your loyal supporters.'

His leering grin provoked no answering smile from Antony. It was true that a chance to seize some funds and stave off his most pressing creditors would be welcome, but a feeling close to panic assailed him. Deep in his heart, Antony knew that he was no administrator and he doubted his power to hold Rome in check until Caesar's return. Discontentments seethed and bubbled in the city and every day brought renewed faction fighting.

'And when Caesar leaves?' he demanded. 'What then? Is he setting up Egypt as a Roman province?'

'No,' said Dolabella smugly, enjoying the drama. 'He's leaving Cleopatra as Queen with three legions to protect her.'

Antony rose to his feet with an oath and paced around the room.

'Three legions! He's not only lost his balls, he's lost his mind!' he exclaimed.

'I know,' agreed Dolabella. 'What's more, he's getting rid of all other possible contenders to the Egyptian throne. The boy King was drowned during the final battle near the Nile, although some say there's a younger brother still alive. But listen to this. There's a sister, Arsinoë, who's being brought to Rome to be exhibited in his triumph. After that she'll be strangled.'

Antony was silent, overwhelmed by an appalled memory of a grave twelve-year-old girl with red-gold hair and a delicate face. A girl sobbing in the arms of her older sister as they stood together at Berenice's funeral service.

'It won't happen!' he said sharply. 'Cleopatra would never stand for it. They're sisters.'

Dolabella smiled mockingly.

'Well, either sisterly love is not all it should be, or Caesar has overruled her on this issue,' he replied. 'I have it on good authority that Arsinoë is going to be executed.'

Arsinoë's first sight of Italy came as a shock to her. Throughout the four weeks of the voyage she had been protected from the full horror of her plight by a haze of disbelief. Like some insect pupa slumbering in a cocoon she had been barely aware of events around her. The ordeals of seasickness, darkness, rotting food, loud, angry voices and close-pressed bodies had scarcely touched her. Now and then something pierced her stupor. The shrieks of a woman prisoner being raped or a man being flogged, an eye-gouging brawl over a mouldy hunk of bread, the howling chaos of a storm at sea. Most of the time she huddled with her eyes closed, pretending she was somewhere else. Until they reached Italy.

The brightness as she stumbled on deck in Ostia was dazzling. The sun seemed to shine with a burning radiance so intense that she cried out and covered her eyes before peering cautiously through the red flare of her fingers. Jumbled impressions swam into her confused brain. Ships riding at anchor, the intense blue of the sea, brick warehouses, umbrella pines, raucous seagulls shrieking overhead. And the wonderful clean, salt tang of the air whipping away the stench of the hold. Then a clout on the head sent her stumbling down the gangplank to join the other captives.

'Sixteen miles to Rome,' said a bored centurion,

hawking and spitting on the pavement. 'We'd better get this lot moving.'

Arsinoë had never walked sixteen miles in her life before. In fact she had rarely walked more than sixteen paces. But she was no longer the same woman who had set out from Alexandria four weeks earlier. For one thing food had been short aboard the vessel. Bread and a scanty ration of salt fish and water. For another she had lost the voracious, insatiable hunger that had driven her for the last eight years since Berenice's death. As she moved unsteadily across the docks in the slave line she had the strange feeling that she could float all the way to Rome.

She didn't quite do that. But she did march along the Via Campana briskly enough to avoid the slave master's lash at first and she even found a kind of pleasure in the journey. After so long cramped in a fetid box it was wonderful to breathe great lungfuls of clean air, to see green fields and spring flowers and all the sights of the countryside. A flock of long-eared, bleating sheep in the care of two worried small boys, a donkey with twin panniers trotting along with a load of firewood, peasants' huts and little villages and green, sprouting vines in neat rows across the hillsides. Italy is beautiful, she thought in surprise. I didn't expect it to be, but it is. The sight of a small, white wayside shrine to Bacchus brought her a stabbing reminder of her own God. For the first time in weeks she tried to pray, but the words stuck like marbles in her throat. Save me, God, and I'll never . . . never . . . She cast around for some suitable bargain. I'll never care about being a princess again. Behind her she heard the cutting swish of a whip and a shrill, feminine cry of pain. Turning she saw a young woman frantically trying to breastfeed a baby as she walked, with one arm now disfigured by a purple weal. A noblewoman of her own class. Rage rose in Arsinoë's throat like molten lava.

'Leave her alone, you coward!' she thundered in a voice of royal wrath. 'Or I'll kill you!'

It was her turn to feel the lash, but she barely flinched as it bit into her skin. With a sudden furious movement she tore it out of the guard's hands and whipped it back across his own face.

'Fool!' she shrieked. 'Will you earn more money by killing your prisoners? Leave the woman alone, I say!'

It would have been enough to have her crucified if she had been any ordinary slave, but she was not. Caesar's instructions had been explicit. Humiliate the Princess Arsinoë in any way you wish, but bring her safely to Rome. Half-blinded by his own blood the legionary still had presence of mind enough to confine his anger to a blow that sent her staggering among the ranks of slaves. A murmur rose like the sighing of a great wind and angry voices began to mutter around her.

'Take care, Roman. Our princess is a living goddess and Dionysus will avenge any harm done to her.'

'A curse on Cleopatra for welcoming these Roman savages! May she perish and Arsinoë reign in her place.'

'Isis, send fire to gnaw the vitals of these men! May they die in agony for harming our royal lady.'

At these words the Roman soldier made a sign against the evil eye and backed nervously away. The centurion in charge, although shaken himself, took hasty action.

'We'll have a rest break of half an hour. Prisoners, fall out and guard your tongues or it will be the worse for you.'

In the green, grassy hollow of a bank with the sound of a stream rippling close by, Arsinoë picked her way through the exhausted captives to find the young mother. She was a girl of about eighteen who must have been pretty before this ordeal. Even now, gaunt and filthy with hair like straw, her eyes were dark and lustrous and her smile haunting.

'Thank you, my lady,' she whispered, trying to set down the baby and prostrate herself.

'Don't bother about that,' ordered Arsinoë sharply. 'We are nothing but two prisoners together now. Or should I say three? Come, give me the child to hold and rest your arms.'

But the baby cried weakly, irritably and threshed its head, refusing to leave its mother's nipple. Yet all its frantic sucking produced nothing. Already the skin was stretched tight over its fragile bones like faded papyrus.

'I've lost my milk,' said the young woman in a haunted voice, unable to stop gazing at the rooting child. 'He'll die soon if I don't get food and rest and clean water.'

Arsinoë bullied a wineskin of clean water out of a soldier, but there was no food to be had. The girl revealed in a listless monotone that her name was Chloe and she was a Macedonian officer's wife who had been captured among the camp followers after Caesar's victory. She was pathetically grateful for the water, but it did little good. The baby died less than an hour after they set out again. Being near a village, the soldiers flung it on a convenient dung heap and laughed at the antics of the grief-stricken mother. Again and again she tried to run back, begged them to let her throw the three ritual handfuls of dust on its body to ensure its passage to the underworld and, when they refused, clawed her face with her nails, flung dust in her own hair and howled like a baying hyena. Arsinoë, watching them, wondered why the power of human hatred was not strong enough to kill.

When they reached Rome it was mid afternoon and the city was gilded by a nimbus of golden light. Up close its glory vanished and it was revealed as a labyrinth of stinking alleys, toppling wooden apartment blocks and noisy workshops. Pigeons roosted on the orange roof tiles of the better houses, pert youths with pans of hot food balanced on their heads darted their way through the crowds, beggars huddled on street corners whining and displaying their sores, runny-nosed children played and urinated in the gutters. The streets were slimy with dog droppings and rotting cabbage leaves and every breath brought the smell of human sweat and dirt and over-crowding. When at last they reached the slave market and were herded into a large barracks behind the square, Arsinoë was relieved to be out of the press and noise of the main thoroughfares, but her relief was shortlived.

An auctioneer and a doctor made their way between the rows of exhausted captives, inspecting teeth and limbs and segregating any cases of skin disease. Most of the prisoners, including Chloe, were stripped naked and placed in a group under a sign reading 'FOR AUCTION TOMORROW', but Arsinoë was cut out from the group like a recalcitrant steer and herded into the auctioneer's office, a poky, badly lit room on the ground floor of the building.

Here two soldiers held her naked and immobilized while the doctor examined her. He took her pulse, pulled down her eyelids, looked into all her bodily orifices and pinched a fold of her skin.

'Seems healthy enough,' he said last. 'Carrying too much fat, but she'll need that where she's going.'

'She'll survive the ordeal then?' asked the centurion.

Arsinoë's skin crawled with apprehension. What ordeal? The doctor made a movement as if he were washing his hands of the whole problem.

'As well as anyone might,' he said irritably. 'But I won't be held responsible if she dies, neither by Caesar nor anybody else. An underground prison is not healthy for anyone and the Tullian dungeon is a death trap. It's damp and badly ventilated and infested with rats and insects. So don't blame me if she perishes of malaria, long before Caesar comes home to lead her in triumph.'

For the first time Arsinoë began to grasp the real terror and helplessness of her plight. Until now she had been sustained by disbelief, by the comforting certainty that rescue would come. I'm a princess, she had told herself over and over on the slave ship. This can't be happening, it will end soon. Now, as she found herself clad in a coarse tunic being dragged along the Roman streets in the spring sunshine, a tidal wave of panic overwhelmed her. She began to shriek and struggle and call on Heaven to bring her aid. The soldiers swore under their breath and cast sidelong glances at the onlookers who gathered to jeer or pity or simply enjoy the spectacle. At last they came out of the twisting alleys into the more open space of the Forum and here at the northwest corner near the temple of Concord, she was dragged out of sunlight into sudden dimness and chill. A huge, surly ruffian clanking a bunch of keys approached them.

'Where to, soldier?' he asked.

'Underground. The Tullian dungeon.'

Arsinoë could not see the warder's expression, but she heard the shock in his voice.

'But she's a woman. That's only for the worst criminals. Men condemned to execution.'

The centurion shrugged.

'Caesar's orders.'

The Tullian dungeon was a subterranean chamber with a vaulted roof of stone. Hoisting a massive block of stone out of the floor, the guard gave a brutal rumble of laughter and shouted into the darkness revealed below.

'Anyone home?'

His voice echoed back, but there was no other answer apart from the drip of water and the sound of scuttling rats far below. Arsinoë took one terrified glance into that dark, gaping hole and recoiled at the stench.

'Let me go,' she begged, backing away. 'Please! Please! I'm a princess, I have friends who'll pay you well!'

It was useless. With more jeering laughter they held her down and looped a rope around her shoulders. Then, as she screamed and wept and fought, they lowered her into the darkness.

'May God curse Julius Caesar!' she shrieked. 'And everyone who serves him.'

Deliberately they sent the rope swinging so that she jarred against one wall. Her fingers touched damp slime and her head ached. Then suddenly, without warning, they let her drop. Gasping and babbling with terror, she found herself on a damp, uneven stone floor. Arms came around her suddenly. A man's arms. She smelt the warm, acrid odour of another human body as he held her tightly for a moment, hushing her screams with his fingers.

'Who are you?' he demanded hoarsely.

CHAPTER SEVEN

On a vessel of a very different sort Cleopatra too was thinking deeply as she made a departure from shore. The state barge of the Ptolemics had been built to dazzle the world with its magnificence. It was a gigantic vessel three hundred feet long and sixty feet high made of split cedar, Milesian cypress and carved ivory with nails and fastenings of red brass. All the rooms in it were adorned with pillars of Corinthian workmanship in gold and ivory. There was a huge banqueting chamber, part of it roofed and part left open to catch the breezes, there were walkways, sitting rooms and sleeping cabins in plenty and there was even a temple to Venus, containing a marble statue of the goddess. And all of it was furnished with a luxury and beauty beyond the power of most men to imagine. As this vessel pulled out into the smooth, glassy blue water at the centre of the Nile, Cleopatra stood in the bow gazing upriver and gave a faint sigh. Caesar was somewhere amidships in the apartment dedicated to the god Bacchus, inspecting the statues there with a connoisseur's eye. She was grateful for his absence. However long she spent with Caesar, she would never quite get over her fear of him. Oh, he could be a charming man. Witty, well read, a fitting companion for her intellectual symposiums with the scholars at the Museum or her taxation meetings with the officials from the treasury. But there was something lurking beneath the charm which made her feel deeply uneasy. All the same, she knew how much she needed him. Her wits had sharpened in the long, nerve-racking months of the siege and she saw clearly the importance of playing Caesar like a powerful fish on a line. Once in the days of her youthful idealism she would have scorned such tactics, but now she was prepared to use every hook and bait and stratagem she possessed to keep hold of Egypt. Without Caesar's soldiers and his continued goodwill the nobles would certainly destroy her the moment he left. Whereas, if she could keep his support, all the things she had dreamed of when she first became Queen might yet be possible. At night she often lay awake, visualizing her goals, as if the sheer force of her will must make them happen. I'll send an expedition to India, she whispered to herself, and I'll give the Museum and Library greater funds than they've ever had so that the scholars can make wonderful machines. Perhaps even machines driven by steam. I'll give women and Egyptians more of a voice in government. And I'll make the Romans realize that they can't treat the entire eastern half of the Mediterranean as if we're nothing but a quarry to be mined by them. Yet I can only do it with Caesar's support. He is the key to everything I want, so I must never let him suspect how much I fear and dislike him. Fear and dislike. Those emotions had been the essence of her dealings with him from the first moment when she crawled at his feet. Even now it stung her to remember that humiliation and the repeated invasions of her body ever since. Just as it had stung her to remember his insistence that Arsinoë be packed off to Rome on a slave ship. Cleopatra had been prepared to pardon her, but not Caesar. Rather than provoke an outright quarrel, she had given in, but she still burned at the memory. Her only consolation was the thought that she had sent agents to Rome to buy Arsinoë if she appeared for sale in the slave market. What more could she do? She was still busy struggling for her own survival and had little pity to spare for her sister. And she could not afford to antagonize Caesar. Much as she longed to see him depart, she must use every ounce of cunning to win his continued approval. Her greatest hope in mounting this expedition up the Nile was to convince him that keeping her as Queen would reward him beyond his wildest dreams. Wealth, adulation, adventure, everything Egypt had to offer must be showered on him during this journey. Perhaps then her own future would be more secure.

A sudden footfall caught her attention and she turned, smiling radiantly.

'Domine.'

He was dressed in the Roman style, but in civilian clothes, not a soldier's uniform. He wore a knee-length tunic, belted at the waist, with long, fringed sleeves which were his own invention. His muscular brown legs were bare, except for leather sandals, and his hair was carefully combed to conceal the bald patch. In bright sunlight such as this, his age was cruelly apparent. The lines around his eyes were seamed as deeply as engravings and his throat had the leathery look of an elephant's hide. He smiled at her and a vestige of the charm that must have hypnotized women in his youth lurked for an instant in his dark eyes. Then he limped across and greeted her in the Roman fashion, kissing her on the mouth.

'You're well?' he asked. 'And the child?'

'Both well,' she agreed, laying her hands on his as he clasped her swollen belly.

In this at least they were in harmony, both of them wanting the expected child with an intensity that surprised them. Cleopatra had always longed for a baby as fervently as any woman, but Caesar was startled and rather amused by the violence of his own feelings. It was thirty-two years since his daughter Julia's birth and he had not expected this fierce, instinctive pride. At first it had only been an occasional flash of pleasure as he pictured a son in his own image. But as the Egyptian Queen's belly swelled, he had found his own emotions intensified alarmingly. His first bout of fatherhood had left him unscathed until the moment when the child was placed in his arms still damp and bloody from the womb. Only then had he felt the terrifying rush of exhilaration and responsibility.

This time he was suffering it all in advance, perhaps because he was fifty-two and knew that he was not immortal. It would be good to leave a strong son in his place. His only regret was that the child was not growing in his wife Calpurnia's womb. Or that Cleopatra was not a Roman noblewoman so that he could divorce his wife and marry her.

'Domine? Is something wrong?'

She was looking at him out of those faintly slanted dark eyes with an odd smile playing about her lips as if she could read his thoughts. Perhaps she could.

'No, nothing,' he said, releasing her. 'The statues in the apartment of Bacchus are very fine. I particularly admired the bronze figure of Mercury.'

'Then you must keep it as a gift when we return from our journey,' she replied in that husky contralto voice which was one of her greatest charms.

'H'm,' he grunted, gripping the carved gunwale and staring at the river which was unrolling before them like a bale of blue silk. 'I suppose there will be other statues well worth seeing on this voyage.'

'Of course, domine. Egypt is a land of wonders, and as its King, it's only right that you should see them.'

He suppressed a growl of laughter. So she was still

harping on that, was she? He had allowed her to talk him into making this dazzling progress through the country, partly to intimidate the populace with a show of Roman power and partly because the adventure appealed to him, but so far he had resisted her blandishments about appearing publicly as King of Egypt. It was the kind of thing that was likely to go down very ill in Rome and might even result in a treason trial. Although he had to admit that being hailed as a king was an experience which could easily become addictive. And of course if the Egyptian people decided (of their own accord) to worship him as the god Amon, he could hardly refuse. A slow smile of anticipation spread over Caesar's rugged features. He was beginning to feel that this voyage was going to be one of the highlights of his life.

He was not disappointed. Soon they pulled away from the lush green swamp land of the Delta into the main tributary of the Nile and the hot, enticing smell of the desert began to fill the air. It was rather like cruising through a landscape painting with only the most restful images to lull the senses. Great, waving thickets of green papyrus, palm trees rustling in the light breeze, blue sky, honey-coloured sand, whitewashed buildings whose brightness hurt the eye. Often they came ashore even at the most insignificant hamlets and the people swarmed out like ants and fell on their faces, shaking with fear at the majesty of the royal couple and the hordes of soldiers who accompanied them. At these times a herald with a shaven head read long, droning proclamations from a papyrus scroll, gesturing often towards Caesar. Jupiter only knows what he's saying, thought Caesar, but he was amused and gratified by the way the villagers gasped, prostrated themselves and banged their heads in the dust after these announcements. He enjoyed raising them graciously to their feet and being shown around muddy potters' studios or village bakeries by people whose eyes were round with awe.

Five days out of Alexandria they reached Memphis, which was as hot as an inferno. Even the pavements seemed to give off a blasting heat and the dappled shade of courtyard gardens with their splashing fountains offered the only respite. But even here the stinging sand was a problem. It was borne in from the desert on a gnawing wind and invaded everything. Hair, clothing, the windowsills of houses. And yet to ride out in the relative cool of the evening to see the pyramids made it all worthwhile. At first the sky was the drab brown of sackcloth, but soon it flushed to wild rose and then lavender and darkest blue. Bright stars began to prick the canopy of the heavens and campfires were lit. Some eerie, wailing chant to the god Horus rang out from the darkness where the royal servants were pitching their camp. And with a strange, prickling sense of misgiving Caesar looked across at Cleopatra in the red glow of the firelight and realized that Egypt was beginning to lay hold of his heart just as surely as the Queen. By dawn his uneasiness had vanished. He climbed the tallest pyramid to watch the sunrise and felt immortal.

Cleopatra, watching him searchingly through each passing day, felt a growing satisfaction with her strategy. It was working, she was sure it was working. Caesar himself would soon leave Egypt – she knew that and felt only relief at the knowledge. But he would not abandon her to her enemies. He would not risk losing the right to be worshipped as a god, nor would he want his unborn child to be harmed in any way. A Roman army would be left to protect her.

Often in the relative cool of the evening, she would look out over the moonlit river and breathe a heartfelt sigh of relief. For the moment, at least, she and her baby were safe.

In her first, blind panic at finding herself in the dungeon, Arsinoë struck out at the man who was holding her. The damp, invisible walls seemed to be closing in around her and she shrieked and shrieked in terror. Suddenly powerful hands gripped her mouth, throttling back her screams.

'Stop it!' he snarled. 'They'll only find some new torment for you if they realize you're afraid. You'll be locked up in a smaller space just to amuse them. I'm your friend, I'll do what I can to help you, but you must stop screaming. Do you understand?'

She whimpered agreement, nodding her head, and abruptly he released her. A muffled sob escaped her and he caught her against his chest so hard that he yanked her hair.

'Filthy barbarians!' he hissed. 'Roman scum! Who are you? Why have they done this to you?'

She drew in breath, her pride stiffening at the memory of who she was.

'I am Princess Arsinoë of the Egyptian royal house of Ptolemy,' she replied with dignity. 'And who are you?'

'Vercingetorix, son of Celtillus, King of the Arverni in Gaul. And a friend of yours, lady, since you speak so hotly against Julius Caesar.'

Arsinoë gave a small, choking laugh that was closer to a sob. Vercingetorix, King of the Arverni in Gaul ... What a barbarous name and what a barbarous origin! No doubt he was little more than some petty chieftain, the sort of man who would have ended up working as a stablehand if he had ever been sold as a slave in Egypt. The sort of man who would not have dared even to speak to her, much less address her as a friend in her grandfather's household. Arsinoë's mouth tightened. Well, her grandfather's household was hundreds of miles away and noble customs would be of very little use here. And, in spite of this man's strangely accented Latin and the squalor of their surroundings, he was as courteous as any diplomat presenting his credentials at court.

'What is it?' he asked.

'Nothing. It seems so ridiculous to be talking like this, as if we were at a formal reception. And look at us! Not that you can even see us for the dark.'

He caught the edge of terror in her voice and his hand closed warmly over hers.

'Pretend we are at a formal reception,' he urged. 'And come and sit with me.'

She stumbled on the damp, uneven floor and gasped as he steadied her.

'There's a stone ledge here which I use as a seat. Can you feel it?'

She ran shaking hands over the shape and nodded, forgetting he could not see.

'Yes,' she said.

'Then sit down. I'll fetch you a drink.'

The ledge was damp with a bone-chilling cold that struck up from below. She heard cautious sounds in the darkness. A clatter, a splashing. Then Vercingetorix returned and sat beside her, putting a metal cup in her hands.

'It's only water,' he apologized. 'But it's not too bad. And I've half an onion and some stale bread if you're hungry.'

Arsinoë gave another choking laugh.

'You're very kind, sir,' she replied unsteadily. 'But I can never eat much at these diplomatic receptions.'

'That's better,' he said warmly. 'A sense of humour is a great aid to survival in this place.'

She gulped some of the water. It was intensely cold and had a rather metallic taste, but it lessened her sense of unreality. Straining her eyes, she looked around, but the darkness remained wholly impenetrable. Panic shook her again.

'How can you bear it?' she cried.

'Steady now, steady. You must learn to think of other things. Tell me about yourself for a start. Why did they send you here? What offence did you commit?'

'I led an army against Julius Caesar,' replied Arsinoë with a touch of pride.

'You?'

'Yes. But I was vanquished in the end and brought here. What about you?'

'The same,' agreed Vercingetorix in a harsh voice. 'Eighty thousand men, but in the end it was useless. My own Gauls were terrified of Caesar, they began to desert me. I did all I could to stop it – any that I caught sneaking away had their ears hacked off or one eye gouged out – but even that didn't halt the rot. They preferred mutilation to fighting Caesar. He's a monster, a demon in human form, but a brilliant general. I don't believe there's a man – or woman – alive who can get the better of him.'

'My sister thinks she can,' observed Arsinoë bitterly.

'What do you mean? What has she done?'

Arsinoë's whole story tumbled out. She kept nothing back. Her love for Cleopatra, her disapproval of her, the way they always seemed to quarrel. How she had

138

felt it her duty to fight Caesar and how viciously he had hated her for resisting.

'But it was our country! Ours!' she finished passionately. 'Why shouldn't we fight to keep it? What right did he have to come and seize it?'

Vercingetorix gave a throttled growl of laughter.

'Right?' he echoed. 'Right? It's a long time since Romans worried about right and wrong, Princess. All they care about is money and battles and glory. You're a brave woman, but you would have been wiser to fling yourself at Caesar's feet right from the start.'

Arsinoë gazed around her in despair, feeling a renewed awareness of the horror that surrounded her. Their voices echoed strangely in the curved space and she could hear the dismal sounds of dripping water and small, scuttling feet. The noxious odours of the dungeon seemed to rise up and assault her like a blow in the face. Damp straw, human sweat and excrement and a dank smell of decay.

'Then what should I have done?' she cried despairingly. 'I thought I was doing the right thing, that God would help me.'

Vercingetorix made a noise low in his throat, like the sound of a wounded animal.

'My gods seem to have forsaken me,' he said wearily. 'I don't know about yours, but I wouldn't trust them too much if I were you. After five years in captivity, you begin to wonder whether they even exist.'

'Five years?' echoed Arsinoë in an appalled voice. 'Do you mean to tell me you've been here five years?'

He made another sound that might have been a laugh if it had not held so much pain.

'Not all in this place, no. I don't think anyone could survive the Tullian prison for that long. No, I'm only brought here from time to time to break my spirit. But

Caesar doesn't want to blind me or kill me yet. I'm to be kept alive to march in his triumph when he's finished conquering the rest of the world.' He spat suddenly and violently on the floor and rattled the chains that fettered his leg. 'Gods, I wish I could ruin that day for him.'

Arsinoë swallowed fearfully.

'What about me?' she croaked. 'Will he leave me here until his triumph?'

Vercingetorix crushed her hand in his.

'I doubt it,' he said. 'I've spent long periods under house arrest with Roman families, sometimes quite decently treated. And you probably will too. This is just a way of softening you up, showing you who is boss.'

Arsinoë drew a quick, unsteady breath of relief. Sunlight, a clean bed, the sky overhead. Would she really see those things again?

'And after the triumph?' she persisted. 'What then? What will happen to us?'

He was silent so long that a chill sense of dread overtook her.

'I don't know!' he hissed at last. 'But we shouldn't give up hope. Not everyone in Rome loves Julius Caesar, Princess. Half the nobles hate his guts and they're simmering with thoughts of revolution. He could be overthrown and we could be set free.'

'And if he's not?' she said unsteadily.

He caught her hair in bunches, framing her cheeks and thrust his face close to hers almost as if he could see her.

'Whatever happens, if you get the chance, live!' he urged. 'Never mind about thrones or pride or anything else. Crawl on your belly to Caesar or anyone else who can help you. But live, Arsinoë! Live!'

*

Three weeks after her return from the cruise on the Nile, Cleopatra went into labour. She was in her own chambers in the palace when the first pain seized her. It was like the ruthless, insistent squeezing of an olive press crushing ripe fruit. She gasped as it bore down on her spine and clapped her hands to her back. Charmion dropped the clothes she was folding and came across to her.

'Are you all right?' she asked sharply.

It was passing now. Cleopatra looked up, her eyes shining. 'I had a pain,' she said joyfully.

The two serving women exchanged expert glances.

'It may be false labour,' remarked Iras. 'You're still four weeks early.'

'All the better!' cried Cleopatra impatiently, lurching to her feet and waddling across the room. 'I'm so sick of having this tied to my belly like a sack of grain. I'm sick of being heavy and clumsy and ugly. I want it over.'

Iras shrugged.

'It'll come when it's ready,' she insisted. 'There's not much you can do to change that. And you'd better sit and rest for a while. If it happens tonight, you're going to need all your strength.'

Unobtrusively Charmion turned the sand glass over so that the grains began to flow. Less than half an hour later Cleopatra gave another gasp, and shot a triumphant glance at her servants. This time the pain was longer and stronger.

'I think you'd better call Olympus,' she said shakily, when it was over. 'And the midwife.'

The midwife was a brisk, plump woman called Lois with greying hair and a professional manner. After a thorough examination, she frowned.

'Well, you can send for the birth chair and keep hot

water and clean towels on hand,' she said. 'She's started, that's sure. But it's all in the back, not the front. We're in for a long night. Long and painful.'

After a couple of hours, Cleopatra was inclined to agree with her. The first euphoria which seemed to have given her wings had now vanished and she was caught in a cycle of back-breaking torment and long, weary walks around the room with Iras and Charmion supporting her. Already her hair was plastered to her head with sweat, her pupils were dilated and she felt a strong temptation to lie down sobbing and pounding her fists.

'Will it be much longer?' she gasped hoarsely at the end of a particularly ferocious pang.

The midwife chuckled.

'Oh, bless you, yes! You've hardly started, my lady.'

'But it's so painful!'

'This isn't pain. Not compared to what will follow.'

By midnight Cleopatra understood that. All semblance of control had fled. She crouched like an animal on all fours, whimpering and moaning. She threshed and screamed and hurled silver cups at her attendants. She cried and begged them to take pity on her, to kill her, to kill the baby. Anything, anything to stop the pain. And still the child stubbornly refused to be born. Olympus with a worried frown left the midwife in charge and summoned the two serving women into the inner room for a hasty conference.

'She wanted Caesar to be present at the birth,' he said without preamble. 'In the old, Egyptian traditional manner with all of us dressed in the robes of gods and goddesses. But I can't allow it. Not in the condition she's in. All the same, you'd better notify him that her time has come, Iras. Tell him she's well and comfortable and we'll let him in once the birth is safely over.'

Caesar was in his own chambers frowning over dispatches from Africa when the black woman arrived. His bowels turned to water at her message and he even felt a chill of panic at the old Roman superstition that it was bad luck to cross paths with a Negro. Forcing himself to remain calm, he offered her wine and sat down to question her.

'How long is it since she started? It's not due yet, is it? What does the midwife say? Is all going well? Is she in much pain?'

Iras gave him a compassionate smile. She had been a fervent admirer of Julius Caesar since the day he executed Pothinus and she found his panic rather touching. Poor old man, he looked more like a grandfather than anything else with that greying hair and wrinkly neck. But he cared about Cleopatra. Yes, he did. And that made Iras warm to him.

'Don't you get upset,' she advised. 'We'll call you as soon as anything happens.'

'Let me come and wait in the room next door,' demanded Caesar abruptly. 'That way I'll be with her as soon as I can.'

He knew he had made a mistake as soon as they ushered him into the chamber. It was fragrant with sandalwood, decorated with exquisite landscape paintings, comfortably furnished with scarlet-hung couches and tables and chests of citrus woods, even equipped with boxes of books. But the walls were too thin. Gods! Were they killing pigs next door? From the squealing and the shuffling footsteps, it sounded like it. Determinedly Caesar unrolled one of the dispatches, sat in a folding wooden chair and tried to read, but the words danced stupidly before his eyes. Africa is in revolt, he thought. I'll have to go and subdue it at once or the war will all blaze up again. Pompeius will

. . . by the gods! Are they killing that girl? That brought him a blind rush of horrified thoughts about Julia's death in childbirth. He rose to his feet, crushing the document in his hand and cursing.

At last shortly after dawn there was a tap at the door. Caesar opened it to find a young woman with red-gold hair and wearing some ridiculous costume gazing earnestly at him.

'Who the hell are you?' he growled.

'The goddess Mut,' she replied with a touch of embarrassment. 'I've come with a message, Lord Amon. Your Goddess Queen – '

'Never mind that foolishness now!' he snarled, ripping the headdress off her head and trampling it on the floor. 'I'm concerned with a woman, not a goddess! How is she? What's happened?'

Charmion gave up the play-acting with relief.

'You're the father of a fine boy, my lord,' she said warmly. 'Congratulations. And the Queen is – '

But he had to see for himself. Pushing past her with an oath, he ignored the swaddled, squalling baby that the midwife held out to him as he entered the room. Oblivious to all else, he flung himself on his knees beside the ivory pale figure that lay in the vast, carved bed. Her cheeks were like wax and there was an ominous stillness about her. For one heart-stopping moment he thought she was already dead. Then he saw the tears that were welling out from below her dark eyelashes.

'What's this?' he croaked. 'Tears? Not from my brave, Egyptian Queen.'

She made a faint sound, half-way between a sob and a groan. It was so unlike her that he felt stunned. Rising to his feet, he sat on the edge of the bed and gathered her into his arms. Her perfumed black hair fell forward and brushed his face, but she was as limp as a rag doll in his embrace. All the same, he felt a rush of gladness simply to know that she was alive.

'Don't cry,' he urged, patting her back. 'I'll take care of you, my love. You must come to Rome and visit me and I'll set up a gold statue of you in a temple so that everyone can worship you. I'll have to go to Africa for a little while, but we'll soon be together again. You'll see. I'll treat you as if you really were my wife. I promise.'

It was the sort of soothing nonsense any man would have babbled when a woman was near death. How could he possibly know that she would recover and demand fulfilment of the promise?

CHAPTER EIGHT

'Don't I know you from somewhere?' asked Cotta, sucking an olive off a toothpick and eyeing Octavian thoughtfully.

Octavian's heart lurched wildly and the room seemed to roar about him. The blood drained from his face and he felt sick and cold. He was agonizingly conscious of each individual chink of glass and cutlery, of the braying laugh of a senator's wife, of his stepfather's deep, measured voice somewhere in the background. He dropped his eyes.

'I don't think so,' he said in a stifled voice.

Perhaps it was the way that the plate of savouries began to tremble in his outstretched hand that betrayed him. Or the sudden wash of colour that scorched his cheeks. Whatever the reason, he found Cotta's relentless fingers forcing up his chin.

'Well, well, well,' murmured Cotta appreciatively. 'Don't be shy. Look at me, dear boy. It's hardly polite to avoid someone who shares such pleasant memories.'

He flashed Cotta a glance of startled dismay and loathing. The senator's eyes were narrowed in unmistakable recognition and a growing gleam of calculation. Octavian began to feel deeply uneasy.

'What's this?' asked Philippus genially, appearing at Cotta's shoulder. 'You've already met my stepson, have you?'

Cotta smiled secretively.

'Yes. We share . . . certain interests.'

'E-Etruscan manuscripts,' blurted out Octavian. 'We

met at the house of Asinius Pollio. We looked at a few things together.'

'Oh?' said Philippus. 'Splendid. Well, you must ask Octavian to show you our library, Cotta. He's got a fine little collection of Etruscan manuscripts there.'

'What a good idea,' purred Cotta. 'It's always nice to escape from these political receptions for a few moments' peace with a kindred spirit. Come along, young man.'

Feeling like a lamb trapped between the altar and the sacrificial knife, Octavian allowed himself to be led away to the library. Once the door was safely barred and they were alone in the dim coolness among the book boxes and sculpted marble busts, he looked apprehensively at Cotta. Cotta smiled.

'Have you been to the Subura lately?'

Octavian's heart sank.

'You won't tell, will you?' he demanded, his eyes wide with alarm.

'Tell? Why should I? But I can't help hoping you might soon make a return visit.'

His hand reached out and stroked Octavian's forearm. Octavian jerked away as if he had been scorched.

'No!' he cried unsteadily. 'I can't – ! I don't ever – '

'Ah. An experiment that didn't work? What a pity. Well, no harm done.'

Octavian gazed at him with overwhelming relief.

'Thank you,' he breathed. 'You promise you won't tell my stepfather?'

Cotta looked amused.

'Philippus? He does rather value the old-fashioned moral standards, doesn't he? I wonder what he'd do to a stepson who disgraced him by unnatural practices? He's an army man, isn't he? Of course the old army punishment was clubbing to death. Do you think he'd go that far? You must be rather anxious about this.'

'Don't tell,' implored Octavian, gabbling in his terror. 'Please don't tell. Anyway, it would incriminate you too.'

Something cold and hard flashed in the depths of Cotta's eyes.

'Incriminate me?' he whispered. 'Why should it? All that I saw as I was walking through the Subura one afternoon was a pretty boy remarkably like you in an alleyway being screwed from behind by another man.'

'That's not true!' cried Octavian. 'You've invented that.'

'Have I? But my reputation is impeccable. If I ever tell my story, do you really think Philippus will believe you rather than me?'

Octavian's throat was suddenly dry and his legs began to tremble so violently they would scarcely hold him.

'But you won't?' he asked hoarsely. 'You won't tell?'

Cotta examined his fingernails and then looked up with an indulgent smile.

'Of course not. But I'd like a tiny favour in return.'

'Anything,' promised Octavian fervently. 'Just tell me.'

'Two thousand denarii. I'm a bit short of cash. Let's say by tomorrow afternoon. You can send it to my warehouse in an unmarked bag.'

Octavian was so outraged that for an insane moment he thought of picking up one of the marble busts and smashing it in Cotta's face. How dare he? The lying, cheating, unscrupulous blackmailer! He could almost feel the satisfying crunch of Cotta's skull beneath the weight. But then there would be the shouts, the footsteps, the explanations.

'I–I can't possibly,' he stammered. 'I don't own that much money.'

'Well, try, dear boy. Try! Otherwise your poor step-father may suffer the pain of receiving a poison pen letter. And we wouldn't want that to happen, would we?'

Cleopatra was still feeling shaken and exhausted from the ordeal of her son's birth when Caesar took his leave of Egypt. During the awkward, dragging months of pregnancy, she had longed passionately for the birth to be over. Time and again she had imagined herself slim and vigorous with a smiling baby tucked under her arm, throwing herself joyfully into the business of governing Egypt. The reality was far different. Her breasts ached and prickled, her stomach was as floppy as an old pig's bladder, the baby seemed to be permanently red and screaming and the mere thought of climbing out of bed was enough to make her burst into weak, miserable tears. Worst of all, she no longer wanted Caesar to leave her, since the prospect of governing Egypt alone was more than she could bear. All she felt able to do was lie with her face turned to the wall, wishing that somebody else would take over everything. Which made his announcement on the fifth day of her lying in all the more of a shock. It was mid morning when he arrived in her chambers and dismissed her attendants.

'I've bad news for you, I'm afraid,' he said, sitting down on the bed.

'What is it?' she asked, her arms tightening instinctively about the baby.

The child whimpered at the disturbance and began to thresh about, opening and closing its mouth in search of her nipple. Unable to find it, he let out a frustrated yell.

'Feed him,' ordered Caesar indulgently. 'I like to watch you.'

Resentfully she dropped her gaze and fumbled her swollen breast free of the clinging robe. She hated his intrusion into these moments of intimacy with her child. Deep down she wanted him to have no claim on the baby, but she knew that was unreasonable. In her rational moments she was fervently grateful for the fact that even at three days Caesarion so unmistakably resembled his father. The fuzz of golden hair on the tiny head, the broad features, the long arms and legs all showed an uncanny resemblance to Julius Caesar and had tapped an unexpected wellspring of pride in the Roman general. He had even begun to talk of staying in Egypt a little longer to watch his son through his first few months of life. Conscious of Caesar's gaze resting tenderly on her, she gripped her nipple between her index and middle fingers and guided it into the howling baby's mouth. The crying stopped magically.

'What's the bad news?' she asked, too absorbed in the rhythmic clamping of the child's jaws to pay much attention.

'I'm afraid I'll have to leave you immediately,' said Caesar regretfully. 'I've just had urgent dispatches from my legate in Asia Minor. His forces have been attacked and defeated by Pharnaces, one of the sons of Mithridates the Great. If I don't hurry there immediately and stamp out the rebellion, he'll try and revive his father's empire.'

Cleopatra stared at him in consternation. A month ago she would have asked for nothing better than to hear this news. Caesar leaving and her kingdom restored to her? She would have danced for joy! Now her mouth sagged open, her eyes blurred and she clutched at his tunic.

'No! No! You can't go! You can't leave me! I'll never be able to cope without you. They'll kill me! And what's to become of Caesarion?'

As if in answer to her question the baby, who had lost the nipple in his mother's frantic movements, opened his mouth and howled indignantly. Much moved, Caesar cupped her breast and guided it back between the tiny lips. As the scalding rain of her tears fell on the downy, golden head, he caught her hand in his and kissed the knuckles.

'Why, sweetheart,' he murmured. 'I had no idea you cared so much about me. I thought you only slept with me for your own advantage.'

Her lips quivered and she looked at him through brimming dark eyes. If she had been honest, she might have replied that he was perfectly right and that the strange phenomenon of childbirth was responsible for her uncharacteristic weakness. Only this morning she had cried for half an hour because Charmion had dropped her favourite drinking cup and broken it. Yet even in the midst of her weakness, she was far too shrewd to waste such an opportunity.

'I don't know how you can say such a thing!' she choked, blinking away the tears. 'I love you, Caesar, and I can't bear to see you leave me.'

Far more deeply stirred than he had ever imagined possible, Caesar drew her into a tender embrace. Inhaling the warm perfume of her hair and acutely conscious of the sucking child at her breast, he felt a pang of some unrecognizable emotion stab through him. Could it be love? Could he really be so foolish? It was madness. Yet in that instant he wanted to seize her and carry her away with him, divorce Calpurnia and marry her, force the Romans to accept her and name this golden-haired child as his legal heir. He ground his teeth at the absurdity of it.

'I love you too,' he said roughly. 'And when these wars are over, I'll find a way of being with you and our son again. I swear it.'

Caesar had little leisure to think of Cleopatra again for a considerable time. Arriving in Asia Minor, he trounced Pharnaces swiftly and conclusively. After the battle, he sat in his tent and wrote a letter to a friend in Rome, describing the campaign. 'I came, I saw, I conquered.'

Blowing out the lamp, he lay down on his stretcher and listened to the night noises of the camp. Drunken victory songs and the clashing of swords on shields, a sentry's challenge, the sound of horses stamping their hooves in the picket lines. A good world, a man's world. He always enjoyed the comradeship, the excitement of shared danger, the euphoria of winning. Yet he could not lose himself in drunken celebration as his men did. He must stay alert to think and plan the next step. So much to do and so little time to do it! At least Egypt was settled – he allowed himself a brief, sentimental image of Cleopatra nursing their baby son and smiled wryly. She had fought him bitterly when he ordered her to marry her surviving brother Ptolemy just before his departure, but she had obeyed him. It would ensure greater stability in Egypt, although Caesar himself hated the thought. If the boy had been old enough to be a true husband to her, he would never have allowed it. He could not bear to think of another man screwing her, but Ptolemy could be poisoned long before that happened.

In the meantime Caesar had his next campaign to

plan. The Pompeians must be stamped out decisively in Africa and Spain. After that affairs in Rome must be sorted out. Those who opposed him in the Senate must be bought off or killed. More important still, he must formally name an heir. While he might maintain the fiction that these bloody campaigns were being fought for the glory of Rome, in his innermost heart Caesar knew better. They were being fought for the glory of his own name. And how was that to be upheld if he left no formal heir to perform the proper religious rites and raise statues and temples in his honour? For a moment he thought wistfully of that golden-haired baby, then he scowled and dismissed the notion. No. His heir must be a Roman. Probably one of his great-nephews, as he had already half promised his family. Octavian was said to be intelligent . . .

He would have time to inspect the boy soon enough. Before tackling the remaining Pompeian forces, he must go to Rome and raise fresh troops. His thoughts began to drift, skimming across the dark waves of the Mediterranean to that ramshackle city clinging to its seven hills. He saw himself returning in triumph and imagined the cheers, the wildly waving crowds, the formal welcome of his Master of the Horse, Mark Antony. An excellent choice, Mark Antony. The finest second-in-command any dictator could possibly have, mainly because he was so admirably second rate. A brave soldier, but not as brave as Caesar. A drunk and a womanizer on a scale so horrendous that he made Caesar look positively virtuous. And, above all, irredeemably stupid. Oh, he could be counted on to keep order and to propose the laws that Caesar wanted but the poor fellow was wood from the neck up. A ditherer, only capable of decisive action when somebody smarter told him what to do. Caesar smiled and turned over, settling for sleep. He was really very fond of Mark Antony. Rome couldn't possibly have been left in better hands.

Not everyone would have agreed with that judgement. The more conservative members of society blenched at Antony's excesses. Driving a chariot drawn by lions, feasting with mimes and jesters, swaggering into the Senate drunk or hung-over. Many grey heads were shaken over Antony and his friend Dolabella. What will they get up to next? was the disapproving murmur. It was not long before the senators had their answer.

Dolabella, perpetually short of money and unlucky at the gambling tables, proposed to introduce a law cancelling all debts. Since it could not be supposed that all citizens would see the charm of such a law, he intended to post armed soldiers in the Forum to ensure its passage. And he urged Antony to do likewise. Antony agreed and they sealed the bargain with a drink. And another. At length Antony lurched off, promising to meet Dolabella at noon in the Forum. All might have gone according to plan if Antony had not met two cooler advisers, Asinius and Trebellius. Half pickled as he was, their assurances that Caesar would not like the law at all began to trouble him. He decided to go home and discuss the matter with his wife Antonia.

The house seemed strangely quiet when he entered, but he made his way from room to room with elaborate softness, hoping to creep up on her and surprise her. In the end Antony was the one surprised. Easing open his bedroom door, he glanced furtively inside and his jaw dropped. Antonia was in bed with Dolabella and there could be no doubt of what they were doing. For a moment Antony gaped in disbelief, then he gave a bellow of rage, unsheathed his sword and charged.

'You bastard! You slimy, conniving bastard! I'll kill you for this!'

Dolabella, wilting fast, escaped from the bedroom with no more than a flesh wound to the backside and fled down the street, modestly covering his private parts. Antonia was hauled shrieking from the bed and dragged about by her hair, babbling pleas for forgiveness along with refusals to surrender her dowry. Antony went raging through the house with his sword, turning the place upside down. The slaves all ran for cover, protesting that they had seen nothing, heard nothing, suspected nothing. And the neighbours winced at the noise and said that it sounded like Master Antony was having another one of them rowdy parties.

When Antony's rage finally cooled enough to allow any rational speech, he drove his wife from the house, with the announcement that he intended to divorce her. Even so, he was still storming about the house, smashing up furniture and drinking deeply when a reluctant senatorial messenger advanced gingerly through the atrium to find him.

'Fuck off!' shouted Antony, hurling a goblet of Tyrian glass at the messenger's head.

'But, sir, there's an emergency in the Forum! Dolabella has occupied the place with armed soldiers to make sure that his law cancelling debts gets passed. The Senate says you've got to come and deal with him.'

A mad grin split Antony's handsome face.

'Oh, I'll deal with him,' he vowed softly, punching one hand into the other. 'I'll slaughter the little runt. Just let me at him.'

Swept along by wine and outrage he rode to his barracks, summoned a troop of soldiers and led them to the Forum at breakneck pace. The mood of the place was already dangerous. Scarlet-cloaked soldiers with unsheathed swords stood all around the perimeter, blocking every exit. An uneasy crowd of civilians milled about muttering in the centre of the open piazza. The men were being forced to file past ballot boxes supervised by grim-faced soldiers, while the women and children were huddling together and crying. High on a podium erected next to the equestrian statue of Julius Caesar, Dolabella's gingery hair glinted unmistakably in the sunlight as he harangued the crowd. Antony's heart almost burst from his breast with murderous rage as he ordered the trumpeter to sound the attack.

'Ten thousand sesterces for the man who brings me Dolabella's head!' he shouted.

With a bloodcurdling war-cry Antony's troops rushed in to win the promised prize. In such a confined space disaster was inevitable. Screams of terror rang through the air as women and children were trampled underfoot. In some fuzzy corner of his brain Antony felt sorry for the civilians, especially when his foot came down on something soft and he looked down through the swirl of tunics and bare legs to see a small girl prostrate beneath him. He tried to drag her up with his free hand and then saw that her head had been slashed half off her shoulders. It lolled sideways, dripping blood, as he dropped her. His eyes blurred with sentimental tears and a renewed flame of rage spurted through him as he waded through the swaying throng of bodies. This was all Dolabella's fault and he must be made to pay for it! A glancing blow from the flat of a sword hit Antony's helmet and he paused, shaking his head and listening to the violent ringing in his ears. The din around him was appalling. The clash of swords, the shrieks of fear and agony, the grunts and snarls of hand-to-hand fighting. And he should never have drunk so much wine. His limbs felt light, flailing, uncontrollable. As if in a dream he lurched through oncoming soldiers, screaming women and bleeding men towards that ginger-haired figure on the rostrum. Then suddenly there was a triumphant roar as some of Antony's soldiers reached Dolabella and hauled him down into the crowd. Antony quickened his floundering pace. In spite of the reward he had offered, he wanted to be the one who dealt Dolabella the death blow.

Suddenly, unbelievably, a toga-clad figure lurched up from the paving stones ahead of him. The back of a ginger head rose tauntingly in front of him. With a savage cry Antony hauled his opponent into a neck lock and stabbed him again and again with his short sword. Then exultantly he hauled Dolabella around so that the treacherous bastard could see who had attacked him before he died. But it was not Dolabella. To Antony's consternation he found himself staring into the unfamiliar features of a sixteen- or seventeen-year-old boy who was choking to death on a torrent of his own blood.

'No!' he shouted as the boy gurgled, rolled his eyes and pitched forward on top of him.

Appalled, Antony hugged him, fruitlessly slapping his face to try and revive him. Then, realizing the futility of it, he shuddered, dropped the still warm corpse and lumbered through the press of bodies to the base of Caesar's statue. Two figures were swaying wildly on the bronze horse's back – one of Dolabella's men and one of Antony's. As he watched, one of them was sent toppling to the ground, breaking his neck with an audible snap. Mastering the urge to heave up his guts Antony cupped his hands and shouted to the trumpeter who was visible on the steps of Venus's temple.

'Sound the retreat!'

It was an ignominious end to a totally ill-advised engagement and Antony's chagrin was only increased when he learned that the total of eight hundred dead did not include Dolabella. Somehow his rival had escaped unscathed in the confusion.

Antony woke the following day with an aching head, a sour taste in his mouth and a feeling of sick apprehension in his stomach. What on earth would Caesar say when he heard of this? With a violent shudder, he buried his head in his hands.

'Oh, shit,' he groaned. 'Oh, shit, shit, shit!'

Caesar had plenty to say when he heard about the incident. It was September when he crossed from Greece into Italy and the pompous elder statesman Marcus Tullius Cicero made it his business to travel south nearly all the way to Brundisium to deliver the news. Pious old windbag! thought Caesar sourly as he listened to Cicero's rolling, mellifluous voice and watched the noble expression of outrage on his dignified, bearded face. No doubt he's only too happy to have something to draw attention away from him. What if I asked him point blank why he supported Pompey in the Civil War? What would he say then, the garrulous old fart? Yet he listened to Cicero, thanked him civilly and rode off towards Rome with a face like a thundercloud.

When at last he came through the cheering crowds to his own house near the temple of Vesta, he was met at the front door by a handsome, rather girlish-looking youth and a serious-faced young woman. Even without the solemn announcement of his name-calling slave, he immediately guessed that he was looking at his great-niece and nephew. They were an attractive-looking pair, his sister Julia's grandchildren, and it gratified him to see them looking so well turned out. Octavia wore the modest dress of a Roman matron, a long stola reaching to her feet, which was saved from dowdiness by its delicate pale blue colour and gold thread embroidery. Her gold hair was arranged in a neat bun on top of her head and a pair of gold and pearl drop earrings hung from her ears. Her younger brother was equally neat in a white tunic with a gold amulet around his neck and the purple, embroidered toga of childhood draped around him. Far too pretty for a boy, thought Caesar. If it weren't for those outlandish eyebrows that meet across his nose, we could enter him in a maidens' choir. But the lad has something on his conscience, some secret that's gnawing away like a fox at his vitals, or I'm no judge of character. That nervous, darting look and the shadows under his eyes are dead give-aways. I must find out what it is when I have time. Smiling genially, he kissed them both.

'How are you, then?' he asked. 'Any children to show me, Octavia?'

'Not yet, Uncle.'

He fancied there was a hint of coolness in the girl's manner. Perhaps she shared her husband's absurd objection to Caesar's prolonged dictatorship? Well, she would soon learn better. And if she didn't, a divorce could always be arranged.

Octavian's embrace too was stiff, almost apprehensive, and he wore the wary look Caesar had seen on the faces of soldiers expecting an ambush. Another republican? No. There was no mistaking the sincerity in the boy's voice as he stammered out a thoroughly disjointed greeting.

'I–I–I'm very glad to see you again, sir. I've always admired your military conquests so much. And I'm very interested in your plans for Rome once this war is really over.'

What was the matter with the boy then? Caesar would have questioned him further, but at that moment Calpurnia came forward into the atrium to join in the greetings. Caesar looked down at his drab, dutiful wife and sighed inwardly. Calpurnia couldn't be more than thirty, but she was turning prematurely grey and her face always wore a strained, watchful expression. Perhaps she worried about his safety while he was away on campaign? He felt that he knew very little about her, considering that he had been married to her for twelve years. All the same, it would be only polite to take her to bed now that he was home.

'Hello, my dear,' he murmured, kissing her on both cheeks. 'What a pleasure it is to see you again. Perhaps we can retire to your rooms and catch up on each other's news?'

As he spoke, he let his fingers rub a small, caressing whorl in the hollow of her back. Calpurnia gazed up at him with grateful brown eyes. Perhaps this time she would conceive the child she had always longed for?

'Oh, yes, Gaius,' she agreed.

He steered her adroitly towards the peristyle and the stairs leading to her bedroom. A momentary thrill of excitement tingled through him as he thought how ardently he would be ascending these stairs if Cleopatra were clinging to his arm. Would he ever see the Egyptian Queen again? Or his baby son? Then another thought struck him, a quite unrelated thought. He turned back to the slave who was carrying his luggage.

'Carus, summon Mark Antony to see me as soon as you can find him.'

Caesar lost no time in reducing Antony to mincemeat the following morning. The Master of the Horse had been expecting the summons and arrived looking unusually subdued, dressed in a simple tunic with a broad purple stripe to show his senatorial rank. Striding into the vestibule of Caesar's house, he cannoned straight into Caesar's great-niece, Octavia.

'Oh, I'm sorry!' she gasped, by no means dismayed to find Antony's brawny arms steadying her. She gave him a small, uncertain smile.

'Not hurt, I hope?'

His voice was a low growl that sent shivers chasing down her spine and his gaze lingered on her with what she hoped was brooding fascination. In fact Antony was trying to puzzle out where he had seen her before. Quite pretty, if you liked that tall, cool, fair type. Antony didn't. Too insipid for his taste. He preferred a woman with tits and a bum, something to get hold of. All the same, he gave her a preoccupied smile. Octavia's heart fluttered and she stepped back a pace. Her lips parted and one hand floated up towards her breast.

'You must be Marcus Antonius,' she said breathlessly. 'Uncle Julius is expecting you. I'll go and find –'

'No need, Octavia. I'm right here.'

Caesar's voice cut through the air like a sharpened sword. A stab of panic pierced Antony as he saw that familiar figure outlined against the flood of light from the inner courtyard. Curse the old bastard, he thought. He's still as dangerous as ever. With his back to the light Caesar held all the advantage. He could see Antony's features, while his own remained mysteriously in shadow. For several heartbeats his gaze scanned Antony, taking in every detail of his bloodshot hazel eyes, his civilian clothes and even the colourful bruise on his cheekbone, a legacy of the brawl in the Forum. Antony shifted restlessly, feeling his bowels turn to water. Then Caesar made a sharp, barking sound that might have been a cough or a snort of disapproval.

'Follow me,' he ordered, turning on his heel.

Antony flinched and hastened to obey. He caught a look of furtive sympathy on Octavia's face and gave her a quick, wry smile before striding off in Caesar's train. Ageing he might be, but he still moved with military haste. He was already half way down the covered colonnade next to the courtyard when the younger man caught him up. Antony glanced at the shady garden with its splashing fountain, cool, green grapevine and stone bench hot from the sun and wished he were eighty years old and safely retired. Instead he felt like a schoolboy again, being dragged off for a beating after failing to learn his Homer. And the room they were entering was not unlike a schoolmaster's lair. The walls were covered with paintings from Greek myths and there were other signs of scholarship. An abacus, sitting on a wooden cupboard, several boxes of books, a map of Africa weighted down by two large stones, a set of mathematical tables for calculating the movement of the planets. All of this impedimenta was arranged with a geometrical precision that struck a cold chill of dismay through Antony. His own office was a chaotic mess of staff lists, legionary memos, empty wine cups and betting tokens. And he never read a book if he could avoid it.

'Before we begin,' said Caesar acidly, 'let me advise you to stop flirting with my great-niece Octavia. She's a respectable married woman and I will not tolerate any scandals in my family. I'll make myself clearer. Touch her and I'll hang you up by the balls from the temple of Vesta. Is that understood?'

'Y-yes, Caesar.'

'Caesar?'

'Yes, sir!'

'Sit down,' ordered Caesar abruptly.

Antony lowered his bulk into a flimsy wooden folding chair and sat waiting. Caesar did not join him. He simply continued to pace while the silence lengthened painfully. Outside in the courtyard Antony heard a snatch of conversation swiftly hushed. It was the girl's voice. Octavia's. And someone else's, naggingly familiar, a man's but high pitched. A waft of bitter-sweet scent drifted in on the warm air. There must be a citron tree in bloom out there, thought Antony, and wished for one passionate moment that he were safely out there with that cool, blonde girl, who looked as if she had never made a scene in her life. Then Caesar spoke.

'I thought you were an excellent officer,' he said calmly, and Antony felt a rush of pride and gratitude at this unexpected praise. 'But I was mistaken.'

Antony's face was a ludicrous study in disappointment. He bit his lip and gazed at Caesar with the stricken look of a whipped puppy.

'You were brave, cheerful, good-natured, popular with the men and quick to seize a military advantage. I trusted you completely. So much so that I made you Master of the Horse. The second highest office that Rome can bestow in time of war. But you've betrayed me.'

'Sir!' began Antony protestingly.

Caesar's open hand slammed down on the table, setting the styluses and writing tablets rattling.

'Betrayed me!' he repeated with emphasis. 'I trusted you to keep good order in Rome while I was delayed by military emergencies overseas and what do I find on my return? Rome in an uproar, eight hundred people dead in the Forum and you prancing about acting the wronged husband like a clown in a farce! What have you got to say for yourself? Answer me!'

'Sir!' cried Antony hotly. 'There was no acting involved. Dolabella was screwing my wife in my own bed! Besides, that wasn't the only reason I intervened. He was trying to bring in a law to cancel all debts and the Senate was in an uproar about it. They begged me to protect the voters.'

'Which you did by slaughtering them?' demanded Caesar savagely. 'No, Antony, it won't wash! You allowed a personal vendetta to cloud your judgement. In addition, there are a dozen rabble-rousing proletarians who are prepared to swear that you were drunk at the time of the outrage. This is the kind of publicity I can ill afford in my subordinates. Everywhere I turn, I hear bad reports of you. Cavorting naked with whores in public fountains, provoking riots, arriving so drunk at the Forum that you throw up all over your toga before important meetings. It is simply not good enough! If this continues, I shall have to dismiss you from the post of Master of the Horse. Your morals are disgraceful.'

Antony had been unconsciously fiddling with a wooden ruler, bending it in his powerful hands as Caesar harangued him. Now it broke with a loud, snapping sound. With an exclamation of impatience, he tossed the pieces aside. Suddenly his annoyance overcame his common sense.

'Don't give me that crap about morals! Who are you to talk? Everybody in Rome knows about the bastard you fathered on Cleopatra!'

Caesar's face was suddenly as pale and cold as a wax funeral mask with only the eyes live and blazing. He took in a breath with a soft hushed sibilance like a hunter stalking his prey so that Antony began to regret his audacity.

'Listen to me,' said Caesar with sinister gentleness. 'My relationship with the Egyptian Queen and her child is nobody's business but mine. And I won't be told by you or anyone else how to conduct it. Is that clear?'

'I don't give a brass as about what you do with your private life,' Antony retorted. 'But you ought to know what the people are saying about you. Gods, you wouldn't believe the lengths they're going to! Some of them claim that you're going to name this Egyptian child as your heir.'

Caesar's ominous control snapped.

'And what if I am?' he roared. 'Is it any of your business or the Senate's? If I want to make my son Ptolemy Caesar my heir, there's nothing you or anybody else in Rome can do to stop me!'

Outside in the courtyard the fair-haired youth Octavian was sitting as close as he dared to the half-open door of Caesar's office. At these words he rose to his feet with his mouth gaping open in disbelief. A swift flush of rage mottled his delicate features. His sister, who was trailing her fingers in the cool water of the fountain darted towards him with a protesting gesture.

'Octavian, you shouldn't – '

'Shut up and listen,' he hissed, clutching her arm and forcing her onto the bench.

His grip was frighteningly strong for someone so lightly built and the look in his eyes frightened her even more. She sat down, massaging her wrist. From the interior of the office came Caesar's voice, no longer so loud, but still resonant with passionate certainty.

'You don't seem to understand, my dear Mark Antony, just how much things have changed in Rome. This may still be a republic, but it's a republic in name and nothing else. Only one man's will counts in Rome any more. Mine! And the sooner you and your backbiting, gossiping, interfering senatorial friends accept that, the better it will be for you. And if that includes accepting Ptolemy Caesar as my heir, by the gods you'd better look as if you like it!'

Antony stared at Caesar in stupefaction.

'B-but you can't do that!' he stammered. 'The consuls won't let you.'

'Consuls!' sneered Caesar. 'What are the consuls worth these days? In any case, they'll be appointees of mine. As a matter of fact, I had even intended to make you consul next year. But I see now that you are quite unworthy of the position.'

The blood rushed to Antony's head at this fresh humiliation. Not even pausing to consider the wisdom of his retort, he hit back.

'I was under the impression that the consulship was an elected office.'

Caesar gave a wintry smile.

'Not any more,' he said. 'And if it depended on merit you'd never win it. You're terminally stupid, Mark Antony. About the only good thing to be said for you is that you haven't the brains to be frightened in battle. Other than that, you're idle, frivolous and incapable of organizing a piss-up in a tavern, much less a city the size of Rome.'

Seething at this attack, Antony turned on his heel.

'Then I'd better get out of here before I wreck any more of your plans, hadn't I?' he snarled.

'Stop! I haven't finished with you.'

Caesar paced negligently across the room and gazed at Antony with contempt.

'You may still be of use to me if you can pull yourself together,' he said. 'I may even consider giving you a consulship at some future date if – '

Antony stared at him in bewilderment.

'If –?' he prompted.

'If you mend your ways. There is a certain marriage alliance that I need and I'm sure you would profit from the influence of a good woman.'

Outside Octavia's heart leapt with a wild and quite irrational hope. She would gladly divorce her dull, middle-aged husband for an exuberant union with Antony.

'Who is it?' he demanded suspiciously.

'Fulvia, the widow of Clodius.'

'No!' shouted Antony. 'I won't do it!'

Caesar smiled.

'Why not? You've divorced Antonia, haven't you?'

'Yes, but Fulvia has a face like the back end of an African baboon. And she reads books on philosophy!'

'Then perhaps you'll learn something from her,' murmured Caesar. 'In any case, if you ever want to enjoy my favour again you'll marry the woman. Is that clear?'

There was a long pause.

'Yes,' said Antony in a strangled voice.

As he marched out of Caesar's office, he was in such a blind rage that he didn't watch where he was going.

The bastard, he thought, the arrogant, scheming, old bastard! One of these days I'll pay him back for humiliating me like this! Wrapped in his thoughts, he almost walked straight into Octavia again. She was standing in the courtyard with her poncey little brother Octavian, who looked as if someone had kicked him in the nuts. And a good thing too, thought Antony viciously. But why should Octavia look so stricken? Mindful of Caesar's warning, Antony gave her a small, formal bow.

'Good day, my lady. I hope I didn't hurt you earlier this morning.'

Her face crumpled.

'No, you didn't hurt me,' she said in a rush and hurried abruptly away.

Antony stood staring after her in bewilderment. Women! He'd never understand them! And Octavia seemed quite pleasant, not like Fulvia. This wretched marriage promised to be one of the worst disasters of his life. With a baffled sigh Antony murmured a farewell and made good his escape.

The moment he had departed Caesar appeared in the courtyard and beckoned to Octavian.

'Come here, boy,' he ordered. 'I want a little chat with you. I want to know what's making you look so worried.'

CHAPTER NINE

Caesar's brutality did not take long to have its effect on Arsinoë. After less than a week in the Tullian dungeon, she had succumbed to a quartan fever and woke one night bathed in sweat and raving in delirium. Alarmed by her cries, Vercingetorix groped his way to her in the chill darkness and encountered her burning skin. He swore under his breath and tried frantically to shake some lucid words from her. In vain. Rattling his chains in fury, he shouted himself hoarse until at last the sleepy guards raised the stone in the roof and shone a lamp into the opening.

'What's wrong, Gaul? Got a bellyache?'

'Did Caesar order you to kill the Egyptian princess? If not you'd better get down here fast. She's on the point of death from a fever.'

This caused worried discussions aloft. A messenger was sent to notify the centurion who had brought Arsinoë to the prison in the first place. He vigorously protested his innocence, but passed the matter on to his superior, who did the same. By dawn the disturbing news had reached one of Caesar's highest ranking supporters in the Senate, Quintus Laelius Severus. While Severus hesitated over the appropriate action, his wife Aelia Trebutia took charge.

'You men are such fools!' she said scathingly. 'The girl will die while you make up your minds. Bring her here at once and I'll nurse her. I'll take the responsibility if nobody else will!'

While the rising sun was still striking red and low through the Forum and morning vapours were rising from the chill pavements, Aelia Trebutia arrived in a litter at the Tullian prison. Within a quarter of an hour she had delivered a blistering attack on the prison management, threatened a senatorial enquiry and whisked Arsinoë into a second litter. When Arsinoë began to flail and scream and utter a long, incoherent monologue about Vercingetorix, Aelia solved the problem by bundling the other prisoner into the litter too.

'Send a guard to my house if you're so worried they'll escape!' she shouted, as her litter bearers set off at a brisk trot.

Ten days later Arsinoë emerged from a long, hot, tangled dream to find a motherly, grey-haired woman bathing her face. She sat up in the bed and gazed around her with a bewildered look. The room she was in was small by Alexandrian standards, its walls painted in a trompe l'oeil fashion to resemble theatrical backdrops inside a red border. The furniture was simple – a bed with covers of brown homespun, a couple of cane chairs, a clothes chest, a cupboard. And the woman looking down at her was dressed as plainly as a slave in a drab homespun robe. Yet Arsinoë had an instinctive certainty that she was both kind and powerful.

'Who are you?' she croaked. 'You took me from the prison, didn't you?'

The woman smiled, setting in motion a network of fine lines around her brown eyes.

'Yes,' she said. 'I'm Aelia Trebutia. It's good to see you're recovering. You gave me a dreadful fright – several times I thought I'd lost you.'

A dim memory came back to Arsinoë of the woman's face swimming in and out of focus during long, feverish nights.

'Why are you being so good to me?' she asked.

The smile on Aelia's lips twisted into bitterness.

'I think enough people have died to gratify Caesar's vanity,' she replied. 'My two sons among them.'

'I'm so sorry,' murmured Arsinoë. 'Were they fighting for Pompey?'

'No. For Caesar. But it made no difference, did it? It makes me sick the way these men have to go playing at soldiers, while mothers are left to grieve and ache for their children. There's scarcely a woman in Rome who hasn't lost a son in these senseless wars. Well, talk solves nothing. You'll need your breakfast and after that I suppose you'll be wanting to see your Gallic chieftain.'

Arsinoë's face flamed.

'V-Vercingetorix?' she stammered.

'Who else?'

'He's here?'

'He refused to leave you that night in the prison and I convinced the guards that you'd die without him. Besides, he had a festering leg wound from the chains which needed treatment. He's well enough now, staying in one of our guest rooms downstairs and anxious for news of you. Do you think you'd feel fit to see him when you've had some breakfast?'

'Yes. Oh, yes!' cried Arsinoë.

After she had eaten a fresh crusty roll with honey and drunk some watered wine, Arsinoë climbed out of bed to find the room undulating alarmingly beneath her feet. Aelia returned in time to scold her as she staggered into one of the cane chairs.

'Dear, dear! You should have waited for me. Look, I've a dress here that might suit you. I've worn mourning clothes ever since my sons died, so I've no use for pretty robes.'

'It would never fit me!' protested Arsinoë.

But it did. She had lost so much weight on the slave ship and in prison that her limbs looked unfamiliar, as if they belonged to somebody else. The robe was made of fine, pale green wool, woven with a pattern of red, gold and white flowers. When Arsinoë had slipped it on, Aelia's maid was called in to dress her flaming hair in a flattering corona on top of her head. At last Aelia pronounced herself satisfied.

'You look beautiful, my dear,' she exclaimed and led Arsinoë by the hand to a huge bronze mirror in her own bedroom to prove it.

Arsinoë stared at her burnished reflection in disbelief. This could not be her, this tall, graceful woman with such regal bearing! She did a tentative pirouette and watched in delight as the delicate folds of material fluttered against her legs.

'Your lover will be very impressed,' commented Aelia drily.

'He's not my lover!'

'Who knows what he has in mind?' retorted the older woman, nodding wisely. 'You take your happiness while you can, my girl. Now, let me show you down to the peristyle where he's waiting. And don't worry about being interrupted. I'll see that none of the slaves disturb you.'

As she floated down the stairs in Aelia's wake, Arsinoë had a curious feeling of unreality. Her heart was thudding wildly at the thought of seeing Vercingetorix again and for the first time she felt that the changes in her life were perhaps not a total disaster. The small, homely details of the villa assaulted her senses with unbearable sharpness. A slave sweeping a mosaic floor paused with his broom suspended in the sunlit dust motes and bowed to them. From somewhere in a kitchen came the sound of clashing crockery and the shouted orders of a cook. An aroma of rich meat soup drifted through the air. I could be very happy in a place like this, thought Arsinoë in surprise, if only I had a good man to share it with. And if only I could be left alone to enjoy it.

She followed Aelia out of the dimness of the house's interior to the bright sunlight of the courtyard. And there he was. He looked up at her approach, his face impassive. This was the first time Arsinoë had seen him clearly and the sight shocked her. It wasn't only his unfamiliar clothing, although that was extraordinary enough. He wore a soft, leather jerkin, laced at the throat over leather garments that encased his legs like tubes. His feet too were wrapped in leather and cross gartered. Yet what really disturbed her was the uncanny sensation that she was looking at a total stranger. He was tall, a good head taller than any man she had ever known in Egypt and broad and powerful with it. His hair was golden and tied back in a braid and his eyes were of that vivid, pale blue that only northern barbarians seemed to have. In the fashion of his country, he kept his chin clean shaven, but had a long, flowing blond moustache. The years in captivity had left their mark in the furrows between his brows and the long grooves that scored his cheeks, but it was his expression that alarmed her. He seemed to stare straight through her with a grim, disapproving scowl.

'Arsinoë?' he muttered.

Before she could stop to think, she launched herself into his arms. Closing her eyes, she almost wept for joy. At least the voice was familiar. That deep, throaty, oddly foreign growl that had sustained her in the prison. And how good it was to feel the steady pounding of his heart through the warm leather. He smelled clean now, not sweaty and rancid as he had in that torture hole, but like pine needles or salt air or open space. Suddenly she became aware that, although she was hugging him, his arms were hanging like lumps of wood at his sides. Her eyes flew open and she saw that he was gazing over her shoulder, deliberately distancing himself from her. Did he find her fat and ugly like the courtiers in Alexandria who had flattered her only because she was royal? The thought was so painful that her eyes stung with tears of humiliation. Releasing her hold, she stepped back a pace.

'What's wrong?' he asked her roughly.

Dropping her gaze, she swallowed hard.

'You think I'm repulsive, don't you?'

'Repulsive?' He stared at her in disbelief. 'What are you talking about?'

'You don't want to touch me now that you've seen me, do you? It's all right, I understand. I – '

Her voice broke and, to her dismay, tears began to spill down her cheeks. As if against his will, he hauled her into his arms and embraced her so hard that her ribs almost cracked.

'Don't be a fool,' he urged. 'Of course I want to touch you, that's the whole trouble. I'd marry you, if I could. You must know how much you meant to me in that hell hole. But what right have I got to think of marriage with the threat of death hanging over our heads? I was a king once. I could have offered you rich jewellery and a fine house and serving women to wait on you. All that is gone, destroyed by Julius Caesar. If I'm ever released alive, I'll be nothing but a slave or at best a freedman. The most I could give you would be a herdsman's cottage.'

Arsinoë stared at him in shock, her lips moving soundlessly. He loves me, she thought, he's trying to tell me that he loves me. A great surge of happiness swept through her like a tidal wave. If only Cleopatra could see me now! she thought inconsequentially. She said no man would ever want me. Looking at Vercingetorix's urgent face, she felt ready to burst with joy.

'I could be very happy in a herdsman's cottage!' she blurted out at last.

Octavian's skin crawled with apprehension as he entered the room so lately vacated by Antony. All his stammered assurances that there was nothing wrong did not seem to penetrate Caesar's consciousness. With a faint, sardonic smile his great-uncle merely ushered him into a chair, barred the door and waited until his excuses petered out.

'And now the truth, please,' insisted Caesar blandly as Octavian faltered into silence.

He eyed the boy searchingly as he took a swift, desperate gulp of air. Embarrassment, guilt, panic were written all over him. Caesar had interrogated too many captives and too many soldiers guilty of cowardice or mutiny to mistake the signs.

'There's nothing wrong!' blurted out Octavian again.

Caesar merely raised his eyebrows and waited. His great-nephew's face blushed an unattractive shade of crimson and he hung his head.

'I can't tell you!' he said in a tormented voice.

'Then let me guess. You're in trouble of some kind.'

Octavian remained silent, but his body stiffened.

'What is it? Gambling, destruction of property, some wild horseplay that got out of hand? Or an unwanted pregnancy of a senator's daughter, blackmail –?'

Octavian gave a convulsive start and his face turned ashen. Caesar paused and flashed him a searching look.

'So that's it,' he breathed. 'You're being black-mailed. What have you done?'

Octavian made a clumsy dive towards the door, but Caesar hauled him back with alarming strength. Depositing the boy roughly in his seat, he felt a sudden rush of uncontrollable rage.

'You little fool! What have you done to discredit me?'

With a pang of alarm, Octavian saw his genial uncle transformed before his eyes into a savage ogre who terrified him. His heart knocked against his ribs and he shrank back gasping for breath as Caesar thrust his furious face close to his. For one panic-stricken moment he feared that the older man would seize him by the throat and throttle him. Then Caesar took a long, deliberate breath and stepped backwards, breaking that threatening spell.

'What have you done?' he repeated in a calmer tone.

'I – ' Octavian's voice came out as a croak. He swallowed and tried again. 'I had a sexual encounter.'

'I see. With some greedy merchant's daughter? Well, that should be easy enough to smooth over.'

'No.' Octavian shot him an agonized glance. 'It was worse than that.'

'Worse? In what way?'

'It . . . wasn't a woman.'

Caesar looked at him in amazed disbelief. The little moron! Didn't he know what uproar any scandal about homosexuality could cause in the Senate? Didn't he have the brains of an ant? This would be shouted on every street corner in Rome by the next market day if word got out. DICTATOR'S GREAT-NEPHEW IN SLEAZY SEX ROMP! The fool!

'Who was it?' he asked in a hard voice. 'I'll need his name and address if I am to do anything to suppress this. Come on, out with it!'

Octavian moistened his lips. He felt a churning sensation as if he were going to be sick at the mere memory of what had happened.

'Publius Valerius Cotta.'

'Cotta? The senator?'

'Yes.'

Caesar's eyes narrowed. Cotta. He had never suspected him of any but normal sexual proclivities and he felt affronted that such a piece of information had escaped him until now. He had always prided himself on his web of contacts in the underworld and the bawdy houses of Rome. But was the boy telling the truth? Or was this merely a random lie designed to shield the real culprit?

'Are you lying?' he demanded suspiciously.

'No,' cried Octavian and his voice rang with conviction. 'It's the truth, I swear it!'

'Tell me what happened then.'

Hesitantly, stammering and refusing to meet Caesar's eyes, Octavian blurted out the whole sorry story. It made him go hot and cold with shame, especially when Caesar mercilessly made him tell every detail of what had gone on. He even had the horrible feeling that his great uncle was deriving a kind of malicious pleasure from his embarrassment. At last, feeling hollow and shaken as if at the end of a bilious attack, he came to a halt.

'Very well,' said Caesar, rising to his feet. 'You did right to tell me, but I warn you, Octavian, not a word to anyone else, or I'll flog you.'

'No, sir, I promise. But please, are you going to do something about this?'

'Yes, Octavian. I'll take care of everything, I promise you that.'

Octavian fell on his knees and kissed Caesar's hand, feeling weak with relief.

'Thank you, Uncle,' he said devoutly. 'I'll do anything I can to repay you. Anything.'

Caesar gave him a wintry smile.

'I'll let you know when it's all sorted out,' he promised.

Three days later, Octavian's great-uncle invited him to go for a walk. They covered several miles through the centre of the city, chatting about books and music and military campaigns as if Octavian's dreadful confession had never taken place. At last Caesar turned into an alleyway next to the Tiber where there was a cluster of warehouses and the air smelled of spices and grain and rope. He produced a key to one of the buildings, opened a door and ushered Octavian inside. Mystified, Octavian preceded him and looked around the dim interior.

'This place used to belong to Cotta,' said Caesar in a conversational tone.

Octavian froze.

'Or rather to his first cousin,' continued Caesar. 'Cotta, being a senator, was not officially allowed to engage in trade. But the building has legally changed hands this very morning. I've now purchased it in the name of one of my freedmen, who thinks it might be useful for his woollen trade. I thought you might like to look around.'

A feeling of profound uneasiness stirred in Octavian's guts as Caesar led him across the brick warehouse to a pile of full sacks set in the middle of the paved floor. For some reason, his breath came faster as Caesar gestured to the gallery above.

'Do you see the hoist beam? The merchants raise sacks on that so that they can store more on the upper level, but it can be dangerous. It's very easy to lose your footing. I expect that's what happened to Cotta.'

As he spoke, he skirted the pile of sacks and Octavian saw a dark shape sprawled on the floor lying ominously still. At the sight he felt his blood congeal in his veins and his heart gave a wild leap of horror. Even though the body was lying face down, he had no doubt whose it was.

'Take a look,' invited Caesar. 'The accident only happened this morning and we haven't even had time to notify his widow yet. It's a shame really. He was moving out his woollen stocks because of the sale and he must have slipped. Of course he shouldn't have upset me. A lot of people who've upset me have suffered accidents.'

Feeling as if he were moving in a nightmare, Octavian stumbled to his knees and turned the body over. It was already cold and stiff, with the eyes wide and the lips drawn back from the teeth in a grinning rictus of terror. A surge of bile rose in his throat and then subsided. It was followed a moment later by a tremulous sense of relief. Cotta could never tell tales of him now. But what kind of man was Caesar to have someone so ruthlessly murdered? He looked up at his uncle and his flesh crawled at the faint, satisfied smile that played around Caesar's lips.

'Aren't you grateful?' murmured the older man. 'Aren't you going to say thank you?'

'Thank you,' whispered Octavian.

Caesar hauled him to his feet, but he did not release him. Octavian felt deeply disquieted at the grip of that lean, brown hand around his wrist.

'I'll expect a reward, of course,' said Caesar.

'A reward?' croaked Octavian.

Caesar smiled more broadly.

'Oh, yes. It seems Cotta and I shared certain tastes.' He shifted his grip and his thumb caressed Octavian's arm. 'What you gave to him, you can equally well give to me. But this time you won't confess to anyone, Octavian. It'll be your little secret with Uncle.'

'What do you mean – you want to go to Rome? Kings and Queens can't just up and leave their countries! Not unless it's a state visit, at any rate. You haven't been invited, have you?'

'No,' admitted Cleopatra.

'Then why do you want to go?' demanded Iras in exasperation. 'Just when we've got Egypt running nicely too! Don't you realize your enemies will start scheming against you once you've left?'

'It's possible. All right, probable. Certain! But I still think I should go.'

'Why?'

Cleopatra drew in breath and looked around the circle of her closest friends and advisers. Iras, the Nubian woman, originally bought as a bedroom slave because she matched the ebony furniture. Trained as a hairdresser, but with a mind as sharp as a razor. Olympus, also a slave captured in Scythia, but now head of the prestigious Alexandrian medical school. Charmion, her manicurist, free born but far from noble – the daughter of a ship's chandler turned merchant. A surge of affection rose inside her. The official council of Macedonian nobles would never give her such honest, unbiased, sometimes outright rude advice as these three. Yet Iras, Olympus and Charmion genuinely cared about her. If she could persuade them that what she wanted to do was right, she would most certainly go to Rome. She was silent for a moment, staring out over the glittering surface of the sea through the open windows as she marshalled her thoughts.

Iras was right. There was no sensible reason for her to go to Rome. It would be far more prudent to remain in Egypt and consolidate her hold on her throne. Yet, as her strength had slowly returned in the months following Caesarion's birth, an overwhelming restlessness had taken hold of her. Caesar was quite clearly bent on conquering the world and, as the mother of his only child, surely she could derive more rewards from his successes? Once, the sum of her ambitions had been to regain Egypt, but now that she had that firmly in her grip, she felt an unexpected discontent. She wanted more. Much more! Cyprus for instance. That had been Egyptian territory, not so long ago. Now, by all accounts, the Romans were making a dog's breakfast of administering it as a province. There had been riots against their rule, calls for a restoration of the Ptolemaic monarchy and Cleopatra would be only too happy if she could gratify the Cypriots' demand. Egypt had no trees of its own and it galled her to have to bribe greedy Roman officials for the shipbuilding timbers that were so urgently needed for Egyptian trade. It was a scandal and one that Caesar could easily put right. Surely if she went to Rome, he would see the sense of her arguments? Surely he would hand Cyprus back to her for the benefit of his son? Her gaze dropped fondly to Caesarion, who was hauling himself up against her knee with a dribbly grin.

'Up!' he ordered hopefully.

Cleopatra shook her head.

'Give him to his nurse, Charmion.'

There was a protesting roar and a good deal of

kicking and struggling as Caesarion was evicted. The moment the door shut, Cleopatra rose to her feet and paced around the room.

'I'll tell you why I want to go to Rome,' she said, struggling to keep the emotion out of her voice and to remain calm and persuasive. 'I want to be formally named a Friend and Ally of the Roman people in the Senate. That way, even if Caesar dies, I should have a better chance of keeping hold of the throne of Egypt.'

'What if you lose the throne of Egypt anyway by going away and deserting it?' cut in Iras impatiently. 'Your brother Ptolemy has powerful supporters who are just itching to get rid of you and marry him off to someone whom they can control more easily. It wouldn't be hard for them to fake a lineage for some docile girl and pretend she's a distant cousin of the Ptolemies.'

'I'm coming to that,' said Cleopatra. 'You've no need to tell me that Ptolemy is a thorn in my side! I intend to take him with me where I can keep an eye on him. I have plans for my little husband.'

'You're going to have him murdered?' asked Olympus with a touch of disapproval.

'I don't think that will be necessary,' said Cleopatra. 'If Caesar does win the civil war, as I fully expect, a vast reorganization of the provinces will be necessary. So many Roman nobles have died in the war already that he's desperately short of good administrators. I intend to ask him to give Cyprus back to me as an Egyptian territory. I'll also ask him to pardon my sister Arsinoë and let her marry Ptolemy so that they can rule it jointly. Then I can make Caesarion King of Egypt immediately.'

There was a stunned silence, broken at last by Iras's throaty, incredulous laugh.

'If you're going to be a megalomaniac, do it in a big way, is what I always say. You're crazy, Cleopatra! He'll never agree to giving up a territory which has been taken over by the Romans.'

'Yes, he will,' insisted Cleopatra.

Iras rolled her eyes.

'Have it your own way. You always do. But if you must go to Rome, I've got only one piece of advice for you. Go in style! Dazzle the Romans. Arrive in such majesty that they'll still be talking about your visit in a thousand years' time.'

The result was that in late July Cleopatra arrived in Italy with a retinue whose magnificence was stunning. She had given her eunuch Mardonius, a past organizer of many successful processions, the task of planning her arrival and the results were spectacular. A string of barges brought the royal entourage upriver from Ostia and crowds of people flocked to the river bank to watch. First came Sileni, half clad in scarlet cloaks, half in purple. Then Satyrs carrying gilded torches decorated with ivy leaves. Then Victories dressed in embroidered tunics and gold jewellery with gold wings on their backs. After this came a hundred and twenty Negro boys in purple tunics, carrying fragrant incense burners full of frankincense and myrrh. Behind them were tableaux of men and women dressed to resemble figures from myth, including the Year and the Seasons. Some of these carried palm branches and others platters of fruit.

The climax of the procession, of course, was Cleopatra herself. She sat on a gold throne set high in the centre of a barge with a canopy of gold silk stretched above her head. Her robes were made of translucent purple silk with a gold embroidered shawl and she wore the gold crown of the Ptolemies in the shape of a rearing cobra on her brow. Magnificent pearls from the Red Sea were coiled around her throat, while her wrists and ankles glittered with heavy gold jewellery. Her attendants were dressed like nymphs, and curly haired boys attired as Cupids sat at her feet, clutching miniature bows and arrows. The air around her was heavy with the scent of sandalwood and cinnamon and the sound of pan-pipes and lyres drifted to the watchers on the bank.

Behind the royal barge came the displays intended chiefly to amuse the crowd. There was a mechanical figure twelve feet high dressed in the robes of the god Bacchus, which could stand up, pour a libation of milk from a gold saucer and sit down again. There was a boat full of exotic African animals including baboons, a lion in a gilded cage, giant pythons and even a giraffe. And there were acrobats and musicians who tossed showers of coins into the crowd.

It was mid-afternoon when Cleopatra came ashore at the landing stage of the new villa which Caesar was building on the west bank of the Tiber. Even *her* audacity had balked at the thought of confronting him in his official residence as chief priest which he shared with his wife. In any case, she had no intention of staying in a horrid, poky little house in the centre of Rome. At least his new villa was reputed to be spacious and comfortable and it should be easy to convince his slaves that she was arriving at his invitation. After all, hadn't he built the place partly to accommodate distinguished foreign guests? Flushed with triumph, she watched as the boatmen threaded stout cables through the iron rings set in stone lions' mouths on the quay. Everything seemed to be going well. It was a perfect day with blue sky, bright sunshine and green, leafy trees rustling in a light breeze. The progress upriver from Ostia had gone without a hitch and she had enjoyed every moment of making her way between the cheering, waving crowds lining the banks of the river. All the same, it was rather a relief now to be carried high above the heads of the crowd and into the private gardens of Caesar's villa.

As the roar subsided behind her, she looked around with interest. The gardens were huge and the dense box hedges planted around the perimeter cut off the noise of the city. Birds sang in the canopies of the plane trees and sunlight fell in dappled patterns on the lush green grass below. Here and there through the trees, Cleopatra caught sight of marble statues and a small building that looked like a temple. From some distant place she heard the splashing sound of a fountain, but the main villa remained out of sight.

'Forward!' she ordered the litter bearers, gesturing at the gravel driveway ahead.

They had just reached the rear of the villa when the sound of horses' hooves came thundering round the building towards them. Leaning out of the litter, Cleopatra saw a snorting bay horse surmounted by a familiar figure dressed in a leather military uniform and flying scarlet cloak. They were coming at an urgent gallop as if they were confronting a dangerous intruder. She bit back a smile.

'Put me down,' she said.

The horse jerked to a halt, sweating and dancing and dripping saliva and Caesar flung himself out of the saddle. He crossed the gravel in two strides, reached into the litter and hauled her out. His face was contorted with rage and his brown eyes were mere pinpoints of glittering light.

'How dare you?' he hissed, shaking her violently. 'How dare you take advantage of my good nature in this way?'

CHAPTER TEN

Cleopatra looked hurt.

'You invited me,' she protested.

'I did nothing of the kind!'

'Yes, you did! The day Caesarion was born. You promised me that I could come to Rome for a visit and that you would put up a statue of me and make people worship me as a god.'

Caesar ground his teeth.

'Do you seriously suppose that I meant you to come here uninvited and unannounced?' he burst out. 'Did you stop for one moment to consider the humiliation to my wife, not to mention the humiliation to me? If you wanted to come and visit me in Rome, why couldn't you write and ask my permission? And why did I have to hear of your arrival through common gossip? Do you realize that I was drilling my soldiers before a group of senatorial onlookers when the message was brought to me of your arrival? Do you know what a fool you made of me? There were hostile senators sniggering into their togas, asking me insolent questions about why I had invited such an important dignitary to Rome without consulting them and I had to – '

He broke off, realizing that one of the garden slaves was raking the same patch of gravel over and over with a suspiciously attentive, downcast look. The fellow was bound to talk, they always did! What was the proverb? A man has as many enemies as he has slaves! Seizing Cleopatra's arm, Caesar bundled her roughly into the loggia and through a doorway leading to a bedroom.

'What do you think you're playing at?' he snarled, once the door was safely closed behind them.

She looked at him assessingly and burst into tears.

'I thought you'd be pleased to see me,' she wailed. 'I've missed you so much and I wanted you to see the baby again. I've left Egypt in safe hands. Truly.'

With a snort of exasperation, Caesar marched away from her and came to a halt by the inner doors leading to an open courtyard. He refused to look at her. She was doing it on purpose, like all women! Weeping to order, so that men would gather them in their arms and rain kisses over them and do anything they chose. Well, he would not give in! Let her sob as much as she pleased. He would not even look at her. Her choking cries slowly died away. Satisfied with his mastery of the situation, Caesar turned with his arms folded and a grim scowl on his face, only to find that Cleopatra had unfastened the brooches at the shoulders of her gown and was standing with her naked breasts proudly displayed. There were still traces of tears on her cheeks, but a sly smile flickered around the edges of her mouth. If one tactic fails, try another, thought Caesar cynically. Then his gaze dropped to those swollen, creamy globes, tipped now with brownish pink buds since she had suckled his child. A shudder passed through him. Even though he recognized her scheming for what it was, he was not proof against the white hot flame of sexual arousal that engulfed him at the sight of her nakedness. The blood rushed to his head and shoulders and his cock leapt into vigorous, urgent life.

'Bitch!' he breathed.

Crossing the mosaic floor, he bunched the remaining fabric of her gown in his hands and tore it asunder. Then he lifted her clear off the floor, flung her on to the bed and launched himself on top of her. She cried out as the bronze cherubs on his breast plate bruised her tender flesh, yet he had the impression that she was enjoying the violence of the encounter just as much as he was. A tremulous light flickered in her eyes and she gave a muffled groan low in her throat as he took his hot swollen organ in his hand and thrust it into her. As always, the first sensation was one of savage rapture. He had raped women from one side of the Mediterranean to the other, but never experienced such an intoxicating sense of power and control. What she gave, she gave unwillingly, yet he saw how unmistakably she revelled in it. Struggling like a tigress, she arched and writhed and fought him, but her own private parts betrayed her. They were hot, slick, wet with the juices of desire. He urged her on, swearing at her, telling her in coarse, staccato phrases what he meant to do to her. And she loved it. He could sense the excitement in her moans, in the way she threshed from side to side, in the shallow, uneven rhythm of her breathing. When at last she convulsed, raking his back with her fingernails and crying aloud, he hauled her against him with almost loving approval.

'Good girl. Good girl!' he whispered.

And came.

Explosively. In a series of tempestuous, thrusting jerks that made the blood thunder in his ears and his entire body feel limp and hollow. After which he collapsed on top of her.

It was a long time before either of them stopped shuddering or panting for breath. When they did, she levered fruitlessly at him with her hands, as if crushed by a falling house beam in an earthquake. He smiled at the image, enjoying the sense of having her trapped. There was no way she could free herself unless he chose. Magnanimously he rolled off her and saw with an odd thrill of pleasure that his armour had left bruises in her flesh. He liked the thought of marking her with his brand as if she were a slave belonging to him. Lazily he reached out and caressed the fleshy curve of her hip. Bending her head, she licked his arm, running her tongue up from his wrist to his shoulder. He shivered pleasurably.

'Are you going to let me stay?' she whispered with her mouth practically in his armpit.

'Yes. Bitch.'

The words were little more than a growl and, to show his annoyance and his comprehension, he followed them up with a stinging slap on her rump. Her outraged squeal of protest filled him with satisfaction. There was no way he could let her go now that she was here, but she need not think he was blind to her tactics. He would show her who was boss!

'Only if you satisfy me in every way,' he added threateningly.

She wriggled against him, fluttering her eyelashes in pretended meekness.

'Yes, domine. And will you introduce me to all your friends in the Senate?'

He frowned at her. What was she really after? A formal alliance with the Senate? Weren't the three legions he had left behind enough to satisfy her? Still, if she was going to stay here, it would be best to put a bold front on it. Pass her off as a foreign dignitary who had come on a diplomatic visit, that was the best way to handle it. And bring her out with proper pomp and ceremony at some major social events.

'I suppose so,' he agreed. 'You can stay and see my triumphal processions in September and I'll see that you're invited to some dinner parties and social occasions. In fact, there's a wedding you could attend in a few days' time, where you can meet all the important people in Rome. One of my officers is getting married. Mark Antony.'

A hot sun was beating down out of the cloudless blue sky when Cleopatra arrived at the wedding a few days later. As a widow of mature years, Fulvia had chosen to be married from her own house, which was a vast mansion on the Palatine hill. Garlands of flowers decked the door posts and the slaves who came running out to meet the Queen's litter were wearing wreaths of scented verbena in their hair. From inside the building came the plaintive, reedy notes of pan-pipes and the upraised hum of chattering voices. As Cleopatra walked in, the uproar immediately died down. After the brilliant sunshine outside, she was momentarily dazzled by the cool interior of the building and she had to blink twice before she could get her bearings. Then she saw that she was standing in a large atrium with a dome-shaped roof, marble columns and an intricately patterned mosaic floor. By Roman stand-ards, the house was amazingly luxurious and even in Alexandria it would have made a fitting dwelling for a wealthy merchant.

But it was not the house which captured Cleopatra's attention. It was the people. At the end of the room, standing out like a large saffron cake in the midst of a platter of ricotta cheeses, stood the bride herself. At the sight of Cleopatra she broke away from the milling crowds of relatives who surrounded her and walked down the centre of the room to kiss her guest on both cheeks.

'Welcome, Your Majesty,' she said in a composed voice.

'May the blessings of the gods be upon you and

your husband on this auspicious day,' replied Cleopatra with mechanical courtesy.

Even as she spoke the words, she felt as if a cold hand were gripping her insides. Could Antony really be intending to marry this lumpy woman? She stared at Fulvia, taking in every detail of the ridiculous flame-coloured bridal veil already slipping askew on her coarse, black hair, her face as red as a slab of butcher's meat with a hairy wart on one cheek and the hint of a moustache on the upper lip, not to mention the snaggletoothed smile. It must have taken cubits and cubits of material to make the bright yellow wedding tunic and cloak large enough to wrap around that massive figure. And Fulvia didn't even have the saving grace of being light on her feet. When she moved it was with the steady, lumbering tramp of an elephant. Can I really be jealous of such a woman? wondered Cleopatra, and then was shocked to find Fulvia's dark eyes resting on her just as searchingly as if she were conducting her own assessment. Antony's bride might not be beautiful, but she was clearly no fool either.

'You must come and meet the other guests,' she invited courteously.

If Fulvia was prepared to do the decent thing and show good manners, there were others who were not. Caesar's influence might have won Cleopatra an invitation to the wedding, but it could not force the Roman nobles to behave politely towards her. As she was led by Fulvia from group to group of the assembled guests, Cleopatra could not mistake the chilliness of their greetings and a cold rage began to burn inside her.

If this had been Alexandria they would have been flinging themselves on their faces to worship her. As it was, she was being made to feel like a beggar or a common street whore. A diseased one at that. As

Fulvia led her around from group to group, performing introductions, she was left in no doubt that she was an unwanted outsider. Time and again, two languid fingers were extended to shake her hand or her presence was acknowledged by the merest lift of an eyebrow before toga-clad shoulders were turned to shut her out. And when Fulvia excused herself to go and greet some newly arrived guests, Cleopatra found herself edged out of a group of chattering women as ruthlessly as if she were a plague victim. Determined not to show her annoyance, she accepted a glass of honeyed wine from a passing slave and began to survey the room with flashing eyes and set chin. Suddenly she became aware that Caesar's gaze was fixed on her in amusement. He was in the midst of a throng of men whose broad, purple-striped tunics proclaimed them to be members of the Senate, but he detached himself from them and threaded his way through the crowd towards her.

'I'm sorry I couldn't come and speak to you earlier, my dear,' he said, laying his hand casually on her shoulder. 'But I was discussing some rather important business. Still, now that you're here, you must come and meet some of my family and friends.'

Draping his arm around her, he led her towards a group of guests. She swayed sensually at the touch of his fingers on her purple silk gown, fully aware of the intake of breath from the women behind her. He might as well have stripped me naked while he's at it, she thought with a spark of amusement. It couldn't have given them more offence than he already has done. But Caesar is quite right. We must make it clear from the start what our relationship is. And if they don't like it, they can screw themselves. With a provocative smile at a couple of scowling old men, she allowed him to lead her across the room and tossed her head defiantly at the whispers that broke out behind her.

'The hide of that woman coming here – '

'I heard she and Caesar – '

'They say the baby is the spitting image – '

Caesar brought her to a halt in front of a quartet of nobles. Three women, ranging in age from the early twenties to more than fifty, and a youth of sixteen or seventeen, all clutching wine cups and looking as if they wished the floor would open and swallow them up.

'Cleopatra, I'd like you to meet my wife, Calpurnia – '

With a flash of hopeless misery in her dog-like brown eyes, the drab matron in the homespun green robe extended her hand and muttered a greeting. Cleopatra gave her a glance of amused contempt. I wouldn't suffer a rival so meekly, she thought, but then she probably hates sex anyway. I may even be doing her a favour.

'My dear friend, Servilia – '

Cleopatra stiffened like a hunting dog at the mention of that name. So this was Caesar's favourite mistress? Still striking looking, even though she must be over fifty, with chiselled features and a tall, lithe figure. No meekness there. The sensual mouth was set with unmistakable hostility. I wonder whether he'll keep sleeping with her now that I'm here? she thought. I suppose she's wondering the same thing . . .

'My great-niece Octavia – '

Twenty-three or twenty-four, golden-haired, blue-eyed, very pretty, very dull. Looks like one of those women in the books about Heroines of Early Rome. 'How Lucretia stabbed herself rather than live once her chastity had been ravished.' I'd stab myself too if I had to wear a gown like that.

'And my great-nephew Octavian.'

Cleopatra glanced up and surprised a look of such venom on the young man's face that she stepped back a pace. She had thought Servilia's gaze was burning, but it was nothing compared to Octavian's. His blue eyes blazed like live coals and there was a curious white, pinched look about his nostrils and lips. Some muscular tic was making the whole left side of his face twitch violently and his hands were clenched into fists. He hates me, she thought with a chill sense of alarm. He really hates me. The young man continued to glare silently at her, ignoring her outstretched hand, until she wondered whether he were quite right in the head.

'Shake hands with the Queen, Octavian,' murmured Caesar silkily. 'Be a good boy now or Uncle will have to punish you.'

Octavian's head jerked back as if Caesar had struck him and for an instant Cleopatra glimpsed something terrifying behind those delicate features. A look of violent malevolence directed at his great-uncle. He hates Caesar too, she thought. I really believe he'd like to kill him. But why? What's happened between –

At that moment the introductions were interrupted by a loud fanfare of trumpets. A sudden outburst of cheering and clapping announced the arrival of Antony.

'The groom! The groom!' shouted the guests.

Some of them even broke into the traditional wedding hymn, 'Io, hymen, hymenaeus', but Cleopatra could do nothing but stand still and stare. Her heart was thundering in her breast and her breath came in long, shallow gulps, for at that moment she was irresistibly reminded of her first view of Antony in his tent nine years ago. Then he had been sweat-stained and naked, dressed in nothing but a towel, while now he was freshly bathed and barbered and clad in a spotless white tunic with a broad, purple stripe. And yet there was not much difference. His dark brown curls still clustered in a riotous halo about his head, his hazel eyes still glinted with devilment and the smile lurking in the dark brown beard was as provocative as ever, while his physique was enough to send any woman into pangs of longing. Massive shoulders and burly arms which would have done credit to a blacksmith, a narrow waist and hips and thighs like tree trunks. Gazing at him with parted lips, Cleopatra was horrified by the pang of desire that shook her. She had always known there was a risk she might encounter him in Rome. It had even been part of the allure of the journey, that delicious secret hope that they might somehow meet ... Yet she had been unprepared for the shock of seeing him alive and breathing before her. It was as if the nine years' separation had never existed. A slow, pulsating warmth began to throb in her groin and a sudden vivid picture flashed in her mind of that fisherman's cottage in Rhakotis where they had held their stolen meetings. Every detail of those sunlit passionate days came hurtling back so vividly that she could smell the salt air of the harbour, hear the cooing of the pigeons on the roof tiles, see the rickety old bed rattling on its base as Antony drove with ever-increasing frenzy into her innermost being. A strange weakness seemed to flow through her limbs and she swallowed and stepped hastily out of sight behind a massive, red-faced senator. It formed no part of her plans for her own advancement to renew her love affair with Antony. It would be too dangerous, too unproductive. Fortunately Antony did not seem to have glimpsed

195

her. Looking around at the assembled guests, he suddenly threw back his head and gave a rumble of laughter.

'Well, what are we waiting for?' he demanded. 'Let's get on with it.'

As he strode down the room towards Fulvia, more than one heart in the feminine crowd felt a sudden flutter and, when he drew back Fulvia's veil and kissed her warmly on the lips, there were sighs of envy and approval. Calpurnia thought wistfully of her own wedding to Caesar thirteen years before and wished that Caesar would show such affection towards her. Octavia fought down a sudden twinge of jealousy and wished that she had a large enough fortune to make her a suitable bride for Antony, while half a dozen other matrons simply wondered what it would be like to be naked and gasping under such a hunk of a man. Cleopatra, who could have told them, had to dig her fingernails into her palms and look away as the ceremony began.

Mercifully it was brief. A squealing pig with a garland of flowers around its neck was sacrificed to the gods and an auspex plunged his hands into the steaming entrails and pronounced the auspices favourable. After this the couple exchanged their vows and Antony uttered the traditional words which would make Fulvia his wife.

'Ubi ego Gaius, tu Gaia. Where I am master, you will be mistress.'

Then the guests burst into congratulations and loud shouts of 'Feliciter! May you be fortunate!' while the ten witnesses solemnly affixed their seals to the marriage contract.

After this, the party became more riotous and informal. The pig was butchered and the slaves set it to barbecue over a brazier of hot coals while others circulated with cups of honeyed wine and plates of nibbles. There were various forms of entertainment to delight the guests. Some chose to watch a rope dancer, others a juggler, while all the children present ran around in a shrieking gang playing complicated games of their own. Out of the corner of her eye, Cleopatra could see Fulvia in her flame and yellow bridal clothes and Antony in white, circulating among the guests, but she did her best to avoid them.

Fanning herself ostentatiously with her hand, she murmured something indistinct about the heat and slipped out into the garden. Very few Roman houses had gardens of any size, but this place was an exception. Built by Catullus more than fifty years before, it was one of the finest villas in Rome, laid out with extensive pleasure grounds behind it. Now, desperate only for some place to regain her composure, Cleopatra hurried down the gravel path until she found herself in a shrubbery full of winding paths. At last she found a secluded spot near the boundary wall, where an artificial grotto created from rocks and cement sheltered a splashing fountain and a huge box hedge hid her from the house. Sinking down on a marble bench, she buried her face in her hands. Caesar was observant and he must be given no opportunity to notice the turmoil she felt when she confronted Mark Antony.

'Cleopatra?'

She jumped at the sound of that familiar voice and turned to see Mark Antony looming above her, clad in his bridegroom's tunic. Her skin cringed as a series of indecent and utterly delectable memories flashed before her eyes. It appalled her to find that the old magnetism seemed to be as strong as ever. She sprang to her feet and stood, rigid and wary, as he advanced towards her with his large hands outstretched.

'It's a very pleasant surprise to see you at my wedding,' he murmured, his eyes crinkling in amusement. 'Haven't you got a kiss for an old admirer?'

She flinched at the warm grip of his hands on her shoulders, the nearness of his body.

'Don't!' she exclaimed in a tormented voice, jerking away from him. 'I didn't come here for that.'

'Why did you come here?'

His gaze was frankly curious. Frankly admiring too. Cleopatra had changed subtly in the nine years since he had seen her, although the changes were not really physical. Even at fourteen her body had offered the lush perfection of womanhood. No, it was not that. Yet there was something disturbingly different about her presence. In those distant days in Egypt, for all her sharp intelligence and character, she had often seemed touchingly naïve. Now a new aura clung about her, a look of experience and cynicism and labyrinthine calculations. It was apparent in the cool glint of her eyes, the wry set of her mouth. Antony found it even more enticing than her youthful impetuosity had been. She's up to something, he thought. But what?

'Why did you come here?' he repeated.

Cleopatra hesitated, feeling the air pulsate with the tension between them. Every nerve in her body was clamouring recognition and the mere sight of Antony disturbed her deeply. He had not changed much. Still the same husky bear of a man with those wild, brown curls, the rough beard that once rasped so thrillingly against her naked flesh, the burly muscular frame. The warmth, the vitality, the raw animal energy that had always flowed from Antony were still there in abundance. It was as if she had come in from the cold and found a blazing fire to warm herself by. But there was more than that. She sensed a current of humour and goodwill that made her long to thrust caution aside and fling herself into his arms. She couldn't do that, but she felt she could still trust him, even with her most secret ambitions. Antony had always been a man you could trust. For all his faults he never revealed a confidence or knowingly betrayed a friend. Besides, he might be able to help her get what she wanted. Abruptly she made her decision.

'I was getting bored in Egypt,' she admitted. 'Everything of importance around the Mediterranean is decided in Rome these days and most of it is decided by Julius Caesar. I wanted to make sure my interests were properly taken care of.'

Antony gave a low growl of laughter.

'I see. And how do you propose to do that?'

'This is confidential,' she warned. 'I don't want anyone else to hear of it, but I want to be formally named a Friend and Ally of the Roman people in the Senate. Then if Caesar dies it will be harder for anyone else to remove me from my throne. I also want to find my sister Arsinoë and persuade Caesar to release her. After that I hope to divorce my brother Ptolemy and make him joint ruler of Cyprus with Arsinoë.'

Antony looked stunned.

'He won't surrender a Roman province,' he said, shaking his head doubtfully. 'But he might spare Arsinoë's life, if you're lucky. I can tell you where she is, although it's not generally known. She's in the home of Aelia Trebutia. In fact I could take you there tomorrow, although we'll have to keep it a secret from Caesar.'

Cleopatra blinked.

'But you've only just got married,' she pointed out. 'Won't your wife object?'

Antony shrugged.

'Fulvia? She'll know nothing about it. In any case, it's not a love match, only a marriage made for political advantage. If men want passion, they find themselves an actress or a dancer. Or an Egyptian Queen.'

Suddenly Antony seemed to lose interest in discussing politics or marriage. With a swift, unexpected movement, he hauled her against him, savouring the warm curves of her body and trapping her ruthlessly between his muscular thighs. Then he buried his face in her hair, inhaling its fragrance.

'Kiss me,' he begged. 'You haven't forgotten those afternoons we spent in the house at Rhakotis, have you?'

Her senses reeled as his mouth came down on hers, forcing her lips apart in a long, devouring kiss. As she felt the powerful thrust of his tongue and the violent, rhythmic caress of his hands on her shoulder blades, she forgot nothing. A throbbing pulse of flame surged through her as she remembered the rented fisherman's cottage in Rhakotis. A square of blindingly brilliant whitewashed stone framed by the blue of the Mediterranean, the searing blaze of the sun reflected off the rooftops and Antony's urgent, skilful hands bringing her to a pitch of frenzied desire, just as they were doing now. She swayed against him, sighing and closing her eyes as his mouth moved down her throat. With a groan of satisfaction he slid his hands inside her dress and cupped the warm heaviness of her breasts. Her eyes flew open and she gasped.

'Listen,' he said thickly. 'I've got an empty apartment near the Circus Maximus. Meet me tomorrow near the shrine of Isis at the third hour and I'll take you to visit Arsinoë. Afterwards we'll go to my place and make violent love from one end of it to the other. What do you say?'

'No,' she breathed, still clinging to him. 'It's too risky. Caesar would kill me if he found out.'

'He won't find out! We'll be careful. I want you, Cleopatra, I want you so badly that I feel as if I'm on fire and I'll make it good for you too, sweetheart. I'll take off all your clothes and – '

'Cleopatra! What in the name of Jupiter are you doing?'

She had not even heard Caesar's approach, but it was unmistakably his voice. Curt, challenging, filled with suspicion. They sprang apart at his words and Cleopatra felt a lurch of panic as dire as if she had just plunged from a cliff top. But the years spent in Oriental diplomacy had not been wasted. In the precise moment when she turned to face Caesar, her features were dramatically transformed. Antony was stunned to see the blurred, gasping, sensual abandonment give way to a nicely calculated mixture of distress, embarrassment and stammering gratitude.

'Thank you, Antony,' she said calmly, touching her fingers to her eyelid. 'I think you've got it out now. It's a horrible sensation having a mosquito fly into your eye.'

Caesar scowled. In that first instant when he had stepped into the grove, he could have sworn that Antony was kissing Cleopatra. And yet Antony was a massively built man whose looming bulk had effectively blocked any clear view of the Queen. Was it really likely that he would have had the effrontery to maul Caesar's own woman with his commander near at hand? Or that she would have connived at it? After all, why would she want a second-rate Master of the

Horse when she already had the most powerful man in Rome as her lover? And her explanation was plausible enough.

'Come along, my dear,' he ordered with only a slight remaining frown. 'Gaius Asinius Pollo wants to meet you to discuss the founding of a public library in Rome. I believe you have more than one in Alexandria.'

Cleopatra looked back over her shoulder at Antony. His lips mouthed a single, silent word.

'Tomorrow.'

Chapter Eleven

The following morning dawned bright and warm so that Cleopatra ordered her breakfast to be brought to her on the terrace outside her suite of rooms. Caesar had gone home to spend the night with his wife so that she was free to think in peace. A frown creased her forehead as she chewed newly baked bread rolls spread with goats' cheese. A night spent tossing and turning, on fire with alternate lust and ambition, had left her convinced of one thing. She could not afford the risk of a love affair with Mark Antony. Even though her secret parts throbbed at the mere thought of him, as if sly, invisible fingers were caressing her, she knew it was too great a gamble. All men seemed to be jealous and watchful by nature, like bulls guarding their herd. And while Cleopatra was no placid cow to be coerced into obedience, some instinct warned her that Caesar would be even more dangerous than any other outraged male if he learnt that he had been betrayed. There was too much at stake to make the hazard worthwhile. Her own kingdom, Caesarion's future. No. Antony must be left to his fat, ugly wife . . .

A pang of resentment stabbed through her at the thought. What a waste, to think of a man like that in bed with Fulvia. Fulvia! What was Fulvia to deserve such a marriage? Rich, well born, Roman. All of those things, yes. But she hadn't a grain of charm or wit or femininity to offer in exchange for Antony's rugged, virile good looks and easy-going nature. And here was Cleopatra herself, chained in wedlock to her younger brother. Life was so unfair sometimes!

As if her thoughts had summoned him, a half-grown youth in Macedonian clothes suddenly wandered out of the shrubbery beyond the balustrade. He paused at the sight of her and his face lit up. Cheerfully he wandered up the stairs and came to a halt opposite her.

'Hello. Are you eating breakfast?' he asked, with the air of one making a shrewd discovery.

What an intellectual giant the boy was! Taking in every detail of his gracefully muscled body, burnished red-gold hair and delicate features, Cleopatra shook her head in faint amazement. Ptolemy's green eyes were long-lashed and just as pretty as the rest of him, but they had a curiously vacant look, like pebbles washed smooth by running water. Cleopatra had had little to do with him until their enforced marriage, but now she was beginning to suspect that he was a drachma short of a full mina. It was odd how many idiots seemed to be born into the royal family, although they were usually strangled at birth or left out to die like any other defective child. Her physician Olympus said it was because of inbreeding. According to him, if you bred animals to their own kin, a disproportionate number of weaklings and malformed offspring resulted, but the survivors were magnificent. Cleopatra smiled. Perhaps she and her brother were both illustrations of the theory in action. Well, even if Ptolemy was a moron, he would do very nicely as a husband for Arsinoë.

'Yes, dear,' she agreed kindly. 'I'm eating breakfast. Sit down and share it with me.'

While they ate, she questioned him about his occupations and his lessons. Horse riding (good), swordplay (good), Latin and rhetoric (hopeless). It seemed he simply couldn't get the hang of foreign languages or the art of reading. Eleven years old and still illiterate! And this little halfwit was supposed to be King of Egypt and eventually beget more children on her! Not if she had anything to say in the matter ... At last, bored by his simple and meandering conversation, she dismissed him with a napkin full of honeycakes, then she settled back on her dining couch to plan her day. It was a stroke of luck that Antony had told her where to find Arsinoë ...

After the magnificence of Caesar's villa and Fulvia's new home on the Carinae, the house of Aelia Trebutia seemed small and modest. Like most Roman homes, it turned its back on the outside world and it was not until she had passed the two rented shops on either side of the vestibule that Cleopatra was shown into a small courtyard and left to wait while a slave went to fetch her sister. Snapping off a sprig of lavender from a vast bank of the plants that filled the flowerbeds, she crushed it in her palm and inhaled its warm, spicy scent. A comfortable glow of righteousness filled her as she waited. She was genuinely fond of Arsinoë and it delighted her to think that she could solve both their problems so elegantly. A divorce and freedom for herself, marriage and the kingdom of Cyprus for Arsinoë. With the pleasant expectation of witnessing tears, humble apologies and an outburst of incredulous gratitude, Cleopatra paced backwards and forwards, humming softly.

'Cleopatra?'

The voice was Arsinoë's, a clear, sweet soprano. Yet, as she swung round to the source of the sound, Cleopatra had the nightmarish sensation that she was looking at an unknown person. This couldn't be Arsinoë, this tall, slim girl with the red-gold hair piled high on her head, delicate features and a graceful figure that curved in all the right places. Could it? The girl advanced towards her.

'Cleopatra? What are you doing here?'

The appearance might be unfamiliar, but the voice was unmistakably her sister's. Could all these months of captivity really have transformed Arsinoë so dramatically? And, if so, why hadn't it reduced her to humility, squalor and despair? There was something disconcerting and almost offensive in Arsinoë's newfound elegance, not to mention the air of confidence that clung about her. She should have looked humble and guilty. Instead she looked wary and challenging as if she, and not Cleopatra, were in command of this interview.

'What are you doing here?' she repeated.

Cleopatra decided to be magnanimous.

'I haven't come to crow over you. I'm here to help you.'

'Help me? How?'

Arsinoë made no move to fling herself at her sovereign's feet, to kiss her robe or beg forgiveness and Cleopatra could not suppress a twinge of resentment. They gazed at each other steadily and the moment when they might have embraced lengthened and then passed. With a flash of renewed annoyance Cleopatra sat down on a stone bench. What right did Arsinoë have to be so arrogant? Didn't she realize how powerless she was? Frowning, she continued.

'I'm visiting Rome at Caesar's invitation and I have a proposal to make to you.'

'What kind of proposal?'

'Well, naturally I don't want you setting yourself up as a rival Queen of Egypt again. But if you will send a letter with your seal to the council in Alexandria forswearing all claim to the throne, I'll try and see you honourably settled. I intend to ask Caesar if he'll let you govern Cyprus. I can divorce our brother Ptolemy and you can marry him and rule the island jointly. It's a trifle unusual, but – '

She got no further. With an impatient gesture Arsinoë interrupted her.

'I can't marry Ptolemy!'

'Why not? It would strengthen your claim to the kingdom of Cyprus.'

'I'm not interested in a kingdom any more.'

Cleopatra stared at her in amazement and then nodded slowly.

'I know you never really wanted to be Queen and that it was only the Macedonian nobles who pushed you into it,' she conceded. 'But I think you'd make an excellent governor of Cyprus, Arsinoë. Even though you always told me you only wanted to rule a household, you're very intelligent and capable. Between us we could reclaim the Empire of our ancestors!'

Arsinoë's words came tumbling out in a rush.

'I don't want to do that. I've met a man, Cleopatra. He loves me and wants to marry me. Like me, he's a captive of Caesar's. If you really want to help me, then I beg you to intercede with Caesar and persuade him to spare both our lives. I wouldn't ask for anything else. If we could just go away somewhere peaceful, we'd be so happy. I don't want much. A cottage, a few acres, anything if I could just be with the man I love.'

Her voice broke and she couldn't go on. Cleopatra stared at her sister in disbelief. A man? Arsinoë with a man? It was impossible, unthinkable! No man had ever looked at Arsinoë before. But then Arsinoë had never looked as she did now. Who could he be? He must be some slave, totally unsuitable, probably uncouth and only after Arsinoë's fortune. Whoever he was, he would have to be put out of the way, but there was no point in arousing Arsinoë's suspicions.

'Can I meet him?' she asked thoughtfully.

Arsinoë's face lit up.

'Yes, I'll call him. He's here in the household.'

She disappeared and returned shortly with Vercingetorix in tow. Cleopatra stared in shock and outright envy at the tall, muscular, blond-haired man who was striding across the courtyard towards her. She had listened patiently when Caesar had talked of his Gallic campaign and she knew at once from the long plaited hair, the flowing gold moustache and the leather trousers that the man was a Gaul and for a slave he looked remarkably healthy and spirited. Those flashing blue eyes did not lower at all when they met her gaze and his mouth tightened as if he were the one doing her the honour and not the other way around. How could Arsinoë, pious, clumsy, ridiculous Arsinoë, have ever made such a man fall in love with her? For he was in love with her, there could be no doubt about that. The way his arm was flung around Arsinoë's shoulders and the glance he gave her as they stepped forward into the sunlight confirmed it beyond doubt. Cleopatra felt a surge of resentment, bitter as vinegar. In that instant she could almost understand why Arsinoë was prepared to give up her royal status to marry such a man.

'Hello,' said Cleopatra. 'I'm Arsinoë's sister, Cleopatra, Queen of Egypt.'

The Gaul's mouth was unsmiling, his blue eyes frankly hostile, and he did not stretch out his hand to her.

'I am Vercingetorix,' he replied. 'And I intend to marry your sister.'

'Vercingetorix!'

Cleopatra almost reeled with shock. Night after night she had listened in Egypt as Caesar strode around her apartments, denouncing the audacity, the cunning, the vile, treacherous ingenuity of Vercingetorix, leader of the Gauls.

'Not the son of Celtillus, the King of the Arverni?' she faltered. 'The leader of the revolt against Caesar six years ago?'

This time Vercingetorix did smile, a bitter, wolfish grin that drew back his lips in a snarl.

'The same,' he agreed.

Cleopatra turned to her sister.

'And this is the man whose life you want me to beg from Caesar?' she demanded. 'Oh, my poor, dear Arsinoë!'

With the smooth-faced guile which she normally reserved for her dealings with diplomats, Cleopatra at last took her leave of Arsinoë. She had made her sister earnest promises of help, but once she was safely inside her litter, she could scarcely restrain her amusement. Poor, silly Arsinoë! Did she really think Caesar would leave two royals hostile to Rome free to wed and breed and raise rebellion? No. She would do her best to save her sister, but Vercingetorix would have to die. No loss, anyway. His hatred for Cleopatra had been almost palpable, so it wouldn't grieve her to see him perish. Chances were that Caesar intended to execute him anyway. If not, Cleopatra would simply have to drop a quiet word in the Roman dictator's ear about Vercingetorix's marriage plans. And once Arsinoë had finished her mourning, she would no doubt be sensible about marrying Ptolemy . . .

As the litter bearers came off the slope of the Esquiline hill and entered the densely packed area of apartment houses in the Subura below, her reflections were rudely interrupted. The first sign of disturbance was the sound of upraised voices like the humming of a hive of angry bees followed by the sound of glass shattering as a bottle hit the side of a building. Cleopatra leaned out through the leather curtains and spoke to the chief litter bearer.

'That sounds dangerous. You'd better see if we can go around it.'

'Yes, my lady,' he agreed. 'You keep your head inside.'

Fear took hold of her as she drew back inside the airless interior of the litter. From outside she could hear more clearly the sound of voices upraised in argument. Then suddenly the vehicle changed direction and went into a side street. She took a deep, shuddering breath, but her relief was premature, for after a few paces she heard the sound of tramping feet and shouting voices up ahead and her own slaves' low cry of dismay.

'Shit!'

The litter swooped suddenly to the ground, so violently that she was flung suddenly against one side of it and struck her head. Outside there was a loud roar of triumph like the sound of a crowd of chariot racers, followed by terrified shrieks from the litter bearers. Then rough hands reached inside and dragged her out. She had a glimpse of a stubbly chin, blazing dark eyes, brown, ruined teeth and smelt a strong odour of garlic as the man who had seized her dragged her forth into the light. From behind him a woman's malignant shriek rose high in the air like the screeching of a gull.

'Here's another frigging Optimate bitch! Come down to collect the rent, have you, love? Or do you just want to see how the poor people live? Well, go on, fellas, show her what it's like to be down in the gutter like the rest of us!'

Cleopatra screamed in terror as the mob came thundering towards her in the narrow alleyway. For one dreadful moment her legs seemed frozen to the ground as if she were caught in the midst of a nightmare while her heart pounded furiously and her mouth opened in a silent scream. Then as if she were pulling herself out of quicksand, she tore loose and turned to run. At that moment, the cry of 'Fire!' echoed through the narrow alleyway and chaos erupted. From the opposite direction a second crowd came surging around the corner, screaming and shoving.

As the densely packed rabble surged to meet her, she felt herself swept off her feet as if by a tidal wave. Instinctively she crouched, wrapping her arms protectively around her head and whimpering in terror. Somebody's elbow slammed into the side of her face, making her see stars, and dense, choking smoke began to fill her lungs. In front of her she saw a child fall to the ground, only to be trampled by the heaving mass of bodies. Then her own legs were knocked from under her. A heavy boot landed right in the middle of her back with crushing force and she tasted the muddy slime of the street. All around her there were shouts, curses, hairy legs, the sweat of human bodies and the almost palpable odour of fear. Incredibly, she saw the litter just in front of her. By some miraculous chance it had not yet been overturned by the crowd. Grabbing the side arm rest, she heaved herself up and catapulted in between the leather curtains. For a moment she lay gasping and spluttering, fighting down the urge to vomit and half asphyxiated by smoke. The vehicle began to rock violently and she feared she would be tipped out into the crowd again. Then the distant sound of a military bugle was heard and, as suddenly as it had begun, the riot ended.

She sat shuddering and counting quietly under her breath to keep herself from panicking. By the time she reached thirty, the smoke had become unbearable and she risked a quick peep through the leather curtains. Now the alleyway seemed almost empty with the only noise coming from the screams and moans of the injured and dying. Her litter bearers had evidently fled. Staggering out of the vehicle, she wrapped a fold of her cloak around her mouth to keep out the worst of the smoke and looked wildly about her for an escape route. As she did so, she saw a familiar figure appear at the end of the alley.

'Cleopatra!' he shouted and ran towards her. 'Aelia told me you were here. I was afraid I might be too late.'

'Antony!'

Too shaken to think, she flung herself into his arms and felt the reassuring pressure of his body.

'Come on,' he urged. 'We must get you out of here. One of those wooden apartment blocks is on fire and the others may go up at any moment. Simon, give me that cloak for her.'

A dark-haired man came forward and flung a cloak of rough, brown homespun around her shoulders. Antony held it in place, giving her a reassuring squeeze as he did so.

'I'm short of men and the mood in these parts is very ugly,' he said under his breath. 'It's safer if they think you're a plain working woman. Come on, we can lie low in my secret apartment until it's safe to go out.'

He dismissed the few soldiers who accompanied him and led her away at a brisk pace. She soon lost her sense of direction amid the twisting labyrinth of back streets and stinking alleys but before long they stopped at a tall brick building and Antony hustled her upstairs to a small apartment on the third floor. It was only a single large room, furnished in a style instantly recognizable as Antony's. Everything in it was flamboyant, expensive and totally vulgar from the naked nymph table legs to the vast bed, draped with scarlet hangings and set beneath a wall painting of a couple enjoying energetic sex in a garish landscape. Cleopatra's lips twitched at the sight. Dear Antony! How ghastly his taste was.

'Are you hurt?' he demanded, barring the door and turning to look at her.

She shook her head.

'No. It was good fortune that you found me.'

'Not fortune. I came to look for you when you stood me up at the temple of Isis. Aelia told me where you'd gone. Are you sure you're not hurt?'

Something about the intentness of his gaze made her feel oddly breathless. She ran her hands over her body and found tender spots that had felt numb until now. Dropping her gaze, she stepped back a pace.

'Nothing serious. A few bruises.'

'Show me,' he said thickly.

She looked up with a gasp and saw that he was advancing on her, his hazel eyes narrowed and his lips parted in hungry anticipation. Before she could do more than squeak in protest, he caught her in his arms and kissed her fiercely. Her senses swam and without any conscious thought she wound her arms around him and kissed him back with a raw, blazing passion to match his own. Catching her hand, he guided it up beneath the leather pleats of his military kilt so that she felt the hot, rough vigour of his swollen cock and testicles. She gasped and a shudder went through her.

Seizing the opportunity, he thrust his tongue half way down her throat. His hands squeezed her soft buttocks and he rammed his pelvis against hers, engulfing her in his bear-like embrace as if he wanted to devour her. She felt the blood thundering in her ears, pulsating in her secret parts, driving in sudden bursts into the tips of her fingers. With a desperate movement she broke partly free.

'I can't!' she cried in a tormented voice. 'Caesar will kill me if he finds out.'

'Bullshit,' growled Antony, hauling her back and sliding his right hand deftly up under her dress until he reached the silken barrier of her loincloth. 'Even when his wife Pompeia was screwing Clodius years ago, all he did was divorce her. And you're only his mistress.'

'Yes, but – '

She broke off with a sudden sharp intake of breath as his expert fingers untied the strings and encountered warm, moist flesh and springy hair. The loincloth fell unnoticed to the floor and Antony found her pleasure bud and began to tease her with maddening, skilful caresses.

'Sweetheart, you're all damp and ready for me,' he breathed into her ear. 'Gods, I've dreamt about this moment for years. Have you dreamt of it too?'

She made some incoherent murmur against the rasp of his beard, but her legs were quivering so much they would scarcely hold her. Of course she had dreamt of it! Silly, romantic fool that she was, she had never quite lost that tenderness for her first lover. Oh, the nights when she had wept over him after he left Egypt! Or the times when she had endured dry, loveless encounters for the sake of political advantage and made them bearable only by conjuring up his image. This is

Antony making love to me, she had told herself, closing her eyes and wincing as Gnaeus Pompeius or Julius Caesar had thrust into her. Antony! Antony! Antony! And now here he was with his arms around her and his huge, powerful, hairy bulk engulfing her and she dare not give way. Even though she wanted him so badly, wanted to inhale that masculine smell of leather and salt and wild parsley, wanted to be crushed in his embrace and taken joyously, she did not dare give way.

'No!' she shouted and tore herself free.

He caught her at the door as she was struggling with the bar. His massive fist came down on it, banishing all hope of escape, and with a despairing whimper, she turned to face him.

'What are you going to do? Rape me?' she hissed accusingly.

His eyes leapt with anger as if she had struck him, but he shook his head.

'No,' he growled. 'I've never forced a woman yet. But I want to know what's going on. I thought you were as fond of me as I am of you. I thought you wanted me.'

This was worse and worse! The hurt look in his eyes made her yearn to reach out and hug him. And, quite apart from that, the way he was looming over her so close that she could feel the heat of his body, left her dizzy with desire.

'I–I am fond of you,' she stammered, moistening her lips with her tongue and dropping her eyes.

'And you do desire me,' he prompted helpfully. 'Don't you?'

She darted him a quick, stricken look.

'No.'

The word was little more than a croak.

'Liar. This says that you do.'

He rammed his hand up between her thighs and withdrew it again, holding up his glistening fingers in front of her face. Then, without taking his eyes off her, he thrust his fingers into his mouth and slowly, voluptuously sucked them.

'I want to taste you,' he murmured, as he withdrew them again. 'I want to feast on you and bring you to the point of madness the way I used to do. Do you remember? I want to make violent love to you for hours on end and make it wildly exciting for you. We're good together, Cleopatra, we both know that. Why waste the chance now that the gods have brought us to each other?'

Her whole body felt as if it were on fire. She twisted beneath the prison of his arms, shaking her head with less and less conviction.

'No. Caesar – '

'Fuck Caesar. This is nothing to do with him! It's between us. The most important thing that any man and woman can do together and I want to do it with you. If I knew I had only half an hour left to live, I'd want to spend it making love with you. Isn't that what you'd want too?'

She was silent, but he took her chin in his hand and forced it up. Her eyes met his and she was lost.

'Yes,' she said hoarsely.

His movements were swift, rough, urgent, but he did not hurt her as Caesar would have done. Breathing as harshly as if he had run a mile in full armour over stony ground, he unfastened her shoulder brooches and proceeded to undress her. Once she was naked, he swept her into his arms and carried her to the huge bed. Dropping her in the centre of the scarlet coverlet, he tore off his uniform and stood gazing down at her.

He had not changed much in the nine years since she had first met him. At thirty-six he was still as muscular and vigorous as ever, although there were now a few scattered flecks of silver in his beard. Looking up at his towering figure, at the breadth of his shoulders, at his lusty cock erect and ready for action and the appreciative gleam in his narrowed eyes, Cleopatra felt a rush of affection. Holding out her arms, she smiled tentatively at him. It felt so good, so warm, so familiar to be crushed beneath that mountainous bulk, to feel Antony's kisses rain down upon her, to hear the deep, resonant growl of his voice. They were both impatient of preliminaries. A few kisses, some mutual sucking and stroking and sighing and he was on top of her, bursting into her with a bellow like a rutting bull.

She abandoned herself totally to the sensual flow of the experience, feeling as if she were speeding faster and faster down a river in spate, hurtling against boulders, spinning in whirlpools and finally plummeting over some heart-stopping edge. At last she came back to earth, gasping and shuddering, to find Antony collapsed on top of her, groaning into her hair.

'You're the best fuck I ever had, Cleopatra,' he said fervently.

'Bastard!' she exclaimed, pinching him. 'That's not the kind of compliment calculated to win a virtuous woman's heart.'

'Well, I'm not calculating and you're not a virtuous woman. You're a sexy little siren.' He fondled her bum appreciatively. 'No decent wife would know half the tricks you do.'

A barb of sudden jealousy pierced her like a thorn.

'What about Fulvia?' she demanded. 'Is she good in bed?'

He sat up and frowned at her.

'I'm not going to discuss my wife with you,' he said with a hint of disapproval. 'It wouldn't be right. She's a decent, dutiful woman and I respect her.'

'Don't talk to me in that moralizing tone!' she flared. 'Decent! Dutiful! Dull! Dull, dull, dull!'

'Now, look, Cleopatra,' he warned. 'You're going too far. Fulvia may not have been my choice, but she shows every sign of trying to be a loyal wife to me. She's discreet, efficient and faithful and I'm grateful for it. In time I believe I'll become very fond of her.'

The sentimental note in his voice infuriated Cleopatra.

'Oh, fond of her? And what if she weren't faithful? What would you do then?'

Antony looked baffled.

'I'd divorce her, of course.'

Cleopatra hurled herself out of bed with such violence that she knocked an oil lamp over. It shattered on the floor, sending a greasy puddle oozing over the mosaic tiles.

'You hypocritical bastard!' she breathed. 'You men are all the same, aren't you? It's perfectly all right for you to be screwing me senseless, but not for your wife to take a lover! And what about me? Supposing I were a Roman woman with an illegitimate child, would you marry me?'

Antony looked appalled.

'Knowing that you'd had other lovers?'

'Yes! Just as you have done.'

'Er. Well –'

'Bastard. Bastard, bastard, bastard!'

She burst suddenly and noisily into tears. He came over to her and put his arms around her, nuzzling her neck.

'I don't understand what this is about,' he confessed.

'No, you wouldn't,' she muttered, scrubbing at her eyes.

But she understood. She had broken her own cardinal rule – never fall in love with a man. In future she would have to be more careful. Much more careful.

Brutus sat in his office at the governor's residence in Mediolanum, scowling at the two letters which lay open in front of him on a small table. It had been a bad morning in any case, filled with tiresome administrative details about embezzling clerks and exasperating provincials, slow to pay their taxes and quick to cause trouble. Being a governor was no job for a man of taste, intelligence and high moral principles. If Brutus had had his choice, he would have taken a chair of philosophy in some quiet, provincial university in Greece and spent his time debating the nature of virtue and wisdom. Instead he did nothing but attend tedious meetings and answer labyrinthine correspondence. And now there were these disturbing letters to deal with.

He picked up his mother's screed first. It was written in her own angular, spiky hand and was uniformly venomous in tone. Although it contained the usual quota of political gossip, the main item in it was a stinging complaint about the young Queen of Egypt who was currently flaunting herself and her illegitimate child around Rome. Reading between the lines, he deduced that his mother had been dumped by Julius Caesar in favour of a younger mistress and could feel nothing but relief on the subject. He had always felt that Servilia's blatant association with Caesar was a serious blot on the family honour. Yet her complaints about Caesar's increasing political ambitions made him deeply uneasy . . .

Even worse was the letter from Porcia, the daughter of his uncle Cato. As he smoothed it out and glanced over the neat, tiny script, he could almost see Porcia's auburn hair, her clear white skin and modest garments and hear her cool, unemotional voice. She must be in her early twenties by now, a young widow and faithful to her husband's memory, unlike many women in similar circumstances. A pang of disgust at modern permissiveness made Brutus stiffen as he remembered how his own wife had cuckolded him with a music teacher. Shaking his head to recall his wandering thoughts, he began to read aloud.

Rome, the Ides of June
AUC 708 (46 BC)

Porcia Cato wishes very great health to her cousin Marcus Iunius Brutus.
My dear Marcus,

If you are well, I am well. I am afraid this letter will grieve you deeply because of the great affection you felt for my father. I have to inform you that he died by his own hand in Africa in April, following his defeat by the forces of Julius Caesar at Utica. My brother was with him after his surrender and eventually persuaded him to go to bed in greatly troubled spirits. During the night he heard a loud groan from our father's quarters. Full of misgivings, he rushed in and found that he had fallen on his sword. My brother immediately called the doctor who was able to replace his intestines inside his abdomen and sew up the wound. Believing him to be safe, they left him to rest. Instead of doing so, he ripped open his wound with his own hands and thus perished. There seems little doubt that Caesar would have spared him in order to display his own clemency, but my father could not endure the humiliation of owing his life to a tyrant. As if his death were not grief enough, we now have to suffer a fresh outrage. It has been announced that Caesar intends to celebrate his military victories by holding four triumphal processions in September. Believe it if you can, but one of these will celebrate his victory over fellow Roman citizens in Africa and a huge painting of my father's suicide will be carried in the procession for the rabble to mock and jeer at.

I try hard not to weep for my father, Marcus, since he died true to the cause that he believed in all his life – the freedom of the Roman republic. It seems to me that the best memorial we can offer him is to remain true to his glorious principles ourselves. There are rumours that Caesar will soon be made dictator for a further ten years, although no foreign enemy threatens Rome. There are even rumours that he hopes to make himself King. I know you owe your present high office to this man, but will you continue to serve him if he makes us all endure such tyranny? I beg you, Marcus, consult your conscience and ask yourself what my father would have done in your place.

Yours,
Porcia

Brutus put up his hand to his aching temple and groaned. It seemed the time was fast approaching when he would have to make a choice about where his loyalties lay.

CHAPTER TWELVE

The first of Caesar's triumphs celebrated his victory over the Gauls and took place twelve days before the Kalends of October. Even before the end of the first hour, when the sunlight was still striking red and slanting across the Campus Martius, the air already held the promise of heat. Caesar's veterans, who had risen in the chill, crisp hour before dawn, were now busy dousing cooking fires, scouring porridge pots and giving a final polish to ceremonial breastplates and leg greaves. Then suddenly a trumpet sounded and, like iron filings near a lodestone, they sprang into orderly formations. Moments later the doors of the great Villa Publica where the general had lodged overnight were flung back and Caesar emerged. A spontaneous storm of clapping and cheering moved like a roll of thunder along the ranks as he strode down the centre of that gleaming guard of honour. Even the centurions were clapping. Time enough for discipline later when they marched through the streets of Rome and civilians shrank back uneasily from the steady tramp of their feet. For now there was a giddy, holiday atmosphere of licence and camaraderie and dirty jokes, for now they were old battle comrades, general and enlisted men, sharing a common past and a glorious present.

'Three cheers for the Imperator!'

The cheers were given with a will, roaring forth from throats that had uttered battle cries from one side of the Mediterranean to the other. Caesar paused, gazing keenly around him, and a slow, shrewd smile split his leathery face. Good old Julius! Fifty-four if he was a day and had been sliced up more times than a side of beef at the butcher's, but he looked every inch a king today. Unlike his soldiers, he was not dressed in a uniform of leather kilt, brass breastplate and helmet with a long, nodding red plume. No. He wore the traditional costume of a triumphant general – a tunic embroidered with gold palm leaves, a sumptuous gold and purple toga and a wreath of laurel leaves. All the regalia of a god-king. Yet his smile had an amazing sweetness and humility as he stood gazing around at his men with eyes that were suspiciously bright.

'You honour me, comrades,' he said huskily.

The unmistakable catch in his voice made them cheer more loudly than ever. What a man! He had brought them loot and glory beyond their wildest dreams and, if many of their fellows had been left blood-soaked and stiffening in the desert sands of Egypt or the chill, damp forests of Gaul, well, that was war. You couldn't blame old Julius for that. And, through thick and thin, he had always stood by his men. Shared the risks, shared the profits. Never a sign of arrogance about him either, not like most of those shitty aristocrats. He'd always buy a veteran a drink or swap a few coarse jokes with him if they met in a brothel. Randy old bastard! It was a pity they couldn't make him a king ... The cheers redoubled.

'Caes-ar!'

'Caes-ar!'

'Caes-ar!'

Then from far back in the ranks, a lone voice shouted hoarsely above the others.

'Caes-ar Rex!' (Caesar the King!)

The general's whole body stiffened and his eyes flashed. For a moment a look of exultation lit his face.

Then, with almost visible effort, he relaxed, smiled, shook his head.

'There are no kings in Rome, my friend,' he shouted back across the heads of the crowd. 'I am a man like any other.'

All the same, he did not seem displeased by the anonymous soldier's words. As he strode towards the triumphal chariot that awaited him a faint smile played about his lips and his dark eyes were narrowed. Yes, the ordinary Roman soldiers knew quality when they saw it and they no longer clung so urgently to those quaint, old-fashioned prejudices about political freedom and independence. Freedom and hogwash! It was all just a plot by a lot of greedy, free-loading senators to keep power and influence in their own hands. None of the nobles would have a bar of monarchy because they feared the loss of their own prestige – yet if one strong and able man were made king, ye gods, what he could achieve! I'd set up a health service, reduce unemployment, reform the education system and reduce our foreign debt in less than a year, thought Caesar fervently. By the gods I would! And receive the wealth and homage I deserve.

'Remember, sir, that you are only a mere man and do not let pride lead you to destruction,' urged a clear, boyish voice.

Caesar started and shrank back, his eyes dilated with shock as he stared at the youth standing gravely in the triumphal chariot. A tall lad of thirteen or fourteen with a halo of brown curls and an earnest expression. For an instant he had the uncanny fear that the boy had read his mind. Then reason came flooding back to him. Of course! It was one of the traditional customs of the Roman triumph that a slave should stand beside the general in his chariot, murmuring cautionary words to him lest the honours of occasion should go to his head. Caesar's smile grew more twisted. Evidently the ancient inventors of this ceremony had known what they were about! No doubt there had been other triumphant generals who had stood in this very place, brooding over their own achievements and longing to snatch the ceremonial crown from the boy's hands and cram it firmly on their own heads.

'Yes, yes,' he said irritably, climbing into place in the gleaming bronze chariot and seizing the reins. 'No need to take your task quite so seriously, my lad. I'm in no danger of forgetting that I owe all my good fortune to my pious respect for the gods.'

And what a load of rubbish that is! he added silently to himself, his dark eyes scanning the crowd. He no more believed in gods than he believed in werewolves (except in a dim, strange way when he saw those odd visions before his epileptic fits, heard those ringing voices . . .), yet he knew the importance of pretence. The common people in Rome were credulous and superstitious, needing to be deceived and kept happy. And the nobles, most of whom were as sceptical as himself, were adroit at using religion as a threat, an enticement, a bargaining counter, a method of blowing smoke . . . Yes, he must be careful. Every detail of this day must go exactly as planned. There must be no ill omens, no blasphemy.

'I see the white horses are without blemish,' he intoned, gazing approvingly at the four glossy creatures harnessed in front of the chariot. 'A fitting tribute to Jupiter Greatest and Best. May he bring his blessing on this day!'

There was a pious murmur of agreement and Caesar took the opportunity to glance about him. Apart from the usual cluster of priests indispensable at any ceremony of this kind, and the ranks of veterans who would soon fall in behind him, there was a seething mass of people milling around, jostling into their rightful places. At this very moment seventy-two lictors were taking their place in single file in front of the chariot. Caesar felt a surge of pride at the sight of them, resplendent in their red cloaks, each of them carrying a bundle of rods and axes over his left shoulder as a reminder of the triumphant general's power to inflict punishment on the citizens. It would be their task to announce his coming in the city, to clear the path ahead and to arrest any troublemakers.

Immediately behind Caesar's chariot, a group of horsemen were now moving into place, among them his great-nephew Octavian and some of his senior officers, including Antony and Dolabella. Caesar glanced at them with a twinge of regret. What a pity he had no legitimate son of his own who could ride there openly acknowledging his proud descent from Caesar! Yet certain decencies must be observed and the only legitimate family member whom Caesar could acknowledge today, apart from Octavian, was his wife Calpurnia. She had come to the Campus Martius to watch the start of the procession from an open carriage, but her appearance disappointed Caesar. Although he had offered her scarlet robes and a selection of pearls brought back from Britain, Calpurnia had obstinately declined. Instead she wore the simple white stola of a Roman matron and she had not even bothered to pluck out the grey hairs which were beginning to sprinkle the centre parting of her hair. Her gaze met Caesar's and she gave him a brief smile. Shy, self-deprecating, anxious. He was conscious of a momentary flash of irritation. Why couldn't Calpurnia enjoy this moment? Why couldn't she revel in being the wife of the most powerful and successful man in Rome as Cleopatra would have done? What a different spectacle that little eastern hussy would have presented if she could have been here for the opening ceremony! Perfumed and painted and decked in transparent gold silk, she would have adored every moment of the glamour and the attention. Yet, rather regretfully, Caesar had decided that it would be improper to include his mistress in the actual parade. Instead, she was sitting under a silk awning outside the temple of Good Fortune, along with the other foreign dignitaries, waiting in comfort to watch it all pass by.

His gaze flicked over the city magistrates, the trumpeters, the wagons with their tableaux and the white, sacrificial oxen to the captives who were lined up in front of his chariot. The blond giant Vercingetorix, clad in his barbarous national costume of buckskin trousers and shirt, with iron chains around his wrists and ankles stood towering head and shoulders above the others. A surge of pleasure which was almost sexual in its intensity coursed through Caesar's veins at the sight. Deliberately, he smiled at the conquered Gaul. To his annoyance, even now the defeated King gave no sign of acknowledging his defeat. Instead he met Caesar's eyes with a defiant, indifferent stare. The bastard, thought Caesar, gritting his teeth. I'll teach him after today's little frolic is over to defy me like that . . .

'Are we ready?' he asked the chief priest, with a lift of his eyebrows.

The priest nodded solemnly and intoned some words in the Etruscan language of a form so ancient that nobody present understood them. Then the incense bearers hastily took their places in front of the lictors, the musical director waved his baton, the zithers twanged into life, there was a creaking and clattering of hooves, and the procession moved off. The route was a long one, across the Campus Martius, through the Porta Triumphalis, a lap around the Circus Flaminius and another around the Circus Maximus, then round the Palatine hill, along the Via Sacra and up to the holy temple of Jupiter on the Capitol. The entire population of Rome seemed to have turned out to watch the spectacle and the air reverberated with the uproar of the crowd. People pressed against the barriers, pregnant women fainted, small boys scrambled along the rooftops and shouted impudent remarks from the stairways of ramshackle tenements. Once away from the shade of the Campus Martius, the air was stifling, filled with the smells of sweat, perfume, horse droppings, dust, leather, takeaway food and sour wine.

Most of the crowd were in holiday mood, only too ready to cheer and roar with laughter at paintings depicting the Roman soldiers triumphant and the Gauls on the run. Yet occasionally there were ominous signs, jeers and catcalls that rang out above the tramp of marching feet and once or twice, disturbing graffiti on the sides of buildings. 'CAESAR, MURDERER!' and 'WHERE ARE OUR BOYS?'

Caesar fought down his annoyance and kept his smile glued firmly in place, even when the soldiers began to shout out a chorus of a bawdy song composed specifically for the occasion. It had always been a tradition of the triumph to allow this form of humour and, however much it galled him, he must put a good face on it. All the same, his hands tightened convulsively on the reins as the soldiers roared out their verses.

'Our bald old general's reached home shores,
Romans lock your wives inside!
All the bags of gold you gave him
Have been spent on Gallic whores!'

A private joke in the barracks was all very well, but
to shout such thing aloud in the open streets ...
Particularly now, when they were approaching the
temple of Good Fortune, where his mistress Cleopatra
sat waiting. To his horror, he realized that they had
begun to sing about her! As they approached the
portico where she sat regally on a cushioned chair of
carved citrus wood a chorus of guffaws broke out and
a stanza was added to their song.

'Egypt's shores were dyed deep scarlet
In battles cruel and long and wild
So Caesar could enjoy his harlot
And leave her with a Roman child!'

A tide of embarrassment swept through him as the
horses trotted closer to the temple. How would she
react to this public humiliation? To his relief, she rose
to the occasion like the Queen she was. Without the
slightest sign of discomfiture, she glided out of her
chair, advanced to the edge of the portico and spoke in
a clear, ringing voice.

'Egypt honours you, my lord,' she announced and
prostrated herself gracefully.

It was as well she did so, for at that moment a stone
came flying out of the crowd opposite and clipped
through the air where she had been standing only a
moment before. Instantly pandemonium broke loose.
A lictor unfastened his gleaming axe, swung it above
his head and strode into the densest part of the crowd.
Women screamed, sunlight flashed blindingly off an

upheld shield on a nearby balcony and the skittish mare on the front offside let out a shrill whinny, tossed her head and bolted.

At once, with practised skill, Caesar hauled tight on the reins. It should have been enough to arrest the horses' flight, but as the chariot swayed and lurched, there was a sudden loud snapping sound and the vehicle overturned. Caesar was flung heavily into the road, a moan of horror and disbelief rang through the crowd and there was a loud clang of mangled metal accompanied by the terrified squealing of horses. With a gasp Cleopatra leapt to her feet and raced down the steps to Caesar's side. He was lying ominously still, half in the dust, half draped on a set of stepping stones with one arm flung up and blood pouring from his nose. She felt frantically for the pulse in his throat and was relieved to find it beating tumultuously. A moment later Octavian, who had jumped off his horse, fell to his knees beside her. Their gaze met over the injured man and a flash of hostility flared in Octavian's blue eyes like the bright dazzle of a sword stroke.

'He's not dead, is he?' he rapped out.

Cleopatra's eyes narrowed thoughtfully. There was concern in the young man's voice and yet the expression on his face was at odds with that concern. For an instant she could have sworn that she saw a glint of savage triumph in those radiant eyes, an almost sensual excitement in the curve of his lips.

'No,' she said bluntly. 'His heart is beating quite strongly. I think he's stunned himself.'

Octavian's mouth tightened and he rose to his feet.

'Then see to him while I reassure the crowd,' he ordered. 'Citizens, calm yourselves. The gods have delivered a warning only. When a mere man is of such divine strength and power and glory as my uncle

Julius, even Jupiter himself grows jealous and offers a check to his pride. Yet truly Caesar is favoured by the gods. For how else could he have survived such a crash? Be patient a moment and soon you will see him rise up to life again as hearty as ever.' (Surreptitiously he prodded Caesar with the toe of his sandal and his smile grew slightly strained.) 'Come, bring another chariot and four new, white horses. Let the triumph continue.'

Down on the ground there was a low groan. Throughout Octavian's speech, Caesar had been lying winded and half dazed but now he gritted his teeth and gave a faint nod of approval. The movement almost made him vomit. He felt as if every bone in his body were broken and he had undoubtedly hit his head extremely hard as he struck the road. For a moment he was content simply to contemplate the dirt where he lay and the rapidly increasing puddle of blood that was drizzling from his nose. Then he groaned and heaved himself into a sitting position. Cleopatra's arms came round him and she pressed a linen napkin to his face.

'Keep still,' she urged. 'Give yourself a moment to recover from the shock.'

It was sound advice and Caesar followed it. She was a sensible girl and kept her head, not like these other fools who were milling about shouting and bleating about ill omens. A doctor was brought forward to see him, but he waved him testily away. There seemed to be chaos all about, with young Octavian shouting orders and another chariot being brought forth from further down in the procession. The worst of it was that discipline seemed to have collapsed completely. Up in front of him the captives had come to a halt just beyond the temple of Good Fortune and were twisting around to see what had happened. Caesar even glimpsed his old Gallic enemy Vercingetorix craning his neck eagerly above the rest of the mob. He felt too ill and dazed to pay much attention, but was conscious of a sharp sense of humiliation that his old enemy should see him in such a plight.

At last the confusion was brought under control. A new chariot had been found and three of the original white horses plus one replacement for an injured mare had been harnessed in place. Caesar's filthy, blood-stained clothes were scrubbed down with cold water and someone retrieved the gold crown which had fallen in the dust. There was a minor check to these preparations when the youth who had been riding with Caesar was found dead with a broken spine and a fresh outburst of wailing and superstitious terror broke out among the crowd. But Cleopatra dealt with this briskly. Snapping her fingers, she summoned some of her attendants from the steps of the temple and offered them to remove the dead body. Then she ordered one of her most handsome slaves in his place.

'I should be honoured if you would let my humble servant attend you, my lord,' she said, hoisting Caesar into place in the chariot and nodding to the youth to steady him with one hand while he held the crown above his head with the other.

Octavian was furious. The bitch was turning the whole incident to her own ends. How dare she place her own creature in the place of honour by Caesar's side? But it might do more harm to have an undignified quarrel about the matter here in the street. He turned to her coldly and spoke.

'Thank you, madam, for your assistance. I believe you may now return to your rightful place among the subject rulers.'

She ignored him. With a bland smile, she strode into the midst of the cluster of lictors who were re-grouping in front of the new chariot. Most of them were men of lower-class origin, many freed slaves, and she deliberately chose one with a swarthy, Syrian cast of countenance.

'The voice of the gods tells me to accompany Caesar,' she announced. 'I should be honoured, good sir, if you would take me under your protection.'

Fortunately, there was not far to go to the Capitol Hill. Caesar was still looking dazed and swaying more than the motion of the chariot would require. At the foot of the stairs leading to the temple, he made a valiant attempt to pull himself together and even man-aged to walk a few impressive paces like a conquering hero before the ground began to undulate strangely beneath his feet. With a muffled groan he lurched forward on to his knees. Before Octavian could dis-mount from his horse, Cleopatra ran forward and spoke to Caesar in Greek.

'Get up!' she hissed. 'Gaius, you must get up! Crawl on your knees if that's all you can do. You must reach the temple unaided.'

Caesar raised his head and gazed dizzily up the sloping steps. To climb them seemed a feat as difficult as winning the battle of Pharsalus but he had always been obstinate. Groping with his hands, he began to drag himself up towards the temple entrance. As he did, Cleopatra turned to the muttering, uneasy crowd and spoke. Her voice rang out in the clear, confident tone of a woman long accustomed to making public appearances.

'Citizens, see how Julius Caesar humbles himself for your sake. So that no harm may come to Rome from the unlucky accident to his chariot, he has made a vow of atonement to the gods. See how he does penance, crawling on his knees to win divine favour for his people.'

Caesar gave a choking hiccup that might have been laughter as he hauled himself dizzily up those appalling steps. Ingenious wench! If he survived this ordeal, he'd reward her quickness of thought. If ... The stairs blurred, his gorge rose, but somehow he kept going.

'Hail, Caesar!'

'Hail, Caesar!'

'Hail, Caesar!'

Not far to go now. She had them cheering and clapping, the noise of it was ringing in his ears, he could see the chief priest of Jupiter Optimus Maximus standing on the top step awaiting him. Then suddenly it all seemed to spin and whirl around him. He barely managed to crawl across the threshold and out of sight before spewing violently all over the temple floor. Later, when the religious rituals were over and he felt somewhat recovered, he summoned Cleopatra to his side.

'I owe you a favour for this,' he muttered. 'What do you want?'

She paused, weighing up her choices. The instincts of a natural bargainer surged in her veins. What did she want? What was the most she could hope to get? For one dazzling instant she was tempted to ask him to marry her and make her Queen of the entire Roman empire. Then sanity prevailed. He was bound to balk at that, especially with so many good, republican eavesdroppers on hand. No. Better to go cautiously, although perhaps in time the same end could be achieved more slowly. A suffocating sense of excitement gripped her as her mind leapfrogged over the obstacles. A divorce for Caesar, a divorce for herself, a marriage between Ptolemy and Arsinoë . . .

'I want you to spare my sister's life,' she said fervently.

The Egyptian triumph was even more sumptuous than the Gallic one had been with all the floats made of richly polished acanthus wood and vast quantities of gold and precious jewellery plundered from Alexandria on display. There were marvellous statues depicting the ocean in chains and tableaux reproducing the main events of the battles in the Nile Delta. There was even a huge, soaring reproduction of the great lighthouse of Alexandria with polished bronze mirrors on the topmost part. Yet everyone agreed that the highlight of this procession was the appearance of the young Princess Arsinoë who had once called herself Queen of Egypt and set up her army in defiance of Caesar. Pale and tragically beautiful with her hair rippling loose about her like a cloud of burnished gold, she wore her rags and chains as if she were quite indifferent to them and seemed to fix her eyes on another world. It touched people's hearts to see her walking so brave and pitiful between the leering guards and a mood of revulsion spread like wildfire among the crowd. Many of them had been brought to Rome as slaves, captured in her numerous eastern wars, and looked on Kings and their families as living gods. It seemed horrifying and almost sacrilegious to them that one of royal blood should be so shamefully treated. Groans and sighs and angry murmurs began to rise among the crowd like the threatening sounds of a storm at sea. When Caesar himself came into sight in his triumphal chariot he was greeted with hisses and boos and shouts of abuse.

'Free the Princess!'

'Caesar have mercy!'

'Peace on Earth, an end to war!'

'Woe to Caesar! No pity for the pitiless!'

Caesar listened in consternation as the grumbles grew louder and louder along every part of the procession route. By the time he emerged from the temple of Jupiter Greatest and Best on the Capitol at the end of the procession, his eyebrows met in a furious scowl and his lips were set, but his mind was made up. He had intended to deny Cleopatra's request, but he saw that he could not risk the resulting unpopularity with the crowd. It was almost a relief to him in consequence when the Egyptian Queen came forward as he reached the foot of the stairs and flung herself at his feet. With a loud, wailing noise, she tore her hair loose from its golden net, scooped mud from the road and smeared it over her face. Then she clutched at his ankles and banged her head on the ground.

'Have pity, Caesar!' she howled. 'Show your god-like mercy and spare my sister's life. Let your rightful anger be softened by the kindness of the Roman people. Hear their prayers and spare Arsinoë!'

The crowd went wild, cheering and shouting and weeping at this heart-rending evidence of sisterly love. Exasperated, but well aware of the propaganda value of showing mercy, Caesar raised Cleopatra to her feet.

'Caesar rules the world, but the Roman people rule Caesar. For the sake of your kind heart, my dear, and the kind hearts of my fellow citizens, I grant this woman her life and freedom.'

The roars of approval that greeted this announcement made him feel certain that he had done the right thing. He was mobbed by the onlookers and caught only a brief glimpse of a bewildered-looking Arsinoë being embraced by Cleopatra, before he was borne away like a floating branch in a flash flood. Pelted with flowers, cheered and fêted and admired, he heard a voice in the crowd take up the cry that his soldiers had used a few days before.

'Caesar Rex!'

'Caesar Rex!'

'Caesar Rex!'

Against all the rules, someone produced the ceremonial crown which he had worn as triumphator and crammed it firmly on his head again. Amid a surge of euphoria he found himself swept along to the front door of his official residence as high priest. The Regia, the royal palace. How apt, he thought exultantly as the shouting began again.

'Long live Caesar the King!'

The front door of the Regia opened and a hush descended on the crowd. His wife came forward with a look of horror on her face and made a sign with her hands to avert the evil eye. To Caesar's shock and outrage, she actually ignored the modesty of a lifetime and spoke directly to the throng of people.

'There are no kings in Rome, citizens. My husband is a good republican like all other loyal Romans. Gaius, take that thing off your head and come inside.'

A fire of indignation blazed through him as he followed her into the building.

'How dare you shame me like that before the people?' he hissed, seizing her by the throat as a slave closed the door and prudently withdrew.

'Are you mad, Gaius? The Senate will accuse you of plotting to make yourself King if you allow such demonstrations.'

'And what if I do want to make myself King? What then?'

She stared at him in horror, barely able to breathe

for the choking pressure of his hand. His glittering eyes frightened her, but she could not believe this was really happening. Half-strangled as she was, she blurted out a protest.

'You can't possibly mean it. You wouldn't bring such shame on your family!'

'Family? What family?' he snarled. 'Fourteen years of marriage and you've never given me a single child. Never! Never!'

As he spoke, he shook her until her teeth rattled in her head. Her wild eyes and terrified whimpering only seemed to enrage him further and he added half a dozen violent blows for good measure. Then abruptly, losing patience, he hurled her to the floor.

'All you ever had as a dowry was your noble birth. I took you out of a slum and made you my wife,' he ranted. 'And what thanks do I get for it? You've done nothing but oppose me with your feeble republican cant! Well, if you don't appreciate all that I've achieved and all that I still hope for, there are others who will!'

Snatching up the crown which had fallen to the floor, he cast her a burning look, then seized a plain old military cloak from a hook on the wall. Without a backward glance, he strode through the house, shouting for a slave.

'Bring me a litter and look sharp about it.'

As he swayed through the streets of the city his thoughts winged ahead of him to Cleopatra. She understood him, she appreciated him, she knew the frustrations of being opposed by fools! If she were offered the chance of being Queen of Rome, she wouldn't cast it aside. Well, he couldn't make her Queen, but he could honour her in a way that would make his disloyal bitch of a wife and these carping, republican senators sit up and take notice! With a grim smile, Caesar leaned out and shouted to the litter bearers to hurry.

The streets were so crowded that it was after sunset when he arrived at his villa beyond the Tiber. He was pleased to find that Cleopatra had washed her hair and changed out of the garments which she had been wearing during her dramatic plea for mercy. He took her to bed and soothed his ruffled feelings considerably by forcing her to do his bidding. At last when they were both flushed and exhausted, he stroked her rumpled hair.

'I have a surprise for you,' he announced.

She dimpled at him. 'I loved surprises. What is it?'

'Get dressed and I'll take you to see it.'

It was close to midnight when the litter pulled up in the yard of a sculptor's workshop not far from the Capitol Hill. There was something eerie about the half-finished statues standing around in the cold bright light of the moon, and Cleopatra felt a strange prickle of misgiving run down her spine as Caesar knocked at the door. Lamplight showed in a thin stripe and then the door swung open with a creak. Cleopatra gave a stifled shriek at the sight of the man who confronted them from the guttering glow of the oil lamp. He was tall and blond and would have been handsome except that one side of his face was hideously disfigured. The left eye was missing from its socket and a series of white scars in the shape of claw marks ran from his forehead down to his chin.

'Nothing to worry about, my dear,' said Caesar, patting her arm reassuringly. 'Brennus is a veteran of the arena.'

'What can I do for you, sir?' asked the slave.

'I want you to transport something to the temple of Venus Genetrix for me.'

'Now?'

'Now,' confirmed Caesar. 'Wake up your master, the sculptor, and get as many men as you need to help you. Cleopatra, you go and wait in the litter and no watching.'

She heard the squeak of wagon wheels and the whinny of the mule being backed into the shafts. Then there was a lot of bumping and swearing before Caesar came back to join her in the litter.

'What is it?' she asked. 'A body?'

That amused him. 'Not exactly. You'll soon see.'

It was only a short distance to the new temple of Venus Genetrix and they arrived there almost as quickly in the litter as the workmen with the cart did. Once again Caesar made her wait while he ordered the workmen about. At last he came to fetch her with a large torch soaked in pitch and blazing brightly held above his head. Ushering Cleopatra ahead of him, he directed her towards an unobtrusive door on the side of the building. There was a squeak of brass hinges, then they found themselves in the hushed interior of the building with the torchlight casting flickering shadows around them and the air heavy with smoke and incense. Caesar stowed the key safely in a fold of his toga and took Cleopatra's arm.

'There's a statue I want you to see,' he announced, guiding her across the central naos to the far wall.

Their footsteps echoed on the marble floor and a strange, creeping sense of curiosity and expectation made Cleopatra's heart beat faster. Then suddenly Caesar held the torch high overhead.

'There you are! What do you think of it?'

She gasped. There was no doubt that the statue was magnificent. Made of beaten gold, it was slightly larger than life-size and set on a plinth so that the viewer was forced to tilt back his head in a gesture of reverence. Yet it was not just the excellence of the craftsmanship that made Cleopatra stand as if she were frozen to the spot.

'I-it's me!' she stammered. 'Isn't it? It's me.'

'Yes, and our son Caesarion,' Caesar agreed proudly. 'Look closely.'

She obeyed and was stunned by what she saw. The statue had been shaped in the traditional pose of the divine mother and child, Isis and Horus. Yet these were not the stylized figures of Egyptian iconography with their timeless, impersonal dignity. No, these were the products of Roman portrait art at its best, where every muscle and sinew bore the stamp of real life. These figures were bursting with so much vitality that they seemed ready to step down from the plinth and stroll away through the temple. Cleopatra in a clinging gown, her breasts thrust voluptuously forward, a sly smile on her lips and even a mocking twinkle in her rock crystal eyes. And the divine infant Horus (alias Caesarion), bearing the unmistakable likeness of Caesar himself, confident, challenging, aggressive, with a mischievous grin on his baby lips.

He held the torch lower so that Cleopatra could read the words cut into the plinth. Slowly she spoke them aloud. 'CAESARION, DESCENDANT OF THE GODDESS VENUS AND CLEOPATRA VII, QUEEN OF EGYPT.'

'What is a statue like this doing in the temple of the Julian clan?' she asked in a stunned voice.

'Well, I made you a promise that I would erect a statue of you in Rome for people to worship. Originally I intended to put it in the shrine of Isis, but now I've decided to give you and Caesarion a place here in the temple of Venus Genetrix, the ancestors of the Julian clan.'

'So you're going to make us members of the family and force the senators to worship us?' she asked in a wondering voice.

'Yes. If you were a Roman woman I'd marry you. But since I can't, I'm doing the next best thing.'

Her eyes shone. She had never guessed that Caesar's infatuation was so powerful. If he was prepared to do this for her of his own accord, wasn't there a chance that he might eventually marry her, whatever he said? Of course, she would have to get her brother Ptolemy out of the way first. She fell to the floor and kissed Caesar's feet.

'Thank you, domine,' she cried fervently.

'Now, now,' he urged, raising her again. 'You deserve it. You've served me well and you're the mother of my child.'

She looked up at him, her eyes bright with ambition.

'I've been wanting to talk to you about that. It's my dearest wish to make Caesarion joint ruler of Egypt with me. But I can't as long as my brother is married to me.'

'Do you want me to have him killed?' he asked.

She flinched. 'No that's too drastic. The Alexandrians would never forgive me. But it did occur to me that you might let him divorce me and marry Arsinoë. You could make them joint rulers of Cyprus.'

'Cyprus?' echoed Caesar in an astounded voice.

'In name only, of course,' said Cleopatra swiftly. 'All the revenues would still come to Rome. And I'm sure you'd find the province much easier to administer if they were in charge.'

He stroked his chin.

'I suppose it's a possibility,' he said slowly.

'There is one snag,' she admitted.

'What's that?'

She took in a deep breath. This was a delicate business and it was important to go carefully.

'Arsinoë has fallen in love with a fellow captive and wants to marry him,' she said in an off-hand voice.

'Well, that might be the best thing, to have her married to some low-born slave. She could never challenge your power again in that case.'

'He's not exactly a slave,' said Cleopatra. 'It's Vercingetorix, the former King of the Gauls.'

'Vercingetorix?' Caesar's face turned a mottled purple. 'The nerve of the man! So he thinks he'll contract a royal alliance and breed more rebellious brats, does he? I'll have him sent to the Sicilian salt mines!'

'Do you think that's enough?' queried Cleopatra. 'He might escape.'

Caesar ground his teeth. 'That's true. Do you think it would be better to execute him?'

'Yes, I do,' she murmured regretfully. 'And the sooner the better.'

An odd look came into Caesar's eyes.

'There's an old custom to do with captives from a triumph. It's fallen into disuse, but I could have it revived. What would you say to ritual strangulation?'

Cleopatra drew a deep shuddering breath and fought down her distaste. I hope by all the gods that Arsinoë never finds out about this, she thought. Well, there was no point being weak; if her plans were to have any chance of success, Vercingetorix must be put out of the way.

'Yes,' she said.

*

When the statue of the divine mother and child was unveiled before a startled group of nobles the following day, Octavian's rage boiled over. He had just enough presence of mind left to keep his features inscrutable, but once the ceremony was over he relieved his feelings by seeking out a brothel in the Subura. There he savagely bungholed a terrified boy of eleven who had been sold into slavery by his destitute parents. Afterwards he summoned an informer, who had already supplied him with profitable blackmail material on several members of the nobility. The fellow was a loathsome, oily law clerk called Syrus, who eked out his salary by selling professional secrets. Octavian's instructions to him were explicit.

'You've got contacts in the criminal world. Use them. If there's any dirt to be dug up on the Egyptian Queen, anything that could discredit her with Caesar, I want to know about it.'

CHAPTER THIRTEEN

Cleopatra continued to see Antony, as she had always known she would, slipping out in disguise to meet him in the tawdry apartment in the Subura. It was unwise and dangerous, but that only added to the spice of the encounters. She envied people who made safety their watchword, but it was not in her nature to do so, especially when she wanted something as badly as she wanted Antony. It was like a fever in her blood, a madness that left her no peace. Yet deep in her heart she knew she had more in common with Julius Caesar. They were both wily, ambitious and unscrupulous, while Antony was impulsive, easy-going and sentimental. She enjoyed pitting her wits against Caesar in arguments which ranged from literature to foreign affairs, while Antony was always left bemused and floundering if she ever tried to start such a discussion with him. And yet it was Antony whom she craved, Antony whose touch made her quiver, Antony whom she loved. Not that she ever admitted it to him.

Her love for him was a weakness which she tried to extinguish by denying it. Even so, there were moments strained against him in that vast, rattling bed, when worse madness overtook her than the simple madness of lust, moments when she felt she would even surrender her kingdom itself if only he would marry her. Usually, of course, it happened when she was reaching her climax. Fortunately, by moaning and shuddering and gritting her teeth, she was always able to hold back the fatal words 'I love you'. Antony had no such scruples. He said them constantly to her, with a sentimental readiness that robbed them of all meaning and he was hurt when she refused to reciprocate. They quarrelled over it as they quarrelled over everything.

'Why don't you ever say you love me?' he complained one afternoon. They had already made love twice and he was sucking her toes as a lazy preliminary to a third bout. 'I tell you that I love you.'

She flashed him a brief glance of mocking amusement. Only this morning she had been formally named a Friend and Ally of the Roman people in the Senate. Later in the day Caesar would be hosting a big party at his villa across the Tiber to celebrate the event. Dizzy with exhilaration at the success of her schemes, she was in no mood to listen to Antony burbling about love.

'It doesn't mean anything when you say it,' she said tartly. 'You've probably said it to dozens of women.'

He looked like a guilty small boy caught with his hand in the cookie jar.

'It would hurt their feelings if I didn't.'

'So you say it even when it isn't true, don't you?'

'Sometimes,' he admitted. 'It's true when I say it to you, though. I do love you, Cleopatra.'

'Why?' she asked recklessly. Foolish, foolish to be fishing for compliments like a breathless young virgin. But she wanted to hear what he would have to say.

He frowned, perplexed by his own inability to put it into words.

'Because you're sexy and clever and beautiful,' he said inadequately. 'Because I was the first man you ever had and I'll never forget the look on your face after I first made love to you that night in my tent in Alexandria. You looked so defenceless I couldn't help loving you.'

She was touched in spite of herself, but she tried to fight off her dangerous weakness with ridicule.

'You sentimental fool! First man, indeed! I had to start somewhere, didn't I?'

He caught her by the wrists and pinioned her against the pillow.

'You do love me, but you won't admit it,' he said hoarsely, with his mouth only an inch away from hers. 'You've loved me since you were fourteen, haven't you?'

A tremor went through her, but she kept her composure.

'Do you really think so?' she demanded coolly.

Deliberately he let his full, hard weight slump against her, crushing her into the feather mattress. Then his hand slid between her legs, slyly caressing her. She arched involuntarily against him with a faint moan.

'You wouldn't do this with me if you didn't,' he said in a tone of triumphant amusement.

She turned her head away, resenting his attempts to use sex to extract admissions of love from her.

'Why do you think I do it with Caesar then?' she taunted, deliberately trying to hurt him.

The flash of anger in his eyes showed her she had succeeded.

'Don't remind me,' he snarled. 'I don't like to think of you screwing with Caesar.'

'I still do it though, Antony. Do you think it's because I love him so much?'

'No,' he hissed, twisting her hair in his hands and punctuating his words with savage, resentful kisses. 'I think you do it because you're a cold hearted, calculating bitch and you want to be made a Friend and Ally of the Roman people! I think you do it to secure your hold on Egypt and get a bit more territory for your son.'

The violence of his lovemaking aroused her. Reaching down, she cupped his hot, hard organ in her hand and began to stroke it provocatively.

'Full marks, Antony,' she purred. 'You're not as stupid as people say you are.'

'Thanks a lot,' he snapped, rolling off her and glancing stormily sideways at her as if he would like to throttle her. 'I know you think I'm stupid and you're right. I am stupid! Oh, if they want someone to lead a cavalry charge or a punch-up in a tavern, Mark Antony's your man. But when it comes to all this government policy and endless Senate committees, I'm useless and I know it. I've never even heard of half the places the Senate wants to seize and make into provinces and I can't really understand what right we have to go around seizing other people's countries anyway. If they left it up to me to choose our foreign policy, I'd say we should give back what we've already taken and mind our own business in future.'

She gave a sudden rueful gasp of laughter and hugged him.

'That's the best piece of Roman policy I've heard in a long time,' she assured him sincerely. 'You're so nice, Antony.'

'Yeah, I'm still stupid though.'

'No, you're not,' she whispered, nestling up to him and beginning to stroke him.

'You're only interested in my prick, not in my brains,' he grumbled.

'I thought you were just telling me you didn't have any brains,' she teased, nuzzling the one attribute he did possess.

'Well, I've got brains enough to know where to put

248

this,' he said hoarsely, seizing her by the hair and guiding her down.

It was a long, tempestuous lovemaking and afterwards she lay dreamily with her head in the crook of his shoulder, watching the rise and fall of his massive, hairy chest.

'The trouble is I was born at the wrong time!' he burst out, as he stroked her tumbled hair. 'This world we live in today is too complicated for me and it's the same thing with loving you. It's too fucking complicated! You're neither one thing nor the other. If you were a Roman virgin I could marry you or if you were a slave girl I could set you up in an apartment and we could see each other openly. I'm fed up with all this secrecy and lying and sneaking about. I hate it. We can't even go to the chariot races or a wine bar together for fear you'll be caught out.'

She gave a brief, bitter shrug.

'Well, that's life.'

'Why?' he demanded passionately, sitting up and pulling her with him. 'Why does it have to be? Why can't we just run off together somewhere and leave it all behind? All the scheming and brown-nosing and empire building? Isn't that what Arsinoë and her boyfriend are planning to do?'

Cleopatra froze at the mention of her sister's name.

'What are you talking about?' she asked in a carefully neutral voice.

'Didn't she tell you?' demanded Antony in surprise. 'I saw her one day at Aelia Trebutia's house. Some Gallic chieftain had fallen in love with her and there were stars in her eyes every time she looked at him. She told me she was hoping to be set free after Caesar's triumphs and that they would go and start a little farm somewhere together. I suppose that's what they'll do now the triumphs are over. I know Arsinoë's been given her freedom and I suppose the Gaul has too. Hasn't Caesar told you anything about it?'

Cleopatra breathed again. What Caesar had told her was that Vercingetorix had been strangled in the underground prison and his body smuggled out at night time to be cremated. Obviously Antony had heard nothing of this and she dreaded the look of disgust and horror which would spread over his features if he ever found out her part in it. She would simply have to tell him what she kept telling Arsinoë in response to her frantic pleas for information.

'No, he hasn't told me anything. But I'm sure it will all work out happily.'

He looked at her keenly, his brows knitting in a puzzled frown. Her heart began beating faster at the strain of the deception and, feeling strangely unable to meet his eyes, she climbed off the bed and padded across to the kitchen corner to get herself a cup of water. After a moment's thoughtful silence, Antony came after her and began to nuzzle her neck and caress her naked breasts. Neither of them saw the watcher behind the shutters of the apartment opposite.

In view of the fine, autumn weather the reception to celebrate Cleopatra's new diplomatic status was to be held outside on the marble patio which extended all the way along one wing of Caesar's villa. As she emerged into the golden sunshine of late afternoon, wearing a purple silk gown and a gold necklace with a string of Red Sea pearls threaded through her hair, a satisfied smile played about her lips. Humming softly to herself, she strolled along to the far end of the patio where the slaves were already laying out the first course of the meal.

Here there was a curved dining seat of white marble shaded by a vine trained over four slender pillars of Pentelic marble. Water gushed out from pipes under the seat, was caught in the stone cistern and then held in a polished marble basin. As a whimsical beginning to the meal Cleopatra had given orders for the hors d'oeuvres to be placed in tiny, floating vessels shaped like birds or little boats which were bobbing about on the water. At the far end of the basin a fountain in the shape of a carved lion's head shot a steady jet of water into the pool beneath. Later on when it grew dark oil lamps would be set in little boats to float about and illuminate the surface of the pool. Cleopatra had no doubt that Caesar's tiresome relations would detest her for these flamboyant touches of luxury. Good. Let them detest her, so long as they realized that it was useless to oppose her. They had patronized her and excluded her when she first arrived in Rome a few short months ago, hadn't they? Then let them suffer the humiliation of seeing that she was now ruling the roost with the Roman dictator. Let them see that it was her home that would soon be the centre of Roman social life, not Calpurnia's! With a sigh of contentment, she sat down on the wide rim at the edge of the pool and dabbled her fingers in the cool water. Yes, everything was going well. Her first ambition had now been realized. Friend and Ally of the Roman people! And she had no doubt that Caesar was coming to depend on her more with each passing day. So what next? Should she simply withdraw to Egypt, content with her achievements? Or should she aim higher? And how much higher was it possible to go? Could he be persuaded to marry her?

A faint, wistful smile played around her lips as she trailed her hand through the water. Caesar, emerging from the loggia, saw her sitting there with the sunlight blazing in a gold nimbus around her head and shoulders and his face softened. How young she looked! Just like a hesitant virgin waiting shyly to be brought to the marriage bed. Creeping forward, he cupped her face in his hands and kissed her.

'What were you thinking, sitting there so pensively?' he teased. 'Were you dreaming of how much power you'll have in Egypt now you're a Friend and Ally of the Roman people?'

'No,' she said with a catch in her voice. 'I was wishing you could marry me.'

The artless simplicity of her reply touched him to the quick. It was always the same with women. Even with the intelligent ones, all their scheming meant nothing once love entered the picture. A gratifying throb of excitement pulsed through him at the realization that she loved him. He had never been quite sure until now, but there was no mistaking the yearning in her limpid brown eyes as she looked up at him.

'Come for a walk before our guests arrive,' he urged, taking her arm and helping her to her feet.

When they were deep in the labyrinth of ivy clad plane trees and clipped box shrubs, he suddenly hauled her into a crushing embrace and kissed her violently. His eyes were dark and strange as he looked down at her.

'If I could marry you, I would,' he said thickly. 'You'd make a fit partner for the first man in Rome, fit even for the King of Rome, but the nobles would never stand for it. Making myself King of Rome would be bad enough, but taking a foreign Queen as my wife? It would be enough to start a civil war. All the same, I sometimes think . . .'

What he sometimes thought he didn't tell her. Instead he suddenly thrust his hand up her dress, tore away her loincloth and backed her into a box hedge. Then with a low groan of anticipation, he hoisted up his tunic, seized his organ and rammed it inside her.

It was an extremely uncomfortable experience for Cleopatra. The hedge was prickling her back and some stinging insect immediately began crawling down her arm. All the same, the delirious prospect of becoming Queen of the Roman Empire had an aphrodisiac effect on her. Her bones turned to watery delight and the juices of desire flowed within her as she pictured herself giving judgements on the Capitol Hill. It was no effort at all to gasp and cling and cry out with delight as Caesar pounded violently away at her and finally convulsed with a long, inhuman moan.

'Oh, Gaius, I don't care about being Queen,' she murmured as his rasping breath slowly subsided. 'I just wish you could be my husband.'

He held her fiercely against him. At any other time he might have suspected her of lying, but her body had secret signs of its own. There was no doubt that she wanted him as hotly as he wanted her, no doubt that she loved him. An indulgent smile creased his face.

'Well, who knows what time will bring?' he muttered half to himself. 'One thing is certain. I don't want you going back to Egypt just yet. I'll have to leave for Spain soon and sort out those damned rebels under Gnaeus Pompeius, but when I return I want to find you here ready and waiting for me. After that, we'll have to see . . .'

Cleopatra smirked to herself as they made their way back through the shrubbery. Everything was going like a dream. She was a Friend and Ally of the Roman people, Caesar hadn't the faintest clue about her affair with Mark Antony and the old man was falling more hopelessly in love with her with each passing day. It was good to be alive.

Her euphoria was shortlived. As they emerged from the shrubbery, they saw that half their guests had already arrived. The entire Julian clan was assembled in a silent, disapproving cohort on the patio in front of Caesar's study. All of them looked gloomy at being summoned to this reception, all except Octavian who stood in their midst with an unholy light of rejoicing in his blue eyes. As Caesar and Cleopatra emerged from the garden, he stepped forward to meet them with an exultant smile on his lips.

'Hello, Uncle,' he murmured. 'Have you been having a good time in the shrubbery with your whore?'

Caesar's face turned plum coloured with rage. He advanced threateningly on his great nephew with his hand upraised.

'How dare you speak of her like that?' he hissed.

Octavian backed out of reach with his right arm raised protectively over his face, but his gloating smile did not waver.

'How else should I speak of her?' he demanded. 'If she isn't a whore, then why was she having sexual intercourse with Mark Antony this very afternoon in an apartment in the Subura?'

There was a sharp intake of breath and all the assembled guests leaned forward as avidly as if a gladiator had just delivered a telling sword thrust in the arena. All eyes flew to the victim of the attack and although no one actually shouted aloud, 'She's had it!' they might easily have done so. Colour drained from Cleopatra's face and she swayed on her feet, looking mortally stricken. With gloating eagerness most of

Octavian's relatives crowded closer but at the sight of that advancing group of malicious Romans, her fighting spirit rushed back. For an instant she had felt as if she stood toppling on the lip of a precipice but now, faced with one of the biggest challenges of her life, she launched herself into space and glided as audaciously as a new-fledged bird. The sensation was almost exhilarating. Once in her youth she had questioned an actor about the secret of holding an audience. His advice came back to her now. 'Believe it's true and you'll have no trouble convincing others.' What would I do if I were really innocent? she thought and the answer came to her. She gave three, gasping, staccato cries and burst suddenly and noisily into tears.

Octavian's announcement had come as a shock to Caesar also. In the past he had always prided himself on being able to think on his feet, but now his feet seemed rooted to the ground. A tremor shook him as if he had a quartan fever and he tried to remember his favourite military maxims. Contain the damage, preserve morale, withdraw and regroup. Yet he could do none of them. Suddenly his shock was transformed into action. With a roar like a trumpeting elephant he lunged at the table, seized a long, iron spit intended for roasting capons and charged at Octavian. The youth gave a long, ululating cry of terror, ducked out of sight and crawled under the table. Caesar's knee flashed up, his foot kicked out and he sent the temporary refuge hurtling to the ground with a crash. Amid the shattered glass, broken plates and flying olives, Octavian found himself pinned against the overturned table with the point of the spit at his throat.

'Curse your lying tongue, you troublemaking little bastard!' snarled Caesar. 'I'll slit you open and hang your liver from the trees for the birds to feed on unless you take back those words!'

At this the guests who had been standing enthralled edged prudently away. All except for Octavian's stepfather, Philippus. A grave, distasteful look pinched his lips and set his shaggy eyebrows in a frown, but he stepped forward unflinchingly and laid one hand on Caesar's shoulder. Caesar did not move the point of the spit from Octavian's throat, but he glanced over his shoulder with blazing eyes.

'Stand back!' he hissed.

'Come, come, Gaius,' urged Philippus soothingly. 'It's ill manners to slaughter your guests and nobody believes my lout of a stepson anyway. All his life he has sought attention by telling tall stories.'

Octavian's indignation overcame his terror.

'It's not a tall story,' he choked defiantly. 'It's the truth! I paid a detective to watch the Queen and you can question him under torture if you wish. He'll tell you – Cleopatra was in an apartment house this very afternoon having sex with Mark Antony.'

His words were spoken with such passionate conviction that all the onlookers turned instinctively to the Queen as if for confirmation. Aware that she was the centre of attention, she took her time about answering. Tears sparkled like jewels in her lovely eyes and her face wore a look of horrified innocence that touched the heart of more than one man present. She tried twice to speak, apparently failed, and caught her full, trembling lower lip in white teeth. At last she shook her head.

'Octavian – hates – me!' she gulped.

It was undeniably true, but no answer to the accusation against her. Caesar, who had at first been sure the charge was one of pure malice, felt the first chill of doubt grip him. In his long experience of love and war, he had come to pride himself on the ability to read people's faces. Now this talent filled him with mysterious horror. Every nerve, every instinct he possessed clamoured the hideous message that Octavian was telling the truth and that Cleopatra was hiding some guilty secret. Why else would she refuse to meet his eyes, why else would she weep and tremble like a mourner at a funeral? A low groan broke from his lips. If she was guilty, he would kill her for it and yet he must know for sure. He must know!

'Cleopatra?' he said, forcing himself to speak mildly. 'Can you offer any reasonable explanation for these extraordinary charges of Octavian's? You weren't really at some seedy apartment in the Subura today, were you?'

As he spoke, his hands clenched so hard on the iron spit that his knuckles turned white. He willed her to deny the charge, to offer any excuse, no matter how threadbare, that would save his honour and hers. Curse the girl! Even if she was guilty, she must not make him the butt of ridicule in Rome! She must defend herself.

'Answer me!' he rasped. 'Were you at an apartment in the Subura today?'

To his consternation, she stood dazed and helpless like some nocturnal animal trapped in the glow of a hunter's torch, too alarmed to make its escape. Her eyes looked glazed, her breath came unsteadily and she made blind, plucking movements at her gown with her fingers. Then suddenly she seemed to lose her nerve entirely.

'Yes!' she shrieked and then she turned away from him. Raising her hands as if she were demented, she began to tear at her hair and pound her breast, keening wildly like a mourner at a funeral. 'Yes, yes! I was!'

Caesar reeled in horror at this admission and dropped the iron spit on the pavement with a loud clang. A buzz of excited speculation ran through the assembled guests and Octavian looked triumphant.

'You seriously mean to tell me that you had sex with Mark Antony in an apartment in the Subura today?' demanded Caesar.

Cleopatra stopped in mid-shriek, her lips parted and her hair disordered like a Maenad.

'Mark Antony?' she echoed in a bewildered voice. 'No, no. I had nothing to do with Mark Antony. Oh, how can you believe such filth, such slanderous lies? Certainly I went to an apartment in the Subura, but not with Mark Antony.'

'What were you doing there, then?' hissed Caesar.

Her lips quivered. She darted him a shy, uncertain glance like a child and then retreated a pace or two, hunching one shoulder defensively.

'You'll be angry–' she began.

'Tell me!' he roared.

She flinched and seemed to gather her courage.

'I went to a soothsayer,' she admitted at last in a rush. 'Oh, Gaius, don't be angry with me! I know you think it's all superstitious nonsense and a waste of money, but I was so worried about what would happen to you in your Spanish campaign that I paid her to cast a horoscope to see if there was any danger for your life. But all was well. She told me you were born under a lucky star and had many years of happiness left to you yet. And she sold me a charm to protect you from your enemies. I'm sorry, Gaius. Oh, say you'll forgive me.'

Forgive her? Caesar's relief was so great that if he hadn't already deified her, he would have done so at that moment. When she cast herself down on the ground and clasped his knees, sobbing and choking, he hauled her to her feet and embraced her warmly. Hardly able to hide his exhilaration as he patted her shoulder, he cast a contemptuous glance at Octavian.

'Poor Cleopatra,' he murmured, stroking her hair. 'So you emphatically deny the charge of Octavian's informant that you went to bed with Mark Antony in an apartment in the Subura this afternoon, do you?'

'Of course I deny it!' she cried indignantly. Then seeing a certain, faint disquiet still in his eyes, she reached up her finger and touched his cheek, gazing at him as earnestly as if they were alone. 'Gaius, I regard you as my husband in all but name and I swear by Isis I will always be as faithful to you as you deserve. But even if I had a mind to cheat you, what possible reason could I have for choosing Mark Antony? The man's a drunken oaf with not a brain in his head to recommend him. Second rate, worthless, a loser! Why would I want him when I have the first man in Rome for my own? If you will not give me credit for virtue, at least give me credit for good taste.'

It was perhaps unfortunate that Mark Antony and his wife Fulvia had arrived just in time to hear this tense exchange. As if to give point to Cleopatra's stinging remarks, Antony was already more than three parts drunk and not in the best condition to deal with the situation. The fact that Caesar had somehow got wind of Antony's relationship with Cleopatra did not worry him in the least. In fact, he was secretly delighted at the thought of the old bastard's humiliation on making the discovery. Nor did he pause to consider the impact of the revelation on his wife's feelings. But one thing did penetrate Antony's fuddled brain – the fact that his passionate, tempestuous little Egyptian Queen was openly abusing him in front of witnesses.

'That treacherous little bitch!' breathed Antony wrathfully as he crashed through the shrubbery. 'I thought she loved me. I'll teach her to talk like that about me!'

Fulvia's fingers closed like iron around his wrist.

'Shut up and let me handle this,' she ordered.

She might be massively built, warty, hairy, and have a tread like an elephant, but by the gods she was magnificent when aroused! It was easy to believe that her father had been a consul and her mother a revolutionary as Antony watched her sail into battle like a trireme under full power. What did they call that manoeuvre where you sailed through the enemy lines and then turned and rammed them? A diecplus wasn't it? Well, Fulvia was doing a diecplus and doing it superbly! Her voice came out firm and resonant as her gaze tracked from Caesar to Cleopatra with equal disfavour.

'I thought we were invited to this reception as a matter of goodwill,' she said with freezing dignity. 'Instead I find that I have come here only to hear my husband insulted. You appear to be operating something midway between a family court and a common brothel, Julius Caesar. But since you find it necessary to conduct this inquisition let me tell you this. Cleopatra may be an ungrateful, slanderous wretch to attack Mark Antony as she is doing, forgetting that it was he who restored her father to his throne in Egypt so many years ago, but she is not an adulteress. If it's any concern of yours, Mark Antony did make love to a woman at an apartment in the Subura this afternoon. I know because I was the woman in question. My husband and I went to inspect an apartment belonging to us which was lying empty and while we were there our natural desires overtook us. This is an embarrassing admission for me to make and one which would not be necessary if Octavian kept his prying informers out of the lives of decently married couples.'

Caesar looked stunned.

'Fulvia,' he stammered. 'I can only offer you my sincerest apologies for this whole distressing incident and beg you and your husband to stay here now as our honoured guests.'

Fulvia drew herself up.

'Certainly not,' she snapped. 'I am far too shocked, outraged and offended.' (Not to mention worried about what Antony may say if we do stay, she thought to herself.) 'Kindly send someone to tell our slaves to bring back our litter at once.'

Cleopatra felt like cheering as Fulvia seized Antony's arm, turned him adroitly and marched him back towards the gates. The remaining guests began to murmur and shuffle and avoid each other's eyes. It was left to Caesar to take decisive action. With a face like thunder, he put out his hand towards Octavian and hauled the youth none too gently to his feet.

'I think it would be farcical to continue with this reception,' he said through gritted teeth. 'I suggest that you all go home and bear this fact in mind. If any slave lets out a word of what has happened here tonight, I'll crucify him. And if any of my relatives does the same thing, I'll disinherit him. I hope I make myself clear.'

Cleopatra's eyes met Octavian's with gentle malice.

'Gaius?' she prompted. 'Don't you think an apology would be in order before your nephew leaves?'

Caesar gritted his teeth so hard that a muscle twitched in his cheek.

'Yes, I do. Kindly apologize to the Queen, Octavian.'

'But I – '

One look at Caesar's stormy face convinced Octavian of the unwisdom of protesting any further.

'Oh, all right then,' he muttered ungraciously as if the words stuck in his throat. 'I'm sorry.'

'In the Egyptian manner, if you please,' purred Cleopatra.

Octavian looked baffled and Caesar with evident enjoyment pushed him down on to the tiles.

'Flat on your face, lad,' he explained. 'That's the way. Now kiss my lady's foot.'

Cleopatra thrust out her graceful toes, encased in a jewelled sandal for Octavian's homage. She felt a brief, moist warmth against her skin, then the boy rose to his feet, glowering. Still she was not satisfied.

'Octavian needs something to occupy him, don't you think, Gaius?' she asked. 'So much imagination and brainpower all going to waste! Perhaps a stint in the army would do him good? I know exactly the solution! Why don't you take him along on your Spanish campaign?'

Octavian stared at his great-uncle in horror. Go into battle? Violence, bloodshed, danger, bad food, dysentery, bedbugs. His stomach churned at the mere thought of it.

'I can't,' he bleated. 'I'll get asthma.'

'Nonsense,' said Caesar briskly. 'You've been living soft for far too long. It's an excellent idea. I'll take you down and get you enlisted tomorrow.'

Once his guests had departed, Caesar did not follow Cleopatra into her chambers but withdrew into his study where he sat deep in thought for a long time. At last he roused himself and decided to go for a walk. His feelings were in considerable turmoil as he strode out of the gates of his villa and along the right bank of the Tiber. By now the evening was well advanced and bright stars shone like jewels in the dark blue vault of the heavens. Even out here where there was still considerable open country, there were a few prostitutes displaying their wares for the benefit of travellers. Several times he passed the leaping, orange flames of a fire, only to see some young woman strutting and posing with her skirt slit to the thigh, her face painted and her breasts exposed. In a different mood, he might have flung one of them a coin and taken her into the bushes or up against the wall of some farmhouse not yet swallowed by the urban sprawl. But tonight he was in no mood for it, being far too tense and overwrought from the fiasco that had just taken place. He stopped on the Pons Sublicius to admire the milky trail of moonlight that gleamed on the waters of the Tiber and was almost bowled over by a rattling, four-wheeled cart on its way to deliver vegetables to the stalls in the centre of the city. He shouted a half-hearted curse at the driver, who raised his whip and bawled back at him cheerfully.

'Blame old Julius Caesar, cock. He's the one that banned us from the city in the daylight hours.'

That brought a wry smile to his lips as he strode on. Yes, he had banned wheeled traffic from the city in daylight and on the whole it had been a sensible move, except when it inconvenienced him as it did now. At least these days the streets were not so congested in daylight and there were no longer traffic jams on every corner. But he had to admit that the uproar at night was unendurable. All the same, he was city bred and his spirits lifted as the racy vitality of Rome took him to its heart. He enjoyed the uproar in the taverns, the smell of frying sausages in the fast-food cookshops, even the mud and the rotting cabbage leaves and the stench of the public urinals as he made his way through the twisting back alleys.

He had no clear destination in mind and was too preoccupied with thoughts of Cleopatra to notice where his feet were carrying him. The shock of fearing her unfaithful followed by the relief of finding her merely gullible and a prey to womanish fears had left him feeling as shaken as if he had sustained a wound or a bad bout of fever. Her earlier words came back to him and he scratched his chin reflectively. There was no doubt that the wench was burning to marry him and he found the realization oddly flattering. Indeed, quite touching. Of course it was out of the question. Such a marriage would create an uproar in the Senate, although that in itself was not necessarily a deterrent to Caesar. No, the real problem was this. He had no objection to being thought a scoundrel, but did not want to seem a fool.

And just how did his contemporaries view his affair with Cleopatra? he asked himself uneasily. At present he had no real doubt that they were both outraged and envious at his coup in seducing the goddess Queen and bringing her to Rome to flaunt before the best society. That was well and good. The outrage and envy of the Roman nobles tickled his vanity. Even if he tired of Cleopatra now and sent her home with rich presents, it would simply be one more episode in the cycle of stories that other men told about him. Caesar and Lollia, Caesar and Servilia, Caesar and Mucia. And did you hear the one about how he bedded the Egyptian Queen? Screwed her his very first night in Alexandria and got her with child. And not only that. He brought her here to Rome to watch his triumphs. Did you ever hear the like? Yes, that's what they'd say in the clubs and taverns.

But the truth was that he didn't want to send Cleopatra back to Egypt even though the triumphs were over now and there was no further reason for her presence. Yet if he kept her here much longer the nature of the gossip might change. People might begin to see him as the conquest rather than the conqueror. The humiliation of that would be unbearable.

He sighed irritably and ran his fingers through his thinning hair. Curse the girl – she had got under his skin like a burrowing tick! He didn't want to give her up, didn't want to give his son up either. But to marry her? Wouldn't that provoke the worst kind of mockery and innuendo among the very men who had envied him for seducing her? He could just hear them at it now. No fool like an old fool, conquered Greece, has captured her savage victor, long in the tooth, short in the wits. No, such a marriage would be a disaster. Not that the political backlash would worry him in the least. On the contrary he rather relished the thought of ramming the necessary legislation through the Senate. And Calpurnia's feelings didn't bother him either. She would simply do as she was told, just as she always had. Fortunately she had always been a dutiful wife and far too frightened of Caesar to argue with his commands. But the question that really worried him was this. Would he look foolish if he married Cleopatra? He paused, turning the idea over in his mind, curiously reluctant to let the idea of marriage go. Reluctant also to believe that he could ever look foolish in any circumstance. Surely by now his dignity was unassailable? Wasn't it? He wondered whose advice he could ask and realized that his feet had carried him without his conscious knowledge right to the house of his former mistress, Servilia.

Chapter Fourteen

Servilia was just about to go to bed when Caesar's arrival was announced to her and with a muffled shriek of mingled excitement and dismay, she ordered the slave girl to ask him to wait while she got dressed again. This was a messy and hurried operation. She had just finished massaging a rejuvenating cream made from bird droppings into the wrinkled skin around her eyes and throat and removing it proved difficult. Olive oil, hot water, scent and towels were instantly demanded and a second slave girl was dispatched to find her best purple gown, gold shoulder brooches and string of pearls.

Fortunately Caesar was only too happy to be kept waiting and amused himself by strolling around the atrium of the house, admiring the portrait masks of Servilia's illustrious ancestors and the fine, Greek statues which adorned the entrance hall. Yes, Servilia had certainly got a bargain with this house, he thought with satisfaction and his eyes narrowed with amusement as he recalled the day of the auction. It had been one of those forced sales of the assets of a senator foolish enough to support Pompey in the civil war and Caesar himself had been the auctioneer. He had knocked the house down to Servilia at a price so outrageously low that it had caused murmurs of discontent even among the subdued crowd who had attended the show. His eyebrows drew together in a frown as he remembered Marcus Cicero's cutting remark on the occasion. 'Well, it was even cheaper than you think. Don't forget that he knocked off a third (Tertia) as well.' A veiled reference to the fact that Caesar had not only had Servilia as his long-standing mistress, but had also seduced her youngest daughter, Junia Tertia. He wondered now whether Servilia had ever got wind of that brief liaison. He thought not, although she probably wouldn't have objected even if she had known. She had brought up all her daughters to be as emancipated in their choice of lovers as she was herself.

At that moment he heard a footstep behind him and turned to find Servilia appearing from the back section of the house. He felt a surge of pleasure at the sight of her. In the soft glow of the lamplight her chiselled features looked as elegant as ever. She was stylishly dressed in a purple robe, gold brooches and a string of pearls. Yet there was no mistaking that she was a middle-aged woman whose hair was turning grey and who had lost the bloom of youth. The sight gave Caesar a feeling of contentment and familiarity, as if he were kicking off shoes that pinched him and drawing on a pair of old, comfortable slippers. Dear Servilia, he could always rely on her! He knew perfectly well that she had been in love with him since the age of fourteen and he also knew that in many ways she hated him. It gave him a thrill of triumph to see that the attraction she felt was always stronger than her resentment. Take this moment, for instance. He had blatantly ignored and neglected her ever since his return to Rome, yet she was still hurrying to greet him with a kiss on both cheeks and a flash of some turbulent emotion in her eyes that reminded him that she was still a woman and a sensual one, in spite of her fifty-four years.

'This is an unexpected pleasure, Gaius,' she murmured in her smoky, rather hoarse voice, letting her fingers linger a shade longer than was strictly necessary on his arm.

'A pleasure for both of us, Servilia,' he replied courteously. 'Tell me, how are your children? Marcus Brutus, for instance?'

There was a touch of constraint in her manner as she led him into the small, front sitting room and closed the door behind them. The antagonism between Caesar and her only son had never been any secret and it was only her relationship with the dictator which had led to Marcus's life being spared after he fought on the wrong side at Pharsalus. But Caesar had always been generous. Not content with letting Servilia's son live, he had also appointed him to high office.

'He's very well,' she said. 'And enjoying the challenge of governing Cisalpine Gaul, thanks to your generosity.'

'Good,' said Caesar approvingly. 'And what about your daughters? I've seen the two older ones at receptions recently with their husbands, but somehow I never seem to run into young Tertia. How is she?'

Servilia stiffened. She was by no means so ignorant about Caesar's brief and torrid affair with her daughter as he imagined and the knowledge had cost her considerable torment. Yet she thrust the thought determinedly from her mind. Junia Tertia, after all, had been old enough to make her own choices, although it was a betrayal that Servilia would never forgive either of them for. She had to make a conscious effort to smile as she gestured to a jug of citron water flavoured with honey which stood on a table.

'Tertia?' she said brightly. 'Oh, she's very well. Spends most of her time quietly at home with her husband. Won't you have a drink, Gaius? I know you're far too abstemious to want wine, but this citron water is very pleasant.'

He took his seat and accepted a cup from her. The room pleased him. For such an expensive house, it was pleasantly bare and simple, reminding him somewhat of an army barracks. There was a mosaic floor with a pattern of seashells round the edge, a few couches and wooden chairs with plain woollen cushions, a couple of three-legged tables and no more oil lamps than were strictly necessary to soften the darkness. It reminded him of the apartment where he had spent his childhood. Servilia waited till he had sipped his drink, heaved a long sigh and settled into his chair before she spoke.

'Is there something particular you wanted to discuss with me, Gaius?' she asked, filling her own cup and sitting down close to him. 'Or is this just a friendly visit?'

He took another sip, letting the tension of the evening slowly drain away.

'I've just had a rather difficult scene with some members of my household tonight,' he admitted. 'Nothing serious, but it was upsetting.'

Servilia's lips twitched. She had heard all about the difficult scene from Caesar's older sister Julia who had called in to regale her with the story on her way home from the disastrous reception. Naturally Servilia had no intention of revealing this.

'Poor Gaius,' she said smoothly. 'Do you want to tell me about it?'

He gritted his teeth and shook his head.

'No. I think I just want to be with you, Servilia. To spend a bit of quiet time. You and I go back a long way, don't we?'

'Forty years now, Gaius,' she agreed. 'Longer than many a married couple.'

He took her hand and squeezed it.

'Were we really only fourteen when we fell in love?' he asked. 'Sometimes it seems like yesterday. I could have strangled your father with my bare hands when he gave you in marriage to Marcus Brutus.'

She bit her lip. Even now that long ago injury had the power to sting. Yet common sense told her that her father had been right. Brutus had made a loyal and reliable husband, where Caesar would have made an atrocious one. Poor Brutus! It was more than thirty years now since Pompey had had him executed at Mutina in one of those endless civil wars, although sorrow had not kept Servilia from finding her way into Caesar's bed after his wife Cornelia died.

'Well, it was all a long time ago,' she said with a sigh.

'It's odd how some things never change,' murmured Caesar. 'I still remember the citron blossom in your father's courtyard the first time I kissed you. I'm fond of you, Servilia. Very fond of you.'

She set down her cup and rose to her feet to fetch the water jug again.

'I'm fond of you too, Gaius,' she said drily, over her shoulder. 'I don't approve of you. But I am fond of you.'

Her astringency amused him. It was never any use coming to Servilia for compliments. To her he was the same ruthless, calculating, horny youth he had been forty years ago. He was rather flattered that she still saw him in such a light.

'Curse you, Servilia,' he murmured amiably, rising to his feet and snatching her in his arms. 'You're the only woman in Rome who doesn't appreciate my worth.'

'Who says I don't appreciate it?' she whispered,

letting her lean, rangy body brush against him. 'I know what a brilliant man you are, Gaius. And what a bastard. There's nobody knows that better than I.'

He had not intended to do more than kiss her for old times' sake, but an unexpected roar of flame leapt through him at the tingle of her lips against his. With a muffled oath, he tore free of her grip, strode to the door and dropped the bar in place, then he returned and plunged his hands down the neckline of her dress. Her breasts had always been small and were now frankly scrawny, with none of Cleopatra's fleshy bounty, but Cleopatra for all her youth and charm did not have the attraction of long familiarity. Servilia's eyes fluttered closed, her thin lips parted, revealing teeth that were gritted as if in pain and a low moan escaped her. Caesar found it all strangely arousing. Servilia was his, his! She had been his for forty years and would be till the day of her death. He possessed her utterly and could trust her as he could trust no other. The thought filled him with an intoxicating sense of his own power and importance.

'On the couch,' he ordered curtly. 'Spread your legs for me, as you did when I came back from conquering Britain.'

It had been more than ten years ago and he had forced her to close her eyes before he dropped a shower of pearls on her naked body. She had cried out in protest at the stinging hail and opened her eyes to find herself endowed with a fortune. There had even been a pearl trapped in the springy triangle of hair at the fork of her body. At the memory he felt himself grow hot and stiff and began to wrench frantically at her clothes.

'Remember how I covered you in jewels?' he murmured thickly, his breath fanning her ear.

'Yes. Yes! Oh, by the Good Goddess, don't worry about unfastening that brooch, Gaius, rip it.'

There was a loud tearing of cloth, a sudden shuddering intake of breath and then the violent rattling of the bronze couch as they slaked their thirst for each other with all the turbulent frenzy of a pair of teenagers. Her body was marked from too frequent child-bearing yet it still had the power to excite him unbearably. He urged her on like a runaway horse till at last her eyes began to shoot gleams of light and her head threshed from side to side. An inhuman cry broke from her lips and her body clenched in a last violent spasm. With a roar of triumph, Caesar thrust deep inside her and came to a stunning climax. For a long time they lay sweaty and shuddering, crushed together until at last their breathing quietened. He rolled off her and lay beside her, caressing her face with his fingers. Yet even as he touched the familiar outline of her cheek, he knew how little the experience had meant to him. Of course Servilia could still arouse him, as any woman between the ages of fourteen and eighty could probably arouse him, but she was not the one who obsessed him. If anything, this experience had only served to make even clearer to him that it was Cleopatra he wanted. Cleopatra who had almost certainly never lain with any other man but him and never would, Cleopatra who was the mother of his son, Cleopatra with her shrewd brain and dauntless ambition and endless wiles, who loved him because he was the most powerful man in the world . . . Cleopatra who must become his beyond any shadow of a doubt.

'Servilia,' he said abruptly. 'Do you think I'm too old to marry again?'

A severe shock jolted through Servilia's body. After what had just passed between them, it was perhaps not surprising that she felt a surge of elation and a wild, ecstatic hope. All the same, this might be only a new twist to Caesar's endless power games.

'Are you thinking of divorcing Calpurnia for some political advantage?' she asked cautiously.

Caesar snorted.

'No. Damn political advantage! I'm wondering if I shouldn't thumb my nose at the entire Senate and simply marry for love.'

'Oh, Gaius,' she breathed, burrowing into his shoulder. These were the words she had hoped to hear fourteen years ago, when Caesar had announced his intention of marrying again, only to disappoint her cruelly by choosing Calpurnia, who was still young enough to bear children. Now, at this late stage, Servilia was touched beyond measure to hear him express these sentiments so unexpectedly. No doubt his bitter disillusionment with the Egyptian Queen had shown him where his true affections lay and since Calpurnia had proved barren and Caesar could have no reasonable hopes of further children, he might just as well spend the rest of his life with the one woman he had always truly loved. 'I think you should,' she added firmly.

'I'm glad you agree, Servilia,' he said, rising to his feet and straightening his tunic before groping around for his shoes. 'I know I can always rely on your advice. You're brave enough not to care about the conventions and I'm sure you can understand how I've come to feel over these last couple of months.'

'Tell me,' she urged softly. 'How have you come to feel?'

He was quite oblivious to the yearning in her voice.

'That I love Cleopatra and want to marry her,' he replied briskly.

'Cleopatra?' choked Servilia. 'You love Cleopatra?'

Caesar smiled wryly as he laced his sandals.

'Yes,' he agreed. 'I love her. She's the mother of my son and I hope she'll give me more children. But she's more than that to me. If all goes as I plan, when I return from Spain, I intend to make myself King with her as my Queen. And when I do, I won't forget your kind advice, my dear. I'll always think of you with great affection.'

Servilia barely restrained herself until she heard the slave girl farewelling him at the front door, but the moment his footsteps had receded into the distance, she picked up the glass jug and the two cups and flung them viciously on the floor. The slave girl came running in alarm but paused uncertainly at the sight of Servilia's flushed face, heaving breast and wild eyes.

'Oh, I see you've had an accident with your best Tyrian glassware, madam,' she said diplomatically. 'What a shame. Shall I fetch a dustpan and brush and sweep it up?'

'Yes,' hissed Servilia. 'And while you're at it, bring me writing materials and the bottle of herba lactaria. I want to write to my son.'

By the time the slave girl had crept out of the room a second time, wearing a subdued expression and clutching a crock full of broken glass, Servilia's rage had abated enough to allow her to stop pacing and sit down at a small table with several sheets of papyrus, a reed pen and some lamp black ink, although she jumped up almost at once to secure the bar on the door again. One could not be too careful, even in one's own house. Caesar had his spies all around Rome. Biting the end of the pen and wrinkling her nose at the trail of greasy smoke which rose from the lamp, she tried to set her thoughts in order. It would be best to do as her son instructed her and write a harmless letter that any prying courier could read without suspicion, adding her secret thoughts in invisible ink at the bottom. Her swift brain reviewed the major events of the last couple of months in Rome. What would it be natural for her to write of? Of course! The triumphs, the reform of the calendar, the private scandals and political gossip which were known to everyone in Rome . . . her pen flew over the papyrus.

Rome
First Intercalary month
AUC 708 (46 BC)

Servilia to her son Marcus Iunius Brutus wishes very great health.

If you are well, I am well. So much has been happening in Rome that it is hard to describe it all. We are living in very exciting times . . .

She went on to describe Caesar's four triumphs, the reform of the calendar, the likelihood of an expedition to Spain to crush the forces of Gnaeus Pompeius, the gossip that Dolabella and Cicero's daughter Tullia really were getting a divorce this time, although she was said to be with child . . . She concluded by signing herself his affectionate mother and then stared thoughtfully at the empty rectangle of papyrus. which would hold her real message. Then she reached for the bottle of herba lactaria, shook it vigorously and removed the stopper. It struck her as bitingly comic that Caesar himself had introduced her to the properties of this plant in their youth and shown her how to write invisible messages in it. Fortunately she did not think that those employees in the diplomatic courier service who were in Caesar's pay were likely to go to the length of scattering charcoal dust on Marcus Brutus's private letters from his mother. No, it would be left to the governor of Gallia Cisalpina himself to decipher this message.

She paused, wondering how best to frame it. Her son's character was the problem, as it had always been. Although he was deeply attached to her, Servilia knew that Brutus had always disapproved of her relationship with Caesar. Brutus himself was pompous, humourless, self-consciously virtuous and seemed to resemble his tiresome Uncle Cato more than his own mother. Perhaps influenced by Cato, Brutus had always vilified Caesar as unscrupulous, power hungry, lacking in integrity and utterly offensive in his dealings with women. It irked Servilia now to admit that there was some justice in her son's complaints. All the same, she needed Brutus's help and it was only fitting that he should avenge the insult she had suffered. Gritting her teeth, she dipped a fresh pen in the bottle of white fluid and began to write.

My dear Marcus,

I believe we are on the brink of another constitutional crisis worse than any we have suffered yet. This time Caesar has gone too far. Believe it if you can, but he has told me he intends to make himself King of Rome and marry Cleopatra legally so that she can be his Queen! Yes. He said this in my own house, though it shames me to admit it. As the Good Goddess is my witness, Marcus, I want no part of any violence against Caesar, but his mad ambitions must be nipped in the bud. It is time he was persuaded to retire and let younger and saner men take office in Rome. My brother Cato lies dead in Utica, stabbed by his own hand

and can no longer act to restrain Caesar's lust for power, nor to defend our family honour. I urge you, my son, not to forget your breeding. Remember how my ancestor Servilius Ahala stabbed the tyrant Spurius Maelius four hundred years ago and how your father's ancestor Brutus drove out the Tarquin kings for the sake of Roman liberty! You are thirty-nine years old, lacking only three years to be eligible for the consulship and there are men who will stand beside you to rid us of this new tyrant. Do not fail us, Marcus. Our freedom is in your hands.

With a blind, despairing movement Servilia flung down the pen and bit the back of her hand as she stared at the apparently blank, harmless papyrus. For a moment it seemed as dangerous and evil a thing as if it were a hooded cobra rearing up to strike. Twice she put out her hand as if to snatch it and tear it up. Her heart was thudding unevenly and a cold fit of shivering seized her limbs. Then the image of Cleopatra nestling in Caesar's embrace and smiling triumphantly as a crown was placed on her head flashed before her eyes.

'No!' she cried. 'No! Curse them both, I won't allow it!'

Like a hawk dropping from the sky, she snatched up the letter, rolled it, dipped it in melted wax and pressed her seal ring into the warm, aromatic blob. Then, with a terrible expression on her face, she kissed the scroll as if it contained a love note written from the heart.

'That will teach you to betray me, Gaius Julius Caesar,' she breathed.

Antony woke the morning after Cleopatra's party with a raging headache, a sour taste in his mouth and a vague but profound sense of misgiving. He sat up and winced as the room rocked like a Gallic transport ship. What in the name of Jupiter had he done the previous night? Then the scene in Caesar's garden rushed blurrily back at him and he groaned aloud. Not that he had taken much part in the action this time. In fact, he had been little more than a bewildered by-stander as Caesar, Octavian, Cleopatra and Fulvia came into headlong confrontation. And, if even half of what he remembered was true, his own political career was probably on the skids by now. Not to mention his marriage.

He dragged out the chamber pot, shouted for a jug of water and had just seen the slave boy vanish with the slops when his wife came in. At the sight of her Antony flinched. Fulvia let out a guffaw of laughter at the sight of his guilty expression.

'I haven't come to punish you,' she announced, sitting on his bed and handing him a cup. 'Here, drink this.'

He sniffed it suspiciously.

'What is it?'

'Egg white, citron, honey and water beaten together over a low flame. My father swore by it for hangovers.'

'I thought you hadn't come to punish me. Oh, well.'

He drained it at a single massive gulp and shuddered. Then he set down the cup and reached for her hand.

'I'm sorry,' he said bluntly. 'I haven't been much of a husband to you. It must have hurt your feelings walking into the middle of all that crap yesterday.'

A wry smile touched the edges of Fulvia's mouth. Nobody had ever worried much about her feelings before.

'You've been a better husband than the other two I've had,' she retorted. 'Clodius used to dress in drag and Curio gambled. Never mind that, though. We've got to decide what to do about this business with Cleopatra.'

He darted her an uneasy look and flushed brick red.

'Y-you mean those lies of Octavian's about how I – '

'Antony, you don't have to pretend to me,' she said patiently. 'I've known for ages that you were having an affair with Cleopatra.'

He stared at her in consternation.

'But how? I've never breathed a word.'

'You talk in your sleep.'

He hung his head and twisted his massive hands together, cracking the knuckles.

'Why didn't you say something before?' he asked unhappily.

She shrugged.

'Good wives are supposed to look the other way, especially wives with a face and figure like mine. And I could certainly understand why you fancied her – she'd charm the birds off the trees. But it's too dangerous for you to continue now, Antony. She'll destroy your whole future if Caesar ever learns the truth.'

Her face was sober, but it held no hint of reproach, only concern for him. Antony felt a stab of shame.

'Why are you being so understanding?'

'Because I'm fond of you. You've always treated me kindly and never made fun of my ugliness. Besides, it's my future at stake too. If you make an enemy of Caesar, I'll suffer and so will the children. He's a vindictive man, however much he proclaims his clemency.'

Antony was silent, thinking of his daughter Antonia from his previous marriage and Fulvia's children Claudius, Claudia and Curio. Would Caesar really leave them destitute or, worse still . . .? He left the thought unfinished.

'You could divorce me,' he said abruptly.

'I could, but I don't want to.'

He was surprised at the twinge of pleasure her words gave him. Surprised also to realize that he didn't want a divorce from Fulvia. She was brisk, plain, practical and as unromantic as a slab of dolomite. But like a rock, she had something strong and comforting about her too. After the sting of Cleopatra's betrayal, Fulvia's loyalty was doubly welcome. His features set into a resentful scowl as he recalled the Egyptian Queen's words on the previous day. He felt angry, hurt and bitter to discover her true opinion of him. What had she called him? 'A drunken oaf with not a brain in his head to recommend him. Second rate, worthless, a loser'? And she had meant it too, the little slut!

'I know you're in love with her,' said Fulvia, misunderstanding his brooding silence. 'But I still think – '

'I'm not in love with her!' burst out Antony. 'I don't know if I ever was. I've always suspected that she was as hard as nails underneath all the perfume and the fine clothes and the caressing ways. But there's something about her, Fulvia! She's like one of those Sirens who lure men on to the rocks and then destroy them. When I'm away from her, I can see it, but once I'm with her I find her irresistible.'

'I know,' agreed Fulvia with a faint, envious sigh. 'It's that husky voice and the way she flatters men and her charm. But you must find the strength to give her up. You must tell her that you can't see her any more.'

Antony had received countless decorations for bravery in battle, but he flinched at these words. Fulvia was right, but her advice filled him with panic and a leaden sense of misgiving.

'What can I say to her?' he muttered. Then his face brightened. 'Perhaps she won't contact me again anyway, perhaps the whole incident scared her off too. She might just let it all die a natural death. What do you think?'

Fulvia shook her head.

'She'll contact you,' she said shrewdly. 'She's so set on having what she wants that she won't give up easily. But I'll see you safely through it, Antony. And, if you'll allow me, I'd also like to help you in regaining Caesar's favour. I've always been interested in politics and my family has a lot of influence in the Senate. If you let me manage your public career, I'm sure you'll go very high.'

Antony suppressed a sigh. He wasn't at all sure that he wanted a public career, but he owed Fulvia something. Picking up her plump hand, he kissed it.

'I'll do whatever you want,' he promised.

Fulvia gave him a snaggle-toothed smile.

'Good,' she said. 'You won't find it too painful, Antony. I don't intend to make you give up all women.'

Antony brightened.

'You don't?' he asked with a twinge of guilty excitement.

For a moment her heavy features looked almost wistful. She would have preferred to have Antony to herself, but Fulvia was a realist. Try to chain him down and within a month he'd be back with that dangerous, exotic Egyptian woman. Better to keep him grateful to her and to have a rival of her own choice.

'No,' she said mildly. 'All I ask is that you choose someone who won't be a political disaster. That actress

Volumnia, for instance. Everyone was scandalized about the way you paraded her around in your magistrate's litter, but the woman herself was no threat to the state. If you were discreet, I'm sure you could resume the liaison.'

A sly smile began to play around Antony's lips.

'Why are you being so generous to me?' he asked.

'I want our marriage to last. Especially now that I'm carrying your child.'

He looked at her in surprise and slowly dawning pleasure, then caught her in his massive arms and kissed her soundly.

The result was that when Cleopatra sent Charmion to Antony's house a few days later to try and arrange a secret meeting, she was told that Antony no longer wished to see her.

It was a fine, autumn day when Arsinoë disembarked in the harbour of Ephesus. She had not wanted to leave Rome with no certain news of Vercingetorix, but the combined efforts of Aelia Trebutia and Cleopatra had persuaded her. Cleopatra had been wonderful, so kind and sympathetic, sharing every detail of Arsinoë's anguish about her missing lover and buoying her up with hopes that he would soon be found. Her plan had been for Arsinoë to sail to Cyprus and wait for news there, but in the end Aelia Trebutia had prevailed.

'Go to Ephesus, my dear,' she had urged. 'I own a small farm there just outside the city and if . . . when Vercingetorix reappears, I'll send him there to manage it with you. In the meantime, I'd feel safer knowing you were in the Sanctuary at the temple of Artemis in the city of Ephesus. I don't trust Caesar even now and he can't drag you out of sanctuary without committing sacrilege.' Arsinoë had obeyed and now she stood with

Ephesus laid out in front of her, praying with all her heart that Vercingetorix would soon be released and allowed to join her.

Somehow the appearance of the city took her by surprise. At the back of her mind she had expected it to look gloomy, like the underworld shores on the far bank of the River Styx, where the dead flitted like formless shadows. Finding Ephesus bright, cheerful and bustling with life offended her. The sunlight which beat down on the marble buildings was so intense that it might have been the blaze of midsummer and she could feel the heat radiating back up from the paving stones on the docks. The ground seemed to rise and fall alarmingly under her feet as if she were still aboard ship and she put out her hand to a huge coil of rope to steady herself as she gazed around at the sight before her. Overhead the sky was like an inverted blue bowl, and the same vivid blue was reflected in the tossing waters of the sea behind her. Trading ships bobbed at anchor in the harbour and the whole area was busy with the normal uproar of a working port. Slaves from the warehouses were loading bales of wool and pottery jars of wine aboard a carrier bound for Athens while sailors on leave shouldered their bundles and disappeared thankfully into the maze of streets leading away from the harbour. Much of the city was built in marble with impressive colonnaded shops and public buildings lining the main street of the Arkadiane which ran half a mile from the harbour to the theatre on the hill. As Arsinoë stood lost in bewildered contemplation, two of the crewmen from the ship vanished into one of the stone offices on the waterfront and returned shortly afterwards with a hired litter and eight bearers.

Arsinoë smiled bleakly and murmured her thanks as they hoisted her aboard, but she left the purple silk curtains open so that she could drink in the details of the city. After the monotony of the voyage, every sensory detail struck her with extraordinary force. The air was filled with exciting scents and she took in deep breaths, almost enjoying the mingled aromas of hot, baked bread, salt air, green, growing things and the spice warehouses with their contents of pepper and cinnamon. Up ahead of them, she could see the vast circle of the theatre set into a green hillside. But as they approached it, the litter bearers veered off to the left and took her past the Palaestra, across some open ground to the stadium and on to the temple of Artemis, which was her destination. As they drew nearer to the temple, she heard the clang of hammers in the silver-smiths' workshop and saw row upon row of souvenir stalls selling statuettes of the Goddess Artemis with elaborate sphinx-like ornaments on her headdress and her skirt and her torso covered with what looked like a huge bunch of egg shaped breasts. The litter took another turn and she found herself inside the temple precinct with a group of white-clad slaves hurrying to help her alight.

'Please ask the chief priest if I may have an audience with him,' she said courteously. 'I wish to seek sanctuary in the temple.'

Once the slave had left with her message, she occupied herself by looking around her. She had never been in Ephesus before and the graceful Ionian columns of the temple were magnificent enough to distract her attention momentarily from her nagging worries about her lover. Yet after a few, rapt moments of contemplating the soaring pillars and echoing interior of the building, melancholy settled on her again like a chill, damp blanket. The return of the slave interrupted her reverie.

'The chief megabyzus will see you, my lady. I'm to take you to his house.'

The priest proved to be a middle-aged eunuch with kind brown eyes and a squeaky voice. She listened attentively as he outlined the rules of sanctuary.

'You must not go beyond the line that is clearly marked a little more than two hundred metres from the temple. That's where Alexander the Great's arrow lodged when he declared this place a sanctuary. He shot his weapon from the rooftop and declared that wherever it landed, within that line anyone could take refuge from his enemies and be under the protection of the goddess.'

'May I have visitors? Messengers and so on?'

'Of course. Any messengers will be sent to you immediately.'

Thus it was that after two months of agonized waiting Arsinoë received her first visitor from Rome. A tall, blond man, unmistakably a Gaul, his face marred by a disfigurement that made her utter a cry of shock. An empty left eye socket with the white, scarred claw marks of a lioness's attack running from forehead to chin. He carried a small urn and his expression was grave.

'Who are you?' breathed Arsinoë with an ominous sense of misgiving. She gestured at the urn. 'And what's that?'

'My name is Brennus. I'm the slave of Milo the sculptor from Rome. I've come to bring you the ashes of Vercingetorix and to tell you the truth about how he died.'

Chapter Fifteen

'Gaius, you really ought to make a new will before you go off on this Spanish campaign,' murmured Cleopatra.

Caesar's brow furrowed and he raised himself on one elbow, thrusting away his mistress's caressing hand and looking at her piercingly. The dark eyes were as meltingly tender as ever, the lips full and pouting and sultry, the naked body as sinuously relaxed as a cat's. Yet he knew her well enough to know that turbulent calculations must be going on behind the languorous façade.

'Why?' he demanded.

Her eyes widened.

'So that Caesarion will be provided for, if anything happens to you.'

'I should have thought the kingdom of Egypt would be adequate provision in the event of my death,' he commented drily.

'But Caesarion's not King of Egypt. My brother is.'

He winced inwardly at the reminder. Little bitch! She knew how he resented the thought that Ptolemy was her husband, especially now that the youth was verging on manhood. Yet Caesar could ill afford to provoke a revolt in Egypt by insisting on a divorce, at least until this Spanish campaign was safely over. Besides, he had done all that was humanly possible for Caesarion already.

'You ungrateful slut!' he growled. 'I've already taken care of Caesarion's future.'

'I know,' she purred apologetically, beginning to

stroke the hair on his chest. 'Don't be cross with me. It's just that I think you could do more for him.'

'Such as?'

She took a deep breath and gambled.

'You could name him as your heir.'

'When and if I decide to make a new will, I already have an heir in mind. Octavian.'

Cleopatra gave a scornful laugh.

'That pathetic little coward! How much credit will he reflect on you? I hear he's come down with a fever and will probably be too sick to go to Spain. It seems a remarkably well-timed illness.'

Caesar flushed brick red with annoyance. Privately he shared her misgivings about his great-nephew, but his family pride was strong. No weakness must be displayed to outsiders and Cleopatra, for all her inroads into his life, was still an outsider.

'He's of noble birth, he has held public offices creditably, he has a shrewd financial brain and he shows promise at picking capable employees.'

'But he's only a great-nephew!' she protested. 'What claim does he have on you?'

Caesar thought wryly of Octavian, stripped and groaning with lust as his great-uncle rammed into him. Some would say that constituted a claim, except that it was a bond which Caesar devoutly hoped to keep secret for ever.

'I have a certain affection for the boy,' he replied primly. 'If nobody better is available, I think he would make a satisfactory heir.'

'I don't understand you!' she cried. 'Octavian humiliated both of us with his filthy accusations at my reception.'

Caesar shrugged.

'I punished him for that.'

It was true enough. He had beaten Octavian so severely that the boy had been unable to walk for a week.

'But he's everything you dislike,' she burst out again. 'He's sly, vicious, physically weak, absolutely contemptible. Why won't you consider Caesarion? He promises to be a much more impressive specimen when he's a man.'

Caesar reflected on what she said. It was perfectly true. Not only did Caesarion bear a remarkable physical resemblance to his illustrious father, but he was healthy, lively and utterly fearless. When Caesar had taken him up on his stallion for a gallop around the Campus Martius recently, the boy had roared with indignation when it was time to be set down again. Yet there was more to being a dictator's heir than courage and an impudent smile.

'He's too young, he's illegitimate and he's not Roman,' he replied repressively.

Cleopatra drew a deep breath of exasperation.

'But he's your son! Blood is thicker than water, isn't it? How can you pass him over when he's your only child?'

Her strident tone irritated Caesar and without thinking he snapped back.

'Caesarion is not my only child.'

The silence that followed was so profound that he clearly heard her unsteady intake of breath.

'What do you mean?' she demanded.

'Exactly what I said. Caesarion is not my only child.'

'But Julia – ' she began.

'I'm not talking of Julia. I have a grown son who is well born, Roman and of appropriate age for high public office. He's not legitimate, or at least he's only nominally so, but in every other way he is suitable to be my heir. I've always done what I could to assist his career, although I haven't always been satisfied with his behaviour. Still, as you so justly say, blood is thicker than water. Who knows? In the end I may even decide to name him as my heir.'

She stared at him in horror at this unexpected reversal of all her plans. Caesar's revelation made her feel as sick and winded as if someone had punched her in the stomach. Her mind raced, summoning up all the possible candidates. The faces of Antony, Dolabella and a dozen other young senators flashed before her mind.

'Who is he?' she asked sharply.

Caesar smiled, enjoying the sensation of watching her writhe like a worm on a hook. Without haste, he got out of bed and began to dress.

'I've no intention of telling you that, my dear,' he said over his shoulder. 'But perhaps knowing of his existence will remind you that Caesarion is not the only pebble on the beach and you, charming as you are, have not been the only object of my affections.'

She almost choked with rage and chagrin as she watched him pull his tunic over his head and fussily tie the belt, but almost at once a new emotion was added to her turbulent feelings. Apprehension. Not only about this unknown son of Caesar's, whose unwelcome existence had just been sprung on her, but also apprehension about his departure for Spain. She had thought herself so secure in his affections, but what if she were wrong? What if her influence began to diminish once he was far away in the western provinces? Would he simply write to her and order her back to Egypt? The humiliation would be intolerable. She thought of Mark Antony and a pang of resentment shot through her. His recent desertion had made her smart, but she had consoled herself with the thought that Antony would soon have to watch her marrying Caesar and do homage to her as his Queen. But what if that never happened? Her eyes filled with tears of anger at the prospect of enduring such disappointment.

'Don't be angry with me,' she begged unsteadily, holding out her arms to Caesar. 'I didn't mean to annoy you. I only want Caesarion named as your heir because it would make me feel that you really love us. I hate being on the perimeter of your life like this.'

His face softened at the tremor in her voice and the tears that were spilling over on to her cheeks. Striding back across the room, he dropped a kiss on her fragrant head. He was on the brink of reassuring her and telling her that he intended to marry her on his return, but after a moment's thought he changed his mind. No, let her sweat it out. She would work harder to please him if she did not feel too certain of his affections.

'Be a good mother while I'm gone and we'll discuss the matter again on my return,' he urged in the pious tone he used as Chief Priest.

'Oh, I will,' she vowed, seizing his hand and kissing it. *Good mother*, she thought irritably. That's all very well, but I can do more than that. I'll achieve so much in Rome he won't recognize the place when he comes back. If I pay out enough bribes, I can get the health service reformed, the calendar set right, the veterans' colonies planned and a start made on the draining of the marshes. I'll make Caesar see that he can't manage without me!

'And stay away from Mark Antony,' warned Caesar. 'I know there's no foundation to the gossip, but I don't want your good name tarnished again.'

★

She had little difficulty in obeying that command since Mark Antony resolutely refused to see her. Even the most austere of senators was startled by the change in Mark Antony and put it down approvingly to Fulvia's influence. He was certainly a changed man since his marriage. He no longer drank to excess, he turned up on time to senatorial sessions wearing a clean toga and he never went near a betting shop any more. It was even rumoured that he kept only one mistress and sometimes left her bed early enough to go home for dinner with his wife and family. Murmurs began to circulate that he might be a fitting candidate for the consulship the following year. If any criticism was made of him, it was that he had been tamed too thoroughly. When orders arrived for him to proceed to Spain, he was actually said to be reluctant to leave Rome, whereas in the past he had always revelled in the prospect of another campaign.

The rumours were true and Antony made his progress up through the Italian peninsula as slowly as he dared. Which was how he came to be staying in a certain inn in Narbonese Gaul one night when two important messages were delivered. Antony had sheltered in worse places in his time as a soldier, but this certainly wasn't the type of accommodation he would have chosen. The walls were grimy with lampblack and enlivened only by a pornographic drawing in one corner executed in red chalk with a certain amount of crude vigour. The air smelled of damp hay from the mattresses and the whole building had a pervasive whiff of untreated sewage from the latrines at the rear. Overhead rats could be heard scuttling around in the ceiling and the food and wine was on a par with the living quarters. Stale bread, dried-up cheese, olives which had seen better days and wine as resinous and astringent as pine-tree sap. Wincing as he swallowed the last couple of fingers of liquid in the bottom of his cup, Antony bade his companion a careless good night and rolled himself up in his woollen military cloak to sleep.

Yet even when his fellow officer had blown out the lamp, oblivion did not come easily. They were both on their way to join their legion in Spain and usually Antony relished the freedom of the road, but this time he felt as if he were tethered to Rome by invisible ropes. Fulvia's baby was due at any time now and he found himself unexpectedly worried about her confinement. It seemed absurd to think of Fulvia bearing a child, particularly since she was about as sexy as a grizzled old senior centurion. All the same, she was a good woman and Antony was surprised by his growing fondness for her. She was not pretty as his earlier wives Fadia and Antonia had been, but she was loyal, capable and as shrewd as a Syrian carpet dealer. She had even been understanding about his disastrous passion for Cleopatra. He winced now as he thought of the scene at Caesar's villa several months ago and all the rage, bewilderment and humiliation he'd felt at the time came rushing back. The sting of her betrayal still felt like a raw wound he could not bear to touch.

The trouble was that he really had believed that she was as much in love with him as he was with her. Of course, he had always known that she was shrewd and calculating with a weather eye constantly open for her own advantage, but he had not thought her treacherous. Gritting his teeth now, he wondered how he had ever been so gullible. Was it really likely that Cleopatra Ptolemy, Queen of Egypt, with her brilliant intellect and formidable grasp of diplomacy, had really wanted anything more than a meaningless sexual romp with

Mark Antony, second-rate Roman soldier and states-man? But she did love me once, he told himself bitterly. When she was still young enough to be impressed by me. His thoughts drifted back to those long ago days in Alexandria. Even then she had been sharper, wittier, quicker to see the point, able to think on her feet and speak as brilliantly as an orator, while Antony himself rambled, backtracked, lost the thread of conversations. Only his masculine vigour and military prowess had impressed her. He could still remember her shining eyes and moist, parted lips as she gazed at him on the parade ground, overwhelmed with admiration for his strength and courage, his capacity for practical action. But the passage of years had made a difference to her. On her arrival in Rome she had been tougher, more calculating, more inclined to follow her head and not her heart.

In the blind, warm throes of passion, it had been easy to believe that nothing had really changed between them. Cleopatra was still his reckless, impetuous darling whose sensual abandon thrilled him to the core. In bed with her in that seedy flat in the Subura, he had been convinced beyond his wildest hopes that she still loved him. To hear her denounce him at Caesar's villa had made him feel as sick and shaken as if one of his own comrades had turned and stabbed him in battle. Even her later denial, her scornful insistence that she had only said those words for Caesar's benefit did not convince him. Deep down, Antony knew with leaden certainty that she had meant every syllable she spoke. Cleopatra might get a primitive thrill out of being crushed beneath Antony's solid heat and muscle and screwed within an inch of her life, but she didn't love him, she didn't see him as her natural mate or partner. To her he was simply an ox of a man whom she petted and indulged, but led wherever she liked with a ring through his nose. It was more than he could stand to be so humiliated by her! It was unnatural for a man to be so driven and thwarted and bemused by a mere woman. He'd like to tan the hide off Cleopatra, then take her to bed and teach her who was boss. He thought of her soft, yielding flesh, the little whimpers of protest and pleasure she would give . . . Abruptly he turned in bed and slammed his fist into the wall, bruising his knuckles and leaving a crater in the dirty plaster. No! He didn't want that at all! By all the gods, wasn't that exactly what he was trying to escape from? Wasn't that why he had picked up with Volumnia the actress again – to try and drive the thought of Cleopatra out of his mind? He punched the plaster again.

'Have you got something on your mind?' drawled Publius, raising himself on one elbow and blinking at him in the dim, red glow from the brazier.

Antony ground his teeth.

'You could say that,' he admitted bleakly, sitting up and reaching for the wineskin. He directed a long squirt to the back of his tongue and then pulled a face. 'What is this rot gut stuff?'

'Caecuban, according to our good landlord. Third-grade paint-stripper, if you ask me. But at least it offers oblivion and you look as if you need that.'

'I do,' agreed Antony with fervour. He thought moodily of Cleopatra, then irritably of Volumnia and anxiously of Fulvia. Curse it! Why couldn't he just fall in love with his wife? Life would be so much simpler.

'What's wrong?' asked Publius.

Antony sighed and came up with the least difficult explanation of his turmoil.

'My wife's expecting a baby any day now.'

294

'Oh, I see. Not much you can do about that, except have another drink and stop moaning. Before you know it, you'll probably have a messenger arriving from Rome to tell you you're a father and your wife wants a nice, gold necklace for her trouble.'

Publius's words proved prophetic. Shortly after midnight, Antony was woken by the sound of horse's hooves coming to a halt outside the tavern. He heard the landlord grumbling and swearing and saw a glow of lamplight under the door. The sound of voices came to him above the rain and the wind and then suddenly the door burst open, precipitating a rain-soaked messenger into the room. With a startled oath, Antony sprang out of bed as he recognized one of his own house slaves.

'Strato! Not bad news, I hope?'

The man grinned from ear to ear.

'No, master. The best news possible. You have a fine son, safely delivered only two days after you left Rome. The mistress is well and sends you her love.'

From somewhere in the depths of his damp cloak, he produced a letter and handed it to Antony, who scanned it swiftly. Suddenly he gave a roar of delight, and hugged the messenger, lifting him clear off his feet. Then he set him down again and snatched up a saddlebag to reward him with a gold coin for his trouble. Publius swung himself out of bed and clapped him on the shoulder.

'Congratulations.'

'Thanks. Bring us another wineskin, landlord, and we'll all drink the baby's health.'

'Not another bout?' muttered Publius, clutching his temples and shuddering. 'I hope you like drinking goats' pee, Strato.'

Antony was still brimming with pride and elation

half an hour later when he sent the slave off to bed down in the barn. A son. A son! He had only ever had girls before, although they had certainly been cute little wenches – he thought of Antonia, with her freckled face and missing front teeth, and his older girls, who had gone with their mother Fadia – but never a boy to follow in his own footsteps. He would teach him to ride and swim and lay bets at the chariot races. No, Fulvia wouldn't approve of that! He blew out the lamp and lay in the smoky darkness, grinning at the thought. The wind howled, the rain rattled against the walls, the fleas continued to bite him even through his rough, military cloak. Suddenly an intense longing to see Fulvia and the boy took hold of him. He began to float on the fringes of sleep, seeing himself riding not to Spain, but to Rome. Down through the green hills of Etruria to the city, along the Via Flaminia and then east to the Esquiline. He would ride right to the front gate of the house and hammer on it and demand to see his wife. He heard the hammering, loudly and clearly, reverberating through his sleep.

'Shit,' muttered Publius's voice groggily in the dark. 'What now? Is that another messenger at the door? Was your wife expecting twins, Mark Antony?'

Antony came fully awake now and realized that the hammering was still going on. He rose to his feet, pulling his cloak around him, but before he could go out to investigate, the door burst open a second time and a soldier came striding in. He checked at the sight of Antony, clicked his heels together and clenched his fist over his heart in the military salute.

'What is it?' asked Antony sharply.

'Bad news, sir, the worst possible news. I was on my way south to take word to Rome, but I heard you were staying here and diverted my course to tell you.'

'Yes, yes. Get on with it, man.'

'Julius Caesar's dead.'

'What? Jupiter! Are you sure?'

'I saw him with my own eyes, sir, borne down in the midst of battle. His men were hanging back on the verge of retreating and in order to give them courage, he charged into the thick of the enemy alone. I swear he must have had two hundred arrows in his shield.'

'But did you see his dead body?' persisted Antony.

'Not exactly,' admitted the soldier. 'But he couldn't possibly have survived. They were on top of him like a pack of hungry panthers in the Circus. My maniple became separated from the others and my commanding officer told me to take the news to Rome that Caesar was dead.'

Antony's mind raced with mingled feelings of shock, disbelief, horror and even a shameful twinge of delight. But rumours were always rife in the confusion of battle and the man hadn't seen the body, he admitted that himself, so the story might not be true. All the same, it was likely enough. And if it were true, it would be insane for Antony to proceed further into hostile territory which must now be held by Gnaeus Pompeius's men. It would also mean that once the news reached Rome, there would be a blood letting of all Caesar's supporters. He must get back as fast as possible and make sure that Fulvia and the children were safe. And Cleopatra? Cleopatra must be warned to make her escape to Egypt! Half the Senate would be after her blood without Caesar to protect her. Then he hesitated, biting his lip and frowning. What if the rumour were false? Caesar would be furious if he did not arrive in accordance with his orders. Still, he would just have to take that risk. He could always think of some excuse later and the gods knew Julius

Caesar was perfectly capable of winning the war in Spain without Antony if he was still alive. He reached a swift decision.

'Wake my groom and tell him to saddle my horse,' he ordered the soldier.

'Very good, sir,' he agreed, turning smartly and leaving the room.

Antony began to pull on his boots.

'Where are you going?' asked Publius sleepily.

'To Rome, to protect my family. And you?'

'No. I've a family in Cispadane Gaul who'll need protection themselves if this is true. It seems we must part here.'

Antony reached out and grasped his hand warmly.

'A safe journey, then.'

Even travelling at the greatest speed he could manage, Antony still found the journey exasperatingly slow. Official couriers could change horses at staging posts and pass on their messages to fresh riders, but Antony had to content himself with the help of friends whose villas were scattered irregularly down the length of the Italian peninsula. Even though he spent every possible hour in the saddle, there were times when sheer exhaustion forced him to spend a few hours under the roof of one or other of Caesar's supporters. There were even times when he dozed off on a strange horse and woke with a start to find his head slumped against the animal's mane, the warm steam of its body rising in his nostrils and some desolate stretch of countryside around him with nothing to see but the black spear points of cypresses rearing up in the moonlight and the chill night skies sprinkled with stars. He had taken the precaution of changing out of military uniform into the sort of clothing a Gallic merchant might wear – a plain tunic, a riding cloak, Gallic shoes –

and thus was able to continue his journey in daylight without attracting attention. At about the eighth hour on his twelfth day of travel, he reached Saxa Rubra, ten miles outside the city of Rome on the Via Flaminia and took refuge in an inn owned by a retired veteran who had served with him in Egypt. The news was not good. Apparently all Rome was already humming with the rumour (still unconfirmed) that Julius Caesar had died in Spain. According to the landlord there had been riotous parties, bonfires where Julius Caesar was burnt in effigy and looting raids on the homes of his supporters. There were some who were stricken at the stories of his death, but by all accounts the general reaction was one of jubilation. It made Antony more anxious than ever about the safety of his family and his ex-lover.

After a hasty wash and change of clothes, he called for wine and writing materials. He wrote two letters – the first a brief note to Cleopatra warning her to be alert to leave the city, the second a document which gave him far more trouble. On his journey south, he had found himself thinking more and more longingly of Fulvia. He knew he was an inarticulate man, not good at putting his feelings into words, knew too that if he tried, he would only begin to stumble and seem ridiculous, so he put it all on papyrus. He wrote about his gratitude for her support, his joy that she had given him a son, his heartfelt wish to put his entanglements with Volumnia and any other woman behind him and devote himself entirely to his wife. When at last the letter was completed, he went outside and saw that the sun was setting in a sky the colour of citron and pomegranate, shading into a deep, threatening charcoal. Wrapping himself in his Gallic cloak so thoroughly that only his eyes were visible, he told the innkeeper to order him a horse-drawn gig. The moment darkness fell, he set out for the city and drove to his own house.

'Who is it?' asked the porter suspiciously, peering through a grille in the door.

'A messenger from Marcus Antonius,' he replied. 'I have a letter for his wife.'

The door creaked open and he was shown in through the magnificent entrance hall with its ancestral images and along the colonnaded peristyle to a room in the women's quarters.

'A messenger from your husband, my lady,' said the slave.

Fulvia caught her breath. She was holding a sleeping baby with a puckered red face and tiny red starfish hands protruding from its swaddling clothes, but she thrust the infant into its cradle as brusquely as if she were setting down a joint of meat. Then she took two or three faltering steps across the room towards Antony, clenching and unclenching her hands and breathing unevenly. In spite of her great size and heaviness of features, she looked unexpectedly vulnerable. 'What news do you have of my husband?' she demanded. 'He's not wounded, is he? He's not – '

She broke off and swallowed convulsively, unable to utter the word.

Antony felt a great wrenching impulse of pity and almost revealed himself in that very instant. Only curiosity made him refrain. He couldn't help thinking that it was a rare privilege for a man to glimpse how his wife felt about him in his absence.

'Don't worry, he isn't dead or wounded,' he said in a deep, gruff voice. Then he thrust the letter at her.

She almost snatched it from his hands, broke the seal and began to read, her dark eyes scanning the words. Some indefinable spasm of emotion crossed her face and tears spilt over and began to run down her cheeks. Antony could no longer ignore the pity and warmth stirring in his own breast. Flinging back the cloak, he stepped forward and hauled her into his arms.

'It's me, Fulvia,' he confessed.

She gasped, sobbed, and then began to laugh. Throwing her arms around his waist, she hugged him back and for the first time he was glad of her size, her solidity, the way she stood like a rock that could not be shifted. He kissed her warmly on the mouth and stroked away her tears.

'I love you,' he said in astonishment. 'I love you, Fulvia.'

When Octavian at last set foot on Spanish soil in early May, it was with the uneasy expectation of finding his great-uncle dead and the province in the hands of the Pompeians. He had suffered shipwreck near the Balearic Islands on his way and wore a shabby tunic begged from a local fisherman when he was finally brought ashore.

'A dangerous coastline here,' said the fisherman, gesturing to the green Atlantic breakers which smashed in cauldrons of foam against the rocks. 'Although Gades is a fine city. Still, you'll be well advised to go cautiously, sir, till you sniff which way the wind is blowing. If the Pompeians are in power, come back to my vessel before nightfall and I'll see you safely on your way to Italy.'

Octavian thanked him, renewed his promises of a fitting reward once funds were available to him and set off for the nearest tavern. There were one or two curious glances from sailors and dock workers perched on stools at the bar, but the place could hardly have been more tranquil. The warm spring sunlight was slanting in through the open windows and the salt tang of the air competed with the scents of new wine and fresh bread. Somewhere in a back room a girl was clattering glasses and singing as she washed up. There was certainly no sign of bloodshed or civil war. Octavian breathed again, but reminded himself that it might only mean that Gnaeus Pompeius's victory was complete.

'I've been travelling for nearly two months,' he said as the tavern keeper set down a pitcher of wine and water. 'Tell me, what's the local news?'

'Good news for those in business,' he replied. 'Caesar's put an end to this pesky civil war that's been ruining trade. Aye, there'll be peace in Spain now with Julius Caesar in charge.'

Octavian's eyes widened.

'You mean he's still alive? I heard he'd died at the battle of Munda.'

The tavern keeper laughed so hard that his body shook.

'We all heard that, but it wasn't true. Seems his men took fright and began deserting, so what does he do but leap off his horse and fling himself into the thickest mass of the enemy? And all the time bellowing at his men, "Come on then, you cowards, will you let me die alone?" Shamed them into turning round and coming back, he did, although the gods only know how he survived long enough for them to rescue him. They say he had so many sword cuts you could hardly see his uniform for blood.'

Octavian shuddered at the thought of such suicidal courage. No help for it now. If Caesar was alive he would have to join him.

'Is there much fighting now?' he asked distastefully.

'Bless you, no, sir,' replied the tavern keeper, polishing a cup on his apron. 'It's all over bar the military parades.'

Octavian sighed with relief.

'Where is Caesar?'

'At Hispalis. You could be there in four or five days if you look lively.'

Hispalis, like Gades, looked remarkably tranquil. Apart from a few burnt-out hulks of ships in the river, there was no sign of war and the people went serenely about their business beneath a clear Andalusian sky. Caesar had made his headquarters in the comfortable palace of a mining magnate and when Octavian had borrowed a military uniform, he asked for an audience with the general. Without delay he was led past the guards and up a marble staircase to Caesar's suite of rooms on the first floor. His heart sank as he knocked at the door. What would his great-uncle say about his long delay in arriving and his failure to appear in Spain in time for the fighting? Yet when Caesar opened the door he looked genial and relaxed and was dressed not in military uniform but in a loose tunic with a purple senatorial stripe.

His eyes widened with pleasure at the sight of his great-nephew.

'Octavian,' he cried, folding him into a warm embrace and hugging him hard.

Octavian was startled, but had enough presence of mind to hug him back. At moments like this he found it hard to believe in the dire secret he and Caesar had shared for nearly two years now and was tempted almost to think that it was a monstrous invention of his own fevered imagination. How could it possibly be true when Caesar was so adroitly playing the part of a proud, indulgent uncle? Then he realized that someone else was in the room. It was a woman, dusky skinned, plump and very beautiful. Her veil and the style of her clothing suggested that she hailed from North Africa and her flushed cheeks and disordered hair made Octavian wonder if she had just emerged from the rumpled bed. His hopes rose. Was this some new replacement for Cleopatra? He gazed at the woman with frank curiosity.

'This is Queen Eunoë, wife of Bogudes, who commanded my cavalry at the battle of Munda,' said Caesar. 'You may leave us now, Eunoë.'

She giggled, fluttered her eyelashes and undulated her way out of the room. The moment she had left, Caesar gave a contemptuous chuckle.

'You wouldn't believe what a fool that woman is,' he remarked. 'She was rather a disappointment in bed too. I don't think I'd have bothered to seduce her if I hadn't had a grudge against her husband. Now you, on the other hand, could never disappoint me in bed.'

With a deft movement, Caesar dropped the bar across the door, turned back to Octavian and embraced him in a manner quite different from his earlier performance. As the dictator's hand fondled his private parts, Octavian felt hot and cold with shame. I hate you, he thought savagely. By the gods I hate you for this. I only wish I could cut your head off, you evil, domineering old man.

Yet shame and fear made him submit, as always. Afterwards he lay staring at the ceiling, torturing himself with worry about what his mother or his sister Octavia would say if they knew of this. Either they wouldn't believe it, or they would be so disgusted that they would hate him for ever. He was often disgusted himself and there were moments when he wished he had the courage to kill himself. And to kill Caesar. Especially Caesar.

'You're quiet, dear boy,' murmured his great-uncle, lazily stroking his flank. 'What are you thinking?'

'I was thinking of you,' replied Octavian with bitter irony.

'How touching. Tell me, why didn't you arrive in time for the war?'

'I was shipwrecked on the way.'

'Really? That's a great pity. You would have enjoyed the fighting. At Munda there were so many corpses that we made a wall and rampart out of them to bar the gates. Then we fixed severed heads on javelins at the top for a palisade. It was quite amusing really.'

Octavian's flesh crawled with a sensation that was half nauseating, half pleasurable as he listened to these gruesome details.

'They tell me the fighting's over now?' he asked cautiously.

'Yes,' agreed Caesar. 'But don't worry, you'll get your turn. I'm planning to invade Parthia as soon as I've settled my affairs in Rome.'

Octavian darted his great-uncle a look of horror. Was he a suicidal lunatic? What harm had Parthia done Rome to justify its invasion?

'I think I might be better at administration, actually,' he said, clearing his throat. 'Working in the treasury, that sort of thing. Perhaps I could do more to help you by staying in Rome.'

'Oh, well, if that's your choice,' agreed Caesar in a disappointed tone. 'Of course, that sort of thing is important too. But I warn you, there are to be no more quarrels with Cleopatra while I'm in Parthia.'

Octavian's lip curled.

'Won't she be going back to Egypt while you're away?'

'Good heavens, no, Octavian! Cleopatra will hardly want to live in Egypt once she's my wife.'

Octavian felt as if someone had hit him in the stomach.

'Wife?' he echoed.

'Yes.'

For once Octavian was so angry that he forgot to be frightened.

'But that's outrageous!' he burst out, leaping to his feet. 'She's nothing but a foreign whore and what's going to happen to me if you marry her? Aren't I going to be your heir any longer?'

'Not if you behave like this,' said Caesar mildly.

'How else can I behave?' raved Octavian. 'That bitch has crawled her way into your good graces and foisted a child on you which is probably not even yours and you can't see her for the whore she is. You can believe what you like, but she was fucking Mark Antony under your very – '

The stinging impact of Caesar's hand jarred into the side of his mouth, stopping his words in full flow. He jerked up his head and gave Caesar a cold, glittering stare.

'Don't speak of my future wife in that tone,' said Caesar very, very softly. 'I want you to do something, Octavian. Go over and lift the lid of that serving dish on the side table.'

With a puzzled frown, Octavian took five or six faltering steps and obeyed. He picked up the lid, stood frozen to the spot for an instant and then dropped it on the mosaic floor with a loud clang. For a moment the image of a severed head, bluish of skin with closed eyes and matted beard, wavered horribly before him.

Then the room dissolved around him in a sickening whirl of grey spots. There was a long, chaotic darkness before he came slowly back to consciousness to find his head pressed between his knees. He groaned and tried to sit up.

'It – it's Gnaeus Pompeius, isn't it?' he stammered.

'It is indeed,' agreed Caesar. 'Or was. My daughter's stepson. A handsome fellow. I knew him from the time he was a small boy and I even had a love affair with his mother. But when he defied me, I killed him. Look carefully at him, Octavian, and let his fate be a warning to you.'

With a faint shudder, Octavian rose to his feet and stood swaying as he looked at the grisly object. Now that his nausea was subsiding, he even found that it exercised a macabre fascination over him. It did not stink as he might have expected, but gave off a faint, rather pleasant medicinal odour. Evidently Caesar had had it embalmed. Yet, as he gazed and his heartbeat grew fast and erratic with terror and excitement, Octavian was not thinking of Gnaeus Pompeius at all. He was thinking of his great-uncle and making a silent vow to himself.

One of these days, you hideous old man, I'll have your head on a plate.

Chapter Sixteen

In mid-September Cleopatra received a note written in Caesar's own hand, summoning her to meet him at his country villa near Labici in the hills southeast of Rome. She obeyed the order with some trepidation. His letters during his absence in Spain had been infrequent and concerned mainly with details of sieges and battles. While she had worked tirelessly to further his interests during the time he was away, she had no clear idea of his present feelings towards her. Would she reach Labici only to be sent on her way to Egypt? Or could she hope for a great improvement in her fortunes? Was he intending to make her his Queen? It was no wonder that she was in a state of high-strung tension as her coach jolted its interminable way up through the hills near Lake Regillus. At least the stifling heat of Rome and the uproar and stench of the city had been left behind to be replaced by clean air, shady forests, vivid green vineyards and the sound of goat bells and children's laughter near the peasants' cottages. The leaves on the trees were still green, but they had a golden tinge and there was a mellow quality about the sunlight that gilded the fields. The villa itself was imposing even by Egyptian standards, two storeys high with a colonnaded entrance of white limestone and an orange pantiled roof. Caesar himself came out from the vast entrance hall to greet her and the leap of pleasure in his eyes encouraged her considerably.

He kissed her warmly, marvelled over the way Caesarion had grown and then sent the boy away with his attendants to have a bath and a nap. Then, with almost indecent haste, he whisked Cleopatra away to the privacy of his own suite of rooms. Scarcely pausing till she was inside the door, he wrenched her clothes off, forced her down on to a couch and took her as roughly as if she were a captive from one of the cities he had so recently besieged. She flinched at his coarseness, but was reassured by his urgency. At least he had not lost interest in her! All the same, his next words took her by surprise.

With a low grunt of satisfied lust, he withdrew from her, reached for a linen napkin and began swabbing himself clean. Relieved that the ordeal was over, she made as if to rise herself, but found herself restrained by his hand.

'Don't move. Let my seed lie where it is for the moment. The doctors tell me it aids conception if the woman remains unmoving for as long as possible.'

'C-conception?' she stammered, appalled by the thought. The agony of Caesarion's birth had left her uncertain that she ever wanted to repeat the experience. 'What do you mean?'

He stroked her cheek with an odd, fanatical look in his dark eyes.

'Simply that I hope to beget more sons upon you. Legitimate ones, this time.'

It took a moment for his words to sink in. When they did, she gasped.

'You don't mean –'

His eyes glittered even more brightly.

'Exactly, my dear. Cleopatra, you're already the mother of my son. I now have the honour of asking you to be my wife.'

It was not the most romantic of proposals, but after her first shock Cleopatra was filled with a rush of elation. After the long, weary months of scheming and hoping, at last success was within her grasp! Now, now she would have real power! Power to protect Egypt from Roman greed, power to foster knowledge and learning, power to regain the territories which had been taken away from Ptolemaic control, power to change the course of history! She turned white and then red and, disobeying Caesar's injunction to keep still, flung herself on him with a cry of joy. He patted her shoulder indulgently, pleased by her obvious devotion to him. To her surprise he climbed back into the large couch with her and put his arm around her.

'I can think of nobody more worthy to share my great destiny,' he said solemnly. 'Together we'll change the face of the world. Very soon now I intend to have myself proclaimed King of Rome. After that I'll push through the necessary legislation to make you a Roman citizen so that we can both divorce our spouses and marry each other. Within a few months I'll make you my Queen.'

'Oh, thank you, Gaius, thank you. You won't regret it, I promise you. But your family, the nobles – '

'My family and the nobles will do exactly as they're told!' growled Caesar. 'I know there'll be opposition, but I'll override it by force if necessary. Young Octavian has already said his piece on the subject and I've sent him off into exile at Apollonia on the Illyrian coast. And if anyone else dares to oppose me, they can expect a similar little holiday somewhere even worse. Now why don't you get dressed and I'll send for my law clerk? I intend to draw up a new will to be signed on the day of our marriage which will provide for Caesarion and any other children you may conceive by me.'

Syrus the law clerk was summoned from Rome and

given a fee of a hundred sesterces for drawing up the will. Twenty-four days later in Apollonia, he was given a further fee of two thousand sesterces for revealing its contents to Octavian. The young man's face went pale with rage as he read the copy of the document and then handed it back to Syrus.

'What's the legal position if that will remains unsigned?' he demanded.

Syrus smiled ingratiatingly.

'You remain as Caesar's chief heir and inherit nearly all of his property,' he replied.

Octavian drew in breath sharply.

'Then it must never be signed!' he hissed. 'I'm sure there must be conspiracies against Caesar's life in Rome. I want you to go back and sniff them out, Syrus. Offer an anonymous bounty to anyone who assassinates him. I'll make it worth your while. You'll receive ten thousand sesterces if Julius Caesar dies before he can marry that bitch.'

Octavian was right about the conspiracies. Aristocrats whose hopes of political office had been dashed and whose property had been seized in punishment for their support of Pompey detested Caesar. So did the middle-class landlords who had suddenly found rents abolished and destructive tenants unable to be evicted, thanks to Caesar. Even among the lower classes, who generally revelled in the bread and circuses that the dictator offered, there were those whose soldier sons had left their bones whitening on the African sands or in the forests of Gaul. Yet the most virulent of all his opponents were the diehard republicans who had admired Cato and none was more unwavering than Cato's daughter Porcia. On his return from Narbonese Gaul Marcus Iunius Brutus had been so smitten by her courage and noble grief that he had divorced his previous wife and married her. Even so, in spite of all Porcia's passionate persuasion, he still balked at the final step of plotting Caesar's murder. There were others who were not so scrupulous. Whenever he appeared in public now, Caesar generally found it prudent to have a troop of Spanish bodyguards with him, although in time he hoped to dismiss them.

It was mid-February before he made his first serious bid to attain the Kingship. He had prepared the ground carefully. Just in case Cleopatra should become pregnant, one of the tribunes in his pay had been bribed to introduce a law legitimizing any future children sired by Julius Caesar on any woman whatsoever. In addition, he had taken care to have various honours bestowed upon him by the Senate and the people of Rome. His birthday was declared a public holiday and statues of him were to be set up in all the temples of Rome and the municipalities. One of the voting tribes was to bear his name, his positions as dictator and censor of public morals were to be held for life. Any son or adopted son he had was to be made chief priest and he was to be given a gilded throne in which to sit at sessions of the Senate and the law courts. More important perhaps than any of these, he had been awarded the right to wear the traditional robes of the ancient Roman kings – a purple gown and high red boots. When several of the citizens on the Alban hill hailed him as King when he was returning from the Latin festival, he decided that the time was ripe for the next stage of his campaign. The venue that he chose was the festival of Lupercalia, a fertility rite whose origins went back hundreds of years to the founding of the city. Before the festival he instructed Cleopatra carefully in what she was to do.

'Now you understand the course of events, don't you, my dear? It would give too much offence to the people if I allowed you to sit on the rostrum with me, but you will be given a place of honour at ground level a short distance away. The ritual is quite simple. The priests called the Luperci run around the boundaries of the ancient village on the Palatine hill and they carry lightweight whips made of goatskin. With these they strike at anyone they meet, but especially at women, because there's a strongly held belief among the people that this will lead to fertility and an easy delivery. I'll ensure that one of the runners approaches you and when he does so, you must hold out your hands to the blow of his whip. That will be a subtle signal to the nobles that I hope to have more children from you. And there will be another twist to the ceremony which won't be subtle in the least.'

'What do you mean?' asked Cleopatra, intrigued.

'Wait and see,' replied Caesar.

The day of the festival was chilly and gusty, with great wracks of clouds the colour of rusty iron scudding through the sky. The runners stood outside the starting point of the cave near the foot of the hill which was said to be the den of the she-wolf which had suckled Rome's founders, Romulus and Remus. Their breath rose like smoke on the frosty air and they stamped their feet and shivered as they rubbed oil into their skins, either as protection against the cold or as a form of ritual anointing. After a lengthy prayer intoned by a priest, a black dog was brought forward, yelping and resisting, to have its throat cut in sacrifice. Then the priest gave the signal for the start of the race and with a roar from the crowd the runners were off. Spectators were spread out all the way along the course, but the finishing line was in the forum where a gold throne had been set up for Julius Caesar on the rostrum so that he could watch the antics of the Luperci below. It was a good-humoured scene. Street vendors did a brisk trade in hot chestnuts and spiced wine to keep out the cold and the crowd roared with laughter and excitement as each new runner made his appearance and lunged among them, flailing at the best-looking women with the harmless goatskin whip. Obedient to Caesar's instructions, Cleopatra waited until the last runner appeared and then stepped forward from her seat and offered her open palms to the lash of his whip. Then she caught her breath as she saw who her assailant was. There was little of consular dignity about Mark Antony at this moment. He loomed above her, his face flushed and his chest heaving from the hectic tempo of the long race. He was naked except for the goatskin loincloth around his genitals and his body was just as hot and hard and masculine as she remembered. Their eyes met and a wordless current of anger, contempt and thwarted desire surged between them. For a moment she thought she saw something else blaze in Antony's eyes, some fierce spark of remembered love, then it flared and vanished.

'A swift pregnancy and a safe delivery, lady!' he said bitterly, then brought the lash down on her hands with unnecessary force.

She cried out at the sting of it and gazed at him as if they were alone together. Then abruptly Antony whirled away and continued on his course, leaving Cleopatra with her breast heaving and her eyes filled with tears. The defiance and hatred and yearning in her expression were not lost on the spectators around them.

'Did you see how she looked at him?' hissed Porcia in a scandalized voice to her husband Marcus Brutus.

'As if it weren't shameful enough that Caesar sends her to the fertility rite like a wedded wife, that foreign harlot looks at Mark Antony as if she lusts after him too. It's an outrage!'

There was worse to come. Antony pounded on doggedly until he reached the rostrum and by some stratagem which must have been prearranged, snatched a gold crown from a spectator who held it outstretched, then flung away his goatskin whip and scaled the podium. Dramatically he set the diadem on Caesar's head, shouting in a loud voice, 'The Roman people offer this to you through me.'

There was a great intake of breath as if they were watching a thrilling moment in the arena. Then a hesitant burst of clapping broke out among isolated spectators scattered throughout the crowd.

'Long live Caesar, King of Rome!' shouted a lone voice.

The stony silence that greeted this showed how few approved the sentiment. A low, uneasy muttering spread among the ranks of citizens. It seemed that Caesar's stratagem had miscarried. Inwardly furious, but forcing a smile to his lips, the dictator rose to his feet and raised his hands for silence.

'Jupiter alone is King of the Romans,' he said calmly. Removing the crown from his head, he handed it back to Antony. 'Take this diadem and offer it to his statue at the temple on the Capitol. And let it be inscribed in the records that Julius Caesar refused the kingship of Rome when it was offered to him by all the people and the consul himself.'

Brutus let out his breath in a harsh rush and slowly his fingers released their grip on the hilt of his dagger.

'Stick fast to that resolve, Caesar,' he muttered under his breath. 'Or your first day as King of Rome will be your last.'

In the echoing interior of the temple of Artemis, Serapion of Alexandria paused to let his eyes adjust to the dimness before proceeding towards the huge, cult statue of the goddess. He was a man in his early forties, his hair already flecked with silver and his mouth marred by bitter lines. The bitterness had its origin on a day fourteen years earlier when he had returned unsuspecting from his work in the royal palace in Cyprus to his home only to find disaster there. A sick rush of hatred still overwhelmed him at the memory of those nightmare scenes. His two little boys picked up by their feet so that their brains could be dashed out against the walls, his wife naked on the bed with blood on her thighs, groaning and whimpering like a wild animal in pain, all the gold and silverware looted . . . It was perhaps merciful that his wife had died within days of her rape and torture. Serapion himself had fled to Alexandria and had continued to suffer. He hated the Romans with a venom that was all the more intense for being kept secret. Only Arsinoë, who had been his mathematics pupil in her youth, had ever guessed the extent of his hostility. Her summons for him to meet her in Ephesus had taken him completely by surprise. He had supposed her dead after her defeat by Caesar and was not at all sure that her survival was a blessing. Serapion regarded life as a torment to be endured, rather than a benefit to be celebrated. Poor girl, she would have been better off dead!

All the same he had come to Ephesus in answer to her summons, leaving behind his comfortable position in the palace treasury in Alexandria. Now he stood looking about him with a perplexed frown, a middle-aged man shaken out of his routine and not welcoming the change. From a back room to the right of the cult statue, he heard the echo of voices and smelled the aroma of charcoal grilled meat spiced with rosemary. Making his way to the source of the sound, he cleared his throat.

'Excuse me, my name is Serapion. I've come from Alexandria to see the Princess Arsinoë. Can you tell me where to find her?'

A temple slave appeared and bowed his head.

'Yes, sir. She's in the guesthouse. Come this way, please.'

Serapion would never have recognized his former pupil. In adolescence she had been massively built, with a moon-shaped face and a heavy tread. Now she was slender to the point of emaciation with her burning eyes the only live thing in the dead pallor of her face. Two lines of bitterness were beginning to extend from the edges of her mouth. One day they promised to be as cruelly etched as his own. She wore a drab garment of brown homespun and no jewellery and her red gold hair, which had been her only beauty, dangled limply on her shoulders.

'Sit down,' she invited bleakly. 'And I'll tell you what you're here for.'

He sat, not relishing the invitation, but pricked by a faint curiosity.

'You hate the Romans, don't you?' she fired at him.

'Yes.'

'Well, I'm giving you an opportunity of having your revenge on them. I hate them too. They've destroyed my life, my sister has – ' Now that she had begun, the words came bursting from her in a torrent, not fully coherent, but charged with rage and pain. 'Listen. Listen and I'll tell you. After I was transported to Rome I suffered great hardships, but I also experienced the greatest joy of my life. I met a man called Vercingetorix who had once been King of the Gauls and I fell in love with him. We hoped to be set free after Caesar's triumphs and to marry and live a quiet life somewhere in exile. But my bitch of a sister Cleopatra and her paramour Julius Caesar ruined that.'

She spat on the floor at the mention of Caesar's name and shuddered as if she had just eaten contaminated food.

'What happened?' asked Serapion soberly.

Fighting to hold back tears, Arsinoë took a long, agonizing breath.

'Cleopatra made me believe that she was sorry for me. She promised she would beg Caesar to spare Vercingetorix's life, but she lied. She lied to me, do you hear? Only Brennus told me the truth.'

'Brennus?'

'A Gallic slave!' she replied impatiently. 'Rome is full of Gallic slaves. He was in the household of another Gaul who had already earned his freedom because of his skill in applying gold leaf to statues. By chance, Brennus overheard Caesar plotting to strangle Vercingetorix and he swears that Cleopatra not only agreed to Caesar's hideous plan, but even urged him on. Anyway, Brennus was loyal to his King and when he told his master of the plot they collected enough gold to try and bribe the guards to let Vercingetorix escape. But then ... all went wrong ... found out ... crucified ...'

Serapion strained forward in his seat, striving to follow her movements as she paced around the room, struggling to make sense of her disjointed speech.

'The guards were caught trying to let him escape and crucified?' he hazarded.

'That's right! That's what I said, didn't I?'

'So Vercingetorix was strangled anyway?'

'Yes.'

The word was little more than a hoarse whisper. Suddenly her face contorted. Dreadful, strangling cries began to issue from her mouth and she buried her head in her hands, rocking and howling as if she were oblivious of his presence. Down the tunnel of years, Serapion heard the inhuman yelps that had issued from his own throat when he discovered his wife and children. With a rough gesture of compassion, he took Arsinoë in his arms and held her until the shaking subsided.

'How did you find out the truth?' he asked.

She wiped her streaming eyes with the heel of her hand.

'Vercingetorix was supposed to come to Brennus for help when he escaped. When he didn't show up, Brennus went to investigate. One of the guards who hadn't been in the plot took pity on him and told him the truth. He also gave him the ashes from Vercingetorix's funeral pyre and a little box containing his few possessions and a letter he'd written to me before he died.' Her face was distorted by another spasm of rage and hatred. 'So now you see why I have to pay them back. I hate them so much, I swear I'd kill them both with my bare hands, except that there's no way I can achieve it without your help.'

'My help?' exclaimed Serapion in a startled voice.

Suddenly Arsinoë stopped pacing and sat down in a klismos chair. In spite of the ravages of grief, she suddenly looked intent and cunning, like a monarch planning her strategy.

'Yes,' she agreed. 'Cleopatra doesn't know that I've learnt the truth and she's trying to persuade Caesar to install me as ruler of Cyprus. I think in the end she wants to reclaim all the land that once belonged to the Ptolemaic empire. If Vercingetorix had lived, I would never have bothered about politics again. As it is I want revenge and I can only have that if I have power. I want to take up the governorship of Cyprus and I want you to come with me to act as my chief adviser.'

Serapion stared at her in consternation.

'How can I help you?' he demanded.

'You worked for my Uncle Ptolemy for years,' she burst out. 'If anybody knows about Cypriot affairs, it's you! If you come with me, I'll restore all the lands and wealth that you once owned and far more besides. I'm told that Caesar will be setting off on an expedition against the Parthians soon, so it can't be long before Cleopatra will be returning to Egypt. When she has had time enough to think herself secure, we'll send assassins to kill her. After that I'll make myself Queen of Egypt with you as my chief minister. We'll train an army and we'll drive the Romans out of Egypt and Cyprus for ever. Will you help me?'

The stunned look slowly melted away from Serapion's face, to be replaced by a look of fierce concentration and bitter, burning hope. He felt in his bones that the plan was lunacy and yet, and yet . . .

'Yes,' he said.

A leaked document revealed that Caesar intended to have himself declared King on the Ides of March. Being confronted with a firm date made the conspirators' resolve harden. Some, like Marcus Brutus and his wife Porcia, were motivated by the idealistic urge to rid the country of a tyrant. Others, like Brutus's cousin Decimus, had the more practical aim of winning the bounty for Caesar's assassination offered by an unknown enemy.

Both groups were equally tense as they waited in the meeting hall adjoining the theatre of Pompey on the Campus Martius. Not knowing that Caesar had been stricken by an attack of dysentery on the point of leaving his house, they grew more and more worried as the hours slipped by and he failed to arrive. Cassius went outside several times to look at the sundial in the nearby garden. Trebonius kept opening his writing case and peering furtively inside to check that his dagger was still there. Marcus Brutus held several anxious, whispered consultations with Decimus, but perhaps the one who suffered most of all was Porcia, the only woman who was a full partner in the conspiracy.

Sitting at home in an agony of apprehension she expected at any moment to be brought news that either Caesar had perished or her husband had done so. As the morning wore on, she grew more and more agitated, sending messengers every half hour to find out whether there was any news. Every distant noise or cry made her start up like a woman in a Bacchic frenzy and rush outside to accost passers-by and beg them for news. With each passing moment her spirits sank lower and lower and her tormenting fears multiplied till at last an overpowering faintness seized her and she sank into a deep swoon from which she could not be revived. Shrieking at the sight of her ashen face and unable to find any pulse, her slaves sent a message to Brutus to tell him she was dead. The news appalled him and his first impulse was to rush home and see with his own eyes whether it was true. Anguish, love and a fanatical sense of duty warred within him. Only now did he realize how much he loved Porcia, but his hatred for Caesar was even greater and he had sworn an oath to do this deed. While he was still pacing restlessly about, his feelings in turmoil, Mark Antony arrived from Caesar's house with a message. It was brief and to the point.

'Caesar gives orders that today's Senate session is to be cancelled. He is feeling unwell and the soothsayer's omens are all unfavourable.'

Brutus clutched at his cousin Decimus's toga.

'Go and see if you can change his mind,' he hissed. 'This is our last chance. Too many people know of the plot already. If we don't get rid of Caesar today, we may all be dead by nightfall.'

At his house in the Regia, Caesar had been genuinely prepared to postpone the day's Senate session. Much as the delay galled him, he did not want a crowd of spiteful soothsayers spreading the word that his kingship of Rome was ill omened from the start. Besides, during the course of the morning, he had been stricken by a sudden attack of the dysentery which had plagued him ever since he left Spain. By the time Decimus arrived, Caesar felt inclined to do nothing except go to bed and slam the door on the whole bickering mob of well-wishers and critics who thronged his house. But Decimus's words changed his mind.

'Gaius,' said Decimus reproachfully, gripping his hand. 'You're not going to disappoint us now, are you? Not when the entire Senate is assembled to see you proclaimed King?'

Caesar sighed.

'I am unwell, my friend.'

'That's a shame,' murmured Decimus sympathetically. 'It seems an ill trick on the part of the gods that you should be sick on the most important day of your life.'

'Well, I suppose the ceremony will just have to be postponed,' said Caesar with a faint, disappointed shrug.

'Nonsense! We'll take care of you, sir. Let me put you into a litter and you can be carried all the way to the meeting hall. And I promise we'll have the business over more swiftly than you can imagine.'

'You're a kind fellow, Decimus,' said Caesar. 'Well, it seems I cannot disappoint so many good friends. I'll come with you.'

He reflected on Decimus's words as the litter jolted across the Forum, past the northern slope of the Capitol and on its way to the Campus Martius. As his friend said, it was ill luck to be sick on such an important day and it was all he could manage to wave and smile at the crowds that thronged the route. When someone tossed a roll of papyrus into his hands with the words 'Read this, Caesar, at once, it is urgent', he simply smiled politely and gave the document to one of his attendants for perusal later. A mistake which was to have deadly consequences, since the letter contained full details of the conspiracy.

When at last the litter came to a halt outside the hall where the Senate was meeting, Caesar caught sight of the soothsayer Spurinna on the edges of the crowd. The man darted him an odd glance and then looked hastily away, as if unwilling to meet his eyes. No doubt he's feeling embarrassed, thought Caesar, now that another one of his wild prophecies has failed to come true. And well he should. What a pack of charlatans these astrologers and fortune-tellers are! Didn't the fellow predict that this day would bring disaster to me? And yet here I am, ready to be crowned King of Rome.

'The Ides of March have come, Spurinna,' he pointed out with malicious amusement.

The soothsayer's eyes blazed and his mouth twisted in a resentful line that was closer to the rictus of death than to a good-natured smile.

'Aye, they have come, but they have not yet gone,' he hissed.

Ill-natured boor! thought Caesar, as he watched the other man slip away into the building. Well, I won't let the spite of a single envious opponent upset me. It's clear that most people here appreciate me. With a benevolent wave, he descended from the litter in his purple robes and high red leather boots. Cheers broke out around him and the entire Senate rose to its feet and applauded loudly as he walked, nodding and smiling into their midst. It had been feared by some that Mark Antony might come to his leader's aid, so Trebonius detained the consul outside under the pretext of an important conversation. As Caesar took his seat in the gilded throne reserved for his use, the conspirators clustered around. Brutus sat tensed forward in his seat, feeling his heart pound and his hands grow clammy as he waited for the prearranged signal. Looking jittery and unnaturally pale, Tillius Cimber stumbled forward, flung himself at Caesar's feet, and kissed his hand.

'H-honoured sir,' he stammered, 'I beg you to recall my brother from exile.'

'I'm sorry,' replied Caesar sternly. 'Your brother wilfully opposed me in the recent civil wars and is my sworn enemy. I am unable to show him my customary mercy.'

'Then die!' howled Tillius. And, lurching to his feet, he tore the toga away from Caesar's throat.

Instantly Casca rushed forward and stabbed wildly at the exposed skin, but his hands were shaking so badly that he only succeeded in delivering a shallow flesh wound. Caesar gave a roar of outrage.

'You villain, Casca!' he shouted and, with astonishing strength, wrenched the dagger from his attacker's hand.

'Help me, brother!' howled Casca, his eyes dilated with terror. As if the starting signal had been given in the arena, they all rushed upon their prey like hunters attacking a cornered wild beast. Hopelessly outnumbered though he was, Caesar had no thought of surrender. Instead he quickly whipped a fold of his toga around his left arm and held it upraised as a shield while with his right hand he laid about him with Casca's dagger. Hemmed in on all sides, he yet succeeded in breaking away several times, darting about the Senate chamber, uttering hoarse cries that terrified his opponents. Then, as he backed snarling into a wall, an attack came from a wholly unexpected quarter. Marcus Brutus rose to his feet and, thinking he was coming to his aid, Caesar lowered his guard.

'May the gods reward you as you deserve, Marcus,' he panted.

'And you likewise,' breathed the younger man.

Too late Caesar realized his mistake. Everything had been blurred, frantic, as chaotic and fragmented as a collision in a chariot race, but suddenly time seemed to slow down. He had the sensation that Brutus was moving towards him very, very slowly with a mad light in his eyes and a strange, contorted smile on his face. Then there was a sudden flash of light, and Brutus's dagger stabbed deep into Caesar's groin. He knew at once that the injury was mortal. There was no real pain, only a kind of searing cold and then a spreading, sticky dampness. It was the shock and the sense of betrayal that hurt him most. Even when the deed was done, he could not quite believe it. His hand clenched on Brutus's arm, his eyes filled with stinging tears and he shook his head in a dazed fashion.

'And you, Brutus?' he cried reproachfully. 'My own son!'

Brutus stared down at the scarlet dagger in his hand and let out an unearthly groan. The bastard, the vicious old bastard! All these years he had kept his son's secret, and now, in one final act of revenge, he had revealed the truth to the entire Senate! And I used to love you, thought Brutus. Curse you, Caesar, I used to love you! Weeping with rage and grief and frustration, Brutus raised the dagger and struck again and again in a frenzy of hostility. Even now he expected the old man to fight back, to pull one of his miraculous escapes, to snatch the dagger out of his hand and beat him for his insolence. But all the fight seemed to have gone out of Caesar. After that first cry of protest, he pulled his toga over his head and sank to the floor in front of Pompey's statue, as motionless as if he had lost all interest in living.

The rest of the conspirators, emboldened by Caesar's weakness, closed in and an orgy of violence began. So frenzied were they that several of them wounded each other in their mad rage. At last, when Brutus himself suffered a deep cut to the hand, he called a halt to the butchery. For a moment he stood gazing down at Caesar's blood-spattered, lifeless body, then he took a long, shuddering breath.

'Well, that's the end of the tyrant,' he announced. 'Our next step is to get rid of his Egyptian mistress.'

CHAPTER SEVENTEEN

Antony was still in conversation with Trebonius when he suddenly heard bloodcurdling cries and the sound of running feet from the nearby Senate chamber. At once he suspected that he had been tricked and swung around to investigate, only to find his way barred by a weasely little man with a knife. Antony was unarmed and hampered by the clinging folds of his toga, but there was nothing he liked so much as a good punch-up.

'Come on then,' he invited, backing away to give himself a few moments' vital time as his eyes darted from the man who was threatening him to his senatorial colleague, Trebonius. As he had suspected, Trebonius too was now brandishing a knife. With an impatient wrenching movement, Antony tore himself free of the clinging folds of his toga and stood crouching slightly in his tunic with his legs wide apart and an expression of anticipation on his face. Then he saw his chance. He had once taken a course in kickboxing from an Indian in Alexandria and at moments like this he found it extremely useful. With an agility surprising in such a massive man, he launched himself into the air, kicking his first assailant in the chest and knocking him flying, then swinging around to seize Trebonius and send him crashing into a flowerbed. Every nerve in his body was clamouring alarm as he set off at a run to enter the hall.

The moment he shouldered his way through the press of bodies at the entrance, he sensed the smell of death. The air was as thick with grunts and groans and cries as that of any gymnasium and the place seemed to be in total chaos. Very few of the senators were sitting in their rightful seats, but most were gathered in a white-robed throng in the centre of the room, like sightseers assembled to gape over a traffic accident. As he shouldered his way into their midst, they fell back, giving him his first clear view of the disaster. A great splash of scarlet was sprayed across the statue of Pompey, disfiguring the carved folds of its garment and trickling from the serene marble smile. Antony caught his breath. At the foot of the statue lay a huddled figure clothed in a long purple robe and white toga with its face obscured. On his knees, hiding the muffled head and moaning softly to himself, sat Calvisius Sabinus, who had tried in vain to protect him. The entire Senate seemed to hold its breath as Antony crouched down beside the elderly senator and drew back the fold of the toga to reveal Caesar's face. The eyes were wide open, there was an expression of horror and disbelief frozen on the features, and, when he touched the lips and throat, he felt no breath and no pulse beat. A spasm of disgust contorted the consul's features as he looked down at his dead leader and then up at the crimson-stained garments of the men who surrounded him. There had been times when Antony had hated Caesar too, but he would never have chosen this method of settling the score.

'You treacherous, murdering bastards,' he breathed as he rose to his feet. Contemptuously he scanned their faces. Brutus, Decimus, Cassius and hordes of others. 'What a mean, skulking, underhand act! Did you do this, Brutus? You who owed him your life after Pharsalus? Or you, Cassius, who were so grateful for the honours he heaped upon you? And you, Decimus, whom he trusted when he was ill? You cowardly scum!'

There was a murmur of anger and the men who had slunk away at Antony's entrance, began to gather around him menacingly with their knives stretched out. Too late Antony recognized his own danger. But as the other conspirators moved towards him, Brutus suddenly leapt in front of Antony shielding him with his own body.

'No!' he shouted. 'We've no legitimate reason for killing Mark Antony. We came here to liberate the republic from tyranny, not to commit murder.'

'And don't you call it murder when you kill your own father?' cried Sabinus in a quavering voice. 'We all heard him name you as his son before he died, Marcus Brutus. May the gods curse you for a foul, unnatural offspring!'

'What's that got to do with Antony?' shouted another voice. 'I say kill him too, before he tries to make himself King.'

There was a chorus of argument and complaint and various shouts and recriminations were raised. Antony could move fast enough when he chose. While the attention of the assassins was diverted, he dived for the doorway and paused to hurl one final reproach at Brutus.

'See if you can control your pack of killer dogs now they're loose, liberator!'

For an instant their eyes met. If Antony had not felt such bitter contempt for Brutus, he might have pitied him. By turns the former governor of Gaul looked dazed, defiant, imploring, utterly bewildered. It was as if he had opened Pandora's box, and was now standing back appalled at the troubles he had unleashed. Antony did not linger to see what happened next. Caesar was beyond hope and he had his own life to save. He guessed rightly that a troop of gladiators belonging to Decimus Brutus whom he had seen loitering in a room near the colonnade might prove a danger to him if he went outside the building dressed in his consular regalia, so he darted hastily into the nearest men's latrines. A slave who was wielding a broom and humming tunelessly gazed up, startled at his approach.

'Take off your tunic,' rapped out Antony.

'Sir, I'm not that way inclined!' protested the slave.

'Neither am I,' snapped Antony. 'I want your clothes, not your body. Now, give me that!'

He had already discarded his toga and it was the work of a moment to haul off his tunic with its purple senatorial stripe and dress in the slave's clothes. He pressed a silver coin into the youth's hand.

'Have you got a cloak?' he demanded.

'Yes, sir. On the hook over there.'

'Forget you saw me,' ordered Antony, as he marched out, drawing a fold of the cloak over his head to conceal his face. He walked until he was out of sight of the building and then paused, frowning thoughtfully. Yes, fortunately he had ordered his groom, Felix, to exercise his favourite stallion on the meadow near the river this very morning. He only prayed that he could find him. Bundling up the cloak and thrusting it under a bush, he ran for half a mile until he neared the river bed. Pausing to draw breath, he saw that his groom was trotting his horse around an oval, making it change legs after each circuit. When Antony ran at him, the groom raised his whip.

'It's me, you fool!' cried Antony, seizing the horse's bridle.

'What are you doing dressed like that, sir?' protested Felix.

'Caesar's been assassinated and if I don't look lively, I'll be next.'

The groom was swift on the uptake, he had to give him that. At once he slid to the ground and thrust the reins into Antony's hands.

'Ride for home,' he urged. 'I'll find my own way of following you.'

Antony swung himself into the saddle and paused. It was the first time he had had a chance to think clearly and the image of Fulvia and his children flashed before his eyes, but Brutus was hardly likely to harm them. Then he thought of Cleopatra and his heart was suddenly as cold as stone in his breast. He must ride and warn her.

'Wait,' he ordered, as the groom turned to go. 'Steal a horse – there must be one somewhere near here. I want you to ride home to my wife and tell her what's happened. Arm all the slaves and fortify the house. I'll join you as soon as I can.'

'But, sir, where – '

Antony did not reply. Turning the horse, he vanished amid a thunder of hooves.

Some time later he trotted across the Pons Fabricius on to the island in the middle of the River Tiber. There he was stopped and challenged by a group of armed soldiers. Their commanding officer Lepidus, looking anxious and grim, recognized him at once and paused in his work of setting up barricades.

'Mark Antony! I'm glad to see you escaped. I was in the Senate when the murder happened, but I couldn't reach Caesar in time to help him. I've got my legion here and I'm fortifying the island, so that we can hold it against the conspirators if there's any more trouble. Where are you off to, man?'

'To fetch reinforcements,' improvised Antony. 'Caesar had soldiers who were to embark on the Parthian campaign camping near his villa across the river. I'll send them back here to join you.'

'Good man,' said Lepidus.

Antony rode on as fast as he dared. When he reached Caesar's villa across the Tiber, he did his duty as a soldier first. First he broke the news of Caesar's death and ordered the soldiers to go to Lepidus and place themselves under his command. He toyed with the idea of telling them to form a protective guard around Cleopatra, but did not trust them – there might be many among them who would be only too glad to see her dead. Instead he told one of her own slaves to bring fresh horses to the side door of the villa. Then he rushed inside the house and searched for Cleopatra herself. He found her in one of the extravagantly decorated rooms in her suite.

'Antony!' she gasped, taking in the details of his servile garb. 'What's happened? Caesar – '

'Dead,' he retorted tersely. 'Stabbed in the Senate by his own best friends and by his own son, if what I'm told is true. Marcus Brutus.'

She shook her head as if to clear it.

'Brutus was his son?' she echoed incredulously. 'I never guessed. I knew he had a grown son, but I thought it might be you or Dolabella or . . . oh, what does it matter? Did you say . . . dead?'

'I saw him, Cleopatra. I held him in my arms. He was hacked to pieces.'

At last his words seemed to penetrate her mind. Suddenly she uttered a low, harsh shriek like the sound of tearing cloth and backed away from him, raising her arm to her mouth and biting on it until the blood flowed.

'No, no, he can't be dead!' she cried. 'I won't let him be. It's another one of his tricks, like the time in Egypt when I thought he had drowned. He'll walk through the doorway any moment now and say it was a mistake.'

'He won't, Cleopatra! He's dead. The only person who'll walk through that doorway today is me.'

Her groans kept coming, rhythmic and urgent as if she were suffering some dreadful physical pain. He tried to touch her, to speak to her, but she twisted out of his grip too baffled and thwarted by this destruction of her plans to listen to reason.

'What use are you to me?' she cried wildly. 'You won't make me Queen, will you?'

'You bitch,' breathed Antony. 'He's dead, I tell you. Dead! Dead!'

At that she began to cry hysterically, darting backwards and forwards like a bird battering itself against a cage, flinging a wine jug and a pair of cups to the floor and crying even more frantically when they smashed. Antony watched in horror, then belatedly took action.

'Stop it!' he shouted, seizing her by the shoulders and shaking her.

'Let me go!' she wailed and tried to claw at his face with her fingers.

Exasperated beyond measure, he drew back his hand and slapped her with stunning force. She gasped and her hand flew to her stinging cheek, but her screaming subsided. Instead she collapsed against him, weeping quietly.

'I'm sorry, I'm sorry,' she breathed, clinging to him. 'Is it really true?'

He nuzzled her scented dark hair, putting his arms around her and hauling her against him, soothing her like a child. All the old, mysterious yearning rose inside him at the feel of her, so warm and defenceless in his embrace.

'Yes, it's true,' he agreed soberly. Then he tilted her chin and looked down into her red, brimming eyes. 'But there's no use grieving. We've wasted enough time already. I must get you out of here, Cleopatra. Marcus Brutus intends to kill you next.'

She stiffened in alarm.

'Caesarion!' she cried.

'Don't worry. We'll take the boy too.'

'We'd better get horses immediately.'

He couldn't believe the change in her. A shudder passed through her, she wiped her eyes and it was like watching Proteus transform from a monster into a human being. She was no longer frenzied, but calm, shrewd, resourceful. Opening the door, she shouted for Charmion to bring Caesarion at once. Then she snatched up a cloak and looked at Antony.

'What about my attendants?'

'It's better if they travel separately. The black woman is far too noticeable. Now, come. There's no more time to lose.'

As it was, they were barely in time. They were just departing by a side gate when they glimpsed a group of armed gladiators trotting up the main gravel driveway towards the house. Cleopatra gasped and twisted in her saddle to look at Antony for guidance.

'Ride on,' he urged her sternly. 'They may not notice us.'

It was a vain hope. At that moment one of the gladiators let out a yell of triumph and pandemonium broke out. Cleopatra's heart felt ready to burst in her chest with panic as everything happened at once. There was a sound of shouting and a loud drumming of hooves, a gleeful cry from Caesarion, then her mare shot forward like an arrow. The hunt was on.

When Antony had left the Senate chamber, a strange indecision settled on those who remained as if nobody now knew quite what to do. A few of Caesar's sympathizers who had tried to help him gathered in a forlorn group around his body. Cicero, who had not been a party to the conspiracy but was shocked and delighted by its happening, began to jot down some notes for a speech in praise of the republic. Dolabella decided to lie low and see what happened when the news was made public. If there was general approval of the deed, perhaps he could pretend that he had been one of the assassins . . . At last Brutus, looking wild-eyed and strange, took his place in the centre of the floor and tried to make a speech about liberty, but nobody seemed inclined to listen. As the assassins milled around, arguing among themselves about what should be done next, one elderly senator made a break for the door. A conspirator made as if to pursue him, but Brutus caught at his companion's arm.

'Let him go!' he ordered roughly.

It was the signal for a general stampede. Crowding close upon each other's heels and casting fearful glances at the blood-stained men in the centre of the chamber, all the remaining occupants of the hall rushed in blind panic to the exit. There was a rumble like thunder as several hundred pairs of feet echoed along the colonnade surrounding the building. Distant shouts reverberated, cries of terror and warning, muffled but still audible.

'Treason!'

'Murder!'

'Run for your lives!'

'Citizens, bar your doors! There are assassins in our midst!'

Cassius glared at Brutus and then spat contemptuously on the floor.

'You should never have let them go!' he exclaimed. 'They'll spread panic all through the city!'

'And what was I to do?' flared Brutus. 'Call in the gladiators and massacre every last one of the senators who wasn't privy to the plot? Don't you think that would spread panic through the city?'

'It's no good arguing amongst ourselves,' protested Decimus, stepping between the two brothers-in-law as they squared up to each other. 'The question is, what are we going to do now?'

'A pity you didn't think of that sooner,' said the reedy voice of the elderly senator Sabinus, who was still sitting awkwardly on the floor beside the dead body of Caesar. Gripping the plinth of Pompey's statue, he hauled himself to his feet and gazed sternly around the faces of the younger men. 'You're fool enough to think you've done a great deed today but you'll soon find that it's easier to tear down than to build up. Caesar had his faults, I won't deny it even though I was his friend, but he was a great man and there's not one among you fit to step into his shoes. All you've done today is ensure that Rome will have another bout of these bloody civil wars that wise men hoped were finished for ever. Well, you may not know what you're going to do next, but I do. I'm going to call in Caesar's slaves and have his body taken away for decent burial unless any of you brave liberators wants to get his dagger out again and stop me.'

'You can't do that – ' began Cassius, but once again Brutus intervened.

'We have no quarrel with dead bodies,' he growled.

'Take his corpse away, Sabinus, and welcome. And tell his wife, Calpurnia, that I . . . that we didn't intend . . . that . . . oh, what's the use?'

With an impatient gesture he flung down his dagger which went clattering across the mosaic floor. Then he put both his hands up to cover his face. For most of the past half hour, he seemed to have been moving in a trance as men do in the midst of battle, operating by instinct, scarcely aware of his own words or actions, too numb to notice any pain. Now as he covered his eyes, he became aware for the first time of the red, sticky fluid that was flowing down his left arm and dripping on to his clothes. And, as if the sight of it had woken his other senses, he felt a sudden, hot, stinging pain. Dropping his hands, he picked up the hem of his toga, bit into it with savage desperation and tore off a long strip of material. Then he tied the fabric round his wound in a hasty, improvised bandage. He would have to get Porcia to see to it properly when he reached home. That thought sent a sudden chill through his body, worse than anything he had experienced on this terrible day. Could he really have forgotten that appalling, garbled message that had been brought to him before Caesar's arrival? A rambling, half-hysterical tale from one of his most trusted slaves that his wife had fallen down in some kind of coma and was believed dead? With the urgency and horror and exhilaration of killing Caesar, he must somehow have blanked it all out of his mind! Now a shudder went through him and he was suddenly frantic with the need to know the truth. Thrusting Cassius and Decimus aside, he headed for the exit.

'Where do you think you're going?' demanded Cassius in an aggrieved tone.

Brutus turned on him, his eyes blazing.

337

'In case you've forgotten, a message was brought this morning to say that my wife was dead.' His voice broke. 'I have to find out whether it's true.'

Cassius shrugged uncertainly.

'Yes, yes, all right,' he agreed distractedly. 'But what are we to do after that? If those senators have gone out and stirred up all the citizens against us, our own lives could be in danger.'

'I'll tell you what we must do,' said Decimus, briefly taking command of the situation. 'We must go and fortify the Capitol Hill. If there's any trouble, it's a strong defensive position and with our gladiators in place we can hold it against an army if necessary. And if there's no trouble, we can say we've gone there to sacrifice at the temple of Jupiter Greatest and Best in honour of the restoration of republic and liberty.'

For the moment they were all in agreement and they filed out, clapping each other on the back and already beginning to relive the greatest moments of the kill, as if it were some event they had watched in the arena. Only Brutus took no part in the boasting, setting off at a run for his house. His breath was coming in long, dragging gulps and the wound in his hand was throbbing and beginning to bleed again when he burst into his wife's bedroom. He found her sitting up in bed, looking as pale as the pillow she leaned against and sipping from a cup of water held by his mother. The relief of finding Porcia alive was so great that, without thinking of the spectacle he must present, he sat down on the bed with a moan of relief and crushed her in his arms. Servilia rose to her feet with a shriek.

'Marcus! You're covered in blood! Whatever has happened?'

Yet where Servilia's face was suddenly ashen with dismay, Porcia in contrast seemed to come back dramatically from death's door. Her pale cheeks flushed, her grey eyes were luminous and even her tumbled red hair seemed to crackle with vitality.

'You've done it, then?' she demanded exultantly. 'You've killed Caesar?'

Brutus had never heard such an appalling cry as the strangled gasp which issued from his mother's mouth. With a strength unbelievable in a woman, she dragged him off the bed and shook him until his teeth rattled in his head.

'What have you done? What have you done?' she howled. 'Answer me, Marcus. By all the gods, is it true what this sly little troublemaker suggests? Have you killed Julius Caesar?'

The anguish and fury in her voice were unmistakable. Brutus, who had had a long, dangerous and extremely harrowing day, felt aggrieved by this lack of gratitude.

'You asked me to put a stop to his ambitions,' he retorted sulkily. 'You wrote to me in Gaul and begged me to do it!'

'I didn't beg you to kill him!' shrieked Servilia. 'Tell me the truth, Marcus, what have you done? Have you killed Julius Caesar?'

'Yes!' shouted Brutus defiantly. 'Yes, I have.'

Servilia moaned and might have slumped to the floor if Brutus had not caught her. She seemed unable to breathe, her mouth opening and closing soundlessly and her face devoid of all colour. Then suddenly she found her voice.

'How could you?' she demanded. 'How could you bring yourself to kill your own father?'

'Father!' gasped Porcia, sitting up in bed. 'What does she mean by calling Caesar your father, Marcus? Is she wandering in her mind?'

Servilia turned on her daughter-in-law like a raging Fury. Her dark eyes smouldered, her grey hair writhed on her shoulders like a mass of snakes and her face seemed to have aged by decades in a single afternoon.

'No, I'm not wandering in my mind, you murderous little bitch,' she said through her teeth. 'And I know very well who lies behind this conspiracy. It's your doing, Porcia, it's thanks to you that I've lost the one man I ever loved. Gaius Julius Caesar and I fell in love with each other when we were fourteen years old and when he got me pregnant I had to be hastily married off to avoid a scandal. But I don't suppose Marcus ever told you that, did he? I don't suppose that you ever knew that it was your own husband's father that you were plotting against? Well, I wish you joy, you precious pair! You've ruined my life and I never want to see either of you again! Oh, Gaius, Gaius . . . how could they do this to you?'

Watching helplessly as his formidable mother gave way to a paroxysm of tears, Brutus began to suspect that liberating the Roman republic from tyranny was going to prove a very thankless task . . .

As for the other assassins, a fresh round of disagreement and discussion broke out among them as they made their way down the Via Flaminia towards the city. In the end it was agreed that Decimus's plan of retreating to the Capitol, while sound, should be postponed for a while. First they would all go to the Forum in a body and try to persuade the citizens that there was no cause for panic. To their surprise they found their fellow Romans remarkably unwilling to listen. Everywhere there was the sound of shutters being closed over shop windows, keys being turned in locks, people hurrying up stairways or diving down alleys at their approach. When they reached the Forum, they found it almost deserted, with a few worried groups of people hovering near its edges as if poised for flight. Cassius tried to make a speech, but while he was still declaiming, a low, keening noise like the sound of wind getting up at the start of a storm spread among the ragged crowd of listeners. Turning to follow their gaze, he saw that Sabinus had been true to his vow to give Caesar honourable burial. Only three of Caesar's slaves had been found brave enough to go and recover his body and now the litter, moving lopsidedly for lack of adequate support, was lurching across the Forum on its sad journey home. The onlookers began to weep and groan as they saw the wounded face and the arms dangling over the sides. A humble flower seller, who had been weaving garlands of fragrant narcissi and blue hyacinths for sale, gathered up all her stock and ran to fling it on the body, sobbing bitterly as she did so. A flute player, who had been busking for small coins in one of the colonnades fell into line behind the three slaves and began to play a melancholy, droning dirge. More people trickled back into the Forum and the tears began to give way to angry muttering and hate-filled glances at Cassius and his companions. Looking uneasily at each other, the assassins decided wordlessly that this might be a good time to withdraw to the Capitol . . .

By the time the cortège reached Caesar's home, Calpurnia had already recovered somewhat from the first shock of hearing about her husband's death. She had cried herself to a standstill and now stood, erect and tragic, in the atrium of their house, waiting to receive him home. But at the first sight of his cold, still body, with the dreadful wounds inflicted on it, all her self-control vanished. She flung herself down beside him, crying and clutching at his hand.

'I warned you!' she sobbed. 'I begged and begged you not to go, but you wouldn't listen! You always had to have your own way and in the end it killed you!'

She was very much touched an hour or so later when Antony's wife Fulvia arrived to share her vigil beside the corpse. She and Fulvia had never been close friends, and there had been times when Caesar had really been far too critical of Antony, but Fulvia was a tower of strength. She held conferences with the undertaker and the kitchen slaves about the funeral ceremony and the family gathering that would follow. With her resonant voice and imperious figure, she had no difficulty in quelling the slaves' laments and sending them all about their household tasks once more. And, in order to spare Calpurnia the worry of being pestered by troublesome bureaucrats, she took all the state funds and official documents which were in the house into her own possession to hand over for safe custody to her husband Antony. As she took her leave of the sorrowing widow, Fulvia's features were set in a mould of grief and sympathy, but the moment she was inside her litter with the curtains safely drawn, a serene smile flickered about the corners of her lips. Caesar's death might well prove to be Antony's opportunity and Fulvia would see that he took full advantage of it. The only thing worrying her now was where in the name of Juno Antony had concealed himself. Everyone had agreed that he had left the Senate chamber alive and well, so where was he? It was a puzzle which must be solved and solved quickly . . .

There was probably nobody in Rome who remained unaffected by the dictator's death. But it was the soothsayer Spurinna who summed up its significance most aptly. The following morning when he sacrificed a sheep and tore out the steaming liver to read the will of the gods for Rome's future, he shook his head with an expression of grave misgiving on his face. All the worst signs were there, spots, deformities, fatal abnormalities of the lobes. Spurinna sighed heavily.

'Julius Caesar's death will bring about great changes,' he said. 'I foresee war, disaster, calamity and a great outpouring of blood.'

Chapter Eighteen

Cleopatra had rarely ridden a horse before and never at such breakneck speed. Every bone in her body felt as if it were being jolted apart and the landscape rushed past her in a blurred and terrifying way. Travellers started and ran for safety to the roadside verges, a chicken squawked and scuttled under a cart, trees and stalls and roadside shrines flashed by in the blink of an eye. Then Antony's horse thundered close to hers, he snatched her bridle and gestured to a dusty track leading up into the hills. A moment later and her horse was sweating and snorting, gravel flying under its feet as it flung itself in pursuit of Antony's stallion. The track took a few more twists and turns and came out in a grove of trees on top of a steep hill overlooking the main road. Drawing Cleopatra's horse into the shelter of a thick stand of cypresses, Antony put his finger to his lips. A moment later, they heard bloodthirsty shouts and the sound of drumming hooves as the group of gladiators rode past on the main road below them. As soon as they were gone, Antony turned to her and spoke.

'They'll search the whole of the Via Campana now,' he said, scowling thoughtfully. 'So I think it's best if we travel by the back roads. By rights, we ought to be on the other side of the river, but I've no doubt they've got search parties out along the Via Ostiensis too, so we'll just have to trust to luck and hope they don't find us. We can cross downstream later on.'

He kept them moving at a gruelling pace for the next couple of hours. If she had not been suffering from the terror of being captured and perhaps seeing Caesarion's brains smashed out on a rock before her very eyes, Cleopatra would have enjoyed that ride. The trees were covered in a new mist of green, there were purple crocuses flowering in sheltered hollows, dappled sunlight danced on the track beneath their horses' hooves and there was no sound but the distant noise of running water and the occasional song of some unseen wild bird. From time to time, they paused on a ridge top and saw peaceful farmland laid out beneath them like an array of green woven coverlets on a market stall, but most of the time Antony kept to the unfrequented woodlands. As the shadows lengthened and the sun began to sink like a blazing red ball in the west and the air took on the chill nip of impending evening, he halted and spoke.

'We'd better look for some shelter until dawn,' he announced.

'Can't we keep riding?' she demanded anxiously. 'I'd feel much safer once we were at Ostia and aboard a ship.'

'I know,' agreed Antony. 'But there'll be no moon tonight and if either of our horses puts a foot in a rabbit hole, we won't be too safe then. Trust me, Cleopatra. I know what I'm doing.'

She nodded, her eyes narrowing as she looked at him. Yes, it was true. When it came to a crisis, Antony sprang into action with a shrewdness and competence that took her by surprise. She had become so used to accepting Caesar's contemptuous evaluation of him that she had almost lost sight of his best qualities. His courage, his capacity for practical action, his compassion. Without his help she and Caesarion might well be dead by now. The thought sent a shiver of dismay through her and she glanced at her sleepy son, nestled

345

in the crook of Antony's muscular arm. Involuntarily her gaze travelled up to the man who held him.

'Thank you for saving us,' she said hoarsely.

He gave her an odd look, half bitter, half reflective, then dropped his eyes.

'You're welcome,' he growled, kicking his stallion into motion once more.

As they picked their way down through the bracken in the thickening dusk, Antony seethed with barely suppressed resentment. Oh, so her royal highness had finally realized that she owed him something, had she? Until now it seemed to have completely escaped her notice that he had deserted his post in Rome to ensure her safety. As usual, all her attention had been focused on herself. Her only concern had been what Caesar's death would mean to her. And it wasn't even as if she cared about the old bastard! She had only been using him, as she would use Antony and any other man who came her way. Her earlier words echoed in his head. *What use are you to me? You won't make me Queen, will you?* His lip curled. No, nothing had changed. Obviously she thought he was completely inept, no more than a muscle-bound bodyguard to whom she might throw a careless smile or word of thanks. So why was he here? Why did he still desire her so fiercely? The thought slipped out before he could censor it and he flushed with shame. The bitch! He didn't love her, he didn't even like her, and, as soon as he had put her safely aboard a ship, he was going to gallop straight home to Fulvia. He thought of Fulvia's massive bulk lying dutifully still like a log and then, guiltily, of Cleopatra's scented softness and sly, knowing fingers. It was almost enough to make him groan aloud, but he took comfort from the thought that Cleopatra was hardly likely to notice his turmoil. Probably too busy

346

raging over how she had lost the chance of being Queen of Rome . . .

Antony might truncate his vowels like a common soldier and spell more barbarously than a Libyan galley slave, but he was shrewd enough. And his assessment of Cleopatra's frame of mind was absolutely accurate. As the fear of immediate death receded, she felt a sense of disappointment so acute that she almost burst into tears. How could fate be so cruel? Just when the sovereignty of Rome was within her grasp, it had been snatched away! She felt utterly cheated and outraged. How could Caesar have been such a fool as to get himself killed? Why had he dismissed his Spanish bodyguard? Why had his monstrous ego always demanded such constant proof of his popularity? Any barber or hot food vendor in Rome could have told him that half the Senate hated him! Fool, fool, fool! Well, it was all very well for Caesar, his suffering was over, but hers was barely about to begin. All that tiresome, painstaking work of bribing senators and forging alliances would have to be done again. And her enemies among the Macedonian nobles would soon be gloating over her misfortune and baying after her blood. Not to mention the enemies she had made in Rome through her attachment to Caesar! If it hadn't been for Antony, they would probably have cut her throat already.

Her bitter expression softened briefly as she glanced sideways at her companion. It had been generous of him to come to her aid, but Antony was always generous. If only he were more forceful and ambitious as well, he could have become King of Rome instead of Caesar. But Antony would be too inept for that, too full of scruples, too worried about offending people, too useless and hopeless and pathetic! Her mouth quirked suddenly and she blinked away a scalding rush of angry, disappointed tears. Why couldn't Antony have been a more suitable tool for her ambitions?

Antony, catching her oblique glance and observing her tears, was unexpectedly moved. So she did still care about him, however contemptuously she had spoken of him to Caesar. A flicker of warmth began to burn inside him.

'Don't cry,' he urged abruptly. 'I'll look after you. I'll see you get safely home.'

Well, at least he's good for that, she thought wearily when Antony finally called a halt outside an abandoned hut. She was almost reeling in the saddle with fatigue and Caesarion, whom Antony had handed up to her while he went to reconnoitre, was a dead weight in her arms. Overhead the stars blazed in a frosty sky and from the dark mass of the woods she heard the hoot of some night bird. Inside the hut there was a creaking sound, followed by footsteps, rustling noises, the crash of something being knocked over and a muffled oath. Then moments later, Antony emerged from the building with a glowing oil lamp sheltered in his hands.

'There's nobody here,' he said. 'We'll have the place all to ourselves – a palace fit for a queen.'

It was hardly that, but Cleopatra had seldom seen a more welcome sight than the humble cottage revealed to her when Antony pushed open the wooden door. In the flickering light, shadows danced on the wattle and daub walls, revealing an unpretentious interior. In spite of the cobwebs that hung in the corners and the thin coating of dust on every flat surface, the place was still dry and habitable. It consisted of a single room with a floor of beaten earth and a ladder leading to a loft above. There were even a few battered items of furniture – a three-legged table, two couches, a store cupboard and a bench and brazier with cooking pots. Antony set the lamp on the table and climbed the ladder to explore the loft. A vigorous fit of sneezing immediately seized him.

'It's dusty up here,' he announced. 'But there's a bed with a sedge grass mattress and some coverlets. Caesarion can sleep there.'

He climbed down again, slung the sleeping child effortlessly over his shoulder and returned to the loft.

Cleopatra waited just long enough to see her son settled, then her eyelids dropped like lead weights and she fell into a deep sleep on one of the battered couches. She woke to the smell of hot soup and found Antony's massive hand shaking her shoulder. She came reluctantly back to consciousness, wishing she could have been left in oblivion.

'Caesarion?' she yawned.

'Dead to the world. I've fed him and put him back to bed. I would have let you sleep on, but I thought you needed some hot food in you too.'

He had found a haunch of smoke blackened bacon hanging from a roof beam and some corn in a store cupboard. With a cabbage from the overgrown garden, he had made quite a palatable meal, but Cleopatra accepted the bowl of soup and the cornmeal pancakes unquestioningly, as if there had been no effort involved in producing them.

Like a weary child, taking for granted its right to be fed and cosseted, she swallowed the hot, smoky liquid and the crisp, savoury pancakes and then lay down again. As her eyelids began to flutter shut once more, Antony felt a surge of irritation. Why didn't she talk, praise him for his foraging, ask about the farmers who had abandoned the hut? Anything rather than this listless indifference to everything around her. It was almost as if she were genuinely grief stricken, but that was nonsense. He knew she hadn't loved Caesar!

'Why are you so upset about his death?' he asked resentfully. 'You didn't care about him, did you?'

At least it got a reaction. Her eyes opened and a spasm crossed her face.

'I hated him if you want to know the truth,' she said with barely suppressed violence. 'I was frightened of him. Sometimes he almost seemed like two people living in the one body. One was charming, the other one was violent, dangerous, almost insane. I used to be afraid that if Caesar ever found out about my relationship with you, he would kill me.'

Her eyes were dilated, a sudden tremor passed through her limbs and her voice was so low that he could scarcely hear it. Antony felt a pang of remorse for upsetting her.

'I wouldn't have let him harm you,' he assured her. 'I would have protected you.'

She almost laughed aloud – his statement was so ridiculous. Did Antony imagine that Caesar would have behaved with decency if he had found himself cuckolded? That he would have come to Antony's house and challenged him to a sword fight or a boxing bout to settle his outraged honour? Did Antony think he would have been given the chance to take Cleopatra under his protection and come out into the open about their love affair? Could he possibly be such a fool? She herself knew differently, knew in her bones that Caesar would have strangled her or cut her throat if he had ever discovered her infidelity. In a way, that knowledge had always added the spice of danger and forbidden excitement to her encounters with Antony.

Yet even though his artless statement fuelled her

scorn, it also touched her deeply. Absurd as it was, she felt a treacherous rush of longing for those vanished days of her girlhood when she had loved him with all her heart and been callow enough to dream that fate might even let her marry him. How childish those fantasies seemed now! There had been the fantasy that her father might seal his alliance with Rome by giving his daughter in marriage to the noble Master of the Horse who had restored him to his throne. And the fantasy that Antony might miss her so much once he left Egypt that he would come back and spirit her away on a mettlesome black stallion. Well, he had almost done that today, hadn't he? Impulsive, reckless, true-hearted Antony, galloping up to save her life! He was a fool for doing it and yet to her astonishment she felt an ache of yearning for him. A yearning that was followed by a fierce blaze of triumph as she reflected that he had deserted his wife in order to protect her. Which must mean (mustn't it?) that he still felt the same insistent hunger for her as she felt for him . . .

Suddenly her listlessness was transformed into unexpected action. Without warning she made a movement towards him, then she was in his arms. He held her protectively, intending only to comfort her, but he had not reckoned on the emotion she stirred within him. Once before in the aftermath of a death, she had given herself to him in a frenzy of passion, which he did not fully understand. Now he had the feeling that he was repeating that odd experience after Berenice's execution. Cleopatra was like some priestess in a hypnotic trance, driven by forces beyond his comprehension. Dimly he felt that she was turning to him as if he were the light of the sun in a cold, frightening world. As if this experience were the one thing that would affirm her right to survive, to go on living. Before he knew what was happening, her lips came up to his. He kissed her reassuringly, but reassurance was evidently not what she wanted. As her mouth opened under his, he felt as a man might feel being sucked down beneath the waves by a sea siren. She was beautiful, deadly, inexorable, and she seemed intent on engulfing him. All the same, the touch of her skin, the scent of her hair, the taste of her mouth filled him with a voracious, aching hunger for her. When she drew up her skirts and lay back on the couch, madness seemed to grip him. He tore off his own clothes and bore her down on to the ragged mattress. All the pent-up emotion of two fiery natures blazed up in that violent coupling. Harder and harder he drove into her until at last her whole body clenched in a paroxysm of release and she cried out his name. A moment later he collapsed, spent and shuddering, against her.

'I love you, Cleopatra,' he muttered. 'You're a dangerous little siren, but I love you.'

She sighed and shook her head with a strange, bleak expression on her face. The joyous sense of oblivion she had felt in Antony's arms was already beginning to fade. Why, why wasn't it possible to hold on to that blinding conviction she always felt in the middle of his lovemaking that nothing else mattered? Why couldn't she keep that warm, fuzzy sense of well-being that Antony seemed to wear like a mantle for hours afterwards? Why did she immediately feel the world rushing back at her in all its implacable brutality and nastiness? And how could Antony be so indifferent to what was happening back in Rome? Caesar was dead, the world was once more on the brink of cataclysmic war, Antony's own career was in jeopardy and yet here he was, nuzzling her cheek and muttering endearments as if nothing else mattered. Impatiently she jerked her head away. He was baffled and annoyed by her abrupt change of mind.

'Why don't you say something?' he snapped. 'Don't you realize I've been unfaithful to my wife for your sake? Doesn't that mean anything to you?'

This time she gave an odd, stark smile. Looking down at her, he had the strange impression that she was drawing away from him, like a voyager on a ship putting out to sea. When she spoke, she did not answer his question.

'Caesar's death will mean more wars, won't it? More bloodshed, more uprisings in places like Egypt, more death and destruction. There'll be nobody strong enough to stop it.'

'I'll stop it. I'm still consul.'

Her eyebrows rose sceptically. That subtle, contemptuous gesture made Antony feel as if she had kneed him in the groin. Hurt and offended, he rolled off her.

'You have a very poor opinion of me, don't you?' he demanded bitterly.

'No,' she sighed. 'I think you're a kind, loyal, trustworthy man.'

'So why do those sound like dirty words when you use them?'

'Because we live in a dirty world!' she flashed back. 'Kindness and loyalty and trustworthiness might be useful if you were out in the backwoods, but in Rome or Egypt, they're a handicap. Cunning and deceit and ruthlessness are much more valuable. Don't you see that?'

He knew she was right and the knowledge filled him with enormous frustration. It seemed that even his best qualities would never be enough to impress her or make her love him. Or at least not while they lived in a world of plots and corruption and political intrigue. Suddenly Antony wished he could turn his back on the whole appalling mess and start afresh somewhere else. Somewhere unspoilt, like the wild lands of Illyria, or the island of Britannia or the remote northern parts of India. A dawning sense of excitement stirred within him. Why not? Why not actually do it, instead of merely thinking about it? At the moment it was a half-formed dream, but what could be easier than to turn it into a reality? This hut couldn't be more than an hour's ride from Ostia, so what was to stop him from setting sail with Cleopatra, not for Egypt, but for somewhere else? Dyrrhachium, where they could strike east into the Balkans, or Massilia, where they could travel north through Gaul to the shores facing Britain?

'Then let's leave this dirty world and go somewhere else,' he said passionately. 'Somewhere where we can start a new life together.'

She stared at him in disbelief, but he rushed on, ignoring her scepticism.

'Britain or somewhere that hasn't been screwed up yet. I could hunt or organize an army for some barbarian prince. We could get married, Cleopatra. You could have my babies.'

A brief twinge of yearning pierced her at his mention of marriage and babies. Then she gave him a faint, pitying smile.

'Don't be stupid, Antony,' she said.

It was past noon when Antony found himself inside the walls of Rome again. With a mixture of resentment and relief, he had left Cleopatra in the safe hands of an Alexandrian merchant in Ostia and with each additional mile that separated them, his preoccupation with her diminished. By the time he rode up to the barred doors of his own house, he was completely consumed by guilt and anxiety about the political crisis in Rome. Fulvia's greeting did nothing to lessen his worry.

'Where have you been?' she scolded as he finally entered the atrium of the house. 'The whole of Rome is in an uproar.'

'What's happening?' he asked with a frown, snatching up a handful of walnuts from a bowl on a side table and cramming them into his mouth.

'Fetch the master a meal and some hot water to wash in,' she said to a hovering slave. Then without pausing to draw breath, she went on. 'The conspirators have barricaded themselves in the Capitol with their gladiators and they're offering bribes to Caesar's discharged soldiers to support them. The Senate is split in two over the issue. Half of them want to vote honours to the assassins, the others want to execute them for treason. At the moment there's a stand off, but it's looking ugly.'

Antony slumped into a chair and thrust out his large feet so that the slave could unlace his dusty riding boots.

'That's tricky,' he muttered to himself.

'Yes, it is,' agreed Fulvia tartly, settling herself in another chair. 'And as the sole surviving consul, you're the one who should be dealing with the situation. This is the very chance you've always needed to take control of Rome yourself.'

She took a cup from the tray the slave was holding, added water to the wine and passed it to Antony. He looked at it with as much horror as if it were a poisoned chalice.

'What do you mean, "take control of Rome"?'

'Exactly what I say. This is your big chance to step

355

into Caesar's shoes and make yourself supreme master of the Empire.'

Antony gave a harsh growl of laughter.

'Caesar got himself killed attempting that,' he reminded her.

'That's because he was a fool! If he hadn't been so hell-bent on naming himself King, he could have got away with it. It's the reality of power that counts, not the title and if you're wise enough to resist empty honours, you'll never have a better chance to help yourself to the reality of power. I'll do everything I can to smooth the way for you.'

He stared at her with as much dismay as though she had just been transformed from a woman into a snake-headed monster. Had he really been married to Fulvia for two years without ever realizing the extent of the ambitions she harboured for him?

'What do you mean, "smooth the way for me"?' he demanded uneasily.

Her eyes kindled.

'You're in the best position of any man in Rome to take advantage of the confusion now and I've done all I can to protect your interests. I've persuaded Calpurnia to entrust the Parthian war chest and all Caesar's documents to me for safekeeping. That means that you can announce whatever decrees you like and claim that they're Caesar's. Nobody will be able to contradict you. You'll have supreme power, Marcus.'

He gazed at her in stupefaction. She was every bit as bad as Cleopatra!

'I don't want supreme power,' he protested. 'At least, nothing beyond what is my constitutional right as the elected consul.'

'Elected consul!' snorted Fulvia contemptuously. 'You know perfectly well that Caesar was moving away from elections to direct appointments and from now on you'll be the one with the power to make them. If only he's named you as heir in his will, your position will be unassailable.'

'Heir?' repeated Antony in a baffled voice.

'Yes! We all know he was about to depart on his Parthian campaign and he must have made some provision for a strong successor in Rome if he got killed. The only other possibilities are his son Caesarion and that little wimp Octavian. Personally I can't see Caesar being fool enough to entrust the succession to either of them. Caesarion's only a child and Octavian's not much better. Eighteen years old and can't handle a sword to save himself, besides being so surly and awkward that nobody could ever take him seriously as a leader.'

Antony was momentarily distracted from his worries by Fulvia's assessment of Octavian which was so close to his own view.

'You're right there,' he snorted. 'He's a sly, underhand, cowardly runt! And I can tell you for a fact all the soldiers were completely browned off when Caesar awarded him military decorations in his triumph a couple of years ago, even though the boy had never been near a battle in his life. It would be more than I could stomach to see him named as Caesar's heir.'

Fulvia sighed.

'Well, unfortunately Caesar's lawyers are being very cagey about releasing the will. But even if Octavian does inherit, it will be up to you to make sure that all he gets is the smallest possible amount of Caesar's private property. It would be a disgrace if he inherits political power that he's done nothing to earn. I advise you to go round and canvass the other senators about it before Octavian gets back from Illyria.'

It was good advice and Antony took it. Although he had no ambitions to make himself King in Caesar's place, he did feel the weight of his consular responsibilities settling on his shoulders like a wooden ox yoke. In the past Caesar had been there as his fellow consul to share the burden, but now he was gone and Antony felt the chilling loneliness of supreme power. Whatever he did he seemed certain to antagonize somebody. For all his brilliance, Caesar had left behind him a legacy of resentment and class hatred. The small farmers turned off their plots of land to provide homes for Caesar's veterans hated the soldiers. The landlords faced with cancellation of debts and no chance of evicting troublemakers hated their tenants. The Senate was a ferment of vendettas with Pompey's silent and malevolent sympathizers ready to turn and massacre those who had profited under Caesar's rule. And here was Antony, thick-witted, raucous, dissipated Antony as the sole barrier between Rome and another vicious civil war. He had never felt his own inadequacies more acutely.

All the same, he had always had the easy knack of talking to people. Now, as he went from house to house asking the views of the senators, he realized that the whole city was like a tinder-dry Calabrian scrubland needing only a spark to set it ablaze. Yet somehow he must damp down the trouble. It did not take him long to realize that his own instinctive contempt for the assassins would have to be hidden. With half the Senate clamouring to raise statues in their honour, it would be foolhardy to demand revenge. Whatever his private feelings on the matter, he felt in his bones that a general amnesty for the crime was the only chance of keeping the lid on the simmering cauldron of political discontent in Rome. At the same time he had no intention of letting all of Caesar's policies vanish into oblivion. In particular he was determined to make sure that Caesar's promise of founding colonies for the veteran soldiers would be honoured. With this end in mind, he conducted himself with unusual discretion. His first act was to order the magistrates to set guards around the city by night and day to prevent any disturbance of the peace. After that he called a meeting of the Senate to be held the following morning in the temple of Tellus near his home. It was a noisy and acrimonious session.

Within the first half hour there were speeches denouncing Caesar as a tyrant and demanding that honours be voted to the men who had killed him. These demands were met by heated retorts from Caesar's supporters and the whole chamber seemed likely to be filled with uproar. Antony's spirits sank, but he knew he must take control.

'Senators,' he announced in a booming voice. 'I've got only one thing to say. If you want to name Caesar a tyrant and reward his murderers, fair enough. But if Caesar was a tyrant, that means all his actions were illegal, doesn't it? So if you do follow that course of action, I think it's only right that anyone who was appointed to a magistracy or received money from the public purse under Caesar should give up those benefits at once. I'm prepared to resign the consulship. Now what about the rest of you? Are you going to give up the salaries and offices you received under Caesar?'

That made them pause. Antony was tempted to grin as he saw the look of consternation that spread like a plague from face to noble face among the assembled senators.

'No? Then I propose the following decree. "That there be no prosecution for the murder of Caesar, but that all his acts and decrees be confirmed for the good of the state." We can't afford any more vendettas for past wrongs. What we need is rec-reconciliation and a fresh start.'

To Antony's surprise a low murmur of approval began to pass around the temple. Even his stumble on the word 'reconciliation' didn't arouse the jeers of derision that similar blunders had brought in the past. Instead somebody near the back began to applaud and soon the clapping echoed round the entire building. Antony's face flushed with pleasure and relief as the vote was carried by a huge majority.

'Now I propose that we have a public reading of Caesar's will,' shouted Lucius Calpurnius Piso as the noise died down.

As they left the building, Piso came over and clapped Antony on the shoulder.

'Good work,' he said approvingly. 'I used to have doubts about my son-in-law's choice of you as his second in command, but now I see he was right. I'll tell you plainly, Antony, that I pray Caesar has named you as his chief heir in the will. There's nobody else who could do a better job of steering Rome towards peace.'

But Piso's prayers were not fated to be answered. When the will was opened and read aloud, it was found that Caesar had appointed a completely unexpected successor to his fortune. Octavian.

The almond orchards were just struggling into bloom so that a pink froth of blossom softened the stark branches around the town of Apollonia when the messenger arrived to bring the news. Syrus had had dealings with Octavian in the past and he looked askance at the pimply-faced youth who came sidling into the quaestorium. Nasty, double-dealing little toad! Still hadn't paid the last instalment of Syrus's commission on arranging Caesar's assassination. And what about all the risks Syrus had taken and the money paid out of his own purse to arms dealers? Untrustworthy, that's what Octavian was. Still, as Caesar's heir, he should have access to a huge fortune. Syrus's eyes gleamed at the prospect, then he composed his features into an expression of lugubrious regret.

'Well?' demanded Octavian. 'What is it? My commanding officer said you had urgent news for me.'

'Ah,' said Syrus mournfully. 'That's so, sir, that's so. I'm sorry to inform you that your great-uncle Caesar is dead. Assassinated.'

Octavian let out a long, unsteady sigh of relief and sank into a chair.

'The gods be thanked! And the will? The will, Syrus?'

'You are named as heir in chief and formally adopted as Caesar's son. May I offer my congratulations as well as my condolences, sir?'

'You may indeed!' agreed Octavian, rubbing his hands together jubilantly. 'Now sit down and tell me the details.'

All the while that Syrus was talking, Octavian's exhilaration continued to grow. Yet it was accompanied by an equally giddy feeling of terror. He wanted the supreme power in Rome, wanted it with a manic intensity he had never experienced before, but he did not want to die as Caesar had done. Every step on his road to power must be taken as safely and prudently as possible. Let others take the risks! Octavian did not intend to suffer a single sword cut on his route to glory. And with care and proper planning, he believed most of the dangers could be eliminated. His mind raced ahead, vaulting over obstacles as Syrus talked. He would not be fool enough to name himself King as Caesar had tried to do. No. Better to be content with the reality of power and forget the titles. And, however much he hated to part with money, he would have to grease the right palms along the way. Lavish government appointments for influential senators, bread and circuses for the plebs. And any rivals must be ruthlessly dispatched . . .

'Are Caesarion and Cleopatra still in Rome?' he broke in abruptly.

'No, sir. They fled to Egypt immediately after the murder. She feared Brutus's gladiators.'

'Curse it!' Still, perhaps he could send assassins to Egypt to dispose of the boy. It was a mere detail, among many. More worrying was the mention of Brutus. If by any chance he had survived after murdering Caesar, he would certainly never countenance similar ambitions in Caesar's adopted son. 'What of the assassins? Torn to pieces by a vengeful crowd, I imagine?'

'No, sir. Mark Antony forbade all further violence for the sake of the state.'

An incredulous rage rose in Octavian's breast. That meddling blunderer! He could have sworn Antony would have rushed bellowing with indignation to slay Caesar's assassins. With luck he would have succeeded and been killed himself in the process.

'Antony's still alive then?'

'Yes, sir. And there's something else you should know. He's persuaded Calpurnia to hand over all Caesar's funds to him for safekeeping. If you want to collect your inheritance, you'll have to ask Mark Antony for it.'

CHAPTER NINETEEN

It was not until she arrived back in Egypt that Cleopatra realized how homesick she had been in Rome. Ignoring the boxes of papyrus petitions and the throngs of secretaries who besieged her from the moment of her return, she managed to slip out of the Lake port in disguise, accompanied only by her attendants Iras and Charmion and a couple of boatmen. On the placid blue waters of Lake Mareotis with no sound but the splash of oars, the rustle of reeds and the occasional cry of a startled bird, she felt an unexpected peace begin to settle on her. How beautiful the light in Egypt was! It clung in a powdery gold nimbus around the heads of her companions and glinted dazzlingly off the white limestone and buildings of the city. The joy of returning home was almost enough to quench the disappointment of her ignominious flight from Rome. As the light craft slipped into the Ship Canal which would take them back through the city to the Eunostos harbour, a feeling of excitement gripped her. There on the right was the fishermen's quarter of Rhakotis and somewhere among those jumbled buildings was the cottage where she and Mark Antony used to meet in secret years before. Suddenly she was possessed by an urgent need to plunge into those twisting streets again, to see and taste and hear and touch the life of Alexandria once more.

Draped in a flimsy, but voluminous covering of the kind Arab women wore, she spent several hours with Iras and Charmion exploring the back streets and the market place near the harbour. She stopped to watch a snake charmer serenading a cobra in a wicker basket with the reedy notes of a pan-pipe. She wandered among the food stalls, sniffing the mingled aromas of onions, fish, hot bread, spices and dates. She threw a handful of small coins into a blind beggar's bowl. She bought a silver charm as protection against the evil eye. And when her sandals began to chafe and her bladder was bursting, she found a respectable tavern where they could visit the lavatories and then have lunch in a secluded courtyard.

'I think the highest achievement of mankind is good plumbing,' she said as she sat down with a sigh of relief on a cushioned couch between her two attendants.

Iras looked dubious and shook her head.

'Good food,' she said with her mouth full.

Cleopatra looked down at the sizzling grilled kebabs, the green salad, the flat bread, the sheep's yoghurt, the dried dates and nuts, and smiled.

'Perhaps you're right,' she agreed.

Later, when they had eaten and rested, they left the shady courtyard with its splashing fountain and walked along the Canopic Way towards the Library and Museum. Iras's younger sister was a medical student there and she wanted to surprise her when she came out of her classes. As they walked, Cleopatra was intensely conscious of all the blessings that her ancestors' rule had bestowed on Alexandria. Take the buildings. The cool, marble columns of porticoes shaded pedestrians from the heat and allowed the caress of a mild sea breeze to penetrate even the centre of the city. And then there were the wide streets themselves with their clean paving stones, unlike the cramped Roman alleys which stank and constantly ran with filth. Most important of all, there were the Library and Museum, where anyone even from the humblest background could hope to become a scholar. Like Iras's sister, for instance. Born to a couple of freed slaves, she was now on the verge of becoming a doctor. What would happen to her if the Romans seized Egypt as a province? Would she ever finish medical school? Would there even be a medical school?

'What's wrong with you?' asked Iras. 'Have you got a pain in the guts?'

'Yes,' replied Cleopatra in an odd voice. 'Yes. I think I have.'

It was a pain that grew worse over the next few weeks as news filtered back with maddening slowness from Rome. What she heard was worrying. Octavian had inherited three-quarters of Caesar's estate and been posthumously adopted. Octavian, adopted! The slur to her own son infuriated her, but worse still was the uneasiness about what Octavian would do with his new-found wealth and status. Of course he was too young and inept to go round annexing new provinces, but with the power vacuum created by Caesar's death, others might well try. Brutus and Cassius, for instance. To her intense indignation, she now learnt that Antony had spared the assassins' lives and that the senate had promised them provinces to rule. What if they were not content with those, but decided to seize more? And what was to happen to the three Roman legions that Caesar had left in Egypt to protect her? Would they be posted elsewhere and would a general revolt follow their departure? If that happened, would Arsinoë be offered the throne in Cleopatra's place? It was all extremely unsettling and she could only do what her ancestor Ptolemy had done during the upheavals following Alexander's death. Sit tight and hope that the warlords would exterminate one another.

There was one bright spot among the dark clouds that threatened her. Arsinoë seemed ready to cooperate with her at last. Indeed, she had sent Cleopatra a very friendly letter. It arrived in early summer by special courier and Cleopatra tore it open at once and read it aloud.

                                    The Temple of Artemis
                                    Ephesus

My dear Cleopatra,

I pray that God sends you all the prosperity that you deserve. You may rest assured that I value your kindness to me in Rome exactly as I should.

I will never stop missing Vercingetorix, but I believe now that he is dead and will not be restored to me in this life. There can be only one way of blotting out my pain. That is to take action fitted to my noble birth and my hopes for the future.

I am therefore writing to ask you to make me governor of Cyprus, if the Roman Senate can be persuaded to accept such a move. There is an Alexandrian treasury official called Serapion on holiday in Ephesus at present, whom I wish to name my chief executive with your approval.

As soon as I hear from you, I will set my plans in motion.

                                    Your loving sister,
                                    Arsinoë

'There! I knew she'd come round if only she were given time to forget that wretched Gallic chieftain!' exclaimed Cleopatra triumphantly. 'Now, if only I can win Mark Antony's agreement, between us we'll wrest

Cyprus back from Roman control. Iras, take down a letter and ask my sister to visit me here in Alexandria before she goes to Cyprus. Tell her not to come until after the Inundation, though. I'll be too busy hearing land claims until after the waters have settled and the new surveys have been done.'

Cleopatra was busy, but not in the way she had expected, dealing with a rush of claims about the new, rich silt. Ominously the Nile failed to rise more than a few feet and it soon became clear that the crops would fail in the following season. Hour after hour was spent in the granaries authorizing the distribution of corn to afflicted regions. Rats which would normally have drowned were found devouring the scarce supplies. And to these afflictions, there was soon added a worse one. Cleopatra returned to the palace one afternoon from a trip into the Delta complaining of a feverish headache and a sore throat. By the following morning her condition had worsened and Iras sent for the doctor in alarm. Olympus's face was grave as he examined her flushed cheeks and heavy eyes, took her pulse and peered down her raw, fetid throat. Shaking his head he retreated from the royal couch and washed his hands several times in vinegar.

'What is it?' demanded Iras. 'What's wrong with her?'

Olympus's reply was brief and terrifying.

'Plague,' he said.

Octavian met with a very cool reception from the senators on his arrival in Rome. Regardless of whether they approved of Brutus's action or not, there were very few who relished the idea of being ruled by a raw and arrogant eighteen-year-old. In the first flush of euphoria at being hailed as leader by Caesar's troops in Apollonia, he had underestimated the difficulty of the task he was setting himself. Now he discovered that being lionized by troops eager for a fat bonus was a very different matter from winning the approval of the ruling classes. Even his own mother and stepfather tried their hardest to dissuade him from accepting Caesar's dangerous legacy. Atia wept and worried about assassination, while Philippus growled warnings that he was not up to the task of filling Caesar's shoes. Octavian ignored them both. From early childhood he had dreamed of power and status with the fervent intensity of one who knew he was regarded as a weakling and their opposition infuriated him. *If they knew how I helped to contrive Caesar's death, they wouldn't dare to despise me like this!* he thought fiercely. *Well, I'll show them! I'll show them all. Not only my parents, but every last one of those Roman nobles who ever sneered at me or patronized me or pitied me for my lack of manliness. I may not be a good horseman or orator or soldier, but I've an instinct for power and plotting that is better even than Caesar's. I'll make myself master of Rome yet!*

The first requirement was money. He must gain control of his inheritance to pay the soldiers, for without their support he could do nothing. And that meant crawling to Mark Antony, much as he hated the idea. He had been appalled to learn from his great-aunt Calpurnia that not only the public funds intended for the Parthian expedition, but also most of Caesar's private fortune had been entrusted to Antony for safekeeping. Accordingly Octavian fought down his dislike and wrote Antony a civil note, requesting a meeting with him. To his annoyance Antony waited several days before replying and then summoned him to an audience in Caesar's villa across the Tiber. Since Octavian had fully expected to receive this sumptuous mansion as part of his inheritance, he was further infuriated by the brazen way that Antony had taken it over for use as public offices. On the day of the interview, Antony deliberately kept him waiting for an hour beyond the appointed time. When Octavian was finally shown into the consul's presence, he was already simmering with indignation. However, he did his best to put a good face on it.

'Good morning,' he said, stretching out his hand. 'I'm very grateful to you for seeing me. I know you must be busy.'

Antony ignored the outstretched hand and nodded to a vacant chair.

'What can I do for you?'

Octavian began well. He praised Antony for refusing to vote honours to the assassins, but a note of irritation crept into his voice as he mentioned their appointment to provinces. And he could scarcely hold back his annoyance when he came to the real point of the meeting.

'I've come to ask you to hand over Caesar's money, which Calpurnia entrusted to your care. There are legacies to other people which as the chief heir I'm legally obliged to pay out, including a gift to everyone registered as a citizen on the electoral roll. There are 300,000 people who are clamouring for their money at this very moment. If you give me enough to satisfy them, I'll be content to wait and borrow the rest from the public treasury on your security.'

Antony smiled incredulously. He was enjoying this.

'Listen, boy,' he said. 'If Caesar had left you the governorship of Rome along with his name, what you're asking would be perfectly reasonable. But in fact the Roman people never surrendered the government to anybody to dispose of, not even Caesar. All the money that has been entrusted to me was state funds and I would be derelict in my duty as consul if I handed a single sestertius over to a private citizen like you.'

'That's not true!' shouted Octavian hotly. He leapt to his feet, almost crying with rage at being so unscrupulously thwarted. 'Most of that money was Caesar's own private property, taken as plunder in wars. If you won't give me what's rightfully mine, I'll be financially ruined. I've already paid out a fortune from my own family's private funds to the soldiers and there's more, much more, still owing.'

Antony smirked.

'Well, that's tough,' he said, savouring the words. 'But I think you're going to have to find the money somewhere else.'

Find the money somewhere else, the words echoed over and over in Octavian's head for days afterwards. But where? The soldiers were getting restive and beginning to murmur. His stepfather Philippus would kill him if he ever discovered the full extent of the fraud that Octavian had already practised in the family's banking business. Time was running out . . . What would Julius do? he asked himself in despair. For an instant the face of his great-uncle flashed before his eyes, complete with the weatherbeaten skin, the glittering dark eyes, the stark, mocking smile. And then he knew the answer. Gamble, Octavian, a voice seemed to whisper in his head. Go for the big prize and if the Senate won't help you, find support elsewhere. He took a long, unsteady breath and found that he was shaking with excitement. Find support elsewhere, yes, that was it! Never mind the elected government! If he could get the army and the people behind him, the

Senate would be too frightened to resist him. And he knew exactly how Julius had always won the favour of the people. With bread and circuses. Well, Octavian would feed them like force-fed geese until their livers were ready to burst and he would spill so much blood to entertain them that the games he hosted would never be forgotten.

Octavian himself had always loved gladiatorial contests, but, according to tradition, these vicious fights to the death had only ever been staged as part of the funeral ceremonies for wealthy aristocrats. Caesar had changed all that at the time of his triumphs nearly two years ago when he had staged high-class, hand-to-hand combats complete with severed limbs, pools of blood and spilt intestines in memory of his dead daughter Julia. Well, Octavian would go even further! There would no longer be any need for a funeral, or even a memorial service before people could enjoy the spectacle of death. Octavian would serve them up all the violence they could possibly want, just for entertainment. And he would win praise for his family piety while he did so. If he held the games in honour of his great-uncle Julius, everyone would say what fine respect he was showing for the dead. The irony of the thought made him smile gloatingly . . .

The Ludi Victoriae Caesaris were held over a ten-day period from the twenty-first to the thirtieth of July. Right from the first day Octavian knew that the games were going to be a smash hit. He arrived with suitable pomp and ceremony and took his place in the stands in full view of the crowd. Only a rickety parapet separated him from the sand of the arena fifteen feet below. Dotted around the arena at intervals were the dark mouths of the passages through which the animals and gladiators would come into the ring, while up above rose tier on tier of wooden seats until the final rim stood out dizzily against the blue sky. There were fully fifteen thousand people in those seats, but it was impossible to see them as anything more than a restless, heaving sea of colour. Only those who were closest to him were differentiated into faces and figures. A young mother with a fretfully crying child, a cluster of schoolboys shooting chickpeas at each other with a catapult, a man edging closer to an unattended maiden.

Octavian waved and smiled graciously at all of them, but at that moment there was a loud fanfare of trumpets from the arena. Down below the procession was just beginning. A priest in a white robe came first, leading a garlanded lamb as a sacrificial victim. After him followed a string of other animals with their attendants and a procession of tableaux of the gods. Last of all came the gladiators themselves, decked out in magnificent armour. A great roar went up from the crowd as they saw these heroes emerging from the main entrance to the ring. There were over a hundred pairs of them armed in all four styles. Mirmillones with fish-shaped crests on their helmets, Samnites with oblong shields and short swords, Retiarii with nets and tridents and Thracians with round shields and curved scimitars.

As they paraded round the ring, women screamed with emotion and bombarded them with flowers, and men clapped and whistled. At last they came to a halt in front of Octavian's party and, raising their weapons in salute, gave a mighty shout. The whole arena rang with the sound and at once a deathly hush fell on the crowd. The priest came forward, wound a fold of his toga over his head and flung something into a brazier, which flared up with a sudden light. The pipers struck up a tune to cover any ill-omened noises and the ceremony began. Octavian caught the sweet, choking odour of incense from the fire, then the garlanded lamb was pushed forward to the makeshift altar. It must have sensed what was to come, for it gave a loud bleat and tried to flee, but the priest held it firmly by its woolly coat as he intoned the prayers. A moment later, as if he were a gladiator himself, he held aloft a knife that gleamed in the sunshine, then with a swift stroke, he cut the little creature's throat. It gave a single convulsive leap and fell dying to the ground, its blood spurting out on the sand. There was a murmur of speculation from the tiers of seats as the priest knelt to inspect the omens. With his dripping knife, he laid open the body cavity and then reached inside to hack at the entrails. The liver came away steaming in his hand and he inspected it gravely for ill-omened signs. When he was fully satisfied, he laid it in a silver dish and carried it solemnly across to the little shrine of the god Mars which the attendants had set down in front of Octavian. Octavian stood up, gazed down at the offering and nodded his approval. At this, a full-throated cheer went up from the crowd and the pipers began to play a lively tune. With the casual efficiency of butchers, the priests began to slaughter the other victims.

Octavian leaned forward avidly, enjoying the animals' panic-stricken bleats and the satisfying fountain of blood that spurted forth each time the knife struck home. And it wouldn't only be animals whose blood would be spilt today. Watching people die would be far more thrilling. As if in response to his thought, all the gladiators stepped forward a pace, held up their weapons again and let out a great cry.

'We who are about to die salute you, Caesar!'

He was pleased that they had remembered to address him by his new, adoptive name and smiled kindly upon them. It gave him a little thrill of pleasure to know that at least half of them would be dead in a few hours, while he himself could sit here in safety enjoying the spectacle. He had already laid bets with a book-maker as to who would survive and looked forward keenly to finding out whether his judgement would be right. With their part in the opening festivities over, the gladiators began to file out of the arena for the serious business of getting ready for the slaughter.

It was every bit as entertaining as Octavian had hoped. After the first man thudded into the sand in a welter of blood, he screamed himself hoarse with excite-ment and the whole experience was made even more enthralling by the frenzy around him. The groans of the dying men, the hoots and whistles and roars of the crowd, the smell from the arena all combined to give him the kind of violent uplift that he knew some men experienced in battle. The scenes below flashed before him as vividly as a series of fresco paintings. A Reti-arius with his belly split open and his guts falling out in tangles over his own net, Octavian's chief military adviser Agrippa leaning forward over the parapet, his face suffused and purple with excitement at the sight, another supporter Maecenas further along the stands roaring himself hoarse as two Thracians grappled for a kill.

Even better in some ways was the killing of the animals. Not the sacrificial victims, but the beasts that were sent into the ring against armed men. There was a bear that whimpered like a baby as four gladiators stabbed at it and an elephant that tried to crawl away on its knees because its feet were so badly wounded. And at least a dozen panthers must have been hacked to death by a troupe of Thracians. Some of the terrified creatures voided themselves in their flight till at last the sand was so stained with blood and dung and vomit that an interval had to be called for cleaning up. And it was while this gruesome task was in progress that the most dramatic scene of all took place.

When the surviving gladiators and animals had gone out to rest and refresh themselves for the next bout of slaughter, the cleaners came dancing into the arena. Even this was organized as part of the show. Pipers played jaunty music, while men masked as the Etruscan demon Charun went round burning the bodies with hot irons to test whether they were shamming. Others attired as Mercury, marshal of the dead, piled the corpses on to stretchers, and young boys, in the guise of winged Cupids, were kept busy shovelling away the blood-soaked sand and replacing it with fresh supplies. After the interval there were several more hours of bloodthirsty combat, but at last the finale came in the form of a display by half a dozen men armed only with knives pitted against a similar number of panthers. Amazingly one of the men succeeded in killing a panther before another beast leapt on him and went for his throat. More amazingly still, he managed to stab the second one to death and emerged from beneath its body, uttering guttural cries and streaming with blood. One eye was dangling from its socket, his chest ran scarlet with claw marks and most of the fingers on his right hand had been bitten off. In spite of this, he managed to stagger across to the patch of sand beneath Octavian's dais and plead for his life.

'Mercy, Caesar!' he shouted, raising his mangled arms.

Octavian looked around at the crowd and felt as if he had been caught in a hail burst. All around, a thunderous echo began to spread as thousands of people roared and drummed their feet and howled for the hero's salvation. Smiling graciously, Octavian turned back to the mutilated man, paused for effect and gave him a dramatic thumbs-up.

The crowd went wild. There were cheers, screams, shouts of joy, roars of approval for Octavian's clemency. In that moment as a doctor and two stretcher bearers came running out to snatch the injured gladiator away, Octavian knew he had done what he set out to do. He had the crowd by the short and curlies. What was more, he knew the secret of keeping their support. Spill enough blood to entertain them and they would never desert him. Only one nagging worry troubled him as the parting music was played and the crowds began to disperse to the public latrines to relieve themselves, to their homes to eat dinner and to the taverns and wine shops to get drunk and relive the best moments of the day's slaughter. How was he going to pay for all this?

Cleopatra's first reaction on learning the nature of her illness was fear for her son. Hauling herself up on the couch, she shouted at Olympus although her words came out only as a hoarse croak.

'Get Caesarion out of here! Do you understand me? Take him right away and shut him up in a high tower with only one attendant. Their food can be passed to them through a hatch and nobody, nobody must come near them until this sickness is over. You can look after me, Olympus, and Iras too, if she's willing. Charmion, you still have a living child. Get out of here and don't come back!'

The progress of the disease was swift and deadly. Soon her mouth was swollen and blocked by ulcers, her tongue became hard to move and began to ooze blood. Then the contagion spread into her chest and every breath became a hoarse, laboured torture. Her whole body was gripped by racking pains and she was shaken night and day by constant retching that convulsed her limbs and wore her out with exhaustion.

Ulcers spread throughout her body and she began to feel as though a furnace were blazing inside her. She flung off every covering that Iras put over her and wept and moaned and babbled about flinging herself into cold water. She was afflicted by a parching thirst which could never be quenched no matter how much she drank. As hours passed into days Olympus and Iras held worried conferences in whispers at the foot of her bed. Sometimes it was doubtful whether she heard them but at other times her wide, staring eyes seemed to follow every movement they made.

Her lucid intervals became less and less frequent. She complained of ringing in her ears and cried out that men with swords were coming to kill her. After eight days she was more often delirious than not and frequent convulsions shook her limbs.

Her suffering was echoed in thousands of huts and mansions throughout the land. In most cases by the eighth or ninth day the victim was so exhausted that he fell into a stupor and a cold chill spread insidiously upwards from his feet, eventually bringing a merciful release as the limbs stiffened in death. Yet there were a few whose constitution or will to live was so strong that they survived even this. Those who survived into the ninth day were often carried off by an evil-smelling black flux of the bowels or a purulent flow of blood from the nostrils accompanied by a violent headache. If they managed to live even through this, the disease often made its way into their joints and sinews and left

377

them alive after a fashion, but often blind, impotent or paralysed. Only a minute proportion of those afflicted ever recovered.

On the ninth day, Cleopatra sat up in bed, shrieking that her head was about to burst. It very nearly did. Without warning, a choking stream of evil-smelling blood shot from her nostrils and mouth and she lurched over the side of the bed, vomiting and fighting for breath. Believing that the end had come, Iras bellowed for Olympus. To her surprise, when he arrived, the Queen was still breathing. She had taken no food for nine days and had vomited back most of the water she had swallowed, but sheer obstinacy seemed to keep her alive. Her eyes burned like live coals in the sunken pallor of her face as Iras washed her and settled her back into the pillows.

'I won't give up,' she croaked as her eyelids fluttered shut. 'I'm going to live.'

Iras thought it was mere bravado, but the following morning Cleopatra was still alive and her breath no longer rattled so agonizingly in her throat. Later in the day she woke up and asked about Caesarion before slipping back into a coma-like sleep. The following day she asked for some food. A week later, although shaky and emaciated, she was well enough to sit out on her balcony overlooking the harbour and demand to know what had happened.

It was not a pleasant story. The plague had swept through the drought-ravaged country, killing thousands. Many of the public drinking fountains had been filled with the bodies of victims trying to assuage their raging thirst. Temples of the gods had become charnel houses filled with the corpses of those who had come to pray for mercy. And all around the outskirts of the city, stinking corpses were being hurriedly thrown into mass graves. It was a tragedy for Egypt, but Cleopatra found some bright spots to comfort her.

'Did Caesarion catch the disease?' she demanded, scarcely daring to utter the words. If her son had died, then she would totter back into her bedroom, take an overdose of poppy juice and slip into a merciful oblivion to join him.

Olympus shook his head.

'Not a sign of it. He's perfectly healthy and asking about you every day.'

'And you and Iras are both unscathed? And Charmion?'

Olympus gave a cautious shrug.

'So far, yes, we're all well. There has been one victim you should know about, though.'

'Who?' demanded Cleopatra.

'Your brother husband Ptolemy. He died last night.'

The news barely touched her. She was so thankful to think that her child had been spared that she could spare little pity for her brother. Besides, all her feelings at the moment seemed woolly and remote and not quite real. She shook her head in a dazed fashion. Then another thought struck her.

'That means he won't be able to marry Arsinoë. Well, it's no loss. Write and tell her I'll find her another husband. And ask her to come and see me as soon as the plague has subsided.'

Chapter Twenty

Just before the onset of winter Antony received a letter from Cleopatra, asking him to appoint her sister Arsinoë as ruler of Cyprus 'in accordance with the wishes of Julius Caesar'. Antony gave a snort of contemptuous laughter at the audacity of the request, but then fell to thinking. Although he still smarted every time he remembered his last encounter with Cleopatra, he could see the advantages of the arrangement. Cyprus was of great, strategic importance and it would be valuable for him to have a loyal supporter there, especially now when the empire was being ripped apart by rival generals who fought like packs of snarling wild dogs.

Antony was a worried man. Only a month earlier, he had barely survived an assassination attempt at Suessa Aurunca by his own bodyguard. Fortunately Antony was a light sleeper. He had woken in time to break the neck of one, stab the second and drag the third attacker away in a headlock to be placed under guard. During the subsequent routine torture, the third man had admitted that Octavian had financed the attempt on Antony's life. More worrying still, two of Antony's legions had now gone over to Octavian in response to massive bribes.

Nor was Octavian the only senator ambitious for power. Antony had tried to restore the republic by abolishing the dictatorship and recalling political exiles, like Sextus Pompeius. His only reward had been to see Pompeius establish himself in Sicily and begin intriguing to win control in Rome himself. Two of the chief assassins, Marcus Brutus and Cassius, had fled to the eastern provinces and were now raising armies and seizing the tribute from the area 'in order to defend the republic'. Well, Brutus might be sincere, but Antony was damned certain Cassius was merely lining his own wallet. Antony himself was fed up with the whole bunch of them and wanted only to go off to his province of Gaul and be shot of the mess. Imagine his exasperation then when he learnt that Decimus Brutus, another of the conspirators, had illegally seized Gaul with an army. And now there was this letter from Cleopatra, equally anxious for a slice of the cake! Well, let her have it! Arsinoë could squat in Cyprus, while Antony went off to Gaul and kicked Decimus's arse.

It proved a harder task than he anticipated. Decimus received reinforcements brought by Octavian and Antony, seriously outnumbered, had no course but to retreat. He crossed the Alps in bad weather and by mid-May was enjoying the mild climate at Forum Julii on the south coast of Gaul. He was infuriated to learn there that Octavian had had him declared a public enemy in the senate and sent the senior commander Lepidus with an army to destroy him. When Lepidus arrived, Antony rode out to his camp under a white flag of truce.

'What is this bullshit?' he asked.

Lepidus looked embarrassed.

'The little runt is a lot smarter than he looks,' he admitted. 'He's got half the Senate in his pay and the other half he's blackmailing to support him. I don't want to fight any more than you do, but he was making some nasty threats against my family. You'll have to come to terms with him sooner or later, Antony.'

It was several months before Antony accepted the bitter truth of this statement, although he did manage to persuade Lepidus to cease hostilities. By July Octavian had eight legions under his command and was demanding the consulship. When the Senate refused, he marched on Rome and resistance collapsed. By August he was designated consul for the following year and the Lex Curiata confirming his adoption had been passed. The assassins had also been officially declared outlaws. When Octavian's vastly increased army marched northwards, Antony at last caved in to Lepidus's insistence that he must negotiate with the young man.

It was a raw autumn day with rain dripping dismally from a leaden sky when they met on an island in the middle of the River Lavinius. Antony found it bitterly humiliating to be forced to meet this pimply-faced boy whom he had always despised so thoroughly on terms of equality. Nor was it made any easier by the look of gloating amusement in Octavian's pale blue eyes as Antony was shown into his tent. How could this little creep have the power to control a quarter of Rome's legions? He still looked too weedy to throw a medicine ball across a gymnasium and the hand he extended was as white and frail as a girl's. Only Lepidus managed to smooth over the awkwardness, sitting there watchful and unruffled as if this were no more than a routine meeting of a Senate committee.

If Octavian was embarrassed at coming face to face with a man he had tried so recently to assassinate, he gave no sign of it. After the first brief flash of triumph in his eyes at Antony's entry, he kept his features carefully expressionless. Yet the truth was that he was in the grip of intense excitement. As he huddled into his warm scarlet cloak and watched his own breath rise in frosty puffs on the air, he was aware that he was in the midst of making history. Years ago his great-uncle Julius Caesar had formed the first triumvirate with Pompey and Crassus, a secret agreement to carve up the power and wealth of the Roman empire among three men. Well, very soon when Antony and Lepidus had signed these documents, a second triumvirate would come into being, far more important than the first. This one would have a veneer of legality, but its intent would be exactly the same as that of the first – to divide up the wealth and power of the Roman empire. Of course Octavian did not intend the arrangement to last for long. As soon as possible he wanted the empire in the hands of one man. Himself. Yet for the moment he did not have the resources necessary to confront both Lepidus and Antony while simultaneously fighting Brutus and Cassius in the east. Besides, he knew in his heart that he was no general. While he always enjoyed watching carnage in the arena, the thought of having his own blood shed made him feel physically ill. Yet somehow Brutus and Cassius must be defeated. The solution was obvious – let Antony and Lepidus defeat Caesar's assassins for him! Afterwards he would find a way to render them powerless. In the meantime, for the next few months or years, he needed their support. And if he had to offer them sweeteners to get it, he was grudgingly prepared to do so.

'Sit down,' he invited. 'And I'll give you a broad outline of what I'm suggesting.'

Antony felt a growing sense of misgiving in the pit of his stomach as he listened to the rise and fall of Octavian's clear, girlish voice. Unimaginable as it seemed, the little rat seemed to have an extraordinary grip on the most intricate details of the empire's administration. He even understood those financial details about revenue and expenses which always made Antony's head ache. Antony still smelled trouble, but he had to admit that Octavian's offer was remarkably tempting. In essence what he was proposing seemed to be a triple dictatorship, but a strictly legal one, or so he claimed. All three triumvirs would be appointed *tresviri rei publicae constituendae* for a long term of years, superior to all magistrates, with the power to make laws and nominate magistrates and governors. Each triumvir would be given a province and Antony was exultant to discover that he was being offered Gaul. Gaul! It would give him control of the entire Italian peninsula. More surprisingly still, as an assurance of his good faith, Octavian offered to take Antony's stepdaughter Claudia as his wife and to resign his own consulship in favour of anyone whom Antony cared to nominate. Twice Antony reached out his hand for a pen and then drew back with the uneasy feeling that it was too good to be true.

'Are you sure this is legal?' he asked for the fourth time.

Octavian did not bother to hide his contempt.

'Of course. I've hired the best constitutional lawyers to draft the legislation. Sign here, please.'

Still frowning and shaking his head, Antony signed. At least he was being confirmed in possession of Gaul.

'There's just one other thing,' said Octavian, producing another document. 'Some execution warrants for men who joined the conspiracy against Caesar. There are seventeen on the list.'

Antony looked more unhappy.

'Execution? Is that really necessary?'

Lepidus clicked his tongue impatiently.

'Go on, Antony, sign. There are only seventeen of

them and most of them would have been glad to kill you too, if Marcus Brutus hadn't stopped them. Let's have an end of constantly looking over our shoulders.'

But it wasn't an end. It was merely a beginning. On 28 November, the day after the triumvirate had been given legal powers in Rome, Octavian had the proscription list of condemned criminals read out in the Forum. Antony, as an ex-consul, had felt it his duty to be present. He stood waiting, stamping his feet against the raw, autumn wind and huddling into his toga in a vain attempt to keep out the rain that was trickling down his neck. As he blew on his frozen hands, he wondered whether this was a huge mistake. Seventeen executions! A lot of senators wouldn't like it and there was no denying that it smacked of tyranny. He shot Octavian a look of intense dislike. Little ponce, standing up in purple consular robes that he had done nothing to earn! Other men had to slog through years in the army and waste their talents in minor offices, organizing Rome's sewerage or doling out pay to the legions in some one-horse village in Macedonia, before they got a crack at the consulship. But not Octavian. No! He had shot right to the top of the heap in one leap, the cunning little bastard. Well, go on, thought Antony savagely. Finish your judicial murders, butcher boy. Let's hear who's on your list. I'll bet my eyes that they are seventeen better men than you!

At Octavian's nod, the herald mounted the rostrum, unrolled a scroll of parchment and began to read. The parchment fluttered in a sudden gust of wind, then the herald's voice droned forth, clear and carrying, but as indifferent as if he were calling a roll at a military parade.

'Be it known that the following people are condemned to death as enemies of the state. Anyone who
kills them and brings in their heads as proof of death
will be rewarded with forty drachmas and a share of
the proscribed criminal's estate. The remainder of
their possessions will go to the official treasury of
Rome. Anyone who harbours these people will also be
placed on the list of the proscribed and be subject to
the same fate, whether male or female. The names of
the proscribed are as follows:

CAESAR, LUCIUS.'

Antony almost leapt out of his skin as he heard his
uncle's name. There had been heated debate in that
rain-sodden tent on the island about the inclusion of
Lucius Caesar on the execution list. It was Octavian
who had wanted the old man killed as one of the most
ardent defenders of the republic. Antony had resisted,
even though he had good reason to hate the old misery
guts himself. Hadn't Lucius voted to declare his own
nephew an enemy of the state for pardoning the conspirators? In the end Octavian had given way, or so
Antony thought. And now here was Lucius's name at
the top of the list! A murmur of shock and disapproval
ran round the crowd and there were frowns and horrified stares directed at Antony. Shit! he thought with a
jolt of stunned comprehension. They think I'm responsible for this! He's set me up, the little rat! A wave of
rage surged through him, rich and hot and murderous.
Buffeting his way through the crowd of lictors who
surrounded Octavian, he snatched at a fold of the
young man's robe.

'What the hell do you mean by proscribing my
uncle?' he demanded.

Octavian looked astonished.

'You gave me his name yourself. I asked if there was

386

anyone you particularly wanted put out of the way. You said, "Yes, my uncle." Now you have your wish.'

'You lying little bastard!'

With a roar of rage Antony spread his hands and lunged for Octavian's throat. Instantly half a dozen lictors smashed down on him with the force of a collapsing building. Finding himself immobilized, Antony spat contemptuously in Octavian's face.

With a cold, glittering look the younger man drew out a linen napkin from the folds of his toga and cleansed his cheek. The faint, superior smile never left his lips.

'Always the hero,' he drawled. 'You're a real Hercules aren't you, Antony? But it won't do you any good. I have more supporters now than you do. Lictors, send the ex-consul home. Herald, continue!'

Antony felt himself thrust out of the surging, muttering crowd of onlookers. Rage burned in his throat like molten fire from Vesuvius. There were troops loyal to him scattered throughout that throng. He could give the order and they would do their best to cut Octavian down. But there were also women and children in the crowd and he had no wish to order a bloodbath. Cursing under his breath, he fought his way free. He must go and warn his uncle Lucius.

Just as he was about to dive into one of the alleyways that snaked away from the Forum, a sudden roar of excitement made him look back. The herald had evidently read the name of somebody standing in the crowd. A quick-witted spectator behind the man had immediately whipped out his dagger and stabbed him in the ribs. He was now busy hacking off the head amid cheers and whistles and shouts of approval. As Antony watched, the bounty hunter completed the job and held the dripping object aloft by a tuft of grey hair. Antony recognized the shocked blue eyes, the overhanging front teeth, the small precise chin. It was the senator Publius Sicilius! Like an actor accepting a round of applause from a theatre audience, his murderer threaded his way through the crowd, ran up the stairs of the rostrum and presented the severed head to Octavian with a flourish. Octavian inspected it, grinned broadly and summoned a slave with a purse full of coins as a reward. Suppressing a shudder, Antony turned his back on the sickening spectacle and made off in search of his uncle. Where would this appalling business end?

Although Antony did not know it, months would pass before it ended and thousands of people would be slaughtered. Anyone who had ever crossed Octavian in any way or merely had the misfortune to own a large estate soon found his name on the lists. Rewards were promised to anyone who brought in the head of a proscribed individual and death was threatened for those who harboured them. Rome was plunged into a nightmare of terror.

Fearful prodigies gave warning of the disasters to come. Dogs howled like wolves, wolves ran through the Forum, cattle spoke with human voices, a newborn infant spoke, statues sweated blood, loud voices of men and the clash of arms and echo of horses' hooves were heard where none were seen. The sun wore a hazy mantle, showers of stones dropped from the sky and lightning fell repeatedly upon sacred temples and images. It was as if the gods themselves were showing their displeasure at the hideous cruelty of humankind.

Some took refuge in wells, others in chimneys, others in filthy sewers. People lay crouched in fearful silence in the attic space beneath their roofs as many an old vendetta came home to roost. Some feared their wives and ill-disposed children, others their freedmen and their slaves. Creditors feared debtors and neighbours feared those who coveted their lands. Some died defending themselves against their attackers, others made no resistance and some committed suicide rather than be taken. But the vast majority of those on the lists were hunted down and had their heads hacked off and taken back to be added to the stinking flyblown pile that adorned the Forum. There were a few cases of heroism when friends or relatives risked their lives to save the victims, but when Octavian did the books at the end of the massacre, he was really quite pleased with the result. The proscriptions had brought in billions of drachmas, certainly enough to finance the next stage of his plans. Better still, most people in Rome blamed Antony for the bloodshed.

In the royal palace in Cyprus, which her uncle had occupied until his forced suicide years before, Arsinoë heard with glee the news of the renewed Roman fighting. She could think of nothing more satisfying than to learn that the hated Roman nobles were shedding each other's blood – unless it was to learn that her equally hated sister was dead. Unfortunately Cleopatra seemed to share the supernatural good fortune that had once blessed her lover Julius Caesar. Even bubonic plague had not been enough to kill her. But die she must! Soon, soon Arsinoë would have to take a hand in engineering her sister's death, although not until her own position was stronger.

Sometimes she wondered if she should have accepted Cleopatra's invitation to visit her in Egypt. There might have been opportunities to stab her sister in the neck with a hairpin or slip hemlock into her wine. Regretfully Arsinoë had decided that the risk of premature detection was too great. Not that she cared a fig about dying! Sometimes she felt as if her whole life had no more meaning than that of a donkey harnessed to a millstone and condemned to plod eternally in the same weary, repetitive circle. Death would be an escape, a means of rejoining Vercingetorix, if the stories of the afterlife were true. Or at least a welcome oblivion and an end to grief. Yet before she could die, she must know that Cleopatra had been punished for her cruel betrayal of Arsinoë's hopes. There must be no chance for her sister to escape. Better, then, to wait until Cleopatra was more vulnerable to attack.

Her opportunity was slow in coming, but in the end it arrived. More than a year after Caesar's death, the three legions which Caesar had left in Egypt to protect his mistress and son were given orders to proceed to Laodicea and join Dolabella in his fight against Cassius. When Arsinoë heard of it she immediately saw her chance. Her eyes were glittering with excitement and her voice was hoarse as she summoned Serapion to share the news.

'We'll never have a better opportunity to overthrow her and seize the throne of Egypt!' she said exultantly. 'We must move swiftly.'

'Yes, we must,' agreed Serapion. 'She must be killed and killed soon.'

Arsinoë's eyes burned like those of a holy man in a desert.

'Serapion,' she breathed. 'You won't like what I'm about to ask you, but listen. Please listen.'

'What is it?'

'I want you to bribe Allienus, the commander of the legions who protected Cleopatra in Egypt to change sides and fight for Brutus and Cassius.'

Serapion stared at her, aghast. When he spoke his voice cracked into the silence like the sound of a whip.

'Brutus? You want me to help Brutus? That murderer who oversaw the seizure of Cyprus and the killing of my wife and children?'

She moved towards him, wringing her hands in a placatory gesture.

'I know, I know,' she soothed. 'I hate the thought as much as you do. It's like a knife in my heart to offer help to any Roman general. But consider what's at stake. If Antony wins, you can be sure he'll send those three legions back to Cleopatra at once. Then we'll never succeed in overthrowing her. But if Brutus wins – ' She paused as if she were seeing some inner vision.

'Go on,' urged Serapion grimly.

'We'll demand his promise to make me Queen of Egypt in return for money and ships to fight Antony. And once I'm Queen, I swear by Vercingetorix's ashes, I'll raise an army that will kill every Roman in Egypt.'

As she spoke she raised her hands and eyes to heaven and a shudder of emotion went through her. Serapion watched her with a brooding expression and then slowly dropped his head and nodded.

'Very well,' he growled. 'It goes against the grain to offer Brutus help in anything, but I'll do as you ask.'

Brutus was gratified but not surprised to receive Arsinoë's offer. The liberty of Rome was so important to him that he would have accepted help from any source whatsoever to preserve it. All the same, he permitted himself a small, sour smile at this further evidence of the innate treachery and deceit of the Oriental character. So Arsinoë was prepared to betray her sister just so that she could seize her place on the throne of

Egypt, was she? So much for the ties of family and honour! These easterners simply didn't have any moral integrity. Yet Brutus had no objection to gratifying her vanity for a few brief months at least. Of course, once the triumvirs were convincingly defeated, he would then make Egypt a Roman province and Queen Arsinoë could commit suicide or go and write her memoirs on some Aegean rock just as she pleased!

What really sickened Brutus was the realization that the moral rot had not only corrupted easterners, which one expected, but seemed to be spreading like a loathsome canker in Rome itself. He had been appalled to learn of the proscriptions that had taken place in his native city. When he and Cassius met in Sardis he was unwise enough to say so as they lay reclining on their dining couches one evening.

'Don't you think it's appalling how Antony has massacred so many people in Rome?' demanded Brutus. 'And I always thought he was an honourable fellow too! A brawler and a boozer and a womanizer, of course, with no brains worth mentioning. But decent. Merciful. Well, it shows you how wrong you can be, doesn't it? He must have a heart of stone to kill like that in cold blood just for his own advantage!'

To his amazement Cassius gave a loud guffaw of laughter.

'And who are we to talk?' he retorted genially. 'Didn't we stab Caesar in cold blood just for our own advantage?'

Brutus went hot and cold with shock and indignation.

'No, we did not!' he shouted. 'We did it to protect the liberty of Rome and to defend our fellow citizens from tyranny!'

Cassius belched rudely and reached for the wine jug again.

'Bullshit! You might have done it for that, but I did it because I hated Caesar's guts and because I didn't see why he should be the only one raking in the profits of government. And it was worth it, wasn't it? Look at us now, lying on jewelled couches, feeding off the fat of the land and all thanks to a bit of well-timed murder. If you ask me, Antony's no better or worse than we are. Not that I intend to let him get away with this little power grab. If anyone's going to be absolute master in Rome it's me, not him. And you, of course. Let's drink to it, brother-in-law.'

He made to fill up Brutus's cup but Brutus struck it out of his hand in horror. The red wine spilt all down the front of his tunic, leaving a spreading stain the colour of faded blood. His breath came unsteadily and he was almost crying as he sprang to his feet.

'Curse you, Cassius! You know I intended nothing of the kind. I'll never make myself master of Rome.'

'Then you're a fool,' growled Cassius, who had drunk too much and was already beginning to slur his words. 'But of course we all knew that. Brutus the idealist, Brutus the philosopher, Brutus the defender of the republic, Brutus who's going to make the Golden Age come back to earth. You're so out of touch with reality, it's a wonder you manage to eat and shit like the rest of us.'

Brutus stiffened with rage at Cassius's coarseness and the barely veiled contempt in his small, piggy eyes.

'If you thought that, then why did you ever ask me to join the conspiracy?' he demanded hotly.

Cassius gave him a leering grin, bit the top off

another wine jar and spat out the pieces. He wiped the back of his hand across his mouth, took a long swig of neat wine and then set down the jar.

'Because we wanted it to look respectable,' he replied. 'And you may be a bloody fool, but you are respectable. The only honest man in Rome, some of the senators call you. Who better to knock off Caesar and give us our chance at the profits of empire?'

Brutus's face was working violently and his hands clenched and unclenched at his sides. Was this the truth that he was hearing at last? Was this really what his fellow conspirators had felt and thought when they all swore their solemn oath to liberate the republic from tyranny? Why had he never realized the depth of Cassius's greed and cynicism? If he stayed another minute, he knew he would draw his sword and stab his brother-in-law to the heart. Springing to his feet he gave Cassius a burning look, turned on his heel without speaking and strode from the room. When he reached his own bedchamber, he slammed his fist into the wall and then slumped on to his bed, rubbing his bruised knuckles and grimacing like an ape. Hot tears of anger and self-pity stung his eyes. Was it for this that he had given up his spotless reputation and taken on the hateful name of 'murderer'? So that Cassius could make his fortune and become a tyrant in his turn? Or Octavian or Antony? Or half a hundred others? He had thought he was doing the right thing, that men would admire and love him for it. That later generations would stand in awe before his statues and venerate him as the guardian of the republic. Instead it seemed that even his fellow conspirators sniggered at him behind their hands. He was a failure, a bumbling fool of an idealist, just as Caesar had always said. Even his mother no longer loved him. Perhaps the best thing he could do was simply to end it all ... And then he thought of his wife Porcia, Porcia who had clung to him with tears in her eyes as he had left Rome, Porcia who cared as passionately for the freedom of the republic as he did himself. No! He could not disappoint her so cruelly. He would commit suicide only when there was no hope left ...

Late one night in the palace of Alexandria the unofficial war council – Cleopatra, Iras, Charmion and Olympus – was in emergency session. Lamplight flickered on an array of papyrus maps and documents and several small three-legged tables were littered with empty beer bottles and plates of half-finished food. Suddenly Olympus flung down his writing stylus with an exclamation of impatience.

'I know you want to remain neutral, but I don't think it's practical any longer. This is the second time Cassius has demanded money and ships from you to help fight the triumvirs. Every other eastern monarch has given in to his demands and contributed to his war funds. Why not you?'

'He can't seriously expect me to help the men who assassinated Caesar!' snapped Cleopatra. 'Look at all I lost by Caesar's death.'

'Agreed,' conceded Olympus wearily. 'But if you won't help Cassius and the defenders of the republic, then you've only got one other choice. You must send money and ships to the triumvirs.'

Cleopatra's mouth hardened into a mutinous line. Her dark eyes gazed blindly through the open window at the heaving silver surface of the sea, but she did not see the serene moonlight or the shadows of the palace towers. What she saw was the dead. The mountains of stinking corpses shovelled into open graves, the orphaned children dying of plague or starvation, their skin stretched over their bones like parchment, the flies settling on their gaping mouths. The despair, the indifference, the horror . . . The field workers she had sent out with emergency food and medical teams were slowly turning the tide, but there was so much still to do if the country was ever to recover.

'Why must I?' she cried defiantly. 'Hasn't Egypt suffered enough? It's a neutral country, isn't it? And it's still recovering from famine and plague! Why do we have to be sucked into wars that are none of our business?'

'Because whichever Roman general emerges the victor is going to come and punish you severely once the war is over, if you don't get involved!' put in Iras. 'You have to make a choice and I say it's better to support Mark Antony. At least he'll reward you handsomely if he's victorious.'

Cleopatra stroked her chin and her eyes narrowed in calculation.

'True, but he won't lop my head off if he's victorious without my help. Brutus and Cassius might. From that point of view, perhaps I should support the assassins.'

'That's outrageous!' cried Charmion. 'You wouldn't really let Egyptian sailors and soldiers fight against Mark Antony, would you?'

An odd, flickering smile began to play around the corners of Cleopatra's mouth. She reached for one of the maps lying on the table and studied it closely.

'No-o,' she said slowly. 'I don't think it will be necessary for them actually to fight, but I'm beginning to think that I'll have to make a show of sending them. In fact, I'll even command the fleet myself.'

Charmion's forehead wrinkled in a puzzled frown.

'How can you do that? You know nothing about naval warfare.'

Suddenly the haunted look in Cleopatra's face was replaced by a flash of her old, reckless energy and flamboyance. For a moment she looked almost mischievous.

'I don't need to know anything. Some mysterious instinct tells me that when we near the coast of Greece, we're going to run into terrible squalls and become forced to put back to Egypt in peril of our lives.'

Two weeks later in brilliant autumn sunshine Cleopatra reclined on the poop deck of the leading trireme of her fleet, sipping honeyed wine and playing draughts with Charmion. Raising herself on one elbow, she looked at the nearest vessel, fifty yards off her starboard side. It skimmed across the tranquil cobalt blue of the Mediterranean like a great wide bird with its bronze ram outstretched like a beak, its brilliantly painted eyes looking to either side and its banks of white tipped oars beating as rhythmically as mighty wings. There was no sound apart from the gentle hiss of waves running past the hull, the splash of the oars and the rhythmic beat of the helmsman's drum keeping the time. All around her the rest of the fleet sped effortlessly on its way. Suddenly a half-naked crewman came climbing up from below decks, his suntanned body reeking and glistening with sweat and prostrating himself before her. 'The captain's compliments, my lady, and the coast of Greece is now in sight. Is it time to turn back?'

'Dear me,' said Cleopatra, rising to her feet and pacing across to the railing. Shading her eyes, she looked ahead to the spot where dark blue smudges seemed to float above the mirror-like surface of the sea. 'Yes, I suppose it is. That looks like terrible weather ahead. Much as I hate to disappoint poor Brutus and Cassius, I fear we have no choice but to return to Egypt. Whoever wins this war must do it without my poor assistance.'

CHAPTER TWENTY-ONE

There was a party going on in Antony's mansion. A wild party. And for the first time in over two years Antony felt happy, or at least drunk enough to believe he was. His wife Fulvia was away at her family's villa in the hill town of Tusculum, recuperating after the birth of their second child, and the house had seemed lonely and echoing without her. Not that things had been going so well between them since Caesar's death. While Antony would be the first to admit that Fulvia was twice as smart as he was, he resented the way she kept pushing him to succeed. Deep in his heart, Antony knew he was born to be second, not first. Yet even though it was a relief to have a month of freedom, he missed her. When the front doorbells jangled, he went forward himself to see who was there, hoping it might be one of his army mates, ready to crack a wine jar and tell dirty jokes. But it wasn't a middle-aged soldier who stood outside. It was a beaming, blonde actress with her lips painted scarlet, her breasts popping out of her silk gown and a wine jar tucked under her arm. Around her stood a motley collection of men and women and people who might have been either, holding torches aloft and chattering in high, lisping voices or deep, resonant baritones.

'Volumnia!' exclaimed Antony.

She gave him a coy look beneath fluttering eyelashes.

'May we come in, darling? I know it's frightfully late, but we've been performing *The Rape of Persephone* (I'm Persephone, of course) and there was the most dreary audience. The rest of the cast decided to walk me home and we popped into a wine bar on the way and, well, here we are! Freezing on your doorstep.'

She shivered theatrically as she spoke and Antony's hospitable instincts were instantly stirred. Stepping back a pace, he flung the front door wide open.

'Of course. Come in. There are hot braziers in the triclinium. Slaves, bring wine and food!'

As he watched the group of actors blow out their torches and file inside, Antony felt a momentary pang of misgiving. Fulvia wouldn't like this. But then wasn't he master in his own house? Anyway, he was fed up with everyone disapproving of him. Hadn't he bust a gut trying to keep the peace in Rome only to have most of the Senate denouncing him as a public enemy? They even blamed him for Octavian's proscriptions. Well, stuff them! Stuff all of them! Why shouldn't he have a little harmless fun once in a while?

By midnight the house was in a shambles but Antony was too drunk to care. The Phrygian flute players were performing at top volume, accompanied by a girl with a tambourine, two actors with painted faces had smashed the best Tyrian glassware in a screaming argument about a pretty boy and Volumnia was lying on a couch beside Antony, alternately pouring wine down his throat and acting out *The Rape of Persephone*. Since they were now up to Act Three, the performance was becoming quite steamy. It was at this moment that the triclinium door opened and a gust of icy air filled the room.

'Fulvia!' groaned Antony.

It took her less than thirty heartbeats to clear the room. For a moment Antony had the appalling fantasy that he was watching a Gorgon at work, since everyone present seemed to have turned to stone. Everyone except Fulvia. Picking up a horsewhip which Antony had flung carelessly in a corner after a morning's chariot race, she advanced on the actors and began swinging. The loud cracks echoed through the room like the explosions of falling trees.

'Out!' bellowed Fulvia.

An actor shrieked in a shrill falsetto as the lash made contact with his delicate skin. It was the signal for a general exodus. Even Volumnia thrust her breasts hastily back into her gown, darted Fulvia a nervous glance and fled to the door. There was a momentary check when one of the actors tripped over and fell to the floor, sending a cascade of silver spoons rattling on the mosaic tiles. Other than that, it was a total rout. When nothing was left in the room except the odour of cheap perfume, spilled wine and stale farts, Fulvia advanced on Antony with a grim expression.

'Sweetheart – ' began Antony thickly.

'Save it,' she grunted. 'You're too drunk to talk sense anyway. I'll deal with you in the morning.'

At first light, while Antony was still nursing his aching head, she came into his room and sat down on his bed. The mattress sagged under her weight.

'Look, I'm sorry – ' began Antony.

'Sorry isn't good enough,' snapped Fulvia.

'It was only a harmless drink with a few friends.'

'Friends? You call those friends? They're nothing but idlers and parasites who'll ruin you if you let them!'

Antony felt sweat break out on his forehead. Shit! Why had she chosen that moment to come home? How unlucky could a man be?

'I didn't think you'd ever know,' he mumbled stupidly. 'I thought you were staying at Tusculum.'

'Well, I received a note yesterday saying that I was urgently needed at home. It's Octavian's doing, of course.'

'Octavian?' echoed Antony in bewilderment. 'How do you know?'

'The little pansy who was stealing the spoons confessed the truth when I threatened to have him branded with a hot iron for theft. They were bribed by one of Octavian's slaves to come here and have a riotous party.'

Antony blinked.

'Bribed? All of them? Even Volumnia?'

'Yes, even your precious Volumnia! Although, to do her justice, she seemed to give value for money.'

Antony flinched at her sarcasm. The news that Volumnia had been paid to try and seduce him sent an uncomfortable pang of humiliation through him. But why? What was the point of it all?

'Why would Octavian do a thing like that?' he blurted out.

'To discredit you with the respectable citizens!' exclaimed Fulvia in exasperation. 'No doubt he'll spread the rumour that you paid for this little bash out of the money you confiscated from victims of the proscriptions. And he probably thought that if I caught you at it, I'd divorce you. Octavian knows you're politically useless without me to advise you.'

Antony opened his mouth to protest at this assessment of his capabilities and then hung his head. The evening which had seemed so much fun was suddenly in ruins.

'You're right, Fulvia,' he muttered unhappily. 'I'm just a useless oaf. Good for nothing!'

Suddenly her brisk, practical voice was almost caressing. She laid one meaty hand on his arm and squeezed it.

'That's not true,' she retorted. 'You're a brave soldier at any rate, and that will count for a lot in the next few months. Brutus and Cassius must be crushed decisively and warfare is one area where you outshine Octavian completely. There's going to be a huge military confrontation in the east and I want you to emerge the hero of it. Do it for me, Antony. Do it for Rome.'

Fulvia's words echoed in Antony's head a month later as he made his way through Greece with a large army. She was right. Soldiering was one thing that came naturally to him and, as he watched Octavian's military ineptitude at close quarters, his own confidence began to grow. Nominally they were joint commanders of the army, but it was soon clear that Octavian didn't know one end of a sword from the other and was a physical coward into the bargain. Antony's initial incredulity and contempt were soon joined by a growing feeling of elation. He vowed that as soon as Brutus and Cassius could be brought to battle, he would crush them utterly. Yet he would treat their followers mercifully. What better way could there be of restoring his own tarnished reputation in Rome? He would not only be a hero, but everyone would see that he was a decent, humane person too.

His opportunity came swiftly. When he learnt that Brutus and Cassius had pitched their camp west of Philippi, Antony attacked. Cassius was routed and his camp plundered. Despairing, he committed suicide. A few days later, while Octavian skulked in his tent and complained of feeling ill, Antony repeated his success and vanquished Brutus. Once the battle was finally over, he summoned his senior centurions. Standing in the freezing autumn rain with his scarlet cloak splashed with mud, he repeated the orders he had given that morning.

'Remember, these are your fellow Romans. Any who surrender are to be fed and sheltered and have their wounds bound up. Provided they swear an oath not to fight me again, they are to be sent back to Rome as free men with their possessions intact. And that's true for Brutus as well. Tell him I'll spare his life if he surrenders.'

A young legionary came thrusting forward through the group of listeners and saluted Antony.

'It's too late for that, sir. We've just found his body. He committed suicide.'

To the young soldier's surprise, Antony groaned as if he had just learned of the death of a relative.

'I want to see for myself,' he ordered.

'Yes, sir. Follow me.'

It was a pathetic sight. They had turned him on his back and he lay with his eyes wide open, his features convulsed in agony and his chill, stiff fingers still clutching the sword with which he had torn open his belly. A silvery mass of intestines hung from his abdomen and his leather uniform was stained with mud and blood. Antony winced. These fucking wars! He had never liked Brutus much, finding him too cold and superior and disapproving, but at least he had been an honourable man. With a twinge of sadness and gratitude Antony remembered how Brutus had stopped the conspirators from killing him after Caesar's death. He would gladly have returned the favour. As it was, all he could do was ensure that his opponent received an honourable burial. Unfastening his magnificent scarlet cloak, he flung it over the corpse, hiding the gruesome spectacle.

'Wrap him properly in that, and have the body burned and the ashes sent to his mother,' he ordered a nearby centurion. 'Charge the expenses to me.'

'But, sir, that cloak must be worth ten thousand sesterces!' protested the officer. 'Wouldn't it be better to –'

'Do as I tell you!' snapped Antony.

Later, when he had visited the wounded from both sides, he went to Brutus's camp to sort out his possessions. Perhaps they would give some comfort to his wife and mother. They certainly brought no comfort to Antony. One of the first things he found was a letter addressed to Brutus and signed by Cleopatra. In it, she promised to bring a fleet to aid him in defeating the triumvirs. Antony had no idea of what had happened to her fleet, but a curious pain gripped him at the thought of her treachery. Bitch. Bitch! If she had to help anyone in this war, shouldn't it have been him? He had a good mind to take Egypt away from her as punishment. Even as the thought flashed across his mind, it was accompanied by the dizzying realization that he had the power to do exactly that if he chose. In fact, he had the power to do anything he liked! With Brutus and Cassius defeated, the triumvirs now controlled the Roman empire. And after today's victory, there could be no doubt as to who was the chief triumvir. If Cleopatra wanted to keep her throne, she would have to crawl to him for it, as she had once crawled to Caesar.

The thought sent a jolt of exhilaration through him that was dangerously close to sexual excitement. He would put her on trial, make her beg for anything he chose to give her! It would be the perfect revenge for the way she had treated him. Seizing a sheet of papyrus, a quill and a pot of lampblack, he began to write, almost stabbing through the papyrus in his urgency. The letter was terse and bitter. It commanded Cleopatra on pain of her life to journey to Tarsus (yes,

Tarsus, that would be his next logical stopping place if he was to take an inventory of the eastern provinces' finances!) and appear before the tribunal of Mark Antony, the Triumvir. There she must defend herself on the charge that she had given support to the enemies of Rome . . .

It was a dismal winter's day when Octavian landed at Brundisium and he had never been so glad in his life to get off a ship. As usual he had been seasick throughout the entire crossing and now, in addition to the nausea he had experienced, he had a strong suspicion that one of his bad sore throats was coming on. With an irritable expression he gripped the ship's railing and watched impatiently as the town came into view. It was a depressing sight. Although the persistent rain had now stopped, the sky was full of grey lowering clouds and strong gusts of wind from the east were stirring up the waves, and hurling drifts of spume in his face. Overhead the incessant shrieking of seagulls was almost deafening and Octavian was heartily sick of the smells of salt air and damp wool that clung about him. His hands, which had been red and stinging from the wind, were now beginning to turn cold and pale and he knew from experience that they would soon be as useless as lumps of ice. All he wanted was a good fire, a warm bed, and perhaps a bowl of beef broth. At moments like this he almost wished he had refused his legacy and remained a private citizen. Almost, but not quite. Suddenly a preposterous vehicle covered in gold and scarlet leather caught his attention on the docks and his spirits revived magically. Only one person could own such a dreadfully flamboyant carriage – Cilnius Maecenas.

The moment Octavian stepped ashore, Maecenas

came forward to embrace him. There was a cloud of subtle perfume, the jangle of gold bracelets, the slithery caress of a silk robe and then the warm imprint of Maecenas's lips on his. Octavian smiled as Maecenas's greetings tripped forth in a lisping flow.

'Darling, such terrible weather to travel! I've been vewy worried about you. I suppose you think it's silly of me but I've missed you dreadfully. Now do let me take you away in my carriage at once. I've a villa not far from here where we can stay overnight.'

As he said this, Maecenas let his hands linger seductively for a moment on the curve of Octavian's buttocks. If he had not felt so ill, Octavian would have been gratified. He and Maecenas had been lovers in the past, and he was pleased to find that the Etruscan noble obviously wanted the connection to continue. Not .that it would have mattered if he hadn't, for Maecenas could still be immensely useful to him. In spite of the contempt with which he was regarded by the more austere members of the Roman nobility, the Etruscan was a shrewd administrator and a capable diplomat. Octavian intended to make full use of his talents in the difficult times ahead, although for the moment all he wanted from Maecenas was a roof over his head and some hot honeyed wine for his sore throat.

'Thank you for coming to meet me,' he said. 'But I don't want to travel in anything so ostentatious as that coach. It might attract highway robbers. We'll take one of the military vehicles instead.'

With a pout and a brief roll of his eyes, Maecenas allowed himself to be ushered into a plain carriage with grey paintwork and brown leather curtains. All the same, he had his revenge an hour later, when after nine miles of jolting along a rough country road, the left front wheel suddenly came off and the vehicle plunged sharply into a ditch.

'Zoe kai psyche, my life and my soul!' exclaimed Maecenas, clutching at Octavian to prevent him pitching through the window. 'I knew we should have brought my carriage. Now here we are, stuck in the middle of nowhere and I dare say there'll be nobody to help us. It's vewy provoking.'

As he spoke, Maecenas opened the door and climbed gingerly out. To their surprise they found that they were not alone in the ditch. Apart from the coachman who was now trying to soothe the frightened horses, there was a small group of peasants in a huddle beneath the shelter of the bank. Octavian wrinkled his nose fastidiously as the stale smell of rancid sweat and dirty rags assaulted him.

'Go and ask those wretches if they can help,' he instructed Maecenas.

With a sigh, Maecenas lifted the hem of his cloak and picked his way along the muddy ditch. As he did so, a dreadful bellowing groan issued from the cluster of figures. Maecenas froze in mid step.

'What in the world is going on here?' he demanded.

At the sound of his voice one of the figures, who seemed to be little more than a bundle of shapeless rags topped by a brown woollen cloak with a hood, detached himself from the group and came slithering across the muddy grass to pitch himself at Maecenas's feet and clasp his knees.

'Oh, sir, help us, for the love of all the gods!' he begged. 'It's my daughter. Gone into labour, she has, by the side of the road, and we've not so much as a hut to call our own since those soldiers drove us out of our farm. Triumvirs' orders they said, a curse on them! And here's my poor lass, like to die and the child with her if we don't get warmth and shelter for them. We've been on the road over a month now, and cruel weather it's been, sir.'

'W-well, what do you want me to do?' stammered Maecenas.

'If we could lift her inside your coach to give birth, she'd have a chance of living, her and the baby. I'm sorry to ask it, but you're not going nowhere, are you? Not with that broken wheel.'

At a loss to know what to do, Maecenas looked at his companion for guidance. Octavian's eyes widened in outrage. What, let some beggar woman into his carriage to deposit blood and filth and worse all over the cushions and leave it unfit for his own use? And all for the sake of some peasant brat who would only turn to brigandage or be one more useless mouth for the Roman state to feed even if he did live? He was about to utter a disdainful refusal when he caught the quick warning twitch of Maecenas's eyebrows and saw that another peasant had moved from the group surrounding the woman and was coming towards them. Even with his cheeks hollow with hunger, he was a great menacing brute, twice Octavian's size, and he carried a nasty looking wooden staff in his right hand. Octavian looked at his fierce eyes, his unshaven chin and thick, dangerous fingers and decided to be charitable.

'Of course,' he said in a voice full of concern. 'Poor girl, you must carry her there at once.'

As it turned out, his charity was unnecessary. At that moment, the young woman uttered another one of her bellowing groans, but this time it was cut off in mid cry by an odd, gurgling gasp. The old woman beside her let out a shriek of dismay, seized her by the shoulders and began to shake her violently.

'Don't die, don't die!' she howled. 'Oh, Rufia, you

must hang on. Here's a gentleman come to help us. He'll save you, you and the baby!'

But it was too late. Octavian took a step forward and saw with fascinated horror that the girl in labour must have taken some kind of fit. Her face was congealed and purple and her lips were drawn back from her teeth in a kind of snarl, as if she were still fighting for breath, but no more sound issued from her mouth, and her eyes were already growing dull and glazed. Apart from the grotesquely swollen mound of her belly, her body was stick thin with limbs that were little more than skin and bone. Her knees were drawn up and splayed apart, and between the gaping thighs Octavian could just see the glistening dark crown of the baby's head. A sudden interesting thought occurred to him. Once in the arena, he had been amused and startled to see a pregnant sow slashed by a gladiator drop a live piglet on the sand which had run away, grunting. He wondered whether the same thing was possible with a human being. It would be very entertaining to slash the girl's belly open and see whether it was possible to get the baby out alive.

Drawing a dagger from the sheath at his belt, he turned to the old man.

'Do you want me to cut the baby out?' he asked with barely concealed excitement. 'It might still be living.'

He was already hunching forward over the girl's still warm body when he heard a low animal growl and the younger man seized his wrist in a grip that almost crushed his bones.

'No!' he hissed. 'Maybe you mean well, sir, and maybe you don't, but my wife and child have suffered enough. We've no milk for the baby, even if you could bring it out alive, and I won't see her butchered like a slab of meat. Let them rest together, now she's dead.'

The young peasant's words seemed to act like a stage manager's signal upon a chorus line. Suddenly the old woman began to shriek and wail. Pulling the girl's dress decently down over her legs, she stretched the body out flat, scooped three handfuls of mud from the bank and dropped them on it as a token of ritual burial and then flung herself down on her dead daughter, raking her own cheeks with her fingernails and ululating loudly. The younger man covered his face with his hands and the older one simply began to cry. Harsh, racking sobs that made tears run down his grey stubbly cheeks and snot drip from the end of his bulbous nose. Octavian stepped back a pace, lifted a folded napkin to his face to block out the rancid smell of the mourners and exchanged a weary, distasteful glance with Maecenas. It was the younger peasant who spoke first.

'I'd like to kill those fucking triumvirs for this!' he said thickly, clenching and unclenching his hands around his staff. 'If they hadn't put us off our farm to resettle their damn veterans, she'd still be alive.'

Even at such a moment Octavian could not resist the opportunity for spite.

'It's not all the triumvirs you should blame,' he said. 'Only Mark Antony. I know for a fact that Octavian did not want anyone dispossessed, but Antony overruled him.'

'Well, he'll soon find the whole of Italy's turned against him, the murdering bastard,' said the peasant, spitting on the ground. 'He's the one that ought to die.'

Cleopatra was stunned and elated to hear of Mark Antony's victory against Brutus at Philippi and she was even more pleased when she learned that he was staying on in the eastern provinces. Who would have thought that of all the warring generals around the Mediterranean he would have emerged supremely victorious? He had always had raw courage, nobody had ever denied that, but she had not believed he would be shrewd enough to survive so long! Of course his wife Fulvia might have been acting as his adviser. Certainly Antony seemed to be doing his best to honour her in every possible way. There were reports that he had renamed the city of Eumenia in Phrygia 'Fulvia' and was issuing coins with his wife's portrait on them. Well, at least she had not accompanied him into Asia and that meant that if Cleopatra played her own pieces cleverly she might soon win a very strong influence over Antony herself. For even if he had given a dazzling display of generalship at Philippi, there were some things about Antony that clearly still had not changed. Secret reports from her spies confirmed that he was drinking and whoring again and that a whole horde of Asiatic flute players and dancers and actresses were wielding influence over his policies. How much better if he were to fall under Cleopatra's influence again! She could safeguard Egypt's independence, perhaps even play on his conscience and win back some of the other Ptolemaic territories previously seized by Rome . . .

When Antony's furious letter reproaching her for her treachery with Brutus arrived, Cleopatra simply read it, smiled secretively to herself and did nothing. Let him cool his heels for a while – his anger would soon give way to uncertainty and then begging. Only when she had received ten letters, ranging in tone from threatening through apoplectic to puzzled and pleading, did she finally give way and promise to obey his summons. But she had no intention of slinking into

Tarsus like a criminal begging for a remittance of sentence. No. Her arrival must provide the most magnificent spectacle the city had ever witnessed.

On a spring morning she came sailing up the River Cydnus in a barge with a poop made of beaten gold, its purple sails billowing in the wind. The oars were made of silver and dipped in time to the music of flutes and pipes and lyres. So heady was the perfume of sandalwood and myrrh aboard the ship that it wafted inland to the watchers on the river banks. Cleopatra herself reclined beneath a canopy of gold, wearing the costume of Venus as depicted in famous paintings throughout the eastern cities. On either side of her stood curly-haired boys, dressed as Cupids, who cooled her with fans. Instead of being sailed by a crew, the barge was tended by the most beautiful of her waiting women, dressed as Nereids and Graces. A roar of excitement echoed along the river banks so that the crowds in the city left the market place in droves to find out what was happening.

Among the watchers was a man called Leon, a Macedonian aristocrat from Alexandria whose father had been killed fighting Caesar in Egypt, whose two older brothers had been sold into slavery for their part in the same war and whose estates had been confiscated by Cleopatra. Orphaned at fourteen, Leon had survived by apprenticing himself to a sword maker in Alexandria. He had learned skills which would be of great value to him in his new profession as hired assassin. Arsinoë had sent him here to kill her sister and he meant to succeed or die in the attempt.

He ground his teeth in frustration as he realized that the gold canopy above Cleopatra's head obscured the view of her from any distance. At first he had hoped to sneak into one of the warehouses overlooking the river with a bow and arrows concealed under his cloak and shoot her as she sailed past, but now he saw that that was impossible. It would have to be a close-up job, done with a knife, and that meant that his own risk of capture was enormously increased. All the same, it would be worth it if only he could find a way of getting close enough to her.

Antony had been sitting in state on his tribunal in the market place awaiting Cleopatra and enjoying the prospect of seeing her humbled before him. In the past, they had only ever met in the most ramshackle of settings. That fisherman's cottage in Rhakotis or the broken-down apartment in the Subura. Now it gave him a little thrill of pride and anticipation to see how she would react at seeing him in the glorious purple regalia of a Roman governor, the dispenser of justice. He squinted up at the sun blazing overhead and sighed. The only trouble was that all this proconsular regalia was damned hot and uncomfortable and Antony had had very little sleep last night. A huge yawn caught him unawares, almost cracking his jaw and his eyelids drooped, fluttered open and then closed again ... He awoke with a start to find the market place emptied of people and himself quite alone on the tribunal. Rising to his feet, he looked around with a baffled frown and then approached a lone beggar who was counting her meagre takings in a corner and packing up for the day.

'Where is everyone?' asked Antony.

She spat contemptuously on the ground.

'Gone to see that there Queen of Egypt down on the river. I don't know why I bothered getting dressed and coming out today. Fair makes you sick.'

Antony smiled wryly as he watched the woman disappear down an alleyway. Her words woke an answering echo in his own heart. He felt like shouting after her, 'Me too!', but then the funny side of it struck him. A wry grin began to spread over his face as he scratched his beard reflectively.

'The bitch,' he muttered admiringly. 'Not even in the city half an hour and she's already upstaged me.'

He could have sent soldiers to drag the Egyptian Queen before his tribunal, but he was too good-natured for that and, in any case, had no desire to appear ridiculous. Instead he wrote her a note, inviting her to dine with him, but was foiled again when she sent back a curly-haired slave boy insisting that he have dinner with her aboard the royal barge and bring any friends he chose. Feeling as if he had surrendered an important tactical advantage to a wily enemy, Antony swore and muttered, but accepted.

The royal barge was magnificent beyond description. As Antony was rowed out towards it over the dark waters of the river he saw that every inch of the vessel was ablaze with lights and a closer inspection only left him more dazzled. He was piped aboard by a dozen handsome boys dressed as Cupids and then led down a companion way with a solid gold stair rail to the banqueting hall below. As he entered the room a heady fragrance enveloped him and he saw that the floor was ankle-deep in rose petals. Jewelled dining couches padded with soft purple cushions were arranged in the form of three sides of a square and overhead there was a stunning display of lights. Lights arranged in squares and circles and triangles; so many lights that the room was dazzling with their radiance and oppressive with their heat. As he paused, drinking in all these details, a gold-clad figure at the far end of the room uttered a joyful cry and came hurrying to meet him.

'Antony!' exclaimed Cleopatra, flinging herself into his arms and kissing him warmly on the lips.

He was taken aback by the artless expression of delight on her face. There was no sign of guilt in her features, just a simple pleasure at the sight of him. For an instant he held her in his arms and felt a twinge of nostalgia at the firm pressure of her body, the scent of her hair, the softness of her skin. Then he stepped back a pace and looked down at her sternly, resenting the way she offered no explanation for her treachery but seemed to assume that all was well between them.

Cleopatra, glancing up at him through the thicket of her eyelashes, had a shrewd idea of what was passing in his mind. She had always been able to handle Antony, and she did not expect things to be any different now. It was over three years since she had seen him last but he seemed very little altered. A few more silver hairs in his beard, a deeper etching of the fine lines around the corner of his eyes and perhaps a new seriousness and firmness of purpose in the hard line of his mouth. But deep down he was probably still good natured, generous and gullible. She was gambling on that. Still, it would not do to show her hand too soon. Smiling serenely at him as if she were simply a hostess at any dinner party, she looked around with mild interest at the men who accompanied him.

'Won't you introduce me to your friends?'

Immediately Antony felt at a disadvantage. He should have come surrounded by Roman officers to lend dignity and authority to his presence. Instead he had invited the two men who had happened to be playing dice with him at the moment her messenger had arrived. Now he introduced them in a gruff tone, as if challenging her to find fault with his love of low company.

'This is Xanthus, a very fine flute player, and this is Herod, the new tetrarch of Galilee.'

Her eyebrows rose slightly but she was as courteous as if they were both consuls.

'You're very welcome, gentlemen. Do come and have a drink.'

As they took their places on dining couches, she scrutinized them sharply, trying to assess their likely influence over Antony. Xanthus she mentally dismissed at once. The broken veins around his nose, the incipient wine gut and the ostentatious finger rings proclaimed him to be another of the parasites who perpetually hung around Antony, flattering him and wasting his resources. It was unlikely that he was of any importance. Herod was another matter. Young, no more than thirty years old, she guessed, he looked tough, intelligent and completely ruthless. If he was acting as one of Antony's advisers, it would be worthwhile getting to know him and picking his brains. He was as tall as Antony but less bulkily built and unusually handsome in a negligent way. He had a cap of dark, close-cropped curls, olive skin, a beaky nose, liquid brown eyes and the whitest teeth she had ever seen. His tunic was of good quality, but faded from repeated washing. Ambitious, poor and dangerous, she summed up. At that moment he looked up and their eyes met. Herod gave her a faint, mocking smile and a thrill of unexpected attraction tingled through her. Then she realized that Antony was talking again.

'Why did you promise a fleet to Brutus?' he demanded belligerently.

'Hush,' she urged soothingly, seizing his arm and patting it. 'I've got guests, we'll talk about it later.'

She flashed him a conspiratorial smile and he seethed inwardly as he recognized her strategy. He had been a fool to come here. Now he would have to cool his heels throughout dinner while she joked and chattered and flirted with the other guests. She would be the one in control of the situation, not him. And she was revelling in it, the little slut! Nor was she the only one enjoying it – he didn't like the way Herod was looking at her one bit. Antony scowled fiercely at the younger man and was answered only with a lifted eyebrow and a sly sideways glance at the Queen. It was the universal male invitation to share the fantasy of undressing a beautiful woman, but Antony felt as outraged as if he had caught some young bastard feeling up his wife. Didn't Herod realize Cleopatra was his? Then suddenly the cold shock of reality slapped him in the face. She wasn't, was she? He had no claim on her. Just because they had been lovers in the past, it did not mean that no other man would ever share her bed again. It was quite possible that after Antony went home tonight, Herod would be invited to stay for a drink and end up spending the night. It was probable even, knowing Cleopatra. She had never been restrained by any ideas of womanly virtue. She did exactly as she wanted, the bitch! The thought made him squirm as if he were lying on a bed of hot coals. He couldn't bear to think of Herod touching her. In fact he hated to think of anyone but himself laying hands on her nakedness. At that moment, while he was deep in these disturbing thoughts, Cleopatra turned and laid her hand on his arm.

'What do you think, Antony?' she demanded.

'About what?' He had no idea what they had been discussing, no idea of anything except that her warm fingers were holding his bare arm, that her dark eyes were raised mischievously to his, that he wanted to screw her senseless.

'We were talking about virtue and women. In particular we were discussing Aristotle's idea that women are a naturally occurring deformity, incapable of true virtue because of their innate imperfection. What do you think? Is there such a thing as a virtuous woman?'

He looked deep into her unfathomable eyes and had a wild fancy that he heard the singing of Sirens and the crash of waves boiling over pitiless rocks. Something gripped him deep inside, a ravenous, urgent need that threatened to devour him. Upending his cup, he tossed off his wine in a single gulp and felt grateful for the surge of heat which it sent through his veins. In that moment he felt a sense of danger more potent than he had ever felt when going into battle. He knew he should get up, leave, burst free into the open air while there was still time, and never, ever set eyes on this woman again. But his head swam with the scent of roses and the heat from the lamps, and she was still there, still hypnotizing him with her gaze. He wiped his mouth with the back of his hand.

'No,' he growled. 'I don't believe there's any such thing as a virtuous woman.'

'Oh cruel!' she cried with a gasp of laughter. 'What a traitor you are, Antony. I had counted on you to come to my aid, but you men always stick together. Still, if there's no such thing as a virtuous woman that also means that women can never do anything wrong, doesn't it?'

He flashed her a baffled frown.

'How's that?'

'Well, obviously we're not responsible for our own actions,' cooed Cleopatra. 'If we do wrong, it's just because of our innate imperfection, so it's no true wrong at all. Which means that you shouldn't blame me, Mark Antony, no matter what I do. I simply can't help myself.'

As she finished speaking, she touched the tip of her pink tongue against the back of her top front teeth. Antony found the gesture maddening, a blatant sexual challenge that tipped him over the edge of common sense. The thought of the fleet she had promised Brutus made him burn as if a gadfly had stung him. For an instant he was unsure which would be more gratifying – to have her over his knee or flat on her back beneath him, begging for mercy. Or both. Rising to his feet, he caught her roughly by the wrist and hauled her upright.

'It's time we withdrew somewhere private to discuss your conduct in the civil war, my lady,' he rasped.

She flinched in mock alarm.

'My guests – ' she began.

'Stuff the guests! You're coming with me. They can all get drunk while they wait for us.'

Out in the passageway he rammed her up against a panelled wall and kissed her so violently that she whimpered in protest. But in fact she was revelling in every detail of his arousal. The way that his powerful, muscular body was blocking all chance of escape, the hot demanding urgency of his lips, the heaving passage of his breath, the bruising force with which he pinioned her against the carved cedar. She knew she had done exactly what she had set out to do. She had goaded him into a frenzy of rage, passionate desire, jealousy, the urge to punish and possess. Yet once his driving need for her had been spent, she knew also that his anger would be transmuted into tenderness and a desire to please her. She would not only be forgiven, she would be rewarded. Antony would want to give her things.

With a thrill of triumph, she flickered her tongue between his lips and licked the roof of his mouth. He groaned softly and hauled her against him so hard that she could feel the unmistakable thrust of his swollen organ through his woollen tunic. Reaching down, she rubbed it teasingly. His hand closed over hers.

'Where's your cabin?' he demanded hoarsely.

'Come,' she breathed into his ear.

Here, too, the floor was ankle-deep in rose petals and there were soft lights burning. The embroidered bed covers were turned back and there were a wine jug and drinking cups on the bedside table, as if she had been expecting company. Yet Antony barely noticed these details in his impatience to possess her.

The moment the door was shut, he unfastened her shoulder brooches and let her silk gown slither to the floor. Beneath it she was naked and her body was just as he remembered it with the high, full breasts, the small waist, the curving hips and the silken triangle of black hair at the junction of her thighs. He dragged her against him and kissed her again, thrusting his tongue half way down her throat. She felt fragile and boneless in his arms, her frame as light as a bird's, but the scent of her hair, the warm yielding texture of her skin maddened him with desire. He wanted her, needed her, craved her as he had never wanted another woman in his life. Suddenly he felt a savage urge to engulf her and possess her, to plough her like a furrow of fertile earth and spill his seed inside her. With a rough impatient growl he seized her in his arms and flung her on to the bed. Then his huge fingers fumbled hastily with his toga and tunic. The heavy, draping material caught about his neck, trapping him momentarily in a hot, clumsy tent of fabric. A moment later he had torn it free. The tunic went next. Then suddenly the warm air was fanning his naked skin and he was poised above her with his cock so hot and rigid that it felt ready to explode.

He looked down at her and saw her watching with a mysterious expression, half mocking, half wistful. He couldn't tell what she was thinking, but it didn't matter. He knew what he was thinking, that she was his. His. His.

He was tempted simply to part her legs and take her violently. Yet even now, when he was furious with her, he wanted her to share the pleasure. He wanted her to gasp and writhe and cling to him, uttering fractured cries and shuddering under his touch. With a gesture that was almost vindictive, he tore the gold net away from her hair so that it tumbled loose about her shoulders and began to kiss her.

His kisses were warm, urgent, deeply stirring. They fluttered over her soft eyelids and down the curve of her cheek. Then his tongue probed her left ear, making her shudder as a tingle of pure delight went through her. She caught her breath, feeling a wave of primitive excitement at the smell and touch and sight of him. He had bathed and trimmed his beard before coming, but the citron scent on his skin only masked the deeper, wilder odour. The indefinable tang, like seaweed or leather which always clung about him in their most intimate moments. His arm was lying across her, trapping her, and she revelled in its weight and hardness. His skin felt like oiled silk, but beneath it she could feel his muscles bunch and harden, as massive as a ship's cables. As his head moved down over her naked shoulder, his beard tickled her skin and she muffled a soft gurgle of laughter. Then his mouth found her breast and she no longer felt any urge to laugh. He tugged her nipple between his lips and began to suck it teasingly. The warm, moist movement of his tongue, the provocative pressure of his teeth, sent answering ripples of sensation thrilling through her groin. With a low gasp, she buried her hands in his curly hair and caught him convulsively against her, as if begging him to continue.

He was only too happy to oblige her. He repeated the same exquisite torture on her other breast and then began to lick her all over. Long, moist, abrasive caresses that made her squirm and giggle and cry out in protest, but that also brought her more and more surely to the edge of madness. At last, when she was clenched and shuddering against him, groaning disjointedly, her breath coming in shallow snatches, he abandoned all play and drove into her.

Her body felt warm and slick and deeply enfolding. He could not hold back a groan of satisfaction at the joy of thrusting so hard up inside her. And there was no mistaking her answering hunger for him. She clung to him frantically, winding her legs around his waist, arching her back and gasping rhythmically as he pounded away at her. It seemed to go on for hours as they grappled and tumbled and sweated in the urgent need to obliterate all barriers and fuse together. But at last he saw the signs of her climax mounting in her face. Her eyes went blank and opaque, her head began to thrash from side to side, her cheeks flushed and suddenly she caught her lower lip in her teeth and uttered a long, strangled moan. Feeling her whole body clench convulsively beneath him, Antony experienced a renewed thrust of vigour and arousal. Crouching over her as if he were urging a skittish mare at a gallop down the final fifty metres of a race track, he muttered encouragingly to her.

'Yes. Yes! Come on, sweetheart. That's my lovely

girl. Oh, forget the slaves! Open your mouth and scream if you want to. Oh, by all the gods . . . You – little – beauty! You – '

His last words were lost in the deep-throated growl of sheer animal enjoyment as he felt his whole body go into spasm and the fruit of his lust explode inside her in a blind, warm end. Gasping and shuddering for breath, he collapsed on top of her, burying his face in her hair and holding her against him.

In the curtained alcove on the far side of the state-room, the assassin Leon held his breath and waited. Perhaps he could have killed them both while they were at it, but Antony was a formidable antagonist and there had seemed too much risk of failure. No. Better to wait. Soon Antony would either fall asleep or leave and then he would have his chance to take out that murdering bitch of a Queen. Half suffocated with terror and excitement now that the moment was so near, he tested the blade of his dagger on his thumb and waited. Before long he heard whispers and a giggle, then a burst of discussion. Something about a fleet.

'Only a hoax, Antony . . . never had any intention . . . helping Brutus.'

' – help me, though, did you?'

'Going to . . . another fleet ready to send . . . too quick for me . . . already victorious . . . so proud of you, Antony.'

There were more murmurs, the creaking of the bed, the sound of kissing. Oh, by all the gods! They weren't going to do it again, were they? Then Leon's luck changed. Through a thin spot in the fabric he saw the blurred shape of Antony rising to his feet.

'I need to take a pee,' announced the Roman general.

'There's a chamber pot under the bed,' she said. 'You can use that.'

Antony looked shocked. He might be coarse and vulgar with his soldiers, but he certainly wasn't going to relieve himself in front of a woman.

'I can't do that,' he said uncomfortably. 'I'd be embarrassed.'

She chuckled.

'Well, go down the hall to the next stateroom then, Senator Modesty. But don't keep me waiting too long.'

As the door closed behind him, Cleopatra leaned back, shut her eyes and sighed contentedly. It was working! Antony was well on the way to accepting her explanation and the rift between them would soon be closed. And that wasn't the only thing she was happy about. She smiled secretively to herself. Antony was also the best lover she had ever had and his talents had not diminished with time. If she played her part carefully, she would be able to keep Egypt safe and perhaps even add to her empire. And for once in her life, doing her duty by her country would be totally and utterly enjoyable!

What made her open her eyes, she didn't know. She certainly heard no sound of any kind, but suddenly she had the alarming certainty that there was someone else in the room. So why hadn't she heard the door open?

'Antony – ' she said uneasily, raising herself on one elbow.

Then her whole body turned to watery terror and a scream burst from her lips as she saw a man advancing on her in the lamplight. His eyes were burning with fanatical hatred and he held a dagger upraised.

Chapter Twenty-two

'Why do you blame me?' demanded Claudia. 'It's not my fault!'

After seven days of repeated fruitless fumblings in the marriage bed, her patience had worn thin. As she snapped back at Octavian, her voice was angry, defiant and resentful. Seeing the unmistakable contempt in her eyes, his own resentment blazed up.

'It certainly is!' he retorted. 'You must have used witchcraft to unman me. I could denounce you before the Senate for that.'

'And let everybody know you can't get it up?' she jeered.

He caught his breath and slapped her so hard that the room rang with the sound and the red imprint of his fingers appeared on her cheek.

She clutched at her face with a gasp of pain and indignation.

'I'll tell my mother!' she threatened.

'You'll tell no one or I'll kill you, do you hear me? I'll kill you!'

A murderous rage overtook him, and he seized her by the throat and began to squeeze. Her contempt was replaced now by terror. She fought him silently, her arms flailing and hoarse, grunting sounds issuing from her throat as she struggled to breathe. She tore out a handful of his hair and managed to land several violent punches which hurt him considerably. She was big for a sixteen-year-old, massively built like her mother, Fulvia, which was part of the reason why Octavian had found her so intimidating. But desperation lent him strength. He squeezed and squeezed until her face turned purple and her eyes seemed ready to pop from their sockets.

'You'll obey me, do you hear?' he shouted, shaking her like a rat. 'You slut! You swear a solemn oath to tell nobody or I'll kill you! Will you swear?'

She could not speak but she nodded urgently. Octavian slackened his grip on her throat and winced fastidiously at the coarse, whooping noise that she made as she fought for breath.

'Put your hand on mine and swear,' he hissed.

She looked at him as if she would rather lay her hand on a poisonous viper, but although her eyes leapt with fear and resentment, she obeyed. Her hand felt heavy on his, hot and sweaty and repugnant.

'I swear I will never tell anyone that you are impotent,' she croaked through her bruised throat.

Fury seized him at her bluntness. He backhanded her again and saw blood spurt from her nose and drip on the sheets.

'Bitch! It's your doing. What man could desire a gross lump of flesh like you, all sweaty and stinking of cheap perfume? It's your fault! Well, I'm divorcing you, so get out! Get out!'

'No, I'm divorcing you!' she shouted hysterically, grabbing her robe and backing away to the door. Alarmed, distraught and overwhelmed with terror, she was still angry enough to want the last word. 'And I know why you couldn't do it, too. My mother says the only reason Julius Caesar made you his heir was because he was sodomizing you! You're queer, that's what you are! I've heard all about you. You hardly ever go with women, and when you do, you only like to hurt them! It's men that you really want, isn't it? If Maecenas were your bride, you'd bed him fast enough!'

She was in the doorway now, screaming at the top of her lungs. There was no chance that the slaves hadn't heard her, but they were evidently remaining prudently out of the way. Maddened by her defiance, Octavian picked up a Tyrian jug, which had been given to them as a wedding present, and hurled it at her. She ducked low and it smashed harmlessly against the open door.

'You'll be sorry for this!' she yelled at him. 'Coward! Bully! Murderer! My stepfather Mark Antony will punish you when he comes back to Italy.'

Once she had delivered this final salvo, she slipped out of the door with surprising agility and slammed it shut behind her with a resounding crash. Was she really going to storm around the house stark naked? Didn't she care what people thought of her? Octavian made as if to follow her, then thought better of it. Bolting the door behind her, he flung himself down on the bed and buried his face in his hands.

'Bitch!' he muttered. 'Bitch, bitch, bitch! How dare she humiliate me like that in front of the slaves?'

He sat for hours brooding over it. After a while he heard the sound of carriage wheels rattling away on the road, in defiance of the law which prohibited traffic at this time of day. Then there was a long silence and eventually the ordinary household noises resumed. The clatter of buckets and mops as the slaves went about their cleaning, the sound of the cook shouting for more charcoal in the kitchen. Yet nobody approached the bedroom door, and Octavian felt sick with apprehension at the thought of opening it. He could not bear the thought of the sly whispers, the knowing looks from his own slaves. There were some among them who knew that his relationship with Maecenas was more than a friendship, but at least it had always been conducted with discretion while they remained beneath Octavian's roof. There had never been any of this public brawling, or the sort of quarrels that belonged in a bawdy house. Octavian was a fastidious person. He disliked scenes and he wanted to be regarded as worthy and respectable even by the sternest members of society. It was for this reason that he had accepted the need to marry, but he had hoped for a wife who was modest, dutiful and retiring. One who would endure the sexual act for the sake of conceiving an heir and would be grateful when it was no longer demanded of her. Instead he had been given this fat, arrogant, assertive slut who thought she had every right to speak her mind, just like a man. Well, what else could he expect from a girl brought up by Mark Antony and Fulvia? Octavian shuddered. It was a relief to be rid of her! But what damage would her departure cause him? In spite of her oath, he had no certainty that she would not entertain the whole of Roman society with the story of his failure in the marriage bed. The little whore! What was he to do? What was he to do?

In the end, hunger drove him out. The slaves who answered his call arrived with downcast eyes, listened to his orders in abject silence and hurried to bring him food, exchanging looks as they left the room. He gritted his teeth in rage, but knew that ordering his steward to have them flogged would only make matters worse. When they returned with a tray of bread, grilled fish, green vegetables and fruit, accompanied by a jug of watered wine, one of them cleared his throat nervously.

'Excuse me, domine. Maecenas wishes to see you.'

Octavian's eyebrows drew together. Was this insolent blockhead baiting him?

'Is this a joke?'

'No, sir. He's waiting in the atrium. He says if it's not convenient for you, he'll go away again.'

'Send him up,' said Octavian curtly.

He was going through a show of eating when Maecenas arrived, but in reality he had done no more than crumble the bread and sip the wine. At the sight of Maecenas's corkscrew curls and plucked eyebrows he felt a brief stab of resentment. Wasn't it Maecenas and others like him who had got him into this pickle? But then his annoyance was followed by a reluctant surge of affection.

'Sit down,' he invited. 'Have something to eat.'

Maecenas was completely urbane and smiling as he sat and sipped some wine and chewed on an olive. After a while he looked at Octavian assessingly and raised one eyebrow.

'How's the honeymoon going?' he asked.

'They've told you, haven't they?' said Octavian bitterly. 'I knew they would!'

'Oh, now be fair. They were vewy discreet,' Maecenas assured him. 'It was the steward Demetrius who summoned me, and he's threatened to brand with a hot iron any other slave who talks about the matter. The only reason he let me into the secret is because he's concerned about your career and your reputation. He shares our tastes, you know.'

'Does he?' demanded Octavian, momentarily startled. 'I had no idea.'

'Well, now you do,' replied Maecenas. 'The question is, how do you minimize the damage? I gather she's left you, has she?'

'Yes, she has,' growled Octavian. 'She's gone running off to tell the whole of Rome that I couldn't – '

He broke off, dropping his head and flushing with humiliation.

'That you couldn't get it up?' asked Maecenas softly. 'I'm sure you could manage it now, though, couldn't you?'

As he spoke, he reached boldly up inside Octavian's tunic and caressed him. With the ridiculous unpredictability of the whole business, Octavian's tool instantly sprang into hot, demanding readiness. Maecenas dropped to his knees before him and lowered his curly dark hair . . .

After a long interval, they lay together on the bed. Octavian felt weak and grateful and pleasantly relaxed, as if he were lying in a hot bath. It was a mood that was dangerously enervating. Soon he would have to get up and face the world, including the hostile, backbiting Roman senators who would seize on Claudia's revelation with glee. He flashed a despairing glance at Maecenas.

'What am I going to do?' he asked in a tormented voice.

'You'll have to improve your image,' replied Maecenas.

'What do you mean?'

'Well,' said Maecenas thoughtfully. 'We need to package you as the kind of ruler that people will feel safe with. Now what makes people feel safe? I'd say peace, harmony, law and order, moral values of the old kind. So we need to associate you with all those things.'

Octavian blinked.

'How?' he demanded suspiciously.

'I'm afraid you'll have to marry again. Although this time you'll have to look for someone who's not so buxom, so strident. There's a skinny, bucktoothed girl of good family called Scribonia who might suit you. Very passive. Wouldn't have the nerve to say boo to a

431

goose. And she's a relative of Sextus Pompeius, so it would be extremely suitable if you want to placate the republicans.'

Octavian pulled a face.

'What else?' he asked.

'Perhaps we could make more of your role at Philippi. Octavian the brave soldier, all that sort of thing. What we need is to get some writers together who could compose poems in praise of you. There's a vewy talented young man who fought on the side of Brutus at Philippi, his name's Horace. I believe he'd do the job well, if we made him an offer.'

Octavian looked dubious.

'But would he do it? If he fought for Brutus, presumably he's a republican, isn't he?'

Maecenas gave a silvery ripple of laughter.

'Sometimes you're exquisitely naïve!' he observed. 'Of course he'd do it. Writers will do anything for money. And the fellow is hard up ever since he had all his property confiscated for the veterans' settlement. At the moment he's working as a clerk in the public service. He'd jump at the chance.'

Octavian's face brightened and then shadowed again.

'Is that enough to repair the damage? If Claudia starts making allegations about my relationship with you, it will do me enormous harm. The Senate might start thinking that Mark Antony is not such a bad fellow after all.'

'Don't worry,' said Maecenas firmly. 'We'll make sure we blacken his character. You can give a few speeches in the Senate denouncing him for lingering in the east, sleeping with Cleopatra, while he should be home in Italy dealing with all the political problems here. Pour on the hatred of foreigners, that always works.'

Octavian smiled faintly.

'I suppose so,' he agreed. 'But it still doesn't establish my respectability, does it?'

'Then we'll go further. We'll start a campaign and call it "back to morality". You can address the Senate about law and order and the sanctity of marriage and offer bonuses for fathers of large families. The conservatives will lap it up. They'll all applaud you as the upright defender of traditional morals.'

As he spoke, his hand trickled teasingly up Octavian's thigh and rose higher still. Octavian choked with sudden laughter.

'Upright,' he mused. 'Yes, I like it, Maecenas. Let's do it.'

As the assassin came hurtling towards her, Cleopatra had the nightmare sensation that her body had turned to stone. Her breath caught in her throat and she stared in disbelief as her attacker loomed over her with his eyes narrowed and his right hand shaking uncontrollably.

'This is from Arsinoë and Vercingetorix,' he hissed and lunged at her.

She was unaware of having moved, but suddenly she found her hand clenched around the neck of the Tyrian wine jug. With a convulsive movement, she dashed its contents into his eyes and followed up her advantage by smashing the whole object into his face. The movement seemed to liberate her. With a piercing scream, she rolled off the far side of the bed, hit the floor in a flurry of rose petals and stumbled for the door, still shrieking with terror. There was a roar of outrage behind her, then a sudden snatch that seemed to tear half her hair out from its roots. Still flailing and shrieking, she was hurtled to the floor with bruising force and rolled on her back. She had a jumbled impression of contorted features spurting blood and lips drawn back in an animal snarl. In that instant she tasted the terror and certainty of death. Then the door burst open with a splintering crash, there was a blur of movement followed by an ominous crack and suddenly it was all over.

Her legs were shaking so violently they would scarcely hold her as she clambered to her feet and she had to clutch at the bed for support. Through a haze of dots she saw that her attacker was lying on the floor with his neck broken, but she still could not grasp the fact that she was safe. Her heart continued to thud violently and her breath came in frantic, shallow gulps. It was all she could do not to burst into sobs or wild laughter as she turned to face her rescuer.

'Thank you,' she whispered unsteadily.

'My pleasure,' said the tetrarch of Galilee.

She's got courage, he thought as he saw the shudder that passed through her slightly built frame and the proud, defiant lift of the head that followed it. A moment ago she had been within a hair's breadth of dying, now she was straightening her wildly disordered hair, covering her mouth with her hand and then feeling blindly about for her clothes as if anxious to restore normality as fast as possible. His gaze rested admiringly on her magnificent breasts, tiny waist and lush, curving hips as she found her silk dress and clutched it in front of her.

'You'd better check whether there are any other madmen here,' she ordered, gazing warily about her.

He admired her cool practicality even as he resented the arrogant note of command. A careful search of the room with his own dagger outstretched revealed no other hidden enemies. He had just finished investigating when Mark Antony appeared in the doorway.

In that first horrified instant, Antony had the wild impression that Herod must be trying to rape Cleopatra. There he stood with a knife outstretched while she shrank back on the bed clutching the silk robe in front of her nakedness and looking stunned.

'Leave her alone!' he roared, lunging at Herod. 'I'll crucify you for this, you bastard!'

'No, Antony! Stop! Wait!' shouted Cleopatra, leaping off the bed and flinging herself between them. 'You don't understand! He saved my life! There was an assassin hidden in the alcove. The tetrarch was protecting me, not attacking me.'

Slowly Antony released his threatening clutch on the front of Herod's tunic. All three of them were jostled together like spectators at a gladiatorial show. Antony felt acutely uncomfortable to realize that Cleopatra was naked and palpitating between them as she tried to hold them apart.

'There was an assassin,' she repeated. 'Herod killed him. He saved my life.'

He swung his head in the direction of her gaze and for the first time saw the huddled body amid the rose petals. Before her eyes Antony was transformed from a suspicious lover into a decisive commander. He sprang into every corner of the room, checking for further intruders and then ran to the door and shouted for his soldiers. There was a rumble of military boots on the companion way and he let loose a stream of orders. She could not help being impressed by the way he took control of the situation.

'I've told them to search the ship and double the guards on this deck,' he said, turning back into the cabin. 'If he had any accomplices, we'll torture them and find out who sent them. Were you hurt at all?'

She shook her head, but without warning, reaction set in and she suddenly crumpled and began to sob. Swearing under his breath, Antony hauled her against him and held her until her shaking subsided. Then he picked up her dress and thrust it at her with an uncomfortable sideways glance at Herod.

'Get dressed,' he urged. 'And then you can tell me about it.'

'I'll be off then, if you don't need any further help.'

'Yes,' growled Antony, giving Herod a curt nod. 'You do that.' As he spoke he was aware of how ungracious he sounded and with an effort he forced himself to clap Herod on the shoulder. 'I see now that I jumped to ridiculous conclusions when I first came in. You'll have to forgive me.'

'Of course,' said Herod smoothly, and turning back to Cleopatra, who had now struggled into her dress, he took her hand and kissed it. 'I hope you'll soon recover from your fright, my lady.'

As the door closed behind him, Antony pounded one fist into the other in exasperation. He could not suppress a surge of unreasoning anger that Herod had been the one to save Cleopatra and not him. And enjoyed getting an eyeful of her nakedness too, the horny young bastard!

'What a business,' he growled. Walking across to the inert body on the floor, he rolled it over with his foot. 'He's badly cut around the face. Did Herod do that?'

'No, I hit him with the wine jug.'

Antony whistled admiringly.

'Good for you. But why should he want to kill you? Do you recognize him?'

She found that she had been holding her breath and let it out suddenly in a long sigh. Without pausing to think, she answered his question.

'No, but I know where he came from. Arsinoë sent him.'

'Arsinoë?' echoed Antony in a baffled voice. 'Why should she want to do that when you've treated her so well?'

'Because – ' began Cleopatra hotly and then stopped. It made her feel sick and shaken to think of Arsinoë's treachery. The scheming, ungrateful bitch! After all Cleopatra had done for her, to lay such a plot, just because of some stupid love affair that had ended five years ago! Somehow Arsinoë must have found out the truth about the part Cleopatra had played in Vercingetorix's death. But what sort of reason was that to kill your own sister? All the same, she did not want to tell Antony the truth about what had happened between them. He was such a sentimental fool that he might easily side with Arsinoë. Instead she laid all the blame on her sister. 'Because she's not satisfied with being governor of Cyprus!' she burst out. 'Because she wants to kill me and take the Egyptian throne as well.'

'I can't believe it!' said Antony in an appalled voice. 'I always thought you were so fond of each other. Well, she'll have to be punished for this.'

'You're quite right,' agreed Cleopatra venomously. 'This time she's gone too far. I want her killed.'

Antony looked taken aback.

'Isn't that excessive?' he asked uneasily. 'Surely it would be enough to deprive her of the governorship of Cyprus and place her under house arrest?'

'No!' stormed Cleopatra. 'She was prepared to kill me, wasn't she? I can't afford to leave her alive! If you place her under house arrest, she'll only go on intriguing and there'll be more and more plots until eventually one of her hired assassins succeeds in cutting my throat. Oh, by the gods, Antony, if you have no pity for me, at least think of the stability of your empire! It's quite clear she hates me so much that she's prepared to intrigue with any Roman general who'll promise to murder me and let her take my place.'

'She wouldn't – ' began Antony and then stopped as a dreadful thought struck him. Perhaps she already had? There had been unconfirmed rumours in Brutus's camp after the battle of Philippi that Arsinoë had sent him soldiers and money. Antony had dismissed it as mere spite, but what if it were true? He began to perspire as he saw the implications of the charge Cleopatra was laying. She saw his hesitation and pressed home her advantage.

'What if she approaches Octavian next?' she demanded. 'He hates me enough to want to kill me. Think of the consequences. Even if you don't care whether I live or die, would you want him seizing Egypt and taking control of the Roman grain supply?'

Antony opened his mouth to protest heatedly that of course he cared whether she lived or died. Then he covered his forehead with his hand and heaved a deep sigh.

'I suppose you're right,' he muttered. 'It goes against the grain to kill a woman, but I don't want you harmed, and I can't afford to let her help Octavian. All right, then. I'll send a detachment of soldiers to Cyprus to execute her.'

Cleopatra's eyes kindled with vengeful triumph, but her brain was still racing, turning over the possibilities. Would Arsinoë have sat passively waiting in Cyprus, knowing that the assassination plot could suddenly blow up in her face? Or would she –

438

'Send some soldiers to Ephesus too!' she urged, clutching his arm. 'It wouldn't surprise me in the least if she's taken refuge in the sanctuary of the temple of Artemis until she hears whether I've been murdered or not.'

Antony looked worried.

'Well, if she has, we're stuffed,' he protested. 'I can't drag her out of sanctuary. It would be a sacrilege!'

Cleopatra throttled down her impatience at these ridiculous religious scruples and tried to look as if she were sharing them.

'I know,' she said in a deliberately anguished tone. 'And it tears me apart to think of hurting her, but at the very least we must try to interrogate her. She might venture outside the sanctuary, and then your men would have every right to seize her. What about that new tetrarch of Galilee who was here tonight? Couldn't you send him?'

She held her breath, waiting for Antony's answer. Did it occur to him as it had occurred to her that a Jewish tetrarch would not recognize the sanctity of any foreign god's temple?

Antony nodded slowly and she breathed again.

'All right,' he said heavily. 'I suppose I could do that. Herod can go after her and force the truth from her. And kill her too, if that's what you insist on! Look, I'd better get back ashore and organize all this.'

'No, don't go!' she begged. 'Stay with me, please, please. I can't bear to be alone after what's just happened. I wouldn't sleep a wink.'

It was true enough that her whole body was still jangling with shock at the experience she had just been through and her scalp felt sore and tender where her attacker had ripped out handfuls of her hair, but she was also mindful of the need to deepen her intimacy with Antony.

As always, he was not proof against an appeal to his chivalry. Hauling her against him, he hugged her hard and nuzzled her hair.

'These are evil times we live in,' he growled. 'But I'll protect you, sweetheart. Go to sleep now and I swear I'll be here beside you when you wake.'

He shouted for his soldiers once more to remove the body, then locked the door, blew out the lights and lay down beside her. As she nuzzled into his embrace, a fierce surge of hope was uppermost in the turmoil of her feelings. It still made her feel shaken and violently angry to think of Arsinoë's betrayal, but Antony's willingness to fall in with her wishes was profoundly comforting. Could it be that fate was giving her a second bite at the cherry? Three years ago she had been on the brink of marrying Julius Caesar and ruling the world. If she played her pieces shrewdly, might she not achieve the same end now with Mark Antony? Could he be charmed into loving her so much that nothing but marriage would sate his need for her? If only she could strengthen her hold over him, all her wishes might still come true! She might still be Queen of the whole Roman empire, and it would be so much more enjoyable than trying to tame Caesar. Antony was generous, loving and wonderfully gullible. She would never fear him as she had feared Caesar. Her last thought as she drifted into sleep was that Herod was a remarkably good-looking young man . . .

'What am I to do, Fulvia? I must take some action before Octavian's propaganda completely ruins my brother. Already the people who have been evicted from their farms are holding demonstrations against Mark Antony in the street. It was Octavian's fault they were thrown out, but it's Marcus who gets the blame for it. It's outrageous!'

Fulvia eyed her brother-in-law thoughtfully. Lucius Antonius bore a remarkable resemblance to her husband. He had the same massive shoulders, bull neck, curly hair and unruly beard. Even his frank, good-humoured features were similar, although for some reason women didn't chase after Lucius in droves as they did with Marcus. Some reckless, dangerous spark was absent. Yet Lucius seemed doomed perpetually to suffer the same political problem as her husband did, especially the worry of being dealt new challenges which he was too scrupulous and conventional to handle. Now he tugged uncomfortably at the toga that covered his consular gown and looked at her for guidance, just as her husband would have done.

'Have you taken any action so far?' she demanded.

'I've given shelter to all the evacuees who have come to my estates or my house in Rome,' he growled. 'And I've told them that it's in Marcus's name. But that's not enough. Every day that little schemer Octavian gains more influence. You know, the veteran soldiers used to worship the ground my brother stood on, but now most of them have changed their allegiance to Octavian. Even the men who are currently serving in the army feel the same way – they're all hoping some-one will be dispossessed so that they can be settled on some nice, rich little farm. You'd think the people who'd been thrown out to make way for them would hate Octavian, but no! Somehow they've been given the idea that it was Antony who ordered their ruin. It seems Octavian can do nothing wrong, and my brother can do nothing right.'

'Octavian must have somebody very clever handling his image,' observed Fulvia.

'He does! It's that rotten Etruscan, Cilnius Maecenas. He's even managed to convince a lot of the conservatives that Octavian is a shining supporter of family values with this new marriage to Scribonia. That's a laugh when you consider what Maecenas and Octavian are really up to! It would be funny if it weren't so harmful. While they're busy bolstering Octavian's image, at the same time they're both busy spreading poison about Mark Antony's vile morals and how he's – '

Lucius broke off and flushed.

'Sleeping with Cleopatra in Tarsus?' finished Fulvia with a wry twist of her lips. 'Don't worry about my feelings, Lucius. I've heard the rumours too, and I don't doubt they're true. What we need to do is take action before the public outcry gets so bad that the Senate demands Antony's expulsion from the triumvirate.'

'That's another thing,' grumbled Lucius. 'The triumvirate! If you ask me, it's a nasty business, and the truth is that it's a dictatorship. We should demand that the Senate abolish it and hold fresh consular elections. What we need is a return to the republic.'

Fulvia stared at him, aghast. Was Lucius a complete fool? Didn't he see that a return to the republic would only lead to more vicious outbreaks of fighting as all the senators struggled for pre-eminence? Nobody in their right mind wanted a republic any more, least of all Fulvia. She wanted Antony to come home and rule Rome, to be king in all but name. No . . . that wasn't strictly true. What she really wanted was to rule Rome herself, but since she was only a woman, she needed a husband for public occasions to smile a lot and glad-hand people while she got on with the real business of government. Of course, she couldn't admit any of this to Lucius, since she needed his support.

'You're right,' she said gravely. 'But I'm afraid it's too late for that. Octavian would never agree to disband his forces so in my view it would be much better to take him by surprise and kill him.'

It was Lucius's turn to look horrified.

'That wouldn't be proper!' he protested. 'He has to be given a chance to do the decent thing and step down.'

Fulvia stared at him in exasperation.

'The decent thing!' she jeered. 'You're just like Antony. You treat wars as if they're some kind of game where you have to play by the rules and not take unfair advantage of your opponent. But do you think Octavian gives two hoots about fairness or decency?'

'Well, I can't help that,' insisted Lucius stubbornly. 'You're only a woman so you don't understand, but it's a question of honour. Octavian must be given a chance to step down voluntarily.'

'You'll be sorry,' predicted Fulvia bitterly.

Her prediction was all too accurate. When Lucius brought his troops to Rome and made a speech in the Senate promising that his brother Mark Antony would restore the republic as soon as he returned to Rome, he was greeted by roars of enthusiasm. But Octavian flatly refused to give up his army or his extraordinary powers. Feeling thoroughly offended and self-right-eous, Lucius then extracted a decree from the Senate permitting him to declare war on Octavian.

Although his stomach contracted at the thought of going into battle, Octavian sought Maecenas's advice. Soon two of his most ruthless and skilful generals, Rufus and Agrippa were sent out to hunt down

Antony's brother. On the high green hill of Perusia, Lucius found himself and his army trapped within the old Etruscan town. Octavian arrived and settled down to starve them out. By late winter their condition was pitiable. Many had died and the survivors were reduced to walking skeletons, their eyes sunken, their cheeks hollow, their limbs little more than bones with a scanty covering of flesh. Even their skin was covered in weeping sores. When Lucius finally walked shakily down that green hillside on a frosty morning to surrender, he was doubly humiliated by the sight of Octavian waiting complacently for him at the bottom. Not only did it go against the grain to yield to a mere youth who had left all the fighting to others, but he could not bear to see Octavian so well fed and smirking when he had left such misery behind him in the town above. But it must be done. He could not allow any more of his followers to die. With a resentful, despairing grimace, he dropped his sword with a thud at Octavian's feet.

'Am I to take it that I have your unconditional surrender?' demanded Octavian, unable to keep the glee out of his voice.

'Yes,' croaked Lucius.

'You may kiss my foot, then,' said Octavian rising from his seat and thrusting his right leg forward.

Even in his last extremity of weakness and deprivation, Lucius felt an incredulous rush of indignation at this order. Weren't they both Romans, both free and equal members of the nobility? And wasn't he the older man, entitled to some measure of respect and dignity? Then, looking into Octavian's ice blue eyes, he saw that there would never be respect, or dignity, or equality again. Groaning inwardly and trying to control the embarrassing tremor in his legs, he slumped to his knees and went flat on his face on the cold, indifferent road to kiss Octavian's foot.

'What will be your terms?' he begged hoarsely. 'You will spare my men, won't you? They were only acting under my orders.'

'We'll see,' replied Octavian, savouring his moment of triumph.

It had been his intention to cut off Lucius's head with his own hands and send it back, gift wrapped, to that bitch Fulvia who had raised extra legions to help Lucius in his fight against Octavian. But Maecenas had dissuaded him.

'If you do that, you risk having Mark Antony come raging back like a lion from the east to avenge his brother,' he had warned. 'And you're not yet strong enough to be sure of victory in such a contest. What would be a far better revenge is to spare Lucius Antonius's life, but slaughter all the officers who followed him. Their families will hate you for it, but they'll hate Lucius even more and suspect that he did some deal with you to save himself at their expense. You'll get rid of your worst opponents and create more antagonism towards the Antony brothers.'

Octavian had pondered and then smiled a secretive smile.

'You're right, Maecenas.'

Consequently Lucius was astonished and grateful when Octavian ordered his slaves to help him to his feet.

'You're a free man,' said Octavian unexpectedly. 'My attendants will give you food and drink and put you in a carriage to take you to Rome.'

'And my followers?' blurted out Lucius.

Octavian smiled sweetly.

'Leave them to my mercy and goodwill,' he advised.

445

Suspecting nothing, Lucius allowed himself to be led away. Only a faint niggling doubt disturbed him. Octavian's mercy and goodwill? During the proscriptions he would have said that he had none, but perhaps he had changed since then. After all, hadn't Octavian just spared his life? Then surely his followers must be safe?

It was not until five days later when he reached Rome that he heard of the massacre that had taken place in Perusia. Appalled, he covered his face in his hands and wept until his eyes were blotched and swollen and his throat was almost closed up. Still deeply shocked, he ordered his slaves to put him in a litter and take him to Fulvia's house. She must hear of this new atrocity.

When she was summoned to the door, Fulvia did not at first recognize the wreck of a man who had just been admitted to the atrium. In the few months since she had last seen Lucius, his hair had turned completely grey and his powerful physique had wilted, so that he looked like a once flourishing plant blighted by frost. His clothes hung about him, his hands were like claws and his face looked like a death mask. She was taken aback when he embraced her.

'Who are you?' she demanded indignantly, breaking free of his feeble grip.

'You don't recognize me?' he demanded incredulously, with a voice that, although weak and reedy, gave him away.

'Lucius!' she cried in horror. 'What on earth has happened to you?'

He sat down and told her. At the end of the recital, he began to weep again, hoarse, wrenching sobs that threatened to tear him apart.

'What has become of us?' he demanded. 'This isn't

the Rome I once knew. All the rules have changed, Fulvia. That boy's a beast, a monster! He didn't even have enough honour to tell the truth about what he intended to do. It breaks my heart to think of my poor lads lying dead there in Perusia, and their last thought that I'd betrayed them. What are we to do now? What are we to do now?'

'There's only one thing we can do,' said Fulvia and there was an odd mixture of bitterness and yearning in her voice. 'We'll have to sail to the eastern provinces and place ourselves under the protection of Mark Antony.'

Chapter Twenty-three

Cleopatra's attraction to Herod was fully reciprocated. As he was ferried back over the dark waters of the Cydnus, his memory was on fire with the events of the evening. It was hard to believe that such violence had ever erupted. Overhead the stars blazed brilliantly in the sky, the dark waters of the river bobbed with fractured reflections of the lamps that blazed all over Cleopatra's barge and the sound of flute music and laughter still echoed clearly across the river. But Herod had seen the corpse of the assassin before they weighted it and flung it overboard, and he knew that what had happened was no hallucination.

When he arrived back at his own austere lodgings, he barred the door and flung himself down on his bed to think. Here there were no purple coverlets, no dining couches studded with emeralds, no drifts of rose petals on the floor. The place was comfortable enough, luxurious even, by the standards that Herod had known in his childhood, but a tetrarch of Galilee was a very small fish compared to the Queen of Egypt and the presence of the Roman triumvir in Tarsus had driven rentals up to an outrageous level. All Herod had been able to afford was this three-room apartment, smelling of mice and with damp patches on the wall frescos. He had only four slaves to attend him and, since they were trained in soldiery not housekeeping, his meals were often badly cooked and his clothes shrunken, rumpled and stained. One day Herod planned to have more. Much more.

For the moment he was simply grateful to have

outwitted the spite of his enemies who had sent messengers to Mark Antony begging to have him removed from office. It was only by hurrying off to Bithynia and intercepting Mark Antony on his progress through the eastern provinces that Herod had managed to win a reprieve. Even so, he was still chafing at the bit, waiting for Mark Antony to honour his promise and send troops and gold to restore him to power in Galilee. While Antony had been quick to grasp the value of having a capable soldier like Herod to defend the frontiers of the empire, he could be infuriatingly vague when it came down to administrative details if no crisis was involved.

Well, Herod would just have to tread carefully, particularly now that Antony's mistress had caught his eye. At the banquet earlier in the evening Herod had been powerfully attracted to Cleopatra but had thought her too dangerous a quarry to pursue, since he could not afford to risk offending Antony. Now, after seeing her naked, he burned to possess her. The trouble was that it would not be easy, given both their positions. Like any red-blooded male, Herod had had his fair share of love affairs, but to offer a queen a love affair might be taken as an insult. He toyed with the idea of proposing marriage instead and dismissed it immediately as both ridiculous and suicidal. Why would the Queen of the richest country in the world want to marry a man who was no more than governor of an obscure northern province of Judaea? In any case, his own people would be up in arms immediately if he proposed marriage to a Gentile. For the millionth time Herod gritted his teeth in exasperation at the touchiness and bigotry of the Jews. They already hated him anyway and treated him as an outsider on the grounds that his mother was an Arab. If he ever married again, it must be to a Jewess of irreproachable lineage. It was for this reason that he had already divorced his first wife Doris and begun courting Mariamme who was a Hasmonaean of the royal line. He could not afford to jeopardize his hopes of that match. Nor could he afford to antagonize Mark Antony. All the same, he wanted Cleopatra, and when he wanted something, he never gave up. Blowing out the bedside lamp, he lay down again with his hands clasped behind his head and continued to ponder. He had already saved Cleopatra's life, which must put her in his debt. Perhaps the chance would come to do her some other service, preferably something which would give him a hold over her. He smiled to himself in the darkness. He would watch, and wait . . .

His opportunity came sooner than he expected. The following day, he was startled to be summoned before Mark Antony and given the commission of going to the temple of Artemis at Ephesus in search of the Princess Arsinoë.

'The Queen believes that her sister Arsinoë was responsible for the assassination attempt on her last night,' said Antony bluntly. 'I want her arrested and brought back here for questioning if you find her.'

Cleopatra opened her mouth as if to protest, and then shut it so hard that her teeth snapped together. Looking from her to Mark Antony, Herod had the impression that they had been quarrelling before he entered the room. With an effort, the Queen kept the look of luminous devotion on her face as her gaze met Mark Antony's, but the signs of tension were evident in the way she gripped the arm rests of her chair and in the faint furrow between her brows.

'Of course, if she attempts to escape on the way

back,' she put in coolly, 'you'll have to take whatever measures you think necessary.'

A gleam of sardonic amusement lit Herod's eyes. He had no doubt about what that meant and he was not surprised as he left the proconsul's palace to be intercepted by one of Cleopatra's slaves and conducted up a back staircase to her quarters. He found her pacing restlessly round and round the room, clenching and unclenching her hands. At the announcement of his name, she paused and looked at him expectantly. He knew it was the custom in Egypt for commoners to prostrate themselves before members of the royal family, but he had no intention of going flat on his face to any woman. He returned her gaze with a provocative stare that stopped just short of insolence. After a moment she coloured and motioned him to a chair.

'Sit down,' she ordered. 'First I want to express my gratitude for your prompt action in saving my life last night. Iras, give the tetrarch that leather purse.'

He was stunned by the weight of the wallet that was placed in his hand and could barely restrain himself from looking inside it to see how much it contained. If those were all gold coins that chinked so satisfyingly against his fingers, he would have money enough to keep himself in luxury for two years! But he decided it was better to seem as cool as if he received fortunes every day. Smiling faintly, he set the purse down on the mosaic floor beside him.

'Thank you,' he said pleasantly. 'You're very generous.'

'I'll be more generous still if you help me in another way.'

'You want me to kill your sister,' murmured Herod.

Cleopatra's eyes widened at his bluntness and she looked hastily around her as if to observe whether they

451

were being overheard. Then she leaned confidentially towards him.

'Yes I do,' she said, in a bitter, rapid voice. 'She's already raised a rebellion against me once in Egypt and I pardoned her for that. Well, now she's tried to kill me and my mercy is at an end! Mark Antony doesn't understand that I'm going in fear of my life. All he can see is that he would be committing sacrilege if he killed someone who was sheltering in a temple sanctuary. But you're a Jew. You don't believe in the sanctity of any gods other than your own, do you?'

Herod gave an odd smile. As a matter of fact, he didn't even believe in his own God, but that was a revelation he could make to nobody. If his Jewish subjects suspected it, they would tear him to pieces and feed him to the wild dogs.

'No, I don't,' he admitted.

'Then you'll do it for me?'

He did not make the mistake of demanding that she name her price or haggling for more money. Shrewdly he judged that willing cooperation would win him most in the long run. Cooperation and another offering whose value was intangible. Approval.

'I'll do it for you,' he agreed. 'Not for any reward that you may offer me, but simply because I believe that what you're doing is right. If your sister has betrayed you twice, your only choice is to eliminate her. It's your duty to Egypt to get rid of anyone who would raise sedition against you.'

Her eyes flashed with gratitude.

'That's what I told Antony, but he couldn't see it and he must never know of this. You must swear by Jehovah to keep it a secret.'

Herod exulted inwardly. Better and better! Now he would have a hold over her that he could use whenever he chose to do so. But he hid his excitement and composed his features into an expression of sympathetic complicity.

'I swear by Jehovah,' he said solemnly, raising his hands to heaven. 'You can trust me. I'll take ship for Ephesus this very day.'

'Wait,' she cried as he rose to his feet. 'I want to come too, and see with my own eyes that this deed is done.'

She was still smouldering over the fact that even after their night of love together, Mark Antony had not yielded to her suggestion that she should join him in the rest of his triumphal progress through Asia. All that she had been able to extract from him was a half-hearted promise that he might come and visit her in Egypt during the winter. And he had made it clear that he expected her to sail home to Alexandria immediately. Well, if she could not establish her ascendancy over Antony immediately, she could and would protect her own back! Every time she thought of her sister, anger burned inside her, as if she were still suffering from the plague. She wanted Arsinoë dead.

'Of course,' said Herod. 'You're the ruler of a great country and you have every right to see that your will is done. But don't be afraid that I'll give in to pity. I was born pitiless.'

Arsinoë found that the tension mounted unbearably with each extra day she spent in the temple of Artemis. Even allowing for storms or flat calms, Leon should have returned from Tarsus by now with his mission accomplished. What had happened? Had Cleopatra escaped? Why did nobody bring her word? When the message finally came that a ship from Tarsus had docked in the harbour, she ran out into the portico of the temple in her desperation for news.

At once she realized her mistake. A detachment of soldiers wearing the uniform of Jewish militia men was marching grimly up the road towards her. There was no reason to suppose that they were coming for her, but Arsinoë's weeks of anxious waiting made her turn in panic and flee back inside the temple.

That too was a mistake. She had barely reached the clear space in front of the huge cult statue of the goddess when a whole army of ominous figures appeared from behind the thicket of pillars. Whichever way she turned, it seemed she was surrounded by soldiers with harsh faces and cold eyes. And then from behind the statue of the goddess herself, came the last person Arsinoë had expected to see alive.

'You!' she breathed.

Cleopatra looked as beautiful as ever in a gold silk dress with a purple travelling cloak around her, but her face was as expressionless as if it were carved from marble.

'Yes, it's me,' she said in an odd voice. 'You didn't expect to see me alive again, did you, Arsinoë?'

There was a long pause as their eyes met and held. A tide of emotion surged back and forth between them. Anger, grief, reproach, the ashes of extinguished affection.

'Why did you betray me?' asked Cleopatra at last.

'I didn't,' cried Arsinoë hotly. 'You betrayed me.'

'That's a lie! I forgave you after you committed treason and raised an army against me in Egypt. I even made you governor of Cyprus. I gave you everything you could possibly want.'

Arsinoë felt a wild urge to burst into hysterical laughter.

'You gave me nothing I could possibly want!' she retorted. 'Only things that were useless to me and you killed my betrothed husband, Vercingetorix. No, you won't meet my eyes, will you? All your charm and deceit won't fool me now! I know the truth, Cleopatra. You killed him out of pure spite towards me.'

For an instant Cleopatra looked guilty and defensive, but then she rallied. Tossing her head defiantly, she looked Arsinoë right between the eyes as if she were taking aim with an arrow.

'It wasn't that at all! All right, I admit that I agreed to his execution, but I didn't think Caesar would spare your life unless Vercingetorix was gone. I only did it to save you.'

As she spoke, Cleopatra almost believed it herself. It was hard to remember now exactly what she had thought and felt except for her urgent conviction that Vercingetorix was dangerous to her and must go. But she had wanted to keep her sister alive. That much was true.

Arsinoë flashed her a tormented look, as if she were half persuaded by her passionate tone. Then she remembered Brennus's vow that Cleopatra was the one who had persuaded Caesar to execute the Gallic chieftain. Her face hardened.

'I don't believe you!' she cried. 'I used to admire you so much, but even when you were young you always relied on deceit to get your own way. You lied and coaxed and charmed until everyone was under your spell. Well, I'm not! I hate you, Cleopatra! I hate you for what you've done to me! You've ruined my life!'

'By saving you from a life of poverty?' jeered Cleopatra. 'By giving you a kingdom?'

'Yes!' insisted Arsinoë. 'Yes! You robbed me of

love, and that's worth more than any kingdom, but I wouldn't expect you to understand that.'

Cleopatra snorted contemptuously. 'And because I don't share your ridiculous sentimentality you were prepared to murder me for it, were you?'

'It wasn't murder,' gasped Arsinoë, taking a deep shuddering breath. 'It was sacred revenge. An atonement of blood guilt owed to the dead. You deserved it!'

'You don't even have the courage to admit what a traitor you are, do you? You should be down on your knees, Arsinoë, begging me to forgive you.'

'Well, I won't!' shrieked Arsinoë. 'If that's what you're hoping for, you can hope in vain! I'm not frightened of dying, I've been longing for it for the last five years. My only regret is that you will escape punishment for your wickedness. But God will remember. God will punish you!'

Cleopatra's patience snapped. She could no longer bear any more of Arsinoë's obstinate hysterical refusal to admit that she was wrong. Why should she endure her raving any longer?

'Kill her!' she ordered coldly.

The soldiers closed in around Arsinoë, but she continued to hurl accusations as they approached. Her voice grew higher and more frantic as they circled about her and memories of the Jewish nurse of her childhood rang in her ears. Suddenly she raised her arms and shouted so that her prayers reverberated around the roof high above.

'Do you hear me, Jehovah? I call on you to curse this woman for her cruelty. May she die in agony and defeat, bereft of anyone she loves! And may anyone who helps her be struck down by your everlasting power and vengeance! Hear my prayer, Jehovah!'

The Jewish soldiers stepped back a pace, muttering and casting uneasy glances aloft. Hadn't she just called on the one true God? Might He not hear her prayer, even in this place of sacrilegious idols? Nobody wanted to strike the first blow and it was left to Herod to step forward with his sword upraised. He cast a questioning glance at Cleopatra and received her nod. Then, snatching Arsinoë by her hair, he drew back her head and cut her throat.

In a rough fortress overlooking the Sea of Galilee, Antony stood looking down over the farmland and pondering his situation. The pastel tones of sunrise with their delicate tints of rose and lavender and old gold had given way now to a cloudless blue sky and the mud brick rampart under his hands was already beginning to give off heat. Looking down at the vivid light green of the walnut trees, the silvery expanses of the olive groves and the sunlight dancing off the ripples on the lake, it was difficult to believe that this peaceful place lived under the constant threat of invasion. Yet it was as a defence against invasion that Herod had constructed this tower he was standing upon and it was because of the constant menace of the Parthians just beyond the border to the east that Antony intended to leave the young tetrarch in power here. There was no denying that he was a capable and resourceful soldier and even his recent handling of the unfortunate affair of Arsinoë had not destroyed Antony's trust in him. He might dislike Herod's hardness and brutality, but he could not fault his courage or his strategic brilliance. No, it was a pity about Arsinoë, but Herod must remain here to provide a buffer state between Roman territory and the threat of Parthian invasion.

Would Cleopatra be distressed when she heard the

news of her sister's death? In Tarsus she had shocked him with her savage insistence that Arsinoë must be killed, but that had probably only been an untypical reaction brought on by her fear for her own life. By now, she had most likely calmed down and would feel as troubled as he had been to hear the news. He tried to picture her back in Alexandria and a pang of unwelcome desire went through him. She had thought him so heartless when he packed her off home from Tarsus, but the truth was that he had not trusted himself to keep her near him. Even the thought of Fulvia seemed to provide little protection against Cleopatra's blandishments, and the strength of his urge to cast aside all his administrative worries and sail off for a long holiday in Egypt had alarmed him. He must act responsibly. He must settle the affairs of the eastern provinces and make Fulvia proud of him. All the same, he could not help lusting for another night like the one he had passed on the royal barge in Tarsus with his arms full of Cleopatra's scented warmth and her body pressed snugly against him.

His thoughts were so full of her that for a moment he thought it was a mirage when he saw a column of marching figures appearing on the road from the sea shore with a purple covered litter in their midst, exactly the kind of litter that Cleopatra always travelled in. He soon discovered that it was no mirage when one of Herod's slaves came to him with the message of her arrival. With his heart thudding like a young boy's, he went hurtling down the staircase of the tower to meet her in the courtyard below.

'What in the world are you doing here?' he demanded incredulously.

She tumbled into his arms as she climbed out of the litter, kissed him warmly on the mouth and, still holding his hands, stepped back to look at him. She looked embarrassed, mischievous, defiant, utterly irresistible.

'Promise you won't be angry,' she urged and a dimple appeared in her right cheek. 'The truth is that I persuaded Herod to invite me here before you ever left Tarsus. I wanted to see you again so badly.'

He should have been angry with her for defying his wishes, but he wasn't. Once the formality of her welcome by Herod was over, Antony hurried her away to his own quarters and took her to bed. There, after an hour of torrid lovemaking, he lay beside her and stroked her hair and her breasts.

'Where did you go after you left Tarsus?' he asked. 'Did you go back to Egypt at all?'

She hesitated, scanning his face to see if he knew the truth and decided he did not.

'No, I went to Cyprus. I thought I might get a chance to speak to Arsinoë, but she wasn't there.'

She held her breath, waiting to see how he would react to this. Surely it must flush him into the open so that he would tell her whatever he knew?

His face shadowed. He was glad to hear that she had gone in search of Arsinoë, presumably in the hope of a reconciliation, but it made the task of telling her the truth doubly hard.

'I have bad news for you about Arsinoë,' he sighed.

He felt her stiffen in his arms.

'What kind of news?'

'Herod found her at Ephesus. If what he tells me is true, she was outside the boundaries of the sanctuary. He tried to arrest her, but she made an attempt to escape and ignored all orders to stop. One of his soldiers shot her with an arrow as she fled.'

'Oh,' said Cleopatra, breathing again. This was the version that she and Herod had agreed upon and his soldiers had been well paid for their silence. 'Oh, I'm sorry to hear it.'

'So am I.' Antony's voice was harsh. 'It doesn't sit well with me to kill a woman and it still worries me whether Herod was telling the truth. What if she really was inside the sanctuary?'

In spite of his boozing and womanizing, Antony was essentially a religious man. He always poured out the first half inch of wine at dinner as a libation to the gods and he was scrupulous about making sacrifices on feast days. If a bad omen happened to him, like tripping over his sandals and splitting his toenail so that the blood ran forth, he would transact no business on that day. And if he saw a raven on his way to the Forum, he always turned back home. His attitude to the gods was rather like his attitude to humans – he hated to offend any of them by a lack of generosity or respect for their customs. Now he could not help worrying about whether Herod had actually exceeded his instructions and, if so, whether the goddess Artemis would inflict her punishment on Antony as the one ultimately responsible. It made him feel deeply uneasy. And it was not the only aspect of Herod's attitude to religion which made him feel uneasy.

'I suppose we'd better get dressed for dinner,' he said reluctantly. 'But I warn you, you won't enjoy it. Herod has some kind of tame prophet who goes into trances and delivers warnings. It's enough to make your blood run cold. I don't understand half of what he says, but it all seems very strange and dangerous to me.'

'What sort of things does he talk about?' asked Cleopatra, intrigued.

'Oh, some character he calls the Messiah,' grumbled Antony. 'He seems to be saying that he'll rise in the east and deliver everyone from slavery and oppression. It sounds like seditious rubbish, if you ask me. And what sort of oppression does he mean? Is this Messiah going to deliver them from Roman rule? I asked Herod about that, but he says I shouldn't worry, that it's nothing of the kind. According to him, the Messiah is purely a religious leader. But the tricky thing is that Herod seems to believe *he*'s the one meant by the prophecies, or at least he pretends he does. It's damned conceited, if you ask me.'

'What does he hope to achieve by it?' asked Cleopatra.

'Money and followers,' growled Antony. 'And it works! I have to admit that it brings him supporters in droves. They're all hoping that he'll cure them of their leprosy or let them off their taxes and he encourages them shamelessly, the ambitious young bastard! If you ask me, he won't rest until he's King of the whole of Judaea.'

Cleopatra blinked. If that happened, Herod would be a force to reckon with.

'I suppose it's possible,' she admitted thoughtfully. 'Hyrcanus the present King has no sons living, does he?'

'No. And Herod is angling to marry Hyrcanus's granddaughter Mariamme, which is an ambitious move. If you ask me, he's hoping that Hyrcanus will make him his heir, but it's not as though he's got the breeding to justify it. He's nothing but the jumped-up son of a temple slave, even though he pretends that his ancestors were high priests in the Babylonian exile. Well, his ambitions suit me well enough. As long as he patrols the frontiers and keeps Roman territory safe from Parthian invasion, he can pretend he's descended from as many high priests as he likes. But pretending he's a god, that's more than I can stomach! He's a completely unscrupulous fellow, Cleopatra. You ought to be careful in your dealings with him.'

'Oh, I will,' she promised.

Antony was right about the prophet. The dinner was a provincial little affair, no better than a struggling merchant in Alexandria might provide. The food was simple – flat bread, olives, fish, chicken and cooked greens, with dates and walnuts for the second tables. And the entertainment was even worse. An ageing belly dancer did the dance of the seven veils, although any man in his right mind would rather have paid her to keep the veils on. There was a flute player who had never really mastered his Myxolydian scales, and the tightrope walker fell off on to the mosaic floor and broke his arm, which was the most entertaining thing that happened all evening. Until the prophet entered the room.

Antony and Herod were busy discussing strategy, using a line of salt cellars to simulate defensive towers built along the frontier of Parthia. They were both ignoring Cleopatra, which exasperated her considerably. She had been prepared to be especially gracious to Herod to console him for the awfulness of his fortress and the poverty of his entertainment. Besides, she believed he was attracted to her and, while she had no intention of being reckless enough to offer him encouragement, she had looked forward to basking in his admiration. She wore a scarlet silk gown, sufficiently transparent to give a discreet glimpse of her breasts while her hair was threaded with seed pearls and she was wearing enough gold jewellery to build ten palaces in place of his nasty little fortress. But instead of receiving smouldering looks, she was being ignored by both of them. She lay fuming silently and did not even hear when the prophet entered the room. She was not even aware of him until his sepulchral voice rang out, reverberating against the domed ceiling far above.

'Woe to the sinners! The Messiah is at hand! He will smite the evildoers even as Jehovah smote Job. Boils will erupt on their skin, worms will consume their flesh, the jackals will feed on their children – '

It was enthralling stuff, better than the old bag with the seven veils at any rate. Cleopatra swivelled her head to look at the prophet and noted that he was suitably dressed for the part. He was cadaverously thin, with a long, wispy grey beard, wild greasy hair and maniacally flickering eyes. In keeping with the austerity of his profession, he wore only a torn home-spun robe, while his horny yellow feet were bare. Approaching Herod, he flung out one arm dramatically with his forefinger extended while his head threshed from side to side in a crazed ecstasy of apparent recognition.

'But blessings will come to those who believe in the Messiah. He will comfort the elderly, succour the widow and her children, heal the lame, cure the blind. His name will be blessed, for He will lead Jerusalem and her people to salvation. Hallelujah! Hallelujah!'

As he spoke, the prophet sank almost to his knees, shuddering wildly as if in the grip of spirits. Cleopatra was reminded of some of her African dancers in Alexandria who were able to bend their bodies backwards so far that they could shuffle under a broomstick in time to the catchy rhythms of whistles and tambourines. The prophet went on shuddering and sinking, and finally fell to the floor as if he were dead. As he did so, a woman came in, dressed in black, wearing a timid expression and clutching two scrawny children by the hand. She went on her knees in front of Herod.

'Help us, master,' begged the poor widow.

With a compassionate smile, Herod drew money from the coin purse at his waist and thrust it into her hand.

His next case was more difficult. A cripple on crutches came in and stood with his face full of yearning and foreboding as Herod rose and laid his hands upon him. A moment later, with a cry of astonishment, the cripple flung aside his crutches and walked. He was soon replaced by a girl whose eyes were wide open, but obviously sightless, who groped her way across to Herod and waited while he spat on his hands and rubbed her eyelids. When she announced tremulously that she could see, half the women in the room burst into tears and there were shouts of acclamation from the men. Loudest of all was the cry of the prophet, who seemed now to rise from the dead, leaping to his feet and uttering Hallelujahs as loudly as a huntsman pursuing a fox. Herod embraced him and pressed another gold coin into his scrawny hand. How appropriate, thought Cleopatra sourly. Even the elderly are being comforted.

'Blessed be the name of the Messiah!' cried the prophet rapturously and loped out of the room with an impressive speed for one so old who had only just risen from the dead.

'Blessed be the name of the Messiah! Herod! Herod!' came the hysterical cries of approbation from all around the room.

Antony caught Cleopatra's eye with an expression of unmistakable disgust. As for her, she had to bite the inside of her cheeks to control her laughter. But when she was getting ready for bed that night, her amusement turned gradually to sober contemplation. Herod's well-orchestrated religious frenzies might involve the shameless exploitation of gullible people, but there was no denying they were effective. She had seen how pledges of money and support had flowed to him after the miracle recipients had gone home. She twisted round to look at Iras, who was brushing her hair.

'This Messiah that Herod's so keen on,' she said. 'Is there any good reason why he has to be a man? Why not a woman?'

CHAPTER TWENTY-FOUR

'Come away from the window,' complained Cleopatra with an exaggerated shiver. 'That night air is like a knife.'

Antony smiled at her frailty and lingered a moment longer, enjoying the frosty blaze of the stars in the dark sky overhead and the cold purity of the air. He was indifferent to cold himself and could have stood here quite happily for another half hour watching the moonlight over the lake, but her weakness amused him. What a luxurious little creature she was. Like a pampered kitten, always wanting warmth and comfort, as if it were her right! Well, she would have all that soon enough when they moved to Egypt and Antony could not pretend that he was sorry to be leaving. It still exasperated him beyond measure to notice the sly way that Herod's gaze followed Cleopatra whenever she entered a room, although his exasperation was equalled by his pleasure at watching the way she snubbed the fellow. Even though he did not suspect her of infidelity, he would not be sorry to be away from this place. He wondered how she viewed their coming departure.

'Are you sorry to be leaving Judaea?' he asked, closing the wooden shutters firmly behind him.

'No,' she said bluntly. 'I've no taste for austerity. Come and get into bed and warm me up, Antony.'

As he climbed in beside her and she moved into the comfort of his embraces, only half her attention was focused on the thrilling rasp of his beard between her naked breasts and the skilful caress of his fingers between her thighs. The rest of her mind was busy scheming. No, she was not sorry to be leaving Judaea. Nor to be leaving Herod. Although she felt an unwilling attraction towards his brooding good looks, she had also begun to think that he was a very dangerous man. He had kissed her this afternoon, luring her into the little hidey hole at the base of one of the towers on a pretence of wanting to show her some maps. Finding herself pinioned against the wall, in the half darkness, she had been horrified to feel her senses flame as Herod crushed her against him and kissed her with expert savagery. She could have forgiven that, but what really inflamed her rage was his insolent remark when she fought him off. He had looked down at her in the gloom with his eyes glittering and murmured, 'Oh, come now. We already share the secret of Arsinoë's death. Surely we can share another little secret?'

Seething with indignation, Cleopatra had kneed him in the groin and made her escape. All afternoon she had worried about whether he would reveal everything to Mark Antony and only now was she beginning to feel more secure. How dare Herod try to frighten her with the implicit threat of blackmail? He had been paid handsomely for Arsinoë's death. Wasn't that enough? Well, now she would leave the insolent little nobody behind to govern his pathetic province while she fixed her sights on the far more important target of Mark Antony.

It was a serious disappointment to her that she had not already managed to extract a proposal of marriage from Mark Antony. After what had passed between them on the night following Caesar's assassination, she had come to think of Antony as her devoted slave whom she could marry whenever she chose. It had been an unpleasant shock to discover that Antony had more pride than she had expected. While he was only too happy to bed her, he had headed off all her hints about marriage, and even her blatant proposals of it, with the curt rejoinder that he could not hurt Fulvia who had done so much to help him. Cleopatra only hoped that in this coming stay in Egypt she could change his mind. To have married Antony three and a half years ago when all he was offering her was a cabin in the wilderness would have been ludicrous. To marry him now when he was a triumvir with the empire of the whole Mediterranean world in his grasp represented the summit of her ambitions. Every attraction Egypt could offer must be used to persuade him! All the things he liked to do would be arrayed before him like sumptuous dishes at a banquet. Feasting, drinking, hunting, fishing, carousing in the taverns – they would do all of them! Antony would have so much fun he would never want to go home. And, of course, the sex would be stupendous. Recalling her mind to the task at hand, Cleopatra wriggled sensually down his body and took his throbbing male organ in her mouth.

Antony did have fun in Egypt. In fact, he had even more fun than when he had first met her, nearly fifteen years before. Then she had been constrained by her youth and her dependent status to sneak out in secret to meet him. Now, as Queen, she did whatever she pleased. She still sneaked out in disguise sometimes, but only for the thrill of it, not because she feared punishment. Between them, they painted Alexandria red. They screamed themselves hoarse at the chariot races and lost huge sums of money on gambling, they drank beer in late-night bars, they went hunting and fishing together and out of pure sentimentality they even hired the little fisherman's cottage in Rhakotis where their love affair had first begun and made the brass bed rattle violently on its base. Every night there was a party and each party was more lavish than the one before. Cleopatra formed a dining club called 'The Society of Inimitable Livers' and its members vied with each other to present the most extravagant banquets. Best of all, she shared Antony's love of practical jokes. Once when they were fishing together, and Antony was catching nothing, not wanting to be outdone by a woman, he bribed divers to go down and attach fish to his hook. Cleopatra, realizing the trick, went one better. The next day she offered the divers an even higher sum to go down and attach dried salt fish to Antony's hook. There were roars of laughter when his catch was brought up. And Antony laughed loudest of all.

The only issue over which they quarrelled was her shameless use of the prophecies concerning the Messiah. One afternoon in the agora, Antony was waylaid by a particularly persistent seller of religious tracts. More in order to get rid of her than for any other reason, he tossed a copper coin into her begging bowl and took the dog-eared rectangle of papyrus which she thrust at him. While he was having a drink in a nearby tavern, he began idly to peruse it and then stiffened in shock as he realized what it was about. Written in a large, straggling, illiterate hand, it was the text of an oracle proclaiming the coming of a Messiah, but with one important difference. This Messiah was a woman and after reading the absurd document several times, Antony had no doubt that Cleopatra was intended by it. He scowled as he spelled out the words.

'And while Rome hesitates over the conquest of Egypt, then the mighty Queen of the deathless King will appear upon Earth ... Three will subdue Rome with a pitiful fate ... A cataract of fire will pour down from heaven . . . And then the whole wide world shall be ruled by a woman's hand . . . Then the judgement of God Almighty shall come.' Perspiration broke out on Antony's forehead. Folding the scrap of papyrus and thrusting it into his wallet, he strode back to the palace as fast as he could go.

'Did you know the sort of rubbish that these religious charlatans are circulating about you?' he demanded, bursting into Cleopatra's private office and waving the offending document under her nose. 'Read that!'

She picked it up, unfolded it and scanned it serenely.

'What are you getting so upset about?' she asked.

'The damned cheek of these people!' roared Antony. 'They pretend it's a religious prophecy, but it's plain as the nose on your face that what they're really saying is that one day you're going to rule the world, and this is God's will. We've got to put a stop to it.'

'Why?' she asked softly.

This single syllable exploded into the air with a strangely ominous sound.

Antony was taken aback.

'Well, because . . . because it's fraud!' he protested. 'You can't convince me that any god dictated that. It's just a piece of trickery to take advantage of people's religious beliefs and make them think that heaven has chosen you to rule the world.'

'And what's wrong with that?' she asked with deceptive mildness.

Antony stared at her, appalled, as an unwelcome suspicion began to form in the back of his mind.

'Did you know about this?' he demanded. 'Did you order it?'

A silvery ripple of laughter escaped her and she looked up at him regretfully but with eyes brimming with merriment.

'Sit down, Antony,' she coaxed. 'Yes, I did, if you must know. And what's wrong with it? Everybody does it! Herod does it. Julius Caesar used to do it. Don't you remember how he was always seeing falling stars or discovering terrible signs in the livers of sacrificial victims whenever there was any legislation he didn't want passed in the Senate? And I'll bet Octavian's got a team of soothsayers churning out prophecies that he's going to rule the world. Why shouldn't you and I do it too?'

Antony's legs suddenly felt so shaky that he was glad of her invitation to sit down.

'Look,' he said bluntly. 'I think it's wrong to make a mockery of the gods – it's just tempting fate. But leave that aside for the moment. What does all this stuff mean about you ruling the world?'

'Not alone, Antony,' she murmured. 'I'd do it with you. Together I'm sure we could rule the entire Mediterranean.'

Antony began to feel as if he were floundering in very deep water.

'But that's Roman territory,' he protested.

'Oh yes,' she said bitterly. 'Roman territory by right of conquest. I know all the arguments but do you really think it's fair for Rome to snatch other people's countries without their permission?'

Antony looked baffled. It was an issue which had always troubled him, even though everyone else seemed to think it was obvious that anyone strong enough to seize a territory had the right to keep it. But Antony had always sympathized with underdogs. He couldn't help feeling that if he had been a poor peasant toiling away on a plot of land, he wouldn't like to have it snatched away from him.

'Well, it's the custom,' he pointed out and then added with a rare flash of shrewdness, 'Your ancestors did it!'

Cleopatra paused, frowning thoughtfully. She had hoped that fact wouldn't occur to him, but Antony was sometimes brighter than he looked.

'Yes, that's true,' she admitted. 'But they didn't pillage and destroy the territories they took as you Romans do.'

'We don't!'

'Yes, you do!' she exclaimed in exasperation. 'You don't know half of the brutality and greed that goes on in your name, Antony, because you always believe what anyone tells you. But I know for a fact that your subordinates are taking bribes and fleecing the provincials right through Asia Minor. In fact, the whole Roman bureaucracy all over the empire is impossibly corrupt. What it needs is strong people at the top who are committed to reform.'

'What kind of reform?' demanded Antony suspiciously.

'Power sharing with the provincials!' she flashed back. 'Do you think it's fair that all the most important government jobs in the east go to Romans who know nothing about local conditions? Why not employ local people to do them? And why are the Romans who are sent out to work in the provinces always such upper-class fools? Why can't intelligent, capable people be given the jobs, instead of senator Haw Haw's youngest son? There's a woman working in my treasury who's worth a hundred of the upper-class idiots who came out with Gaius Rabirius when my father was alive. She would have done the job of financial manager ten times better than he –'

'A woman?' Antony went as rigid as if he had just laid his hand on an electric eel. 'Do you mean to tell me you want to employ women in important administrative jobs?'

'Why not? Here in Egypt we have women who are mural painters, doctors, scholars in the museum, political advisers – '

Antony stared at her with an appalled expression. He felt as disoriented as he had one night at a banquet when he had peered at his reflection in the concave surface of a silver spoon and found to his drunken amazement that it was upside down. The idea of a world where women worked side by side with men, or even ruled them, overwhelmed him with a sense of strangeness and bewilderment. Could Cleopatra really want women to hold important posts and make political decisions openly and not just in private?

'That's outrageous!' he said sharply. 'It's ridiculous. If that's all that your oracles are about, then they belong in the fire.'

Rising to his feet, he crumpled up the scrap of papyrus and flung it into the brazier of hot coals where it burned with a hissing blue flame.

'It's not all that they're about!' she shouted hotly, leaping to her feet. 'They're about preparing the way for a new regime of peace and prosperity with you and me as god King and Queen, looking after our people. That's what the eastern provinces need – it's what the whole Roman empire needs!'

The words 'peace' and 'prosperity' echoed uncomfortably in Antony's mind. Thinking of all the slaughter he had witnessed over the last twenty-five years, he was almost tempted to agree with her. He swayed like a man on a precipice above a hot spring, being assured that the waters below were healing, but unwilling to take the risk of plunging into them. Then he thought of the agreement he had signed with the other triumvirs and stepped back a pace.

'I can't make you a partner in governing the empire,' he muttered. 'Not formally, anyway. I've taken an oath to Lepidus and Octavian.'

'And do you think Octavian cares about his oath to you?' she demanded passionately. 'Don't you think he'd take the first opportunity to remove you from power if he could?'

Antony winced. He knew that what she was saying was true, and yet he had always regarded oaths as sacred. Even if Octavian was a treacherous little shit, did that give Antony the right to break his sworn word?

'What do you want from me?' he demanded in a harassed voice.

'I want you to marry me and make me your Queen,' she said simply.

'I can't marry you! I can't even make a full pact to give you power anywhere except in Egypt and Cyprus. It would be treason on my part. Treason and sacrilege.'

She crossed the room in three strides and snatched the front of his tunic in her fists. Looking down at her impassioned features, the tension in her muscles, the blazing determination in her eyes, he was shaken yet again by his need for her.

'Would it? Would it?' she cried. Then suddenly her face contorted and she laid one hand on her belly. 'Even now when I'm carrying your son or daughter in my womb, would it be treason and sacrilege for you to marry me and share the Roman empire with me?'

When the almond blossom began to appear in pink

drifts in the orchards around Alexandria, the first ship of the season arrived from Athens. It brought with it a cryptic message from Fulvia which made Antony's pulses thud with alarm. All it said was this:

Fulvia to Antony wishes health.

If you ever cared about me or the boys, come to me at once in Athens. We are staying in a rented villa at the foot of the Acropolis next to the tavern of Arion and the Dolphin. I need you desperately.

Antony could hardly control his anxiety as he hurried to pack and book a passage to Greece. What could have happened? He thought he had left Fulvia safely in Rome and it was not like her to panic or make a great issue out of a small one. Had one of the children died? But, if so, surely she would have written and told him? He should never have spent so much time here with Cleopatra. Guilt made him irritable and when Cleopatra became tearful and begged him not to leave, he flared up and they quarrelled. By the time he watched the towers of Alexandria slip out of sight beyond the ship's churning wake of foam, he was completely consumed by apprehension and annoyance. He had never intended to hurt anyone and now here was his wife in desperate straits and his mistress blotched and tearful and refusing even to say goodbye to him. There were times when he wished he could become a celibate hermit and be done with it! The news which reached him at the port of Tyre that the Parthians were massing for an invasion of the eastern provinces did not make him feel any happier, but there was little he could do about it immediately. He sent sealed orders to Italy where he had twenty-four legions, instructing them to sail east and deal with the menace. Then, praying that he was not deserting his own duty, he sailed on for Athens.

The city was as lovely as ever on a flawless spring day. Almond blossom, later here than in Alexandria, frothed in pale pink drifts over the trees and the sky was light blue with skeins of white cloud. He decided to walk the five miles from the port of Piraeus to the city, glad of the chance to stretch his legs and enjoy the sights and sounds. After so long cramped up in the prison of a ship, it was a pleasure to see goats grazing in small green allotments, to hear the clang of stonemasons' hammers, to smell the aroma of fresh bread from bakeries and to stop in a tavern for a cup of resinated wine and a plate of dried fish and olives. Anxiety about Fulvia did not allow him to linger long and he was soon standing outside the gates of a rather dilapidated villa at the foot of the Parthenon. He rang the bells loudly and an unfamiliar old slave with a bent back and a grizzled beard arrived to let him in.

'What can I do for you, sir?' he asked.

'I'm Mark Antony, Fulvia's husband,' he replied. 'Is she at home?'

The porter blinked, clearly taken aback. No doubt he would have expected a triumvir to arrive with a huge retinue, but there were times when Antony was impatient of ceremony.

'Yes, sir,' he said slowly, scratching the side of his nose. 'But she's asleep at the moment.'

Antony blinked. Fulvia, asleep? When the sun was almost directly overhead? Impossible! While Antony had been known to snore until noon after a drinking bout, Fulvia was always up at the first hour. What could be wrong?

'You'll be wanting to see your sons I suppose, sir,'

said the old man, ushering him into the dimness of the entrance hall. 'I'll send their nurse to bring them.'

Antony was seated in the sunny courtyard when the two little boys arrived shortly afterwards with a careless-looking slave girl. Antyllus gave a shout of joy at the sight of his father and ran forward to hug Antony's legs, while Iullus, the younger one, hid his face in the slave girl's dress and clearly did not recognize him. Although they were both bright eyed and curly haired, Antony had a vague feeling that they did not look as clean as they might have done. Antyllus's tunic was ripped and Iullus had a runny nose which had not been wiped. Coaxing them on to his lap with a box of honey and sesame cakes brought from Egypt, Antony did his best to repair the damage with a linen napkin dipped in the water fountain.

'Where's your mother?' he asked the older boy when the greetings were over.

'Asleep,' said Antyllus glumly. 'She sleeps all the time now.'

Antony's uneasiness grew.

'Go and wake her at once,' he ordered the slave girl.

'I can't, sir,' she whined. 'She's taken poppy juice. She'll sleep till evening now.'

In fact it was just before sunset when Fulvia emerged unsteadily into the courtyard, blinking at the light as if it hurt her eyes. He was shocked by the change in his wife's appearance and could scarcely believe it was her. In the two years since he had last seen her, she seemed to have wasted away. Her eyes looked hollow and sunken and her once massive frame was now gaunt. She held two of her fingers pressed into her diaphragm as if holding some oppressive pain at bay. Moved by an incredulous feeling of pity, Antony stepped forward and took her in his arms. Uncharacteristically, she burst into tears.

'Fulvia,' he said in dismay, stroking her lifeless hair which hung in rats' tails around her shoulders. 'What's wrong? Are you ill?'

'Yes, I am,' she said in a hoarse croak. 'But it's not only that. You won't want to hold me when you hear what's happened. Oh, Antony, I'm sorry. I'm sorry. You trusted me and I've failed you.'

As she spoke, he became aware that she smelled. A strange, sickly sweet, nauseating smell, as if her body were rotting from within. He stiffened, trying to conceal his distaste for fear of hurting her.

'Sit down,' he urged, moving around to the far side of a stone table and benches to put distance between them. 'Tell me all about it.'

She smiled grimly as if she recognized his manoeuvre for what it was.

'My illness first,' she said with a touch of her old arrogant disdain for anything that tried to get the better of her. 'The doctors say it's some kind of internal cancer and they can do nothing for me. I've a few months left at the most.'

Antony half rose to his feet, looking appalled, but she seized his hand in her scrawny one and pushed him back down into his seat.

'I haven't finished,' she insisted. 'That's not what counts any more. You need to know the dangers you're facing in Italy.'

'Dangers?' he echoed, as baffled as if she were speaking a foreign language. 'What dangers?'

'Octavian is doing his best to turn the entire country against you. Lucius won the consent of the Senate to wage war against him, but Octavian defeated us.'

'You made war on Octavian?' asked Antony in

478

horror. 'But I had sworn an oath of non-aggression against him! How could you do such an underhand thing?'

Fulvia gave a dry, choking laugh and shook her head, so that her hair surged round her shoulders like a cloud of ashes. Antony noticed that it had gone quite grey.

'Underhand,' she whispered. 'Oh, Antony, you poor fool. You can't afford to cling to your outmoded ideas of honour or you'll be the next to be ruined. There's nothing non-aggressive in Octavian's attitude towards you. You've only one chance of survival now. You must make a pact of alliance with Sextus Pompeius and kill Octavian before he kills you.'

'No,' shouted Antony, thumping his fist on the stone table. 'I will not forswear an oath.'

'Then you'll die for being so stupid,' snapped Fulvia. For an instant she looked at him with her old ferocity and then she caught her breath. Suddenly, as if she were tired of the whole business, as if it were a game she was no longer interested in playing, she motioned to the slave girl to step forward with a flask of some liquid. Putting it directly to her lips, Fulvia swigged urgently from it, then shuddered and let her head collapse in her hands. Antony opened his mouth to protest, but realized that he was already too late.

Shuffling to her feet, Fulvia made her way back to the pillars that supported the peristyle. Leaning on one of them for support, she looked back at him, blinking as if she saw him only blurrily. Twice, she opened her mouth, as if to give him further instructions, but her strength was not equal to it.

'Take care of the children,' she begged at last, and then vanished.

For the next few days, Antony was so overwhelmed

with anger and disbelief and a sense of betrayal that he was paralysed into total inaction. He felt that everyone had wronged him, Octavian, Fulvia, Cleopatra. All he wanted was to be open and honest and to play by the rules, but it seemed there were no rules any more. What was he to do? On the night Fulvia died, Antony took the two little boys to their room and tucked them clumsily into bed himself. Six-year-old Antyllus cried, but four-year-old Iullus, although upset, clearly didn't understand what was happening.

'Is Mummy coming to tell me a story?' he asked.

Antony flinched.

'No,' he said distractedly. 'No, Iullus. I'll be looking after you from now on.'

'Oh,' said Iullus, eyeing him askance. 'Are we going to keep living here?'

Antony bowed his head, feeling shaken and strangely lost without Fulvia to advise him. Where were they going to go? Should he send the boys back to Rome to the care of a relative? Or would he be sending them into danger if Octavian was so hostile towards him? Or now that he was a widower, should he simply go back to Egypt and marry Cleopatra? He stared helplessly at his two little boys, feeling as if his brain had turned to porridge.

'I don't know,' he said huskily. 'I wish by all the gods that I did.'

Octavian was exultant as the messenger from Gaul left the room. He rose to his feet and paced around with such a bright, glittering look in his eyes that Maecenas was reminded of Julius Caesar plotting the invasion of a new territory or the downfall of a political rival.

'Now I've got Mark Antony just where I want him!' announced Octavian, brandishing the letter in the air.

'Remember how I told you that his legate Fufius Calenus died suddenly in Gaul? Well, the minute I heard of it, I sent orders to Calenus's son telling him that Mark Antony wanted all eleven legions handed over to my control until further notice and the little moron fell for it! Now the entire province of Gaul is mine and eleven legions. Eleven legions! When Antony arrives back in Italy, he'll find the gates of Brundisium barred against him and my next step will be to put legislation through the Senate to strip him of his powers as triumvir.'·

Maecenas looked dubious. 'You'd better go carefully,' he warned. 'In my opinion it's too much too soon. How do you know Antony hasn't formed a defensive alliance with Sextus Pompeius or one of the other naval commanders who were exiled after Caesar's assassination?'

Maecenas was right. Alarmed by Fulvia's warnings, Antony was not sailing blind into Octavian's trap. Sextus Pompeius, Pompey's youngest son, had been living by piracy ever since his defeat by Julius Caesar in Spain. Antony's kindness in recalling him from exile after Caesar's death had given him a somewhat easier life with Sicily as his base. Now he returned the favour by sending envoys to Antony in Greece offering an alliance against Octavian. Antony's reply was typical.

'I can't break my pact with Octavian until I know for sure that he's dishonoured it,' he said. 'If he's kept the terms of his oath with me, I'll do my best to reconcile him with you, Sextus. If he has betrayed me, then I'll be honoured to accept your alliance.'

Sextus was not the only pirate of noble birth to warn Antony of Octavian's intrigues against him. On the Adriatic coast Antony received a message from

Domitius Ahenobarbus, a red-bearded giant of a man, who had taken part in the conspiracy against Julius Caesar and been an outlaw ever since. Domitius's warning was even more blunt than that of Sextus.

'That little bastard Octavian is out to get you, Antony. I'm bringing my fleet along as an escort to make sure that you land safely on Italian shores.'

Even so, it was not until Antony sailed into the harbour at Brundisium and found the city gates shut fast against him that he really believed what he had been told. For once he lost his temper.

'That creeping little toad!' he shouted as the bronze gates remained obstinately closed. 'Lock me out of my own country, would he? I'll teach him a lesson!'

Blazing with anger, he set about blockading the town and sent forces further up the coast. He also sent word to Sextus Pompeius who was only too happy to join the struggle against Octavian. In Rome, Octavian was alarmed to be informed by his chief military adviser Marcus Agrippa that the situation in southern Italy was looking grim and he had better march south and negotiate with Antony.

Encamped near Hyria a few miles inland from the coast, Antony was beginning to enjoy himself. He had won a brilliant cavalry victory the previous morning and was relishing the prospect of crushing Octavian decisively and stripping him of all his honours. The news of the loss of Gaul and his eleven legions there had not discouraged him in any way, but only fuelled his incredulous rage against his younger partner. In his present frame of mind, he would gladly have ripped Octavian apart with his bare hands. But on that evening he had two visitors who changed his mind.

The first was a retired veteran who had fought beside him at Philippi. He ducked in under the leather tent flap looking ill at ease and shuffling from one foot to the other as Antony's batman introduced him.

'Sir, this is Aulus Pupius Balbus, a retired veteran who served under you at Philippi.'

Antony rose from his folding chair and gripped the other man's hand warmly.

'It's always a pleasure to see an old comrade in arms,' he said heartily. 'Sit down and take a cup of wine with me, and tell me what brings you here.'

The veteran lowered himself on to Antony's camp bed and looked unhappier than ever as he accepted the wine cup. He took a hasty gulp, gritted his discoloured teeth and dropped his gaze.

'You see, sir, it's like this,' he muttered. 'After I was honourably discharged from the army, I was settled on a small farm near here, thanks to Octavian. I'm doing well in my retirement. I've got a roof over my head, a full belly and I've married a local girl. Even got a kid on the way after all these years. There's a lot of us Philippi veterans in the same situation. Well, now Octavian's sending a recruiting agent around our farms telling us we've got to join an emergency legion and fight against you.' He took another gulp of wine and rubbed his sweaty palms down the coarse woollen tunic that covered his thighs. 'I don't want to fight again, sir. Especially not against you. But if we don't, Octavian will take our farms away. Ain't there some way you can make peace with him?'

Antony felt as if he had received a javelin thrust straight to the heart. He sat for a further quarter of an hour drinking with the old legionary and reassuring him that he would bear no malice against him, whatever his decision. Yet after the grizzled veteran had shaken his hand, wrapped himself in his cloak and stumbled out into the cool night air, Antony slumped down on to his camp bed with a weary sigh. He should have foreseen this! What the hell was he to do? He couldn't allow Octavian to go around evicting these tired old men from their homes, but that was what would happen if he continued this war. There would be more bloodshed than ever. And for what? So that Mark Antony's pride could be intact? So that he could hold up his head and proclaim that he hadn't let that little runt get the better of him? Was it worth it when he considered the cost in other people's lives?

He was still pondering miserably over this when his batman appeared once more outside his tent. His voice came through the leather, slightly muffled and with an undertone of amusement.

'Sir, there's a lady here to see you.'

With a startled oath, Antony sprang to his feet. There were prostitutes among the camp followers, of course, there always were, but for once Antony had not been involved with them. Ever since Fulvia's death, he had felt so guilty and depressed that he had taken no interest in women, particularly with this political crisis hanging over his head. Had Domitius Ahenobarbus sent him a whore as a friendly joke to raise his spirits?

'Send her in,' he ordered.

The woman who came creeping into his tent did not look like a whore, even though he could not catch the slightest glimpse of her features. She was completely swathed in a cloak of soft brown lamb's wool and beneath that she wore a veil of Chian silk so that Antony had the eerie impression that she had no face. Her whole body seemed to shrink inwards on itself as if she were filled with misgivings at finding herself in such a place.

'Won't you sit down?' asked Antony courteously,

waving at the folding chair. 'Would you feel more comfortable if you had an attendant with you?'

'Yes,' she stammered. 'Thank you. No ... I wouldn't. I've left my maid outside. I wanted this conversation to be secret. Oh dear, this is so difficult!'

Antony dismissed his interested batman with a curt nod and a frown of warning against eavesdropping. Then he crossed to the tray of drinks on the folding table and looked back over his shoulder at his guest.

'Won't you let me see you?' he coaxed. 'It's so hard to have a conversation with someone invisible, and you won't be able to join me in a drink with that veil thing over your face.'

Her fingers trembled visibly as she drew back the hood and then unwound the veil from around her head. He judged that she was about thirty years old with blonde hair caught back in a respectable bun, blue eyes and sweet, rather sad features. The delicate earrings in her ears and the tasteful gold necklace around her throat suggested that she came from a prosperous family and her accent was unmistakably patrician. Antony had the oddest feeling that he had met her somewhere before.

'Don't I know you?' he asked.

The colour rushed up into her face.

'I'm Octavia,' she said unsteadily. 'The sister of the triumvir.'

Antony was so shocked that the silver spoon dropped from his hand and fell on the tray with a clatter. He looked at her in consternation.

'Octavia!' he echoed. 'What in the world are you doing here?'

She caught her lower lip in her teeth and took a deep, unsteady breath.

'If you're offering me a drink, I'd be glad of it,' she said in a rush.

Intrigued and disturbed, Antony spooned honey into two cups, added wine and cinnamon and hot water. Then he turned and passed one of them to Octavia.

'Does your brother know you're here?' he demanded.

She blushed again in obvious confusion.

'No, and you mustn't tell him,' she implored. 'He thinks I'm safely within the town of Brundisium.'

'Then why have you come to see me?' demanded Antony, utterly baffled. 'You must know that your brother is no friend of mine any more.'

'I do know it,' she agreed despairingly and gritted her white teeth as if she were some raw recruit about to launch into battle for the first time. Her words came out in a staccato rush. 'And I'm sorry for it. I think Octavian is behaving abominably, but he's half mad, you see, just like Uncle Julius. So that's why I've come here, to offer myself to you.'

'What?' Antony was so stunned that he was almost rooted to the spot. 'What do you mean?'

'I'm proposing that you and I should make a marriage alliance,' she said hastily, spilling out the words before her nerve could fail her. 'It's the usual thing to seal an important political agreement and we're both free agents now. I heard about your wife Fulvia – I'm so sorry – and I've recently been widowed too. It's the only answer, don't you see?'

Antony had never felt more baffled than he did in that moment.

'No, I don't,' he said blankly.

'It will save Italy from another civil war,' urged Octavia passionately. 'My brother can't possibly fight you if you're married to me. Oh, please, Antony, it's our only chance of keeping the peace.'

Chapter Twenty-five

'There's a trireme flying Mark Antony's flag in the harbour,' announced Iras, hanging out the window and squinting.

Cleopatra felt as if a sudden shaft of sunlight had pierced the gloom of her feelings. It was months now since Antony's abrupt departure and, apart from a brief euphoria when she learnt of Fulvia's death, she felt as if she had spent the entire time at the bottom of a black pit. As with Caesarion, pregnancy and child-birth had left her feeling ill and exhausted. Even now, seven weeks after the birth of her twins, Alexander Helios and Cleopatra Selene, she was subject to sudden outbursts of violent weeping. The birth itself had been painful and hideous, and afterwards her breasts had hurt so much that she had handed the task of feeding over to two wet nurses. Then she had suffered an irrational despair, as if she had left her babies out on a bare hillside for vultures to devour. As if all that were not bad enough, seven-year-old Caesarion was jealous and sulky, the Macedonian nobles were deeply disapproving of her single motherhood and the political news from Parthia and Italy was worrying. Now, with the arrival of Antony's ship, she felt the same powerful feeling of joy she had experienced once in the Alban hills outside Rome when, in the aftermath of a storm, five fingers of light had suddenly descended from a charcoal grey cloud and transformed the grimness of the landscape with their radiance. She could think of only one reason for Antony's return. He was coming to ask her to marry him. She knew he was!

Yet it was not Antony who arrived from the harbour, but one of her own slaves whom she had sent with him as a parting gift. Uneasiness pumped through her veins as the black-skinned Nubian youth prostrated himself at her feet.

'Get up,' she commanded. 'Where's Antony? What news do you bring?'

The boy looked around unhappily, as if he were checking the escape routes.

'It's not good news, my lady,' he mumbled. 'He's married again.'

'Married?' She could not believe it, could not take it in. It was too shocking, too cataclysmic! 'Did you say married?'

'Yes,' he agreed, backing away nervously from the wildness in her eyes.

She pursued him, clutched his arm.

'Who?' she demanded.

'Octavia,' he blurted out. 'The sister of the triumvir.'

Suddenly she released his arm and uttered a terrible cry as if he had struck her to the heart. With a frenzied movement she tore off the gold and pearl hairnet which had been one of Antony's gifts to her. Then she snatched the string of pearls around her neck and jerked it so hard that the tiny white balls flew like hailstones all over the mosaic floor. Lastly she seized her green silk gown and ripped it to shreds, as if she were mourning the death of her children. Low, whimpering cries choked from her throat as she flung herself on the floor, hitting her lip so hard that she left a smear of blood on the tiles.

'No! No! No!' she shrieked in frenzy.

'You'd better go,' advised Iras, seizing the messenger's arm and steering him to the door. 'In this mood the Queen might well have your tongue cut out for offending her so deeply.'

Iras was experienced enough to allow Cleopatra to cry herself to a standstill before she intervened. At last she raised her blotched and swollen face and Iras took pity on her, hoisted her up and helped her to her bedchamber.

'I thought he loved me,' she moaned as she allowed herself to be laid back against the pillows.

'I'm sure he does.'

'No, he doesn't! He's marrying that Roman bitch! And she's Octavian's sister.'

'I'm sure he doesn't care about her,' said Iras soothingly. 'It's only a political marriage.'

'And that's supposed to comfort me?' she demanded hysterically, starting up against Iras's restraining hands. 'Of course it's political! And that means she'll be the one queening it over the entire Mediterranean and I'll be abandoned! Abandoned! Oh, I wish I were dead!'

Iras sighed wearily. Sometimes she longed to slap Cleopatra's face. Of course everything she was saying was true, but why did she have to be so obsessive about the things she wanted? Didn't she still have three fine, healthy, living children and a kingdom to call her own? Whereas all Iras had was an urn containing her son's ashes and a small bedroom on the top floor of the palace. With a feeling of exasperation she saw that she was in for a weary day of listening to endless tears and recriminations and disconnected reminiscences of every moment Cleopatra had spent in Antony's company, when all she really wanted was a bit of peace. But she was Cleopatra's slave . . . and her friend. Sighing, she pulled a chair up to the bedside and prepared to listen.

It went on just as long as she expected. Iras had to listen to every detail of Cleopatra's first meeting with Antony, the stratagems they had used to carry on their love affair while her father was alive, the way she had hated Caesar and how Antony had been the only one who had kept her sane while she lived in Rome, how she had always loved him and would have married him if only her duty had allowed it, how he had even proposed to her in a wooden hut the night after Caesar's assassination, but Fulvia and Octavia and all those other scheming Roman bitches had been determined to ruin her happiness. Then there was a day-by-day account of their time together in Tarsus and Judaea and a retelling of the fishing episode in Alexandria. By the time they got on to the suicide threats and the fresh outbursts of frenzied weeping, Cleopatra's eyelids looked as pink as a pair of boiled shrimps and Iras's left leg had pins and needles. It was an immense relief when Charmion opened the door and entered the room with a fresh piece of news.

'Guess what?' she said, advancing rather gingerly to look down at Cleopatra. 'Herod the tetrarch of Galilee has come to visit you.'

Feminine to the core, Cleopatra did not want any man, least of all Herod, to see her dishevelled from weeping. Yet she was intrigued to know what had brought him to Alexandria and after a couple of hours lying down in a darkened room with slices of cucumber over her eyes to take away the swelling, she invited him to have dinner with her.

By the time he was shown into an intimate apartment adjoining her bedchamber, she flattered herself that she looked considerably better than most women of twenty-nine. Her raven dark hair was coiled into a smooth knot on top of her head and threaded with amethysts and pearls. Her face had been carefully made up with white lead and pounded poppy juice and a fragrance of rose petals hung about her. Her dress had come all the way from China and was made of an amethyst-coloured silk with little medallions of gold let into the hem. Her shoulder brooches were gold, too, and she wore a necklace of twisted gold acanthus leaves around her throat. As she lay reclining on her cushioned dining couch, she had the complacent feeling that she was looking her best. Certainly Herod seemed to think so. When he was shown into the room, his eyes narrowed in unmistakable admiration at the sight of her.

'You look very beautiful, Cleopatra,' he said, going on one knee to kiss her hand.

She shrugged, half annoyed by his breach of protocol in using her first name and failing to prostrate himself to her, but also ridiculously flattered by his interest. After Antony's rejection, it was like balm to her wounded heart.

In Rome she might have come immediately to the point and asked him what he was doing there, but in the east matters were handled differently. Common courtesy required that she ply him with food and drink and small talk before broaching the reason for his visit. She noticed that his tunic was shabby, that there was a new gauntness to his face that showed off the fine sculpted lines of his bones and that he ate ravenously of everything. Freshly baked bread, fried fish from the river, roast guinea fowl, vegetables, sweet pastries and fruit. Yet his drinking of wine was abstemious, as if he were a man with a mission who must keep a clear head. At last when only the nuts and raisins remained, and the slaves had withdrawn from the room, she decided it was time to question him.

'To what do I owe the honour of your company?' she asked with a hint of tartness.

He looked directly at her and she noticed that his dark eyes were surrounded by ridiculously long, silky eyelashes.

'I need your help,' he said frankly. 'I've been driven out of Galilee by my enemies.'

'Really?' She popped a grape into her mouth and crushed its sweetness on her tongue, savouring the sense of power that his plight gave her. 'What kind of help do you want from me?'

'I want you to lend me money so that I can go on to Rome and ask Mark Antony to restore me to my position as tetrarch.'

She was enjoying this more and more. Lounging back on her couch, she thought of his hints of blackmail in Judaea and knew he was thinking of them, too. How pleasant it was that she now had the power to make him squirm!

'Why should I want to help you?' she asked silkily.

His mouth set in a tough, resentful line. She knew he was hating every moment of this interview and it made her feel like an official torturer gleefully giving the rack another twist.

'Because I can keep the Parthians at bay! I'll stop them from overrunning the eastern Roman provinces and perhaps even taking over Egypt. I'm a capable soldier.'

'Are you?'

At his sharp intake of breath she knew she had gone too far and a strange sense of terror and tempestuous delight thudded through her veins as he sprang from his dining couch and loomed over her. Her heart plunged with excitement as he seized her by the wrists, hauled her to her feet and kissed her savagely.

'I'm also a capable lover,' he growled.

Her heart was hammering so violently that the amethyst silk on her breast was heaving with its movement. Her senses swam and her legs would scarcely hold her, but she fought to remain cool.

'Really?' she retorted. 'You come with a sworn testimonial from grateful customers, do you?'

His eyes leapt with such rage that she thought he would hit her, but all he did was to tighten his grip on her so that she found herself clamped in the muscular prison of his arms.

'No,' he snapped back. 'But I do give obligation-free demonstrations of my skills.'

'You're a sleazy, scheming swine, Herod,' she breathed.

'And I've no doubt you're a qualified judge! Tell me, how are your preparations for the arrival of the Messiah progressing, Cleopatra?'

'Better than yours, darling. I haven't been driven out of my kingdom, at any rate. My subjects still believe that I'm a living goddess, whereas yours obviously believe that you're a living devil.'

He caught her by the hair, forcing back her head and kissed her naked, quivering throat with sinister gentleness. An unexpected excitement surged through her at his nearness, at the tense urgency of his virile physique, at the ruthless energy that radiated out from him.

'As a matter of fact, I believe you're both,' he murmured. 'A living goddess and a she-devil. Kiss me again.'

The blood roared in her ears as his mouth came down on hers and she strained against him, matching his passion with equal fervour. As they grappled and clung together, his hot breath tickled her ear.

'Come to bed with me,' he whispered hoarsely.

'Why should I?'

'Because you want to. The only good reason that there is. I've lusted after you from the first moment I saw you and it's the same for you, isn't it?'

'No,' she lied.

He laughed, a hoarse, smoky sound, then he slid his fingers adroitly up between her thighs and brought them away, glistening.

'And this is just because you hate me? All right, I'm not fussy! Hatred will do as long as it has this effect on you. As a matter of fact, hatred can be a very powerful aphrodisiac.'

He was right, as she soon found out. She was aware that she disliked and distrusted him, but she found his arrogance shamefully erotic. A gasp of outrage escaped her as he bunched the amethyst fabric of her gown in his fists and ripped it off her in a single, violent movement. She heard the gold brooches strike the floor and felt the slither of silk about her ankles. But the realization that she was naked apart from her jewellery sent a hot arrow of desire through her most intimate parts. As she stood with flushed cheeks and heaving breasts, Herod inspected her mockingly from under half-closed lids. To her shame and annoyance she felt the blood begin to throb like fire through her veins and a mysterious heat uncoiled deep within her. With a swaggering step Herod strode in a circle around her, as if she were a slave stripped for his inspection on the auction platform. She endured his scrutiny in silence with her head tilted defiantly and her mouth twisted, but she could not hide the evidence of her response. It was apparent in the sudden hardening of her nipples, in the tilt and sway of her hips as he drew closer.

The elusive, masculine tang of him filled her nostrils as he approached. She took a quick, shallow breath and closed her eyes briefly. Oh, gods, it was unbearable! She could feel the heat radiating off his body, smell that odour like leather or salt or wild parsley, sense the dangerous power that lurked in his tensed muscles. She did not even like the man, in fact she hated him. Yet her body seemed to have a will of its own. And what it wanted appalled her. To be flung back brutally on that cushioned couch, to be seized in those ruthless, possessive arms, to feel his hot, hard cock thrust into the wetness that pulsated in waves of fire between her legs ... With a faint shudder, she forced her eyes to open.

'You want it, don't you?' he demanded, leering down at her with an insulting mixture of amusement and triumph.

'No,' she hissed.

'Liar.'

He thrust his hand between her thighs again, moving his fingers with such adroitness that she moaned softly. Desperate to escape the madness that was overwhelming her, she grabbed at his wrist and tried to haul it away.

'Good,' he growled throatily. 'There's nothing I like better than to take it by force.'

They grappled in a silence broken only by the frantic clamour of her breathing, but she knew from the start that it was useless. He did not carry an ounce of spare flesh, but his lean physique held an unbelievable strength. The muscles in his arms stood out like whipcords as he seized her wrists and forced her hands effortlessly up to the level of his torso. Amused by her struggles, he held her wrists as if they were manacled together. They might as well have been. His grip was as inescapable as solid iron.

'Admit that I'm your master!' he taunted.

'Never!'

'Then I'll have to teach you a lesson. Rebellious slave women are always taught to obey.'

Panting and gasping with outrage, she felt his grip tighten. She had thought it painful before, but now skewers of hot iron seemed to lance down the backs of her arms.

'Kneel and suck my cock,' he ordered.

'You bastard!' she gasped.

'Go on, bitch. Obey me and enjoy it.'

The dreadful thing was that she did enjoy it. Shrieking and struggling, she found herself forced to her knees before Herod adroitly transferred his grip, leaving his right hand free. Then he hoisted up his tunic, exposing a swollen, throbbing organ of impressive size.

'If you bite me, I'll kill you,' he warned. 'Now suck.'

With a vicious movement he caught her by the hair and thrust it into her mouth. The hot, hard size of it almost choked her, but her body seemed to melt and flow with the juices of desire. A low whimper escaped her and she gave herself up with total abandonment to the satisfaction not only of her own desires, but of his.

For a short time he stood with his legs straddled, thrusting ruthlessly into her and enjoying her subservience. But when she suddenly stiffened and moaned, he took a more active role.

'You're not coming yet,' he hissed, snatching her by the hair and hauling her off him. 'I'm the one who's master here and I'll choose the moment when you get your satisfaction. And it won't be until I've had mine. Turn over!'

With a rough movement, he turned her over, exposing her plump, soft buttocks. Positioning himself behind her, he drove in as if he were a stallion covering a mare. She braced herself for pain, but there was none. Her body was so slick with wanting that she felt only a deep, savage satisfaction at the cruel force of his thrusts. Even when he cupped her breasts mercilessly and pounded her as hard as if he were a battering ram at a city's gates, she felt only an intoxicating pleasure. And when at last he reached his climax, erupting into her with a hoarse groan of triumph and biting her shoulder, she stiffened and cried out in equal frenzy.

He did not hug her afterwards, as Antony would have done. Instead he simply rolled off her and lay with his eyes closed, looking as if he had just devoured a huge meal or enjoyed a win at the races. Blank, sated, self-contained. With her heart still racing and her pulses thundering, Cleopatra glared at him resentfully. But as her breathing slowly quietened, she had to admit silently to herself that he had left her fulfilled, as well as humiliated. There was no doubt about it – Herod was a damned good fuck! Probably the best she had ever had, although there had been moments with Antony . . . She pushed the thought away. She was not going to think of Antony any more! After his betrayal and desertion, this new Jewish lover was exactly what she wanted, virile, sensual, but with a streak of ruthlessness so unmistakable that she would never make the error of falling in love with him. And no doubt he was a capable soldier too since he was Roman trained. Perhaps he was even capable enough to recruit and drill an entire Egyptian army which could repel any future invasions? The thought filled her with excitement of an entirely different kind and she hauled herself up on her elbows and trailed a finger down Herod's muscular, hairless chest.

'I have a proposition to put to you. Don't go to Rome, stay here instead. I'd like to make you a commander in my army with an annual salary of half a million Roman sesterces.'

The sum took his breath away and he was even more stunned when she rose to her feet, padded across to a carved chest and drew out a wallet full of gold coins.

'There you are,' she said. 'Your first year's salary in gold denarii, if you accept my offer.'

'And what would Mark Antony say to that?'

'He'll say nothing to it! Since he has married Octavian's sister, we have had very little to say to each other.'

Herod was stunned by this news.

'Did you say . . . he's married?'

'Yes, didn't you know?'

'No, I didn't.'

He shook his head to clear it. This changed everything! Why should he waste his time courting Cleopatra when she had lost all influence over Mark Antony? It had been a pleasant evening's entertainment cocking a leg over her, but he would be a fool to waste more time on her. What he must do was head off to Rome at once to the real source of power.

She saw his frown and guessed some of what was passing in his mind. Picking up the wallet, she weighed its heaviness temptingly in front of him.

'There's a lot of confusion and danger in Rome at the moment. You'd do better to stay here. I can make you a wealthy man.'

Herod continued to eye the gold coins covetously. It was more money than he had ever seen in one place in his life and it could all be his. What she was saying was true. She would make him a wealthy man and he

498

would have the not inconsiderable pleasure of screwing his employer regularly. Besides that, he could always demand more money once he had made her truly dependent on him. The prospect was tempting, very tempting. And yet was it sufficient for his ambitions? He had never fancied himself as anyone's servant, least of all a woman's.

'Well, are you going to stay?' she coaxed.

'I'll sleep on it,' he replied, reaching between her thighs with a gesture that showed sleep was the last thing on his mind.

When she woke in the morning, the space beside her in the bed was empty and she was immediately struck by the hideous suspicion that she had been tricked and violated. Leaping out of bed, she shouted for Iras.

'Where's Herod?' she demanded.

'Gone,' was the grim retort. 'He must have sneaked out in the middle of the night. When I realized he was missing this morning I organized a search party, but it was too late. Apparently he was seen boarding a trading vessel bound for Rome at dawn.'

Cleopatra explored further and uttered a choking cry of wrath.

'He's taken that wallet of gold coins with half a million sesterces in it!'

'Half a million sesterces? Well, I hope he was worth it,' said Iras scathingly.

With a howl of rage Cleopatra picked up the pottery lamp which sat by her bed, smashed it on the floor, then tore apart a feather pillow and flung that down in the pool of oil which was leaking from the broken lamp. After that she stormed around the room, punching the walls and groaning. At last she collapsed on her bed in a flurry of feathers and let out her breath in a long wail.

'Everybody betrays me! Everybody!' she hissed. 'Well, I'll teach them a lesson, Iras, both Herod and his precious Mark Antony! Bring me writing materials. I want you to write a letter to Sextus Pompeius asking him to set up a blockade of ships around the Italian coast and intercept all the Egyptian grain carriers so that no more food gets through. If I can't have what I want, Rome can starve!'

The blockade soon began to cripple Italy. Bread disappeared from the bakers' shelves and while the nobles simply shrugged their shoulders and bought on the black market at outrageous prices, the poor began to starve in their thousands. The shortage of provisions drove up food prices to outrageous levels and soon the urban plebs were reduced to selling their pitiful clothes and furniture and cooking pots in the streets just in order to eat. With one of the mysterious reversals of public opinion, Octavian was given the chief blame for this. When he appeared in the Forum he was stoned by a furious mob and only Antony's intervention saved him from certain death. After his first terror was over, Octavian fumed in silence as he sat holding a pad to the bleeding wound above his left eye, while the litter jolted through a jeering crowd to Antony's house. It galled him to be in his brother-in-law's debt and to see the looks of dog-like devotion that his sister kept casting at Antony, even while she was supposedly dressing Octavian's wound.

He had always worshipped Octavia and he would have preferred her to live a life of chastity and mourning after the death of her husband Marcellus, instead of which she seemed to have fallen for Antony's leery charm just like any common whore. Octavian had been white with fury when she had publicly announced her intention to marry Antony in front of an assembly of veterans at Brundisium, but with all the old soldiers cheering and whistling, he had been unable to prevent the match. Now the thought of his failure galled him. He must get rid of Antony, but how? How? The man was a fool, a drunken halfwit with his brain in his testicles and someone of Octavian's superior intelligence should be able to outwit him easily. Yet for once Octavian was baffled. There must be some way of depriving Antony of his share of the empire, but for the moment he was unable to see it.

Had he but known it, Antony was within a hair's breadth of giving up political life anyway. He was fed up with the intrigues and the corruption and all he longed for was a quiet life. Octavia's timid, undemanding companionship had given him a measure of peace, but what he really wanted was a complete escape. Even his private life was not totally happy. He missed Fulvia and felt appallingly guilty that she had had to leave Rome without him. There were even times when he blamed himself for her illness and death. Who knew where cancers came from? Might they not be the product of sadness and disappointment? Well, disappointing people was the one thing Antony was good at! Look at Cleopatra too! That thought filled him not only with a pang of guilt but with a stab of illicit desire. He had received secret word of the birth of her twins and longed to sail east and see them, to explain to her why he had contracted this marriage with Octavia. He had already tried once to explain it in a letter, but the blunt, illiterate phrases had seemed unconvincing, even to him. 'I thort it was my duty . . . I never wanted to hurt annybody . . . I still love you, Cleopatra.'

In the end he had torn it up and burnt it. Apart

from anything else, it seemed disloyal to Octavia. None of the mess he was in was her fault and she had done her best to comfort him for Fulvia's loss. She even told him that she was looking forward to meeting his two little boys, who had been left behind in Athens, and he knew that her sweet nature would make no distinction between them and her own three children by Marcellus.

Bowing to necessity, Octavian reluctantly made a truce with Sextus Pompeius and the blockade was called off. There were no longer any frail, translucent waifs begging for bread in the streets and when Octavia presented Antony with a daughter in early September, for the first time since Fulvia's death, he was almost happy. He sat by Octavia's bedside, awkwardly holding under one massive arm the red-faced bundle with its spiky thatch of black hair, and gripping his wife's fingers with his free hand.

'Why don't we leave it all for a while?' he asked. 'Go off to Athens and spend some time together?'

She looked at him with incredulous joy dawning in her face.

'Oh, yes, Antony!' she breathed. 'Oh, yes, please.'

Octavian was relieved by their departure. If he could not be rid of Antony, he wanted him as far away from Rome as possible. Indeed, he was beginning to hope that he might be able to persuade Antony to mount an expedition against the Parthians and get himself killed in battle. The brainless oaf was bound to jump at the chance of performing a military exploit that Caesar himself had planned, but failed to execute. Well, that would keep for a while longer. At the moment Octavian was occupied by a more pressing matter. For the first time in his life he had fallen in love with a woman.

Livia, the wife of the ardent republican Tiberius

Claudius Nero, had been on the proscription lists, but had managed to flee to Sicily with her husband and little son. Now she was back in Rome under an amnesty and Octavian found himself obsessed by her. Tall, beautiful, haughty, she had repelled all his advances, but that only increased Octavian's fascination with her. He wondered what it would be like to stroke that long black hair, to lie beside that marble white body, to possess her utterly. Her very coldness intrigued him. She was like a statue of the virgin goddess Diana and Octavian wanted her more insatiably than he had ever wanted anything. To him she seemed like a symbol of purity and unattainability. If he could possess her, he felt that he would die happy.

Only two obstacles stood in his way. The fact that Livia seemed unswervingly loyal to her husband Tiberius and that Octavian's own wife, Scribonia, was shortly expecting a child. If Scribonia gave him the heir that he longed for, he did not feel that he could reasonably divorce her. Well, at least not yet. On the other hand, if all she produced was a worthless girl, nobody could blame him for taking such an action. On the day that Scribonia gave birth to a screaming, red-faced daughter, it was almost with a feeling of relief that Octavian formally issued her with notice of divorce. After which he sat down and wrote to Livia, begging her yet again to accept his hand in marriage.

CHAPTER TWENTY-SIX

Antony shifted uncomfortably on the cold marble seat and wished for the tenth time that he had accepted the offer of a cushion. Even in the sheltered, southward-facing courtyard, it was cold in Athens at this time of the year and the brazier of scented pine cones glowing orange near the speaker's podium did little to drive off the chill. It was enough to give a man piles, sitting around like this for hours on end! Grumpily he vowed that he was never coming to another book reading again, not even to please Octavia. It was all very well for her, she actually seemed to enjoy this sort of thing and he could see how she was obliged to be here, since Athenodorus had dedicated the book to her. But where did he fit in? And why did his wife have to be a patron of philosophers and architects? Why couldn't she be a patron of horse trainers and wine sellers and hunting shop owners? Antony would gladly come along and give her moral support in that case.

As it was, he shifted restlessly yet again, received a warning frown from Octavia and subsided. Discontentedly he tried to draw his wandering attention back to the lecturer's droning voice. The pretentious old windbag had got off the subject of virtue (thank the gods!), and was now burbling on about some character called Timon. This geezer had apparently become so fed up with all the shit he had had to take in public life, that he had become a grouch and a hermit. Well, Antony could identify with that! He was tempted to do the same thing himself. Perhaps then he'd never have to listen to another bloody stupid lecture or book reading in his life. He stole another gloomy glance at his wife and yawned surreptitiously. Shit! Why hadn't anyone told him what a pain this culture stuff could be? He was grateful to Octavia and he wanted to please her, but all these lectures and theatre performances and concerts of ancient music were boring him rigid. Even her attitude to sex depressed him – she seemed to think it was some perverted invention of his own. Although she was anxious to please him, she had obviously been brought up on the maxim that 'women don't move', and making love to her was about as exciting as performing necrophilia. Several times recently Antony had sneaked out to the bars near the Roman agora, got drunk, got laid and returned home considerably refreshed only to wake the following morning with a pounding head and a bad conscience. He also found himself dreaming frequently and guiltily of Cleopatra.

Suddenly Antony realized that the lecturer was almost at the end of his roll of papyrus. Perking up at the reviving prospect of hot wine, sausages, bread, and the big tits of the barmaid in the tavern opposite, Antony looked alert and attentive and clapped loudly as Athenodorus finished reading. Then he realized that he was the only one applauding. Octavia leaned across to him and whispered.

'That's only part one. There are three more parts to come.'

Antony rolled his eyes and groaned audibly. Abandoning all pretence of paying attention, he huddled down into his cloak, closed his eyes and let his thoughts drift again. Oh, what he would give for some action! If only he could be out on campaign, leading a cavalry charge or fighting hand to hand with a short sword or getting drunk in the officers' mess. His horoscope this morning had predicted news of battles from afar and the possibility of a love affair. It might even be true. The astrologer who had cast it was a slave given to him by Cleopatra before he left Alexandria and he had proved time and again to be uncannily accurate. Yet Antony could see no real prospect of a foreign war unless the trouble in Parthia blew up again. At the moment the military situation around the Mediterranean was at a stalemate like a board game of Robbers, where no player was strong enough to take out his opponents but all were glaring suspiciously and biding their time. Lepidus was settled happily enough in North Africa, and Antony and Octavian had divided most of the rest of the empire between them, while Sextus Pompeius had been bought off with Corsica, Sardinia, Sicily, the Peloponnese, a handsome sum of money and a promise of a future consulship. Only in the east was there any promise of action. Herod, the tetrarch of Galilee, had come to Antony several months earlier in Rome with a tale of Parthians massing on the Syrian borders. Alarmed by the news, Antony had strengthened the Roman troops in the area and made Herod King of Judaea to deal with the problem. He had no doubt of Herod's military talents, but he would give his eye teeth to be part of the action himself when it finally blew up.

Antony's head nodded, his beard spread out on his chest and he began to snore softly. Octavia was just about to nudge him awake when there was an interruption. A Roman soldier entered the courtyard, stood at attention and scanned the rows of white clad philosophers.

'Urgent dispatches from Syria for the triumvir Mark Antony,' he announced.

Only too grateful for the interruption, Antony

sprang from his seat and led the messenger into one of the empty lecture halls that opened off the peristyle.

'What's the news, man?' he demanded.

The sealed letter was clutched in the messenger's right hand, but Antony knew from experience how long winded dispatches could be. It was often best to get a quick oral summary first.

'It's serious, sir. You had heard, of course, that your legate Ventidius won some important engagements against the Parthian cavalry?'

'Yes, yes. Get on with it!'

'Well, it seems there's been a complication. The surviving Parthians took refuge with Antiochus of Commagene in the city of Samosata and you ordered Ventidius to take it by siege. There are allegations by Ventidius's second in command, Clarus, that he's accepted a bribe of a thousand talents from Antiochus to make the siege a deliberate failure. Clarus says that something will have to be done about it.'

'It certainly will!' agreed Antony exultantly, punching his right fist into the palm of his left hand. 'I'll have to go there and take command myself. You know, it's an odd thing, but my horoscope predicted something exactly like this only this morning!'

What Antony did not know was that Cleopatra's astrologer had bribed the military messenger not to deliver his news to the triumvir until after the horoscope had been cast. He also did not know that a summary of the message had been sent back to Cleopatra in Alexandria. By the time Antony set sail for Syria to subdue the Parthians she knew every move he intended to make and was laying her own plans accordingly.

*

On the fifteenth day before the Kalends of February in the seven hundred and sixteenth year from the founding of the city, which was the date scheduled for his wedding, Octavian woke up in bed with Maecenas and almost immediately found himself embroiled in a quarrel. It was a beautiful morning, although it was winter. Cold, pale sunlight filtered in through the half open shutters and against a cloudless blue sky birds could be seen in the leafless plane trees in the garden, fluffing up their feathers against the chill air. Octavian felt dizzy with excitement at the thought that Livia was at last to become legally his. Three days earlier her second son Drusus from her first marriage had been born and there was now no further impediment to her marriage to Octavian. Scandalized tongues might wag at the unseemly haste of the divorce and remarriage coming so soon after the birth, but Octavian was fiercely exultant at getting what he wanted. There were even rumours that Drusus was his son, but Octavian knew to his regret that this was untrue. All the same, Livia's evident fertility left him in no doubt that she would soon provide him with an heir. He was all ready to leap out of bed and begin dressing in his bridegroom's tunic when Maecenas's arm came round him.

'Just one more bout, darling,' purred Maecenas, 'before you take this dreadful step.'

'It's not a dreadful step,' retorted Octavian in exasperation. 'I love Livia and I want to marry her and last night was supposed to be the end of all that. Stop it, Maecenas . . . Don't touch me there . . . It's . . . Oh, damn you!'

He surrendered, as he'd known he would. Afterwards Maecenas lay beside him with a smug expression on his heavily powdered face and let his fingers trickle teasingly down Octavian's hairless chest.

'We've got to stop all this,' said Octavian in a tormented voice, jerking away from those seductive caresses.

'Why?'

'Because I'm getting married!'

Maecenas's plucked eyebrows rose.

'What's the connection? I know you need an heir, I'm not complaining about that, but half my sweethearts are married men. Every park in Rome is full of them. They hang about there lurking, positively lurking, in the bushes, lying in wait for young men who are drunk and short of cash on their way home. Why, my first introduction to Rome was when I came down here at eleven years old on holiday with my parents and there was a flasher who used to leap out of the bushes in their gardens across the Tiber. It was vewy impressive. I actually thought it was a new species of plant with an odd sort of stamen – '

'Shut up!' cried Octavian fiercely. 'It's no joke.'

'Dear me,' sighed Maecenas. 'We are cross this morning.' Licking his finger, he dabbed at the corner of his eye. 'Do you like my new make up? It came all the way from Egypt.'

'Don't talk to me of Egypt!' snarled Octavian. The very word was enough to bring him out in hives, reminding him as it always did of Cleopatra. 'I'm serious about this issue. We must stop seeing each other.'

'But why?' repeated Maecenas plaintively. 'Why?'

'Because I want to become respectable! Not only for Livia's sake, but for my own political future. I don't know if you realize it, but the vilest things are being said about me in Rome. If you'd been in the theatre yesterday, you would know what I mean. One of the actors came on stage pretending to be a eunuch priest of Cybele, the mother of the gods, and as he played his timbrel another actor exclaimed: "Look how this pervert's finger beats the drum!" Well, of course, the words had a double meaning in Latin. They could equally well have meant, "Look how this pervert's finger rules the world!" and that's the way the audience took it. They all cracked up and started roaring with laughter, whistling and cat calling and shouting my name. If you'd been there, you'd know why I was upset about it.'

As a matter of fact Maecenas had been there, although not in Octavian's company. He was enjoying a quiet little intrigue with the actor Bathyllus and had observed the whole comedy from backstage and been much entertained by it. Still, recognizing that Octavian was not amused, he composed his features into an expression of sympathy.

'That's dreadful, darling.'

'Yes, it is! I ask you, how is my "Back to Morality" campaign to have any credibility when people call me names like that?'

Maecenas shifted, stretched, reached down and stroked Octavian's genitals absent-mindedly. Octavian thrust away his hand as if he had been burnt.

'Don't you think you're going too far with this campaign?' asked Maecenas mildly. 'Winning votes and support is all very well, but aren't you getting just a teeny weeny bit carried away by your own propaganda?'

'It's not just propaganda, Maecenas,' said Octavian, sitting up and clutching his knees. 'Deep down, I've always felt troubled about the way I've been living my own life. I was strictly brought up, very strictly brought up, and when I was a youth I was more or less raped by an older man. I've told you all this, how it made me feel filthy, guilty, shamed – '

His voice began to shake and Maecenas patted him soothingly on the shoulders.

'I know, duckie, rape is nasty, nobody denies that. But at least you did discover that you liked it in the end.'

'I'm not sure of that!' retorted Octavian in a tormented voice. 'As a matter of fact, I often hate myself and now I feel I want to put it all behind me. Marrying Livia will give me a chance to do exactly that.'

'So you want to become respectable?' Maecenas's tone was full of incredulous amusement.

'Yes! And what's wrong with that? I want to make Rome respectable too. I'll bring in laws prohibiting adultery and encouraging marriage for the sake of producing children and I honestly think I ought to punish homosexual rapists with castration. They deserve it!'

'Oh, don't do that,' protested Maecenas in alarm. 'Just think, you might change your mind about all this moral fervour and you don't want to lose your own dangly bits, do you? If it comes to that, I don't want to lose mine. Why don't you just stick to punishing women and prohibiting them from enjoying sex? I've no objection to that. I'm warning you though, the voters won't like it!'

'I'll make them like it,' vowed Octavian, his eyes beginning to glitter. 'I'll hold rallies in honour of the family and get those tame poets of yours to write wedding hymns, I'll offer tax relief for large families and I'll only associate with men of irreproachable conduct. You will have to change, Maecenas. As a matter of fact I think you ought to get married too.'

'Oh, gods,' cried Maecenas faintly. 'Where did you put that bottle of Caecuban? I think I need a drink.'

'What's more,' continued Octavian, now in full flow, 'I'm sure it will work! I think it will bring me the support of the conservatives and make Livia respect and admire me.'

'Well, I think you're out of your fucking mind, sweetheart. Livia already respects and admires your power and money, and that's all she's interested in. If you think you'll have a good time taking cold baths, delivering sermons and turning moral, I won't try to stop you, but don't expect me to change.'

There was still a coolness evident between them when they arrived for the wedding ceremony at Livia's house. Octavian was sternly dressed in a white tunic with a purple stripe, but Maecenas was deliberately outrageous, scented, curled, wearing a saffron yellow shift the same colour as the bride's gown. As they came into the courtyard for the feast after the ceremony he leaned across confidingly to Octavian and spoke.

'I'll tell you one thing. If you go too far with this ridiculous morality campaign, it will only have the result of making Mark Antony more popular than you. A lot of people adore reprobates.'

'He's not a reprobate any longer,' said Octavian coldly. 'He's married to my sister.'

'Yes, darling, yes, but for how long?'

Cleopatra looked around the circle of her advisers. Olympus, Iras, Charmion.

'Mark Antony has written, asking me for money and troops for his Parthian campaign,' she said. 'What do you think I should do?'

She hated herself for the eagerness with which she had torn open his letter and the pang of disappointment with which she had read its contents. There had been not one word of a personal nature in it. No endearments, no reference to their twins, no indication that he cared about them although she knew he had received the information of their birth. She fought to subdue the barbed pain in her breast. Why should she care? He obviously didn't! Yet her anger continued to gnaw at her. Her first, white-hot impulse had been to write back and tell him to stuff himself but she knew she mustn't. That would only reveal the hurt which she was determined to hide and, besides, she must handle a letter of this kind not as a woman in love, but as a sovereign making a tricky political decision. Only one question must concern her. Egypt's advantage.

'What should I do?' she repeated.

There was a moment's silence as they shuffled and exchanged glances. Charmion was the first to speak.

'I think you should hedge your bets. Send him enough money and troops so that he can't complain of your disloyalty if he wins, but not so much that it will cripple Egypt if he loses.'

'Iras?'

Iras was silent for a moment, scowling thoughtfully. When she spoke there was a faraway look in her eyes, as if she were gazing down a long tunnel into the past.

'He's been messing around with this Parthian campaign for more than a year and nothing conclusive has been achieved. If Egyptian help managed to tip the balance now, he might be grateful enough to do whatever you wanted. When you were younger you used to claim that you wanted to win back the empire that your ancestors ruled. Do you still hope to do that? If you do, this might be the best chance that you'll ever have. If you help him conquer the Parthians, I'm sure he'll hand over more territory to you. He might even divorce Octavia and marry you. Do you want those things badly enough to take the risk?'

Cleopatra winced. Did she? It was true that in childhood she had drawn maps of Alexander the Great's conquest and chanted the strange, barbaric names to herself, half-hypnotized by their music. Parthia, Sogdiana, Bactria. And she had drawn another map – smaller but still of respectable size, showing the territory her ancestors had managed to keep after Alexander's death. Coile Syria, the cities of the Phoenician coast, Cyrene in North Africa, Cyprus, Arabia, Judaea. She remembered now the childish vows she had made, that one day she would win them back.

'Yes, I did have dreams of restoring the empire of my ancestors,' she admitted. 'I thought it was my destiny.'

Olympus snorted impatiently.

'Destiny! You'd do better to concentrate on holding what you've got.'

'Are you saying I shouldn't help Antony, then?' she asked.

Olympus shrugged.

'I was sold into slavery in my youth,' he said, 'so I have no trust in the benevolence of destiny. My philosophy is that it's best to be like the Nile reeds and bend with the wind, not like the proud oak trees that defy the elements and get uprooted. It's all very well to dream of ruling the world, but dreams are dangerous things and rulers are tempting targets.'

'Some people fulfil their dreams!' retorted Cleopatra, stung by his patronizing tone. 'Alexander the Great did.'

'Only when he surrendered the dreams and accepted them as reality. There is a difference, you know. The reality is that he suffered hideous spear wounds and raging fevers, that he was physically burnt out and died, sweating and hallucinating, when he was only thirty-three years old. That was the cost of realizing his dream. Is that the sort of cost you're prepared to pay?'

Cleopatra tossed her head defiantly.

'I might be!' she retorted.

Yet his words made her pause, because she knew there was truth in them. She was thirty-two now, almost the age Alexander had been when he died, and she was hardened and cynical enough after the knocks life had delivered her to know that glory was not easily won. Sometimes simply plodding on from day to day was difficult enough. There were moments when she was seriously tempted to give up all her old ambitions and content herself with watching her children grow, and passively accepting whatever life sent her. Caesarion was nearly eleven now and the twins were three. She adored them when she remembered them, but she was usually too deep in work even to notice them. A twinge of sadness pierced her as she remembered Selene's sad little face peering around her office door only that morning.

'Play with me, Mummy,' Selene had begged.

'I can't, darling, I'm too busy.'

She was always too busy. But if she gave up her dreams of power, wouldn't she have more time for her children?

Even as the thought crossed her mind, she knew she could not do it. She could no more stop being ambitious than she could stop breathing. Her eyes turned opaque and she stared vacantly at Olympus, but she didn't see him. What she saw was the harsh terrain of Parthia, columns of marching soldiers, creaking siege engines and Mark Antony in the scarlet cloak of a

Roman general. Oh, yes, Mark Antony! She might hate him for abandoning her and preferring Octavia, but she still dreamt of him. His warmth, his crushing embraces, his booming laughter. He was the father of two of her children and yet he had never even seen them. Tears pricked her eyes as the daydreams came thicker and faster. She saw herself arriving in Syria with the twins, Antony embracing her, gaping at the troops and money she had brought him, hurrying off to defeat the Parthians and coming back, flushed with gratitude, to marry her.

'You're a fool!' said Olympus sharply, as if he saw all that was passing before her eyes. 'You forget that I grew up in Scythia and was riding a horse over those treeless steppes before I could even walk. Roman armies are useless in that kind of terrain and climate. The Parthians will be able to defeat them without even firing an arrow.'

'How?' challenged Cleopatra.

'There are two great weapons that the land itself supplies. Cold and hunger. The Parthians will retreat within their defensive walls and once the winter comes on, if the Romans don't have adequate siege machinery to break in, they'll starve and freeze to death. I'm warning you again, stay out of it.'

Even as he spoke, he knew it was useless. He saw from the look of stubborn yearning in her face that she would go to Antony's aid. What was it about that pair? They were so mismatched, and yet it was like watching a Mars of polished iron and a lodestone Venus drawn inexorably together. What would be the final result of their turbulent union? Olympus had the ominous feeling that it was bound to lead to disaster.

When Cleopatra came to Antioch in Syria, her arrival was not the exuberant, impromptu affair that her entrance into Caesar's chamber in the bedroll had been eleven years before. This time it was a carefully orchestrated public event which had seen many days of preparation. She was in a fever of anxiety as her attendants fussed around her on the morning that her ship was due into port.

'I've got crow's feet around my eyes!' she wailed as Charmion stroked delicately with a brush at her lower lids.

'No, you haven't.'

'Oh, gods, is that a grey hair? Pull it out, Iras, quickly. He'll think I'm hideous, won't he? Charmion, tell me honestly, have I changed much since I was fourteen?'

'You look better than ever,' said Charmion diplomatically. 'And anyway, Antony is bound to look much older than you do. He's forty-five now, remember?'

Charmion was right. Antony's beard and temples were shot with silver and Cleopatra saw that there was a hint of a paunch beneath his barrel chest as he came striding down the chief reception room of the governor's palace to meet her. Even so, he looked as burly and powerful as ever in his purple consular gown and the frank admiration and delight in his hazel eyes sent the old familiar yearning coursing through her veins.

'Cleopatra!' he exclaimed joyfully, helping her down out of her litter and kissing her on the mouth. 'I've missed you so much. It's wonderful to see you! You look magnificent.'

His gaze rested warmly on her scarlet dress, her gold jewellery, the lush curves of her body. There was no mistaking the leap of desire in his eyes and his hand lingered longer than necessary on her arm as he guided her to a couch. She felt a mixture of resentment and answering attraction at his welcome. If he had missed her so much, why hadn't he written? Why hadn't he explained what his feelings were? Angrily she reminded herself that she was here for reasons of diplomacy, not love.

Over dinner they discussed the politics of the east and of Rome. The meal was of uneven quality. The local fish was excellent, but the roast wild boar was charred in places and half raw in others. It seemed that Antony still let his slaves take advantage of him.

'I'm fed up with Rome,' he summarized at last. 'Octavian is a little prick. He's as devious as Caesar, but he hasn't got Caesar's physical courage. And even though Julius could be a vindictive old bastard if you'd harmed him, he never did the dirty on you if you hadn't. Octavian's different. He pretends he's friendly, but he stabs you in the back. I hate him.'

While they were drinking a sweet dessert wine accompanied by raisins and walnuts, he suddenly set down his cup, laid one massive hand on her bare arm and spoke in a low, hoarse voice.

'Come to bed.'

The simple words made the tiny hairs on the back of her neck prickle. As if the years had rolled away and she were fourteen again, she felt molten fire throb through her veins. Pride told her to refuse, to shake off his touch, to say something that would wound him to the core, and then ambition whispered that this might further her interests, might bring her dreams closer to fulfilment. But it was not pride which made her reach up, cup his face in her hands and kiss him until her whole body ached with need. It was something else, something she didn't want to name.

It was four years since they had made love and their union was turbulent. Yet even while they were rutting and groaning and panting like wild beasts, there was a deep, satisfying familiarity about it, too. Perhaps it was this which made Cleopatra blurt out the words she hadn't intended to say. While their breath was still coming in thundering gasps, and they were still shuddering in the aftermath of passion, she suddenly bit Antony quite viciously on his imprisoning forearm.

He yelped.

'What's that for?'

'Why didn't you ever write to me?' she demanded accusingly.

He let out a long, shuddering sigh.

'Shit! I'm sorry, Cleopatra. I did try, but I'm no good with letters, I can't spell, I can't say what I want and it wasn't the kind of topic where I could ask anyone to help me. In any case, what could I tell you? How could I explain why I decided to marry Octavia?'

'Why did you?'

'To keep the peace,' he said gloomily. 'Octavian was threatening another civil war and it seemed the only way to stop further bloodshed. She suggested it and I agreed.'

'Are you happy with her?'

He heaved another long sigh and reached for a wine jug by the bed.

'No,' he said morosely, splashing the liquid into two cups and handing her one. 'But it's not her fault. It's just that we're as different as chalk and cheese. She's a good woman and I've no complaints about her. We've had two daughters together and she looks after my boys by Fulvia as if they were her own. But she's so bloody virtuous that I feel stifled, Cleopatra. And I know I don't make her happy. She thinks I'm coarse and rowdy and vulgar, and I am! I like to put my feet on the furniture and drink wine with my army buddies and scratch my backside, but I can't do any of that.

She fills the house with scholars all the time, architects and poets and philosophers. Philosophers!'

'What's she like in bed?'

'I can hardly remember,' groaned Antony. 'It's so long since we've done it. And she doesn't like it anyway. She thinks it's dirty and nasty. Sometimes I feel it's like screwing a Vestal Virgin. Mind you, I feel sorry for her, she's just as miserable as I am, but the truth is that the whole thing was a big mistake.'

'Then why don't you leave her?'

He looked at her with a stunned expression and shifted uneasily. To divorce a wife who was unfaithful was one thing, but to pack off a blameless woman?

'She's given me no cause,' he muttered.

'But you're both miserable!' cried Cleopatra. 'You'd probably be doing her a kindness by divorcing her.'

'And then what would I do?' he growled. 'Marry some other prissy little senator's daughter?'

'No. Marry me!'

He made a sound that was half way between a laugh and a groan.

'In some ways there's nothing I'd like better, Cleopatra. But it's impossible. You're Queen of Egypt, how could you live in Rome?'

'I don't need to live in Rome,' she cried impatiently. 'We could live in Egypt. You like it there, you've always said so, and you know I won't spoil your fun. You could go to the races, fishing, hunting, whatever you wanted to do. And as for your career, you've already admitted that you're fed up with Rome and the empire is already divided in half, isn't it? So let Octavian keep his half, and you settle here in the east. You don't need to go back. Ever!'

It was madness, but as her words tumbled out, he realized that he was tempted, seriously tempted. He had always done his best to serve Rome, but he had never been appreciated. Now he felt oddly touched by the discovery that Cleopatra still loved him even after all these years. What she was offering, although crazy, was insidiously attractive. He could have a good life with her, and she needed him, as Octavia didn't. If he moved to Alexandria, he could take charge of the Egyptian army and keep the country safe from invasion, whereas Octavia only wanted him at home to make small talk. He thrust down the uneasy suspicion that Octavia would be bitterly hurt if he left her.

'I'm a senator,' he objected. 'If I married a foreigner, the marriage wouldn't be legal in Rome.'

'I don't care! It would be legal in the east, and that's what counts to me.'

It was odd to think of being married to Cleopatra after all these years. How long was it since he had first screwed her? Seventeen, eighteen years? That was a long courtship! He grinned at the thought, but found himself liking the idea. As he slipped into sleep, he squeezed her bottom appreciatively. It would be nice to know that she would always be there, warm and comforting against him. Suddenly he felt too tired and too stupefied to resist her any longer. He didn't know what was right or wrong any more, he only knew that he needed her more than ever. He spoke slowly, his tongue slurred by drowsiness and wine, and his words came as a surprise to both of them.

'All right, I'll do it. I'll marry you.'

Chapter Twenty-seven

'Antony, I beg you, don't go through with this marriage.'

Domitius, the red-bearded pirate, looked uncharacteristically grave as he spoke. Even though he was holding the small jewel-studded box containing the ring intended for Cleopatra's finger, he felt it his duty to go on trying to argue Antony out of his madness until the last possible moment. But Antony simply continued to whistle serenely, adjusting the wreath of flowers on his head and winking at himself in the large bronze mirror hanging on the wall.

'It's too late, buddy,' he said. 'We've already hired a priest, the animals are outside waiting to be sacrificed, the witnesses are lined up, the wedding gifts are on display and the crowds are waiting for the big show.'

He jerked his thumb at the open window where the autumn sunlight was pouring in and a dull roar like the surging of the sea could be clearly heard, interspersed by occasional shouts of 'We want the Messiah!'

'That can all be cancelled,' said Domitius irritably. 'I'm begging you, Antony. Stop and think! This wedding will give Octavian exactly the excuse he needs to knock you off once and for all.'

Antony uttered a growl of scornful laughter and brushed a piece of lint off his wedding tunic.

'He doesn't need an excuse, he hates my guts.'

'Well, think of the ordinary citizens then,' urged Domitius. 'They'll say it's treason.'

'Not in the east they won't,' flashed back Antony.

'They're in raptures about it here. Listen to them outside shouting for the Messiah and her husband.'

'Husband,' groaned Domitius. 'Shit, Antony, that's the whole problem! Why do you have to marry the woman? You could keep her as your mistress and nobody will care. You can screw her as much as you like. Do it hanging upside down from the Colossus of Rhodes or the Pharos of Alexandria if you want to, but don't make her your wife! All this crap about the goddess Queen and the promised Messiah is only going to scare the life out of the Romans. They'll say she's planning to take over the world and destroy the empire.'

'Let them,' said Antony indifferently. 'They can say what they like, I don't care any more.'

Domitius seized him by the arm.

'Listen, I've even heard rumours that you're planning to give her some of the Roman provinces as a wedding present. If there's any truth in it, don't do it, I beg you. It will only cause trouble. Let her interfere unofficially as much as she likes, but don't hand any land over to her publicly in front of witnesses. It will be political suicide.'

Antony looked stubborn. As a matter of fact, the rumours were perfectly true. He had already promised Cleopatra that as her wedding present she would receive a large estate in Crete, the kingdom of Chalcis at the foot of Lebanon, the entire Phoenician coast from the mouth of the Eleutherus to Sidon, a cedarwood estate in Cilicia and the profitable balsam woods near Jericho. She had actually asked for the whole kingdom of Judaea because of some mysterious quarrel she had had with Herod, but Antony had put his foot down about that. He needed Herod exactly where he was, at least until the Parthians were defeated.

'It's no use arguing with me, Domitius,' he insisted. 'My mind's made up and I wish to heaven you'd stop looking as if you're going to a funeral instead of a wedding. I want this to be a happy day for Cleopatra.'

It was a happy day for Cleopatra. In fact, it was the happiest day of her life. She felt ready to burst with elation and triumph as Antony slipped the ring on her finger and they exchanged their promises. Olympus had been wrong! It was possible to make dreams come true and soon the whole of the eastern empire would be under her control. Once Antony had defeated the Parthians, he might even go on and conquer India. Soon the whole world would be at their feet, worshipping them, just like this rapturous crowd that was bombarding them with flowers and shouting, 'Long live the Messiah and her consort!' She smiled radiantly at Antony and, in defiance of all propriety, hugged him as if she would never let him go.

With the arrival of spring, Antony set out on his Parthian campaign. He was as anxious as Cleopatra to bring it to a swift conclusion, especially now that he had learned that she was pregnant again. His plan was to take Ecbatana, cut off Babylonia from Parthia proper and finally annex Babylonia and establish a new frontier. It was a huge challenge for a single campaigning season and every moment of time would count. Striking north through Melitene he travelled along the Euphrates to Carana and there held a review of his troops. It was the largest army he had ever commanded. He had sixteen seasoned legions, totalling sixty thousand men, ten thousand Gallic and Spanish horse, and thirty thousand auxiliaries, including sixteen thousand Armenian cavalry and the forces of some of his client kings. There was also an enormous siege train, including an eighty foot battering ram, since he intended to operate in a country devoid of good timber. If he could not conclude the campaign in a single season, he meant to take the Median capital of Phraaspa and continue on to Ecbatana the following season.

Unfortunately the train of wagons and siege equipment made his progress maddeningly slow and he divided his army. Leaving two legions to escort the wagons, he pushed on ahead with his main force. When Monaeses, the commander of the Parthian forces, learnt of this, he was exultant.

'The stupid bastard!' he exclaimed. 'Sometimes these Romans make it so easy I'm ashamed of myself.'

Antony and his advance force did not catch a single glimpse of the Parthians as they pushed further and further into the interior of that hostile country. But for the wagon train it was another matter. One morning in the red light of early dawn they were woken by a terrifying chorus of whoops and the thunder of horses' hooves. Within half an hour the two legions were annihilated and their eagles captured. The siege train was burnt and all the food was stolen. By mid August Antony found himself in front of the walls of Phraaspa without so much as a stick of firewood to batter down its gates.

He was too proud to retreat, but the Parthians stood on the ramparts and jeered at him, repulsing his attacks without difficulty. Soon the Roman army had eaten up all the food in the neighbourhood and then in October the cold set in. One night as he sat shivering in his tent, forcing down an unappetizing meal of boiled rat, a deserter came and offered to guide the Romans back to safety by a route through the hills.

The appalling retreat to the Armenian frontier lasted for twenty-seven days. In all his years as a soldier,

Antony had never endured such misery. He was racked with guilt and despair as he watched his gaunt-faced, hollow-eyed soldiers struggling to march in a square and to beat off the hit-and-run attacks of the Parthians, who nipped at their heels in spite of the hilly ground. At night time it was so cold that the wine and water froze solid in the skins and men frequently awoke with their toes and fingers lacking all feeling. Many lost limbs to frostbite, some even lost their noses and staggered along with gaping holes in the centre of their faces, as if they were already turning to grinning skeletons. The griping pains of hunger eventually subsided, but the weakness which followed did not. Time after time Antony heard a muffled thud and glanced back to see another legionary drop lifeless amid the rocks and snow. He did his best to encourage them, to give them heart, to keep them going. Over and over he reminded them of Xenophon and the march of the ten thousand who had travelled a much longer journey through even worse territory and arrived safely at the Black Sea. But in his heart he feared that they would all leave their bones whitening on those cruel hillsides and he blamed himself for the disaster. The worst moment of all came when they were parched with thirst and they reached a river, but their guide warned them that its waters were unsafe to drink. Antony went round among the men, trying to persuade them to last out a little longer, but many ignored his orders, flung themselves into the freezing waters and drank their fill. Their relief did not last long. Those who had yielded to temptation were soon seized by cramps and vomiting and died, retching horribly, by the water's edge. Antony covered his face with his hands and wept and groaned, blaming himself for their plight. He longed to die with them, but his duty to the survivors and a dogged need to see Cleopatra again, kept him slogging on until at last they came in sight of a second river. The guide called a halt and turned to Antony, his face transfigured with relief.

'We're safe now,' he said. 'From here on there's plenty of food and water and we're only six days' march from the boundary between Media and Armenia. You'll get home now, sir.'

After Antony's departure for war, Cleopatra set out to make a leisurely tour of inspection of the new territories which had been given to her as a wedding present. While she was pleased by the prospect of owning the Phoenician coastal cities, the gift which gratified her most was the balsam groves of Jericho. Every time she pictured the expression on Herod's face when he learnt that he would have to hand them over, her heart sang inside her. It would be the perfect revenge for the way he had robbed and insulted her at their last meeting. And her revenge would not stop there. Her next step would be to ask Antony for the Gaza strip, which was the terminus of the profitable spice trade with Arabia. And one day she planned to own the whole of Judaea.

Because of her pregnancy, she took the journey slowly, enjoying every detail of the brilliant blue sky, the dry hills and the small villages with their silvery olive groves and the splashes of vivid green, cultivated land which surrounded them. She knew there had been recent violence in Judaea – it was the kind of country where there was always violence – but with her large escort of Roman soldiers, she felt perfectly safe. And in this tranquil countryside where the only sound was the braying of donkeys or the splash of water in the irrigation channels, it was hard to believe that blood had been so recently and thoroughly spilt.

Yet Herod's seizure of the Kingship had been brutal and efficient, which was only what she would have expected. With Mark Antony's backing he had deposed the previous ruler Antigonus, who had been intriguing with the Parthians, but the transition had been far from easy. Orthodox Jews, accustomed only to having a member of the priestly Hasmonaean family as both their King and high priest, had been outraged at the prospect of a half-Arab outsider on the throne. They had fought violently to destroy Herod and he had been even more violent in crushing them. Even his marriage to Mariamme, the Hasmonaean princess, had not succeeded in subduing the resentment of the survivors. Cleopatra knew that beneath this peaceful exterior, rebellion still seethed and the thought gave her pleasure. While the Orthodox Jews were hardly likely to welcome her as their ruler any more than Herod, if she found the right puppet to represent her, perhaps something could still be arranged.

She went first to the Dead Sea area where Antony had promised her control of the bitumen monopoly hitherto held by Malchus, the ruler of the Nabatean Arabs. Malchus had cheated her recently on some large spice deliveries and she enjoyed seeing the expression on his face when she handed over the document signed by Mark Antony which formally deprived him of his rights to the bitumen lease. The taste of revenge was even sweeter than the prospect of the profits to be made by selling the bitumen for embalming corpses and killing grubs in vineyards. Confronted by the cohort of tough Roman legionaries who surrounded her, Malchus could do nothing but seethe and mutter and accept his defeat. Cleopatra did not linger long. The smell of the bitumen made her feel queasy and in any case she had a larger grudge to settle. Her grudge with Herod.

Turning northwest again, she soon covered the short distance to Jericho, but was disappointed to find that he had not yet obeyed her written summons to meet her there. While she waited for his arrival, she amused herself by strolling in the balsam groves. There were twenty square miles of trees and their scent was overpowering. From now on, she would be the one to market the famous 'Balm of Gilead' which was renowned from one side of the Mediterranean to the other for curing headaches and cataracts. An added bonus was the groves of date palms known as 'hangover palms' for the strength of the date wine that they produced. The profits from this trade too would now be hers. With a satisfied sigh she made her way back to the royal lodge to take her afternoon rest. For once even the aches and pains of pregnancy could not depress her spirits. As she entered the coolness of the colonnade, Iras came to meet her.

'Someone to see you,' she said.

'Herod?'

'No. His mother-in-law, Alexandra.'

Intrigued, Cleopatra allowed herself to be led away to a shady courtyard where a plump woman of about forty with a shrewd face lay on a cushioned couch. At Cleopatra's approach, she rose to her feet and then prostrated herself on the paving stones. Pleased by the courtesy, Cleopatra helped her up and waved her back to her couch. She tried to hide her curiosity and impatience as they went through the usual mideastern rituals of eating smoked almonds and olives, drinking honeyed wine, sampling plates of chicken and wild rice and green vegetables followed by little honey cakes rolled in sesame seeds and discussing the outrageously high price of Chinese silk before they came to the point of the meeting.

'I'm honoured that you should come to visit me here,' said Cleopatra at last, approaching the subject obliquely.

'The honour is all mine,' replied Alexandra. 'I believe you could do much to help me.'

'In what way? If it lies within my power, I would be only too pleased to help such a gracious guest.'

The two women exchanged secretive smiles, pleased with the subtle progress they were making.

'I will be honest with you,' said Alexandra. 'My daughter Mariamme is married to Herod, but the match was not of my choice. There are many Jews who have no cause to love my son-in-law.'

And you are among them, thought Cleopatra silently, feeling her ears prick up. So Herod was hated even by his own mother-in-law? Well, well, how interesting!

'I can see that his personality might not please everyone,' she said.

'He's a conceited upstart!' flared Alexandra, her hostility overpowering her diplomacy. 'I never thought I'd live to see the day that a man who not only doesn't belong to the holy Hasmonaean line, but is actually half-Arab should be King of Judaea! At least Mark Antony didn't make him high priest as well, that would have been more than we could endure! But what has happened is almost as bad. Herod has nominated his own candidate to the high priesthood and my son who should rightly have had the place has been passed over.'

'I see,' said Cleopatra in a voice resonant with sympathy. 'I can understand how hurt and offended you must be by this. Tell me, how old is your son?'

'Aristobulus? He's sixteen.'

'Young for a high priest, but coming from such good family, I'm sure he would acquit himself well in the position. Do you want me to speak to Mark Antony and see if he'll reconsider his decision?'

Alexandra's face flushed with gratitude and triumph.

'Yes,' she agreed passionately. 'That's exactly what I want you to do.'

'It may be a difficult undertaking,' Cleopatra murmured reflectively to herself.

'I'll see that you're repaid with my utmost loyalty if you do this for me! Not all Jews want Herod to continue as King and we are not all bigoted and suspicious of foreigners. There are many who would welcome a Queen as our ruler. Especially if a woman of priestly family like myself believed that she was the Messiah.'

The two women exchanged smiles.

'I think we understand each other very well,' purred Cleopatra.

Alexandra had only just taken her leave when Iras returned to announce the arrival of Herod. Cleopatra did not think it wise to receive him in the privacy of a courtyard without a single attendant. Instead she summoned him to meet her in the banqueting hall with a hundred fully armed Roman soldiers forming a guard of honour for his arrival. He marched between the threatening walls of men with his face set in a black mask of anger and outrage. This time there were no courteous prostrations. Instead he came to a halt in front of Cleopatra's chair and gritted his teeth before he spoke.

'To what do I owe the honour of this visit?' he demanded.

She leaned back, smiling.

'I've come to collect a debt,' she said. 'Five hundred thousand sesterces.'

Herod's eyes flashed with anger but he glanced briefly behind him at the lines of Roman soldiers.

'You shall have it,' he growled.

'I've also come for your balsam groves and date palms,' she added, smiling even more radiantly.

For a moment it looked as though he was going to choke with outrage and disbelief.

'Wh-what are you talking about?' he stuttered. 'Mark Antony confirmed me in possession of those groves. They're a major source of income for this country.'

With a fluid movement of her hand, Cleopatra summoned Iras to bring her a document on a salver.

'Mark Antony has changed his mind,' she said. 'You may like to read this so that you understand the conditions of the lease in future. I am now the legal owner of the monopoly on the groves. I'm also taking over the lease of the bitumen monopoly on the Dead Sea from the Arabian King Malchus. If you read Antony's directions carefully, you'll see that it's your job to act as my agent in both cases. The Arabs will continue to harvest the bitumen, but you will send the profits to me. Naturally my inspectors will remain here to see that you discharge the task honestly and you will be given a commission for your labour. A small commission. The same principle will operate with the balsam groves and the date palms. You will continue to do the work, but I will receive the profits. Any questions?'

Herod's face turned purple with rage, and his hand travelled instinctively to the scabbard of his sword.

'Oh, I wouldn't do that,' warned Cleopatra pleasantly. 'Not with so many witnesses. And I don't think poison would be a good idea either. Mark Antony would be sure to guess who was responsible for my death and you wouldn't like to lose your entire kingdom, now would you?'

Herod gave an incoherent groan of rage, but he knew when he was beaten.

'You bitch,' he said thickly.

Cleopatra fluttered her eyelashes at him, remembering how he had groaned and convulsed as he reached his climax inside her at their last meeting. But she had no regrets. On the whole, she thought, this was even better than sex.

Octavian winced at the uproar as he approached Antony's house on the Carinae. This mansion had once belonged to Pompey the Great, who had adorned the front entrance with the bronze prows of pirate ships which he had captured. During the civil war Antony had bought it for a song from Julius Caesar, but the once noble dwelling had gone steadily downhill under his careless custody. Drunken actors had vomited on the expensive embroidered coverlets, dancing girls from Gades had stolen pieces of valuable silver plate from the dining rooms, while boisterous ex-soldiers had damaged the exquisite pastoral frescos in the reception rooms while showing off their skills at knife throwing. Now, to judge by the din that issued forth from inside, it sounded as though Pompey's battles with the pirates were still in progress. Yet Octavian knew from bitter experience that it was only his nieces and nephews letting off steam. With the great December festival of the Saturnalia fast approaching, when gifts were exchanged and parties held, his sister was probably indulging the children more shamefully than ever. Octavian's lips pinched in a thin, disapproving line. Why couldn't Octavia keep her brats under control and bring them up properly as he was endeavouring to do with Julia? While he spent very little time with his daughter, Octavian had made sure that she had a nurse who believed in rigorous discipline and would certainly not allow shouting, rough play or foolishly indulgent presents. Ringing the doorbells, Octavian was ushered inside by an elderly doorkeeper, but almost found himself knocked down by a shrieking, milling crowd of children who were evidently playing Blind Man's Buff around the stern ancestral statues and sacred death masks which adorned the atrium. Scowling horribly, he swore under his breath as a bright-eyed, curly-haired little girl of about five, too busy looking over her shoulder to watch what she was doing, hurtled straight into him, kicking his shins and muddying his toga. His sister Octavia came laughing to the rescue.

'I'm so sorry, Octavian, it's nearly Saturnalia and the children are over-excited. What brings you here?'

'Is that Antony's daughter?' demanded Octavian disapprovingly, trying to brush the dirt from his garment.

'Yes,' said Octavia fondly, her gaze following her curly-headed daughter, who was now turning cartwheels on the mosaic floor. 'She's exactly like her father, isn't she?'

'Exactly like him,' agreed Octavian venomously. 'And it's him I've come to talk to you about. Can we go somewhere private?'

Once they were settled in her sewing room at the back of the house, surrounded by the comfortable clutter of spindles, a weaving loom and hanks of brightly coloured wool neatly arrayed on shelves, Octavia looked at her brother with apprehension. She had

had no letters at all from Antony since his departure for the east and knew only that he had set out on his campaign against the Parthians. A little ache of grief and apprehension rose in her heart each time she thought of him and she tried to keep busy caring for the children and making the house as comfortable as possible for his return. There was plenty to occupy her with her own son and two daughters from her previous marriage, Antony's two boys by Fulvia and the two little girls they had had together and none of the seven more than nine years old! She loved Antony and knew he did not love her, but he had always been kind and it hurt her to discover that he would not even spare the time to write to her. So far she had remained in blissful ignorance of his marriage to Cleopatra, for Octavian had threatened with death anyone who betrayed the news to her although it was not compassion which had made him take this step. He wanted to be the one to tell her of Antony's treachery and he wanted to choose the time and the circumstances of the telling. Antony's absence in the east had given Octavian a heaven-sent opportunity to get rid of his other rivals without interference. Only this morning he had received word from a reliable source that Sextus Pompeius had been killed in Sicily and Lepidus had agreed to give up all power and go into voluntary retirement on his estate at Circeii. The moment had arrived for his sister to learn the plans that he had for her.

'I have some bad news for you, Octavia,' he said solemnly. 'You must brace yourself. It concerns Mark Antony.'

Horror leapt in her eyes.

'He's not – ' she croaked.

'Dead?' Octavian gave a thin smile. 'Not to my

knowledge, but you may wish he was when you hear what he's done to you.'

Octavia's heart began thudding tumultuously from the rapid succession of fear and relief. She looked at Octavian warily, not trusting his sympathy. Only a blind woman could have failed to see how much her brother hated her husband and Octavia was not blind.

'Why, what's he done?' she asked flatly.

'He's married Cleopatra.'

The shock was so bad that for a moment she felt as if a dagger had stabbed her straight to the heart. Her first impulse was to cry out, to run shrieking about the room, tearing her hair and scratching her face as if she had just received the news of a death in the family. Yet the avid, almost gloating look in Octavian's eyes restrained her. She saw that that was exactly what he wanted to witness and revulsion seized her. Why should he derive entertainment from her suffering? With an effort that took all her will, she sat perfectly motionless, fighting down the dizziness and hysteria that threatened to engulf her.

'When did this happen?' she asked quietly.

Octavian would not meet her eyes.

'Last year, I believe.'

'And it's only now that I'm told of it?'

'News travels slowly from the east.'

'Not that slowly! Why didn't you tell me before, Octavian?'

'I didn't want to upset you.'

'And now you do?'

He rose to his feet and glared down at her as if she were one of the fallen women he was so fond of attacking in his speeches about morality.

'Of course not,' he spluttered indignantly. 'The very

536

idea is preposterous! I've come here to try and minimize any pain the news might give you.'

'Have you, Octavian? How generous of you. And how do you propose to do that?'

He sat down again, leaned confidingly towards her and took her hand. She snatched it away.

'I want you to divorce him at once! I've just had word that Sextus Pompeius has been killed and Lepidus has decided to retire from the triumvirate for reasons of ill-health. Now that Antony has shown himself in his true colours, I believe the only proper action – '

He got no further. With a hiss like a scalded cat, Octavia sprang to her feet, spun round and stood glaring down at him, her entire body shaking.

'No!' she shouted. 'I won't do it and for once you can't bully me into it, Octavian. I don't know what the details are of your scheme, but I'm sure I can see the main outline of it. You want to be sole master of Rome, don't you? And you want me to help you by distancing myself from Mark Antony and turning the sympathy of the ordinary people against him? Well, I won't do it! I made vows to him when I married him and I regard those vows as sacred and binding.'

'Sacred and binding?' sneered Octavian. 'How sacred and binding do you think his vows to you were?'

Octavia turned away her head to hide the scalding rush of tears that sprang to her eyes.

'That has nothing to do with it,' she insisted. 'Whatever Antony may or may not have done, I'm a free, adult woman and I have the right to run my life as I choose, without interference from you!'

'Free, adult woman?' echoed Octavian incredulously. 'There's no such thing! In our class, marriages have always been arranged by men for the political benefit of the entire family. Women simply do as they're told.'

'Not this woman!' said Octavia through her teeth. 'Now kindly leave my house.'

She stood there, glaring and defiant, until she heard the echoing clang of the bronze front doors. Only then did she sink down on a chair and begin to weep.

At the end of the winter, accompanied by all her children, including the new baby Ptolemy Philadelphus, Cleopatra braved the dangerous sea voyage from Egypt to her new Phoenician territories. There she waited in mingled anxiety and hope for Antony's return from his Parthian campaign. Surely he must have been successful by now? With such a huge force, how could he fail?

One afternoon she was sitting in an upper room in a beam of pale winter sunshine, studying a map of Armenia, when the door creaked open behind her. She swung round, not immediately recognizing the greyhaired, wild-eyed stranger who lurched into the room. She had a blurred impression of a face covered in a network of tiny lines, of wild, imploring eyes, of a beard that was almost pure white, of a huge, gaunt frame, hung about by a rag of a cloak. She opened her mouth to scream, wondering if this was another crazed assassin, but something familiar in the awkward, shambling movement of this pitiful creature stopped the cry in her throat. As he stumbled across the room and pitched to his knees in front of her, her voice came out in a hoarse, disbelieving croak.

'Antony?'

He clutched her dress in his hands and buried his face in her lap, then his broad shoulders began to

shake as terrible, wrenching sobs issued from deep
inside him.

'I've lost my army, Cleopatra. You must help me!
Help me! Help me!'

Chapter Twenty-eight

At first he was so relieved to have her warm and solid and breathing in his hands that he did not notice anything else. It was enough to feel the rounded firmness of her thighs and inhale the fragrance of her skin. Dimly he noticed how her muscles stiffened, but it was not until she spoke that he realized the impact his announcement had had on her.

'What do you mean, you've lost your army?' she demanded sharply. 'You had over a hundred thousand men, you can't have lost all those.'

He flinched at the accusing note in her voice.

'Not all of them, no,' he said dully. 'But over thirty-seven thousand of them. It's a disaster! You can't begin to imagine how bad it was.'

'But what happened?' she cried. 'Did the enemy take you by surprise and slaughter them?'

He shook his head and tried twice to speak, but could not utter the words for the tears that clogged his throat. At last he managed to blurt out the truth.

'No more than a few hundred at most were killed by the enemy.'

'Then what happened?' she demanded, her voice rising to a shriek. 'Why did those men die?'

'Hunger and cold,' he muttered. 'My siege equipment was captured and we were unable to take Phraaspa. We were forced to retreat in unspeakable conditions.'

'And where were you when your siege equipment was captured?' she asked scathingly.

'Miles away. I divided the army so that I could go

ahead faster. I wanted to get the campaign over and come back to you.'

'You fool!' she shouted, springing to her feet and storming across the room as if she were charging into battle herself. 'I warned you and warned you not to do that before you left. I told you what Caesar said to me about his own plans for the Parthian campaign, that it was of the utmost importance that the siege equipment be guarded at all times and that no harm must come to it, because it could never be replaced.'

'Don't talk to me about Caesar!' flared Antony, rising with some difficulty to his feet. He had sustained a bad fall in the mountains of Armenia and his right knee still pained him. 'I'm tired of having every word Caesar ever said crammed down my throat!'

'Oh, are you?' she jeered. 'Well, it's a pity you didn't pay attention to it in the past! Caesar would never have let himself get into such a predicament as this. You're not half the man he was!'

Antony stared at her in amazement and horror. He could not believe that these venomous, wounding words were pouring from her lips. All through the marrow-chilling cold of that hideous retreat with the horrors of starvation and dysentery and enemy attack, the only thing that had kept him going was the image of her. He had thought of her warmth and laughter and love as if it were a blazing beacon fire on a freezing night. Sometimes the only way he had managed to force his weak, stumbling legs to take another step was to whisper to himself, 'I'm going home to Cleopatra.' Now he was dumbfounded and pierced to the heart by her rejection. Worst of all was the feeling that he deserved it.

'I'm a disappointment to you, aren't I?' he demanded bitterly.

'Yes, you are!' she spat, not even bothering to hide the angry gleam of tears in her eyes. She folded her arms and bit her lower lip to try and still its quivering. 'I wish I were a man! I could do so much with the opportunities you have, but all you do is throw them away!'

'It's not that easy!' he growled, striding across the floor and seizing her by the arm. 'All right, you don't have the opportunities that men have. But you don't have to endure the horrors we go through either. You weren't out there starving and freezing, chucking your guts up, sleeping in mud, watching your companions die. What do you know about it?'

Their eyes met and held, Antony's angry and imploring, Cleopatra's bitter and implacable.

Her breath came in a long, shuddering gulp.

'I know I trusted you to defeat the Parthians and you failed me,' she said.

Her words rang in the air, as harsh and pitiless as the crack of a whiplash. Antony's head jerked back as if she had struck him. Then he gave her a long, cold, sorrowful look, as if he were seeing her clearly for the first time.

'If that's the way you feel, perhaps I should take myself off so that you can find a man who won't be such a disappointment to you!'

'Perhaps you should,' she agreed.

Cleopatra woke up three times that night and each time she was still burning with rage and disappointment. Once Antony came and knocked at her closed door, but she ignored him and after a while the footsteps withdrew. He did not come back again and when she enquired of his whereabouts the next morning, she was told he had gone down to the barracks to be with his men. At the back of her mind she felt that she ought to make peace overtures to him, but she didn't feel peaceful at all, she felt furious! How could he have been so stupid? It wasn't bad luck, it was ineptitude that had brought this defeat upon them and now all her hopes of extending their empire were in ruins! What upset her most was the thought of Octavian sitting there in Rome gloating over the news and rejoicing at her humiliation! And all because Antony was such a useless oaf. It was more than she could bear. By late afternoon, although disappointment and irritation still weighed like a stone in her breast, the first blaze of her indignation had died down. She might have been prepared to make peace, if Antony had not come home from the barracks roaring drunk. Sitting in her rooms awaiting an apology for his loss of so many soldiers whose equipment and rations she had funded, she was even further outraged when she learnt that he had rolled straight into his own quarters and fallen on to the bed in a snoring stupor without even calling a slave to remove his boots. The next morning Antony, hung over and embarrassed, decided not to risk his dwindling self-esteem with any more bumbling apologies. Instead he went out for a hair of the dog that had bitten him. A stalemate was beginning to develop.

After almost a month of this mutual antagonism and bitterness, a ship arrived from Rome bearing a letter from Octavia. Antony opened it with a mixture of reluctance and curiosity. He still felt guilty about the way he had treated Octavia and he no longer even had the satisfaction of feeling that his own heartless behaviour had brought him happiness. Cleopatra seemed to hate him. She no longer let him into her bed, she threw him glances that would have wilted a melon on a vine and she didn't seem to have the slightest appreciation of all that he had given up in order to marry her! If Octavia too was writing to reproach him, he would start to feel like some unfortunate criminal in the arena, being attacked by lionesses on all sides. But there were no reproaches in Octavia's letter. It was as cool and sweet and sensible as she was herself. Antony's lips moved soundlessly as he spelt out the words.

> Rome
>
> The Kalends of March
>
> A U C 718

Octavia to her husband Antony wishes very great health.

(Antony winced at the word 'husband' and went on reading)

My dear Antony,

I was very upset to learn recently of your misfortunes in Parthia, but I am glad to know that you are safe and well. To be honest with you, my brother Octavian is putting pressure on me to divorce you formally, but I am reluctant to do this. I still consider myself your wife, if you are prepared to have me, and I would never reproach you for any other entanglements you may have become involved in. In case you should wish to make a second attempt at defeating the Parthians, I am sailing for Athens, bringing soldiers and supplies with me. I very much hope that you will see fit to meet me there. All the children are well and send you their best love.

> Your wife Octavia

Antony was still gaping in astonishment at this letter, when he heard a footfall behind him. Swinging around, he saw Cleopatra with the hurt, watchful expression on her face which he had grown used to over the last month. Her gaze slid away from his and she made a movement as if to leave.

'I'm sorry I disturbed you,' she said coldly. 'I didn't know you were here. I thought you were down at the barracks drinking with your companions again. Excuse me.'

'Wait, don't go,' he growled, seizing her by the wrist and forcing her down on to a chair. 'There are things we must discuss.'

'Are there? What sort of things? Where you can get the best price on wine? Or what to do with sixty-three thousand unemployed soldiers.'

Antony swore under his breath.

'Stop being such a bitch!' he shouted. 'I know you hate me, I accept that. And I probably even deserve it, but we can't go on like this. We're destroying each other and I can't stand it! We've got to make some kind of a change.'

'What kind of a change?' she countered suspiciously.

He sat down too, clutching the letter in his hand, and drew a long, agonized breath.

'Do you want a divorce?' he asked.

Whatever she had expected, it was not this. Suddenly the armour of rage and grief and disappointment which had protected her from Antony's misery and confusion over this past month was pierced by an unexpected pain. A divorce? She had been angry with him, had blamed him, even hated him, but she had never considered that.

'Why?' she challenged. 'Do you want a divorce?'

He closed his eyes and rubbed his eyelids in a weary, defeated gesture.

'I don't know what I want any more,' he burst out. 'But if you want me to leave, I will. Octavia has asked me to come back to her and I think it's an offer worth considering.'

A mysterious chill of horror surged through her as if the ground had begun to tremble beneath her in an earthquake. Octavia? Octavia! She had thought Octavia banished, safely left behind in Rome, too much of a bore and a goody-goody to be a threat to her. But it seemed she was wrong. She stared at Antony with a stricken expression, suddenly realizing that she might be on the verge of losing him and realizing, too, how much he meant to her. Not only because he would work loyally, if ineptly, to further her plans, but because he was a good, kind man who didn't deserve to be treated as she had treated him. With a sudden gasp, she burst into tears and flung herself into his arms.

'Don't leave me,' she begged. 'Please don't leave me. It makes me so miserable to think of it.'

Antony's first impulse was to crush her against him and promise that he would always take care of her. He had never been able to bear the sight of a woman in tears. But for some reason an uncharacteristic spurt of resentment restrained him. Her stinging attack, coming at a time when he was in trouble and in most need of support, had wounded him deeply. Dimly he remembered a conversation he had once had with Fulvia about Cleopatra's charm and caressing ways and a warning sounded in his head like the echo of a military trumpet ordering a retreat. He wanted more than anything to bury his face in Cleopatra's hair, to feel the warm softness of her arms winding about him, but he knew that if he did he would be lost. For a moment he stood rigid, enduring her embrace without response, and then he shook her off. To her bewilderment and dismay he stood looking down at her with an unfamiliar, scrutinizing coldness in his eyes.

'I can't make any decisions about it now,' he said roughly. 'I need time to think about what you really want from me.'

Without another word or a backward glance, but with a new look of purpose in his face, he strode from the room. Thoroughly alarmed now, Cleopatra ran after him, her sobs coming faster, but he thrust her roughly aside and made good his escape. When she pursued him to his rooms, she found herself shut out by two tough-faced Roman legionaries and, unable to endure the humiliation of their knowing glances, she retreated furiously to her own chambers. Later in the day, when she sent Iras to Antony with a letter of apology, she received even worse news.

'They said he's gone hunting,' said Iras. 'He told them he might stay away for a couple of weeks and after that he might go and join Octavia in Athens.'

With a groan of horror, Cleopatra flung herself down on her bed and wept. She had never been able to endure being thwarted and the violence of her tantrums in childhood had alarmed and infuriated her attendants. Iras, left to cope with hysterical sobbing, smashed plates, a complete refusal to eat and disjointed outbursts of abuse, began to feel wearily that nothing had changed. As the days slipped by, Iras's initial annoyance gave way to a chill feeling of apprehension.

'She's not eating a thing!' she reported anxiously to Olympus. 'Not a thing! And she's more depressed than she's ever been after any of the other babies. She won't even look at Ptolemy Philadelphus when his nurse brings him into the room. And she won't speak to the other children either. All she does is lie there and cry and the flesh is simply falling off her. I'm really worried about her.'

'You must speak to Antony when he comes back,' advised Olympus. 'From what you've told me, it's a mixture of guilt and fear that he's going to leave her for Octavia that has brought on this crisis. He's probably the only one who can help her.'

Antony was only mildly concerned on returning from his hunting trip to be told that Cleopatra had been weeping and refusing to eat. Another one of her theatrical displays! he thought grimly. She had always been able to turn on tears or laughter or breathless passion to suit her needs and he did not suppose that this occasion was any different. Obviously his threat to leave her had given her a jolt and a good thing too! It was high time that she stopped dishing out cruelty to other people and learnt for herself how painful rejection could be. Yet when he yielded to her attendants' desperate entreaties and went to her rooms to visit her, he was shocked by the change in her appearance.

She lay propped against a pile of pillows and her face was as pale as bleached linen. Tears trickled silently from beneath her closed eyelids and her body had a frail, wasted appearance beneath the shapeless grey woollen robe that she wore. Her black hair hung in wild disorder about her shoulders and she did not even look up when Iras announced him, but simply gave a small, choking sob which sent a tremor running through her entire body.

'Has she been crying ever since I left?' whispered Antony in an appalled voice.

'Near enough,' agreed Iras. 'And she won't eat either. That's what really worries us. Please see if you can talk to her.'

He felt helpless and abandoned, as the black woman slipped out of the room, closing the door silently behind her. Clenching and unclenching his hands awkwardly at his sides, he tiptoed across to the bed and was mortified to notice how his sandals squeaked. Looking down at his wife, he was overwhelmed by a wave of pity and affection for her. He didn't like to think of anybody suffering like this, but he could not help feeling a surge of pride and astonishment at this dramatic evidence that Cleopatra cared so much about him. He would never have believed that he had the power to hurt her so much and her misery made him feel guilty, protective, responsible. Hesitantly he reached down and touched her hair. She flinched and jerked away from him.

'I wish you'd just kill me and be done with it,' she said desperately.

The change in her voice upset him more than anything. It had always been one of her chief beauties – that smoky contralto, full of sensuality and warmth and laughter. To hear it reduced to this lifeless croak was more than he could bear. Suddenly he sat down on the bed, sending the mattress plunging with his weight and cupped her face in his big, warm hands and kissed her red, swollen eyelids.

'Stop behaving like a baby,' he begged, 'and tell me what's wrong.'

Her eyelids slowly opened, revealing bloodshot eyes that made her look as if she had been on a bender for the past two weeks.

'You don't love me any more!' she wailed.

The absurdity of it made him laugh. Dropping his head, he nuzzled her tearstained face.

'Sometimes I wish that were true,' he growled. 'But it isn't. I don't always like you, Cleopatra, but I don't think I could ever stop loving you, any more than I could cut off my right hand.'

She looked up at him with a mixture of anguish and hope.

'Is that true?'

A shudder went through him and he let out a long sigh.

'Yes, it's true,' he said.

She sat up then, winding her arms around his neck like a vine clinging to a massive oak tree.

'So you won't leave me and go back to Octavia?'

For a moment he felt a twinge of alarm, as though he were throwing away his last chance of choosing the path his life would follow. Then he looked down at her woebegone face and was touched again to see the ravages of grief upon it. They were neither of them growing any younger, but he still found her as bewitching and infuriating as ever, and there was no doubt in his mind that she was the one woman he wanted beside him for the rest of his life. Gently he stroked her tumbled hair back from her face.

'No, I won't leave you,' he promised.

Two weeks later Octavia, sitting patiently in Athens, received a note from Mark Antony. The message it contained was brief and brutal. It ordered her to send on the troops and equipment to Antony and return to Rome herself. And, while Antony was in such a conciliatory mood, Cleopatra persuaded him to take the Gaza strip away from Herod and give it to her. Her shock and dismay at the thought that Antony might leave her had been genuine, but once the whole unhappy episode was ended, Cleopatra was not dissatisfied with the outcome. In fact she sometimes reflected that it was amazing what a little dieting could achieve.

Nevertheless she was determined not to risk losing Antony again and to that end she now did her utmost to be agreeable. At her suggestion they returned to Alexandria for a period of rest and recuperation. But there was little rest involved. Wanting to show him how different she was from Octavia, Cleopatra organized a frenzy of parties and entertainments. Once again as they had done five years before, they attended chariot races and wrestling matches, disguised themselves as humble working people and roamed around the waterfront bars, drank heavily and spent a lot of their time in bed. Was Octavia dull and virtuous? All right, Cleopatra would be outrageous and flamboyant! Was Octavia boring in bed? Then Cleopatra would be wildly sensual and inventive! Yet this time there was a quality of desperation about their gaiety that had been lacking in the past. Over them both there hung the ominous cloud of the Parthian defeat and the knowledge that a confrontation with Octavian was looming ever closer.

When Cleopatra introduced Antony to the vapours of the Indian hemp plant which she sometimes liked to inhale, he took to the practice with a fervour that startled her, since it offered a dulling of his regrets and anxiety in a way that nothing else did. Seeing how much he enjoyed the detached, floating feeling that came from the use of the plant, Cleopatra chose her moment carefully to broach an extremely delicate subject with him.

It was late at night. Earlier in the evening they had been up on the roof of the Museum in the astronomers' observatory, looking at the vast, inverted bowl of the night sky together. After that they had gone for a walk to the waterfront where they had eaten fried sausages and hot, crusty bread and roared out sea shanties with a bunch of drunken sailors from Rhodes. Now in the silence after midnight Antony lay sprawled on a couch in the flickering lamplight while Cleopatra assembled the metal steamer which Olympus had built for her. The hot stones and the hemp seeds went into the top over a pan of water kept boiling by a charcoal-fired brazier beneath. All the user had to do was draw closer and inhale the clouds of steam which came off this contraption. Once the water was bubbling merrily, she ushered Antony over to another couch conveniently close to the vapours.

'Mmm,' he murmured, inhaling the pungent fumes deeply. 'That's good stuff. Where did you get the idea for this anyway?'

Her voice came from the far side of the room, echoing oddly. He wondered why she did not come closer and join him.

'From Olympus, my physician. He's from Scythia originally and it's an old custom of the nomads there. These days he uses it mainly for pain relief with his patients.'

'Pain relief,' muttered Antony, closing his eyes. A pleasant dizziness was already beginning to invade his senses. 'That's what I need, pain relief! So I'll never have another nightmare about my soldiers freezing to death, or about Octavia reproaching me . . .'

His voice trailed away and Cleopatra eyed him searchingly through the billowing white haze of vapour. Was it the right moment? Too soon and he would be shocked and refuse her request. Too late and he would become incapable of any coherent discussion whatsoever. She decided to chance it.

'Well, all that's in the past,' she murmured soothingly. 'And you must put it behind you, darling. What we need now is something to pep up the morale of the empire's inhabitants here in the east and send a clear message to Rome that you're still a winner.'

Antony nodded slowly. A winner! Yes, that's what he was now that Cleopatra loved him again. In fact, he felt ready to conquer the world.

'I could try another invasion of Parthia,' he mumbled. 'Now that I know the right strategy to adopt.'

She turned away to hide the expression of consternation that flitted across her face. Only when she had composed herself did she look back and smile at him.

'All in good time,' she cautioned. 'I think it would be better to tackle Armenia first. After all, that's a conquest that's well within your powers, it would be a shorter campaign and the people back in Rome would be just as much impressed by it. Besides, you've got a sound excuse for it. Didn't Artarvasdes, the Armenian King, help the Parthians against you in your last campaign?'

'Yes, he did, the treacherous bastard!' snorted Antony, scratching at his beard and then yawning widely. His words came in a slurred monotone. 'And that was after he'd formally surrendered to me ... Like a fool, I trusted him and didn't take any hostages or leave a garrison behind. Then he turned against me and joined the Parthians ... If anyone deserves to be taught a lesson, he does.'

'Then do it!' urged Cleopatra. 'And afterwards I'll give you a magnificent triumphal procession in Alexandria.'

Antony lurched upright and blinked at her with a startled expression.

'Alexandria? But the triumphs have always been held in Rome for hundreds of years! It's a tradition.'

'Not everything traditional is necessarily good! And, anyway, do you want to go back to Rome?'

Antony scowled, sucking his teeth. The top of his head felt ready to lift off, but he struggled to concentrate on what she had said. *Do you want to go back to Rome?* Did he? It was several years now since he had set foot on Italian soil and he knew he was not welcome there. To all intents and purposes Octavian had locked him out of Italy, even denying Antony the right to recruit soldiers on Italian soil, which had been one of the conditions of the triumvirate. If Antony went back, he might have to fight to force his way to Rome. There was no doubt that he could do that, but did he want to? Besides, if he went back to Rome, he would have to confront Octavia and that prospect filled him with apprehension and guilt.

'No, I don't suppose I do,' he muttered, subsiding on his couch. 'All right then, I'll trounce the Armenian King and we'll hold a triumph in Alexandria better than any triumph that's ever been held in Rome! Thassa promise!'

Cleopatra was quietly exultant as Antony marched off to war. This time he was surrounded by prudent officers and she felt certain that the task of reducing Armenia was well within his powers. It would be good for morale in the east for Antony to win a victory and it would be one more step towards the realization of her dreams. Antony might not realize it, but holding a triumph in Alexandria would send a powerful symbolic message to the Senate in Rome. As far back as the days when she was Julius Caesar's mistress, Cleopatra had always dreamed of transferring the capital of the Roman empire to Alexandria instead of Rome. Once this ceremony was held in her home city, she felt the battle for prestige would be more than half won. The next step would be to set up an Alexandrian Senate as a rival to the one in Rome and pack it with her own nominees. Perhaps if she proceeded carefully, one day there would even be women among its members!

Antony's luck seemed to have turned and this time he swept all before him. In a brilliant and lightning-swift campaign he invaded Armenia, conquered the country and captured the King, Artarvasdes and his younger sons Tigranes and Artarvasdes. Only the eldest son Artaxes escaped and fled to Parthia for refuge. On Antony's return to Alexandria, the city witnessed two extraordinary spectacles. The first was Antony's triumph. It took place on a mild autumn day with just a hint of crispness in the air and it seemed that every inhabitant of Alexandria turned out to see the spectacle. Cleopatra sat in state on a golden throne, high above the heads of the crowd, and Antony entered the city in a triumphal chariot followed in procession by his Armenian captives, whom he presented formally to the Queen. In every respect, the ceremony followed the rituals of a genuine Roman triumph, with one exception. Antony was too tender-hearted to execute any of his captives and even King Artarvasdes's life was spared.

The triumph was followed by a ceremony which was even more important. In a huge gymnasium on the north side of the Canopic Way a vast crowd of people sat waiting impatiently. There were representatives from every city in Asia Minor and even from as far east as India. Black-skinned Nubians sat next to olive-skinned Syrians and dusky traders from the Punjab. Sparkling white Roman togas brushed against purple Macedonian military cloaks and green silk dresses all the way from China, while the babel of more than twenty languages filled the air. High on a silver tribunal, Antony and Cleopatra sat on twin gold thrones and at a lower level on other thrones, sat their three children and Ptolemy Caesar, nicknamed Caesarion. While Caesarion was dressed in the white, purple-bordered tunic of a noble Roman youth, Alexander Helios wore Median garb, including a tiara and an upright headdress, and his twin sister Cleopatra Selene was resplendent in the flowing robes of a North African girl. Two-year-old Ptolemy Philadelphus, clad as a miniature Macedonian soldier in a tunic, boots, a short cloak and a broad-brimmed hat, provoked adoring sighs from the women in the audience. There was a holiday mood with the air thick with the scent of sandalwood and myrrh and pipers playing cheerful tunes as the people took their seats. At last Mark Antony rose to his feet and lifted his arms for silence. The roar of the crowd slowly subsided and he stepped forward to the edge of the tribunal and began to speak. Cleopatra had written the speech and coached him carefully in it, but he still felt his stomach plunge nervously as he looked around at the blurred faces. This was probably the most important speech of his life and he didn't want to make a muck of it!

'Citizens of Alexandria,' he announced in his booming baritone which carried to the topmost portion of the stands. 'We are gathered today to celebrate a new era of peace and prosperity for the Mediterranean empire. I have the honour to present to you my wife Cleopatra, who in the past was formally married to Julius Caesar. I also present to you the legitimate son of that marriage, Ptolemy Caesar. What I am about to do today is done in honour of Julius Caesar's memory and in accordance with his wishes. I therefore declare that Cleopatra is Queen of Kings and Ptolemy Caesar

King of Kings, that they are the joint monarchs of Egypt and Cyprus and the overlords of all other kingdoms surrounding the Mediterranean. To my dear son Alexander Helios, I give the kingdom of Armenia and the overlordship of Parthia and Media. To my other son, Ptolemy Philadelphus, I give Syria and Cilicia and the overlordship of all client kings west of the Euphrates and as far as the Hellespont. To my daughter Cleopatra Selene, I give the kingdoms of Cyrenaica and Libya. And I declare myself supreme ruler of the inhabited world, east and west alike, in equal partnership with my beloved wife. Under our rule we want all nations to live in peace and prosperity.'

The news of Antony's triumph in Alexandria and his subsequent donation of Roman territory to Cleopatra and her children caused a sensation in Rome. Octavian held an emergency council with his chief advisers Maecenas and Agrippa to discuss the matter.

'In my view, this can be legally regarded as treason and gives a solid ground for declaring war on Antony,' he said exultantly. 'What's your opinion, gentlemen?'

Agrippa frowned. He was thirty years old, the same age as Octavian, but looked much more both because of his premature baldness and the sternness of his features. Politically he was ultra conservative, approving of family values, traditional morality, the worship of the gods and capital punishment, but he still had a lingering admiration for Mark Antony's skills as a soldier.

'It may be treason,' he growled, 'but you'll have a hard time persuading the legions to fight him. Mark Antony's always been a popular man in the army and, if you ask me, it's a rotten shame that he ever got entangled with that foreign bitch. They say she's got him on drugs now. And worse! Sex parties, dancing in public, wearing Greek clothes. I don't approve of any of it, myself. But you won't easily turn the Roman soldiers against him.'

'What do you think, Maecenas?' asked Octavian.

Maecenas brushed a few specks of imaginary dust from his own Greek gown which had been made of transparent silk on the island of Chios and which everybody said was the next best thing to genuine Chinese material. Silently he breathed a prayer of thanks to the gods that he was not a xenophobic buffoon like Agrippa, who seemed to take a pride in leaving his legs unshaven and smelling like a hairy goat under the armpits. But there were plenty of other Romans who shared Agrippa's prejudices against everything foreign or cultured, and perhaps that prejudice could be exploited.

'What about just declaring war on Cleopatra?' he suggested cunningly. 'And don't mention Antony. That way you won't upset the soldiers, because she'll be the enemy, not him.'

Octavian and Agrippa exchanged admiring glances.

'That's not a bad idea,' said Octavian. 'The only problem is my wretched sister Octavia. She flatly refuses to leave Antony's house or to give up custody of his children and, until he formally divorces her, I have no way of legally forcing her to do so. That's the only remaining obstacle in my way. If I declared war at the moment, she'd kick up a fuss, even if I only named Cleopatra as my opponent. But if Antony would send her a formal letter of divorce, Octavia would have to give up all hope of a reconciliation. I'm telling you, if only we can get that letter of divorce, we'll have every excuse we need to go to war.'

CHAPTER TWENTY-NINE

'Antony, you can't just sit and wait for Octavian to come and destroy you,' said Cleopatra passionately. 'Everyone says he's raising new legions to prepare for war against you. You must strike first!'

'I don't know,' said Antony, shaking his head unhappily. 'I hate to think of deliberately starting another civil war. There's been enough bloodshed already.'

'There'll be more if you don't! And you know how it will end, don't you? Octavian will capture me and drag me in triumph through the streets of Rome, then he'll kill me. I know he will.'

'He wouldn't –' began Antony and then stopped. It was easy to utter the glib, reassuring words, but was there any truth in them? He knew that Octavian hated her and he had a cruel streak like his great-uncle Julius Caesar. Turning the idea over in his mind, Antony realized uneasily that it was all too likely. With a sigh, he raised his hand to his forehead and rubbed it wearily. 'What do you want me to do?'

'I want you to declare war on Octavian! Heaven knows you have plenty of grounds for it. He's broken nearly every clause of your agreement as triumvirs.'

It was true, but Antony still balked at taking that final step.

'I'll tell you what,' he said. 'I won't declare war, but I will strengthen my defences and raise new troops to be ready in case he does.'

'That's not good enough!' she burst out. 'I know why you won't do it. It's because you don't love me. You want to go back to her, don't you?'

Antony groaned.

'No!' he shouted. 'That's not true. I do love you! I married you, didn't I?'

Her face crumpled as if she were about to cry.

'You may have married me, but you don't regard it as a true marriage, do you?'

'I do!'

'Then why haven't you ever divorced her?' she cried passionately.

They were at it again. Time after time Cleopatra had battered him with this complaint and usually Antony became obstinate and blustering, feeling all the more resentful because he could give her no satisfactory answer. How could he say that he didn't have the heart to inflict that final cruelty on Octavia? Although he had never written to her, he always secretly asked for news of her from any visitors who came from Rome and it had eased his guilt to know that she seemed outwardly serene. What was more, he felt that at least by continuing to live in his house, she had achieved some means of independence from the schemes of her brother. If he divorced her, wouldn't Octavian just marry her off to someone else with a total disregard for her wishes? Yet perhaps Cleopatra was right. There was no doubt that she was the one who was his true wife now and it might be better for everybody if he made a clean break.

'All right,' he said, gritting his teeth. 'I'll do it. You draft the letter of divorce and I'll sign it.'

Once the decision was taken, he felt as if a great burden had been lifted from him. In the autumn they sailed together for Ephesus and began recruiting new troops. Antony told Cleopatra of his plan to summon all the client kings who held their territories under the overlordship of Rome and demand that they swear an oath of loyalty to him personally.

'Well, don't summon Herod,' she begged. 'I don't like him and I don't want him as an officer in our army.'

Antony was exasperated by her directive, even though she was the one who had put up the twenty thousand talents to fund their war chest. Although Herod had once saved her life, there seemed to be some kind of long-standing antagonism between the pair of them whose origins baffled him. In some ways his sympathies lay with Herod. Even though he had only been a lowly tetrarch when Antony had first met him and owed all of his present territory and status to Antony, it must have galled his pride to give up part of that territory to Cleopatra. It was hardly surprising if Herod had resented the order to hand over his balsam groves to the Egyptian Queen and her subsequent seizure of the Gaza strip must have made him even more indignant. But why did she hate Herod so much? Antony could see no reason for it and for once he decided to go behind Cleopatra's back and overrule her. After all, Herod's military advice would be invaluable when it came to planning a campaign against Octavian. Yet when the Jewish King arrived in Ephesus and Antony asked his advice, he got more than he bargained for.

There was a nip in the air and the red glow of the setting sun was beginning to turn the streets to beaten copper when Herod's arrival was announced to Antony. He had been busy drilling the cavalry and paused only to dismount, knowing that the smell of horse sweat and leather which clung about him would not trouble an experienced soldier like the Jewish King. Wrapping his scarlet cloak warmly about him against the evening chill, he walked the short distance to the rented building just outside the temple sanctuary which was being used for the headquarters of the campaign. Herod looked very much as he had seen him last, tough, muscular and carelessly handsome, but with a few flecks of silver in his beard. With a shock, Antony realized that the 'young' tetrarch must be over forty by now. The two men shook hands and Antony waved Herod into a seat and offered him wine.

'I want to ask your advice,' he said, when the preliminary courtesies were over. 'I don't want to be guilty of starting a war, but I have every reason to believe that Octavian intends to foist one on me. I want your opinion on the best strategy I should follow in such a case.'

Something sinister blazed in Herod's eyes. This was the moment he had been waiting for, the moment to give Antony his frank advice without any danger of an intermediary suppressing or distorting it. But it was a dangerous moment. It might bring Herod the revenge he craved on that bitch Cleopatra, but it might equally well destroy him. He took in a deep, shuddering breath.

'You want my advice?' he demanded. 'All right, I'll give it to you. I think the smartest thing you could do is to kill Cleopatra and take Octavia back as your wife.'

Antony reeled as if he had been struck by a shot from a ballista. Shaking his head in a stunned fashion, he glared at Herod.

'Are you out of your senses, man?' he growled. 'How dare you speak of my wife like that?'

'No, I'm not out of my senses,' retorted Herod. 'And the reason I dare to speak of her like that is because no one else will dare to speak the truth about her. She's a scheming bitch, Mark Antony, and she cares nothing for you.'

'Shut up!' roared Antony, rising to his feet with

such violence that he knocked over the citrus wood table which held his cluttered array of documents. The blood thundered in his veins as he snatched the front of Herod's tunic and shook the Jewish King like a cornered rat. 'I'll kill you for these insults!' he bellowed. 'Take it back or I'll smash that pretty face to pulp.'

'It's the truth,' insisted Herod doggedly. His hands closed over Antony's wrists and the two men strained and sweated like fighting bulls. 'She cares for nobody who gets in the way of her schemes. She killed her sister Arsinoë and she'd just as readily kill you!'

Suddenly Antony had the appalling sensation that everything about him had dwindled into slow motion. A chill feeling gripped the pit of his stomach and the floor beneath him seemed to heave unsteadily as if he were trying to walk on water. Even Herod's intent, angry face seemed to dissolve into a pattern of moving grey dots. He no longer attempted to strangle Herod. Instead he shuddered and sagged against him as if for support.

'What did you say?' he whispered through frozen lips.

Herod felt a fierce blaze of exultation. *I've got him now!* he said to himself. Yet with a show of consideration he guided Antony back into his chair and sat down himself, facing him.

'It's the truth,' he said. 'Cleopatra ordered Arsinoë's death and she stood by in that very temple up yonder and watched to see that the killing was done to her satisfaction.'

Antony felt sick. As sick as he had felt in the mountains of Armenia watching his men die. This couldn't possibly be true, Cleopatra would never do such a thing! She had been fond of Arsinoë and in any case had been miles away in Alexandria when Arsinoë had met her death trying to evade capture. Trying to evade capture . . .

'I thought you gave me your sworn statement that Arsinoë was killed by one of your men while trying to resist arrest outside the temple sanctuary!' he blazed.

Herod shrugged and gave him a brief, wry smile.

'That was what Cleopatra told me to say,' he said. 'And I was too afraid of her influence over you to do otherwise. But the real truth is as I have just told you. Arsinoë died within the temple on Cleopatra's orders. There are people still living here in Ephesus who can verify that and I saw it with my own eyes.'

He did not add that he had done the deed with his own hands. If that fact emerged in a subsequent enquiry, he must weather it as best he could. At the moment his chief hope was to blacken Cleopatra's character so thoroughly that the Roman triumvir would make a complete break with her and perhaps even restore Herod's lost territory.

For a moment Antony was too shaken and appalled to say anything. Horrible as the story was, it had the ring of truth. He could not endure the shame of bribing temple attendants to give evidence against his own wife and he had no heart for torturing anyone to extract the truth from them. But he could and must question Cleopatra. If what Herod said was true, then everything he had felt for her was based on a lie. He had always known she was wilful and calculating, but he had not believed her totally heartless. If she had been capable of such savagery once, could he ever love her again? While these thoughts ran through his mind, he gazed at Herod with a blank and stricken look and then realized that he must say something to bring this interview to an end. Suddenly he felt a renewed rush of antagonism towards Herod. All very well for the slimy little bastard to sit there calmly, saying he had only obeyed Cleopatra's orders, but he was a free man, wasn't he? He could have refused! Rising to his feet, Antony scowled at his tormentor.

'Well, you've given me your advice,' he said sourly. 'But I must tell you I've no intention of taking it. Nor do I have any intention of detaining you here any longer. I believe the rents from Malchus's Dead Sea bitumen monopoly are badly in arrears and you're the collecting agent for the area, aren't you? Well, you can go and exact payment from him. That's your next military assignment, King Herod. Good day to you.'

The look of outrage on Herod's face was small compensation for the turmoil Antony felt as he walked slowly back to the lodgings he shared with Cleopatra. She looked up at his entrance with a bewildered expression.

'What's happened?' she demanded. 'You look terrible, like an old man. Are you ill? Has something happened to one of the children?'

He shook his head, still unable to reconcile the graceful, feminine reality of her with the image of a murderess who would kill her own sister. Then, dreading the answer, he put the question to her.

'Cleopatra, did you kill Arsinoë?'

In the temple of Vesta in Rome, the youngest of the Vestal Virgins, a fourteen-year-old called Cornelia, flung a log of wood into the fire pit and retreated sulkily as the flames blazed up. It seemed stupid to her to have a great, roaring orange fire like that going in mid summer when the place was already stiflingly hot. But if the sacred flame was ever allowed to go out, disaster would fall on Rome and, what was more, the chief priest would flog her mercilessly if she was in charge at the time it happened. Slouching back against the circular marble wall of the stylized hut, she sat down in a luxurious cushioned chair and picked up her plate again. Mmm, roast pheasant with asparagus. And later there would be honeycakes to follow. At least Vestal Virgins ate well and there were other benefits too. They were given a huge 'dowry' by the state on their acceptance into the order although most of them would only ever be wedded to the service of the goddess. Still, a few had managed to survive the thirty years' service required and marry afterwards. Cornelia, who had been a Vestal since she was six, hoped to be one of them. And they always got the best seats at the theatre and the right to manage their own financial affairs.

Yet there was no denying that on the whole the life was boring. Nothing to do but tend this stupid sacred flame and, as you got older, file all the wills and leases and legal documents and deposits of money that were entrusted to the Vestals by the most important men in Rome. Today there wasn't even anyone to keep her company, since four of the six had gone out to the theatre and the chief Vestal Virgin, Junia, was busy trying out a new filing system. Watching the billowing smoke eddy out through the circular hole in the roof to disperse in the bright, blue sky, Cornelia wished passionately that something interesting would happen.

Her wish was fulfilled. She had just finished eating the pheasant and embarked on the first of the honeycakes when there was a cry of outrage from the doorkeeper and the sound of tramping boots outside. Cornelia set down the plate and rose to her feet. She had just sufficient time to glimpse a cohort of armed soldiers outside before a slightly built man in the purple-bordered tunic of a senator entered the marble hut. With growing curiosity she recognized the triumvir Octavian. Usually he sent a slave to announce his visits. What could he be doing here so unexpectedly?

'Good morning,' he said in a clipped voice. 'I'd like you to call the chief Vestal Virgin. There's a will that I want to inspect.'

'Yes, sir.'

She hurried away and returned moments later with Junia, who was thirty-five years old, tall, dark and formidable.

'What can I do for you?' asked Junia.

'I wish to inspect the will of Mark Antony.'

Junia looked shocked and affronted.

'I'm afraid that's quite impossible. We can only release legal documents to the people who deposited them here with us. Mark Antony's will is no concern of yours.'

Octavian took a step closer and Cornelia saw a strange, glittering look appear in his eyes.

'It is every concern of mine,' he said softly. 'Two of his followers, Plancus and Titius have come to me from Ephesus with the news that Mark Antony's will formally bequeathes provinces of the Roman empire to Cleopatra and her children. If that is so, it is tantamount to high treason. I demand to see that document!'

Before Junia could answer, there was a fresh disturbance. Suddenly a woman broke through the cordon of soldiers outside the building and ran into the marble hut with her blonde hair in wild disorder and tears running down her cheeks.

'Don't listen to him!' she shrieked hysterically. 'I'm Antony's wife. I forbid you to do this!'

'Be silent, Octavia!' thundered the triumvir. 'You

are no longer Antony's wife. He has now sent you a formal notice of divorce and the marriage is at an end. Madam, I must ask you again to bring me that will, or I'll order my soldiers to enter the temple premises and seize it by force!'

Junia's eyes flashed indignantly.

'That would be sacrilege!'

'Not at all!' retorted Octavian. 'I was clearly instructed in a dream sent by the goddess Vesta last night that this was what I must do.'

Junia's eyes shot sparks as fiercely as the sacred fire, but as Octavian raised a hand to summon the soldiers she made a decision.

'I cannot allow you to desecrate the temple,' she said bitterly. 'Cornelia, go and fetch Mark Antony's will.'

Shortly afterwards, while his sister struggled in the grip of two muscular soldiers, Octavian tore the seal from the document and scanned its contents with growing satisfaction.

'Excellent,' he said half to himself. 'Exactly the sort of material I need to discredit him.'

Stepping forward, he raised one hand and stared into the leaping flames of the sacred fire. His voice echoed ominously in the confined space of the temple.

'I call on you, almighty Vesta, to witness that I now declare war upon Cleopatra, Queen of Egypt, and vow to bring about her destruction!'

The ship heeled violently in a sudden, roaring gust of wind and the captain shouted at the crew to drop the sails which were flogging dangerously against the mast. Overhead, branches of lightning lit up the dark clouds with a white tracery of patterns and were followed almost at once by a reverberating boom of thunder.

Great walls of green sea water smashed against the sides of the ship and came hurtling across the deck, drenching the passengers. Cleopatra staggered and clutched at Mark Antony to keep her balance. There was a distant sound like the drumming of horses' hooves and then down came the rain in a steady, drenching torrent that blotted out the other ships in the fleet and made navigation even more difficult.

'It's a bad omen,' said Mark Antony, gripping the railing and staring out over the heaving, grey seas.

'It's bad weather!' she shouted in exasperation above the roar of the wind. 'Octavian will be experiencing it too.'

Antony turned back to her and brushed a strand of wet hair back from her face.

'Well, this is where we part company, sweetheart,' he said. 'I'll transfer to my ship now. And remember whatever happens, you're to stay clear of the battle. I don't want you involved in any danger. Is that understood? If anything should go wrong and I realize we're losing or that you're in danger, I'll run a red flag up my mast. The minute you see that you're to turn tail and flee for Egypt immediately. There are to be no arguments and no discussion and I've told the captain the same thing. Do I have your promise?'

She stared at him rebelliously.

'But I want to be involved in the battle,' she protested. 'My sailors are every bit as good as yours.'

'I know that,' said Antony impatiently. 'But I'd never forgive myself if you came to any harm. Give me your promise, Cleopatra, or I swear I'll call off the battle even now.'

For once she saw that he was implacable and dropped her gaze.

'All right, I promise,' she muttered.

He took her in his arms and kissed her.

She felt a momentary pang of fear as she felt his cold, metal breastplate against her cheek and the stiff, leather pleats of his kilt and the damp wool of his cloak. What if this was the last time she ever saw him? Then she pushed the thought away. No. By tonight he would be victorious, the emperor of the entire Roman world, with her as his empress. Rising on tiptoes, she kissed him again with passionate urgency.

'May the gods go with you, Imperator,' she said.

As Antony went over the side of the ship into the smaller vessel that was tossing violently below, he cherished the memory of her face for a moment and wondered whether he could achieve all that she required of him. Sometimes he had the dreadful suspicion, even after all these years of turbulent involvement, that she was merely using him, that she saw him only as a second-rate tool to achieve her ambitions. The evidence of her cruelty and indifference towards Arsinoë had shaken him badly. Yet she had met all his accusations with the plaintive retort, 'What else could I do? She tried to kill me, didn't she?' It was true, but it pained him obscurely. Was there any room in Cleopatra's heart for love and pity? Or was it all taken up by ambition? He had even thought once more of leaving her for Octavia, but could not bring himself to do it. Whatever her faults, he loved her. He only wished he knew whether she loved him. With a sudden shake of his head, he thrust the question ruthlessly from his mind. From here on he must concentrate purely on the battle.

He knew that he would find Octavian's fleet to seaward of him and he meant to use the wind when it shifted, as it generally did at midday, to turn their left and drive them southwards, away from their camp.

Once they were broken or dispersed, he could starve their camp out. This storm was a setback, but as soon as it blew itself out, Antony intended to put his plan into action.

At first it seemed that all was going well. The winds abated and the following morning, the second day of September, dawned bright and clear. Both fleets came out and lay on their oars, waiting for the wind to veer. When it did so, Antony and Agrippa raced to turn each other and the ends of their lines met. Fierce fighting took place and Cleopatra watched from the rear of the fleet in an agony of apprehension. Because of the distance and the confusion, it was impossible to say exactly what was happening, but twice she saw ships raise all their oars in token of surrender and wondered anxiously whose they were. The air was thick with uproar. The crash of bronze prows as ships were rammed, the fast, rhythmic, synchronized splash of banks of oars, the yells of battle and the cries of the wounded mixed with the hiss and rush of water surging past the hull. After a time the fighting came too close for comfort and the captain gave orders for her trireme to retreat some distance. It was while they were in the midst of this manoeuvre that the helmsman gave a shout.

'Sir, the red flag is flying from the mast of Antony's ship! I saw it clearly.'

They all turned to look, but an enemy trireme was now blocking their vision and bearing down fast upon them. In that instant the captain made a decision.

'Hoist sails and head for Egypt,' he shouted. 'At the double.'

He was not to know that the helmsman was a traitor in Octavian's pay, bribed to seize just such an opportunity to create confusion and trouble between Mark

Antony and his wife. And Octavian had guessed Antony's weakness all too shrewdly.

Looking up from the roar and press of the fighting, Antony was horrified to see Cleopatra's ship spreading its sails and heading for the open sea. What had happened? Why was she retreating? Had Octavian's men boarded her vessel and taken her captive? Fear for her safety flowed through his veins like a chill dose of hemlock and he turned to the helmsman and bellowed an order.

'Hoist sails, man, follow the Queen's ship. Some disaster must have happened to her.'

The rest of Antony's fleet was shocked and appalled to see their general turning tail and heading for the open sea. Believing that he must be running away, captain after captain stared after him in stunned horror and then gave the orders to raise the oars in token of surrender. Octavian, standing on the prow of his own ship, turned to Agrippa and let out a yell of triumph.

'We've done it!' he cried, flinging himself into Agrippa's arms and thumping him on the back. 'We've tricked the bastard! We've won!'

CHAPTER THIRTY

It was nearly two hours before Antony caught up with Cleopatra's ship and went on board. At first he was relieved to find her unharmed, but his relief rapidly gave way to baffled fury.

'Why did you run away if you were in no danger?' he demanded.

'Because you told me to retreat!' she shouted. 'You ran up the red flag on your mast.'

'I did no such thing!' stormed Antony.

A heated argument ensued and it was discovered that in the confusion of the retreat the helmsman had handed over his place to another sailor and slipped away in a small boat. Cleopatra was outraged when she realized that Antony had left the rest of the fleet to fend for itself while he came in pursuit of her.

'Why on earth did you follow me?' she raged.

'I was worried about you. I thought Octavian's troops might have captured your ship and taken you prisoner.'

'You fool! He's probably there off the cape of Actium accepting the surrender of our entire fleet right this very moment, thanks to you.'

With a groan, Antony pushed her aside and made his way up to the prow of the ship. For the next three days he sat there almost motionless with his head in his hands, staring at the sea and agonizing over what had happened. He knew that she was right and he took it hard, blaming himself for the wreckage of all their hopes. And yet he could not repress a feeling of bitterness for her lack of sympathy. After all, he had deserted his men in order to try and save her and was this all the thanks he got? It was just like the retreat from Parthia all over again!

By the time they reached Egypt, Cleopatra had recovered from her first throes of disappointment. Some of the fleet had succeeded in escaping from Greek waters and following them and she now gave orders for all the ships to be hung with victory garlands and for the crews to sail into the harbour cheering and playing music in order not to lower the morale of the citizens of Alexandria. The stratagem gave her a few hours' grace and she arrested and executed all those who might have raised a revolution against her if they had known the truth. When at last Antony came to join her in the palace, she tried to rally his spirits.

'It's the end of all we've worked for,' he said miserably.

'No, it isn't!' she cried. 'You can still defeat Octavian with your land army and, even if that fails, we could sail to Spain and seize the silver mines and start a new empire there. Or we could take all our treasures and move to India! We're not beaten yet, Antony. We're not beaten until we give up.'

'I have given up,' said Antony moodily.

To her horror, he seemed to mean it. She had half-expected Octavian to sail immediately to Egypt and launch an attack upon the capital city, but Octavian was too cunning for that. He preferred to wait and let despair do its work. Day after day the number of desertions in Antony's forces increased and Antony's spirits seemed to sink lower with each fresh betrayal. Where he might have spent his time drilling the army, or making plans for their escape, instead he took a house near the Pharos and installed himself there in a state of bachelor squalor.

'What was the name of that geezer, the one Octavia's tame philosopher told me about?' he asked his friend Lucilius. 'The politician from Athens who got fed up with all the shit he had to take in public life and became a hermit?'

'Timon,' was the reply.

'All right, well I'll call my house after him. It'll be the Timoneum and I'll be another Timon! I won't have anything to do with people any more. I'm fed up to the back teeth with the lot of them. From here on I'm just going to live on my own and get drunk.'

He proceeded to do this with single-minded fervour. Cleopatra was incensed to find herself turned away when she arrived at the door, or worse still, greeted by a stubbly-faced, bleary-eyed Antony who staggered around smelling of sour wine and clutching a wine cup in his hand. When she tried to persuade him to listen to her schemes for battle or flight, he simply stared at her with blank incomprehension. At last she lost her temper.

'You ought to be ashamed of yourself, you drunken, spineless layabout!' she shouted.

'Oh, piss off!' retorted Antony rudely and slammed the door in her face.

She could not rid herself of her bitterness and disappointment, but if Antony would not help her, she would have to plan alone. Rumours arrived that Herod had deserted to the victor of Actium and that Octavian's land army was now moving through Judaea and advancing towards the borders of Egypt. If Antony would take no action, then she would! Knowing how much Octavian had always resented her son Caesarion, who was Julius Caesar's genuine son, while he himself could only claim the fiction of a legal adoption, she sent her eldest child away to India. Even though

Caesarion was now sixteen, it broke her heart to see him go, but she hoped soon to join him herself. Her plan was to have a fleet of ships portaged across the isthmus at Heroopolis and into the Arabian gulf so that she could set sail to India. It might have worked if it had not been for Malchus, the King of Arabia Petra, who was only too overjoyed to have this chance of avenging the loss of his bitumen monopoly. Hearing of her plans, he sent troops to attack and burn her ships and she was forced to retreat back to Alexandria.

As for Antony, he finally sobered up when he heard that Octavian was in Syria and fast approaching the land border of Egypt. Unable to control his shaking hands, he summoned his friend Lucilius to his side.

'I want you to write me a letter,' he said. 'Tell Octavian I'll commit suicide if he'll give me his sacred oath that he'll leave Cleopatra and the children unharmed.'

The letter was duly sent, but Octavian made no reply. As the menace of his army drew nearer, a pall of alarm and despondency hung over the city of Alexandria worse than anything that had been experienced since the time of the plague. Antony and Cleopatra were still not speaking to each other, but she had built herself a mausoleum which was not yet completed near the temple of Isis. The lower part was crammed full of all her treasure, gold and jewels, ivory and spices, and the aisle ways between the display cases were heaped with logs of wood and twisted rags soaked in pitch. Her plan now was to offer to abdicate her throne and to ask Octavian to give it to Cleopatra Selene or Alexander Helios. If he refused, she intended to throw a torch into the treasury and burn it all and herself with it.

On the last day of July, word came to Antony that

Octavian's advance cavalry had reached the outer suburbs of the city. It was after midnight and in the stillness of the great city Antony suddenly heard a distant uproar as if a troop of revellers were making their way through the city. Suddenly he felt that he could not bear to die passively, but must make one last attempt to turn defeat into victory. Calling for his slave Eros, he ordered him to set out his military uniform and help him on with his breastplate and leg greaves. A renewed vigour flowed through him as he felt the familiar weight of his sword in his hand and he marched out to the barracks and started to muster his soldiers. As a bright red sunrise began to turn the surface of the sea to a great flaming mirror of beaten copper and the fires of the lighthouse lost their power in the strengthening daylight, Antony posted his infantry on the hills in front of the city and sent out his ships to attack those of the enemy. His heart was thudding with renewed excitement and hope as he heard the steady beat of the oars and watched the triremes skimming across the harbour.

'I'll save you yet, Cleopatra,' he vowed silently to himself.

But, oh, gods, what was this? As his triremes sailed close to those of Octavian, he witnessed a sight which pierced him to the heart with horror. He was too far away to hear the order, but in perfect unison all the rowers suddenly raised their oars straight above their heads in token of surrender.

'No! No!' howled Antony.

Shock and rage almost overwhelmed him at this fresh betrayal, but they were followed at once by fear. He must warn Cleopatra of the danger she faced! In spite of his heavy armour, he set out at a run for the mausoleum near the temple of Isis.

Hearing shouts and the approach of soldiers, Cleopatra gave orders for the drop doors to be closed and bolted. Then she retreated with Iras and Charmion to the upper floor, waiting in alarm to see what was happening. A steady hammering began at one of the doors below. A portico covered the entrance and she was unable to see who was there.

'Go down and find out who it is,' she instructed Iras.

The other woman obeyed and soon returned.

'It's Mark Antony,' she hissed. 'He says he needs to talk to you urgently.'

Cleopatra's mind raced. Antony! All her bitterness over his feckless behaviour in the last few months came welling to the surface. This was a fine time to come and tell her that he needed to speak to her when Octavian was at the very gates of the city! Why couldn't he have done something sooner? She was sick of him, sick of him! Let him go back to his pathetic Roman wife and make his peace with his rotten brother-in-law. She would find some way of sailing away to India and confound all of them.

'Tell him I'm dead!' she said stormily. 'Tell him I've already committed suicide.'

Iras rolled her eyes, but obeyed. Standing in the dimness of the entrance hall with the litter of wood and treasure around her feet and the smell of pitch in her nostrils, she shouted through the barred door in a strained voice.

'You're too late. She's already dead. She committed suicide.'

Antony felt as if his heart had stopped beating at this appalling announcement. Dead? Dead? It was too dreadful to grasp. Clutching at one of the pillars of the portico for support, he felt a chill tide of horror surge through him. Oh, gods, it couldn't be true! Not his impetuous, spirited darling, who had never known the meaning of the word defeat! She wouldn't give up like that, wouldn't leave him, wouldn't desert the children . . . But if she had, then it was all his fault! He should never have given way to despair after his defeat at Actium! Hadn't she tried time and time again to rouse him from his torpor, to urge him to be a man and fight? But he had been too busy wallowing in his own misery to care about hers and even her boundless optimism must have had its limits! If only he had come sooner they might have comforted and cheered each other, they might even have gone off and grown old in exile together. Instead she had killed herself and it was all his fault! A sudden, scalding rush of tears blinded him and he clenched his right fist and slammed it into the pitiless wall of the building.

'No!' he roared. 'No, no, I can't bear it.'

Dreadful, racking sobs wrenched his body and he wept as he had not wept since the retreat from Parthia. And all the time the thought gnawed at the back of his brain that Octavian was coming closer with his army to demand his final humiliation and surrender. All at once he saw what he must do and with hasty, fumbling fingers, he tore off his helmet and breastplate and snatched his sword from its scabbard.

'Cleopatra,' he said hoarsely. 'I won't grieve for you any more, because I'm coming to join you at once!'

Then with a long, horrible cry as if he were charging into battle, he raised the sword and thrust it straight into his guts. On the other side of the locked door, Iras heard his terrible, bellowing cry and guessed too late what he had done. Pulling back the small, sliding panel which covered the peephole, she looked out and caught a horrified glimpse of Antony, groaning and writing on the ground. She was just about to try and haul back the barrage of bolts and bars that secured the door when she saw several Roman soldiers running towards him. At the same time Cleopatra's voice came echoing down the stairs.

'What's going on down there? Has he gone away?'

Iras's legs were shaking so much they would hardly carry her, but anger lent her strength. In a sudden rush she went flying up the stairs.

'No, he hasn't gone!' she hissed. 'He's stabbed himself and it's your doing, Cleopatra.'

'Oh, gods!' shrieked Cleopatra, shrinking back and covering her face with her hands. 'I never thought he'd do anything like that. Is he dead?'

'Not yet,' said Iras bitterly. 'He botched that too, just the way you accused him of botching everything else.'

There was no mistaking the shock and horror in Cleopatra's face and Iras's anger turned to pity as she saw the Queen's white, stricken cheeks and wildly dilated eyes.

'We've got to help him,' she cried. 'Can we get the doors open?'

'Not easily. There are so many bolts and bars and keys you'd need a locksmith and half an hour to do it.'

'We must do something! I can't just leave him there to die.'

'There are some soldiers outside,' said Iras slowly. 'If they put him on a litter, we could haul him up through the top floor window.'

Charmion came to their aid and together they went to the window and called down to the soldiers below. A shouted conversation established that Antony was still alive, but sinking fast. Iras flung a stout coil of rope over the hoist beam and the soldiers below caught the other end. Working hastily, they improvised a makeshift stretcher out of some cloaks and cushions purloined from the nearby temple of Isis and the three women hauled him up. He was almost more than their strength could manage and tears poured down Cleopatra's face as she groaned and strained at the rope. Smeared with blood and struggling with death, Antony stretched out his hands to her even as he dangled in the air. When at last they got him inside and laid him down on the floor, she flung herself down beside him and tried to wipe the blood from his stomach and his mouth. His hand caressed her hair weakly.

'Sweetheart,' he gasped. 'They told me you were dead ... So thankful ... Escaped ...' There was a long pause as he seemed to choke on the blood that was bubbling from his mouth. Then he coughed and spoke again. 'Stuffed it up ... Failure, even at this.'

'You're not, you're not,' she wept.

'I wasn't a failure at one thing, though,' he croaked. 'I loved you ... better than any other man ... ever did.'

'Oh, Antony,' she wailed. 'Don't die, don't die! I love you! Please don't die.'

With a dreadful groan she buried her head against his shoulder and sobbed as if her heart would break. He clutched her with his arm and his wandering eyes tried to look at her. But the effort was too much. Suddenly he vomited blood again and his lips made one more effort to frame a word. She raised her head and strained to catch it.

'Sorry,' he breathed.

Then his eyes rolled up into his head and his arms dropped to his sides.

She could not believe the horror of it. Could not believe the mess, the pain, the waste of it all! Her hair was soaked with his blood and her eyes were streaming. As she clutched at his limp hand, the realization gripped her that he was dead and suddenly she gave way completely. Tearing her clothes and hair and shrieking wildly, she clung to him in total abandonment. This was not just a show of mourning, but real grief. She felt ready to burst with love and pity. Why hadn't she ever seen how much she cared about him? Why hadn't she told him how good and kind he was? Why hadn't she thanked him for all he had done for her? Not only the kingdoms laid at her feet, but the little kindnesses which might have happened between any husband and wife. She remembered how he had mended her broken sandal strap with his own hands, how he had brought her boxes of honeycakes and flower garlands from the market, how he had given their children rides on his shoulders. It was gone, all gone, and she had never told him how much it meant to her! Had Arsinoë suffered like this when Vercingetorix was taken from her? If she had then it was all Cleopatra's fault! She had thought ambition and success were what counted and she had never given love the importance it deserved. But Antony had. Now she buried her face in his chest and groaned.

'Oh, Antony, I wish I had my life all over again. I'd do it all so differently.'

While she was still weeping over his lifeless body, there was a sudden disturbance outside the door downstairs. Still numb with shock, Iras went down to investigate.

'Who is it?' she demanded, opening the spyhole and confronting the Roman soldier who was pounding relentlessly on the closed door.

'My name is Proculeius. I want to speak to the Queen.'

'You can't. She's with Mark Antony.'

She made as if to shut the sliding panel, but he jammed his fist in the hole and spoke through the tiny remaining space.

'Listen, I know all that's happened. One of Antony's bodyguard came running to Octavian and told us he'd committed suicide or was near enough to dead. Octavian sent me as his messenger. He wants you to tell Cleopatra that he's got no intention of killing her, that he'll treat her and the children kindly and she's not to do anything rash.'

He watched her through narrowed eyes, trying to guess whether she would be deceived. What Octavian had actually said was this: 'Tell the bitch whatever lies you need to keep her alive, but make sure she doesn't set that monument on fire. I want her treasure intact and I want her displayed in my triumphal procession in Rome before I kill her.'

'I'll tell her,' said Iras coldly. 'But I don't think she'll believe you.'

With a sudden vicious thrust, she forced Proculeius's hand out of the opening, skinning his knuckles, and slammed and bolted the sliding panel.

He swore under his breath and turned to his companion Gallus.

'Try to keep them talking,' he mouthed. 'I've got an idea.'

Once more the hammering began on the lower door and, with an exasperated cry, Iras came back down the stairs.

'What do you want now?' she shouted, without opening the sliding panel.

'I've got another proposal to put to you,' began Gallus. 'But Cleopatra will have to hear it herself. I promise you, it's worth her while.'

Grumbling to herself, Iras went back up the stairs. She had just returned with a distraught Cleopatra, when there was a sudden shriek from the room above.

'Mmmph! Let me go, you Roman pig! Cleopatra, look out! They've got a ladder! They're inside the building.'

After that everything seemed to happen in a jumbled blur. Cleopatra had just snatched up her dagger to stab herself in the breast when Proculeius came hurtling down the stairs and disarmed her with a force that almost broke her wrist. Iras ran to fetch the torch and kindling, but he sent her flying against the wall so hard that she hit her head with a loud crack. Then, unsheathing his sword, he turned its tip towards each of them in turn.

'I come only with friendly intentions,' he said.

Cleopatra gave a wild burst of hysterical laughter at that.

'As friendly as Roman intentions usually are!' she said bitterly. 'Are you threatening to kill me, officer? Do me a favour! Strike now!'

Proculeius dropped his eyes and looked discomfited. 'There's no need for you to die,' he muttered, avoiding her eyes. 'Octavian is prepared to spare you.'

'So that he can drag me in his triumph through the streets of Rome? No, thank you! You may have stopped us from burning this place down, but you can't stop me from starving myself to death.'

'If you do yourself any wilful harm,' said Proculeius, not without a twinge of guilt, 'Octavian has given me orders to cut your children's throats with my own hand.'

Cleopatra's mouth twisted.

'I see. Two ten-year-olds and a six-year-old! And this is the man whose mercy I'm supposed to trust?

All right, Roman. I'll come with you for now, but don't imagine that I'm fool enough to believe your promises.'

An unnatural calm descended upon her and she left the building moving like a sleepwalker in the custody of two burly Roman guards. Her earlier anguish about Antony had been replaced by a dogged determination to finish the hard tasks that remained to be done. What she must do was give Antony honourable burial and make some attempt to safeguard her children. After that she would kill herself. Yet even to achieve these dismal aims, she would have to convince Octavian of her desire to live. As she was marched into the palace, she tossed her head defiantly.

'I am still Queen of Egypt,' she said with freezing dignity. 'And I wish to be accommodated in my own quarters with proper food and drink and my own attendants about me. Kindly inform Octavian that I am disgusted by his unprovoked invasion of my country and I will meet him in a few days' time to discuss it after I have had time to mourn the death of my husband.'

This message was reported back to Octavian, who was delighted by it, since it provided clear evidence that the callous whore intended to go on living. Well, he had expected no less! Let her have her comfort and her companions! It would make it all the easier to lure her to Rome where she would find a very different kind of life in the Tullian dungeon.

'Give her whatever she wants,' he ordered. 'It will give her something to look back on when she's put on parade in Rome and executed.'

One of the officers sent to deliver Octavian's message was Cornelius Dolabella, the son of Antony's old rival. Dolabella could not help pitying the Queen and he was moved by the stark look in her eyes as she took his hand and begged him to do all he could to protect her children.

'Do you know what Octavian's plans are for me?' she demanded. 'If you have any pity at all, I beg you to tell me.'

He hesitated and then gave in.

'He's going to send you and the children to Syria in three days' time,' he muttered, casting a glance over his shoulder at the barred door beyond which Roman guards were stationed. 'He intends to parade you all in his triumph. After that . . . I don't know.'

She caught her breath and crossed over to a side table, then returned with a letter.

'Will you give this secretly to Octavia?' she begged. 'Ask her in the name of Antony to do her best to protect his children.'

Her voice broke and she could not go on. Blinking away tears, she drew the gold and amethyst ring off her finger and pressed it into his hand.

'If you have a wife of your own, give this to her,' she added.

The next day Antony's funeral took place in the palace gardens. Octavian had given permission for it to be held, both in order to ensure Cleopatra's continued cooperation and also to avoid the unpopularity which a memorial service in Rome might provoke, but it was a tiny band of mourners who gathered around the funeral pyre. Antony's children had been forbidden to attend and only Cleopatra and her companions were there. Yet everything had been done according to proper custom. She had washed the body with her own hands and dressed it in a senatorial tunic and a spotless white toga and put a coin in his mouth to pay his ferry fare to the underworld. She had even paid a craftsman to make a wax death mask of his face, although she did not know in what atrium it would ever be displayed. As the slaves moved about, piling the fragrant pine logs at the foot of the pyre, her own face was set in a frozen mask of grief. Somebody handed her a torch and, bending forward, she touched the tip of it to the piled logs. There was a crackling sound, as wisps of smoke rose into the air, then suddenly, with a great whoosh, it burst into an inferno of bright orange flames. Driven back by the sudden heat and acrid smoke, she picked up jars of myrrh and sandalwood and emptied their fragrant spices into the flames. It did not take long until all his mortal remains were consumed, but when at last she was given wine to quench the smouldering ashes, she felt as if she had woken from a long trance. The pain of it was almost more than she could bear.

'Of all the dreadful things that have ever happened to me,' she said to Iras, 'these last few days I've lived without him have been the worst. I want to go home now.'

Late that night she summoned Iras, Olympus and Charmion to her chambers. Ever since she had left Antony's funeral pyre, Dolabella's words had been echoing in her head and her mind had been full of thoughts of Arsinoë. She could not endure to be dragged through the streets of Rome and made a ridiculous spectacle for the amusement of the common mob as her sister had been. No. The time had come for action and she was determined to die like a queen.

'Olympus,' she said when they were all seated. 'You promised me once that if I ever needed to die with dignity, you would give me the means to do so. That moment has come. Tomorrow I want you to send me a swift and certain means of death. Will you keep your promise?'

Olympus felt the tiny hairs on the back of his neck rise in horror at her words. Yet he could give her no comfort and offer her no hope beyond the bitter gift that she asked. With a silent shudder, he bowed his head.

'I will,' he said.

Rising to his feet, he kissed her hand, prostrated himself on the floor in front of her, then rose and left the room, shaking his head and sighing.

For an instant Cleopatra gazed after him with a desolate expression. Then suddenly her chin came up and she continued, as if this were simply another of their meetings to discuss matters of policy.

'Iras,' she said briskly. 'Take this document and guard it well. It's my sworn declaration that you're now a free woman and there's a jewellery box over there in the cupboard. I want you and Charmion to divide the contents and leave while you're still able.'

Iras gave Cleopatra an unwavering stare.

'I'm not going anywhere,' she said at last. 'My only child has already passed to the underworld and I've nobody else but you and Charmion. I'll stay with you.'

'You're to go!' snapped Cleopatra with a return to her old arrogance. 'That's an order!'

'You can't order me around any more. I'm a free woman,' said Iras stubbornly. 'That document says so.'

Cleopatra gave a choking laugh, then turned to her other companion.

'Charmion, persuade her.'

Charmion shook her head.

'No. I'm staying too,' she said with dignity. 'I'm a

widow now and my only daughter's married. We three were together at the beginning and we'll be together at the end.'

Cleopatra tried twice to speak and failed. At last she said huskily, 'I don't think there's anything in the world as important as good friends. All right. All right. We'll do this together.'

When day broke, they all bathed, dressed in their best clothes and ordered a sumptuous meal. They were still reclining at table when a man arrived at the door with a basket full of figs. The Roman soldiers blocked his way with their swords, but he smiled placatingly.

'Come on,' he coaxed, 'it's only a basket of harmless fruit. It was sent by her doctor Olympus.'

The soldiers looked at each other doubtfully. Then one of them spoke.

'Go on. Give it to her and get on your way.'

Inside the room the three women received the basket of figs in hushed silence. Only when the messenger had left and the door was barred behind him, did they carefully take out the fragrant purple fruit.

'Look, the basket's got a hollow base,' said Charmion. 'Oh, my goodness!'

She took a quick, sharp breath and stepped back, allowing the others to glimpse the writhing mass of cobras in the lower compartment. A chill feeling invaded Cleopatra's veins, but she forced herself to remain calm as she reached inside the flexing coils and disentangled a single snake. She moved so quietly that it remained unafraid and went sinuously gliding up her arm as if it were caressing her. Her breath came in long, heaving gulps, there was a distant ringing in her ears and her throat felt dry, but she was proud to discover that her voice was quite steady.

'How appropriate,' she said, swallowing hard and wishing that her dizziness would recede. 'That's really very imaginative of Olympus. He must have remembered the Egyptian belief that anyone bitten by a cobra becomes a god. Well, we'll all be deities now. Unless you've changed your minds?' She looked at her companions and saw the same fear and agonized purpose in both their faces. One after the other they shook their heads. 'Well, then, let's go bravely and go together.'

Deliberately she raised her hand and struck the snake violently on the side of the head, enraging it. It reared up with a hissing noise, its hood extended, and lunged. She felt a sharp pain, followed by a rushing sensation and a bright, blinding light. The room seemed to roar and whirl about her as she stumbled to a couch and collapsed upon it. An uncertain smile curved her lips and she reached out her arms.

'I'm coming, Antony,' she breathed.

In general I have tried to make the historical background of this story as authentic as possible. However, there are some subjects on which I have allowed myself the licence of a novelist rather than the caution of an historian. Most important of these is the fact that there is no evidence suggesting a love affair between Arsinoë and Vercingetorix. In addition, my account of the early involvement between Antony and Cleopatra is based purely on a single line in Appian, saying that Antony fell in love with Cleopatra when she was only fourteen years old. Similarly, Julius Caesar's sexual involvement with Octavian is based on the hostile allegations of his political enemies which may well have been false. There are also several minor points where I have felt free to simplify history. For instance, the gold statue of Cleopatra in the temple of Venus Genetrix was not finished by the time of Caesar's triumphs, so that he and Cleopatra would only have viewed a clay copy, Fulvia's death took place in Sicyon after Antony had already left Greece and some details of the battle at Actium are highly simplified. It is also worth noting that, owing to the primitive astronomical knowledge of the Romans, their calendar was in wild disorder until it was reformed on the advice of the Egyptians. Thus in the early chapters of the book the months were out of phase with the seasons so that September, for instance, was really July. In 46 BC, sixty-seven extra days were inserted into the calendar to solve this problem.

Readers may be interested to know what happened

to the surviving characters after the end of the story. Iras and Charmion, faithful to death, died with Cleopatra. Olympus lived on and wrote a biography of her, which has unfortunately not survived. Octavian became the first emperor of Rome and lived until a month before his seventy-seventh birthday. Seeing Ptolemy Caesarion and Antony's eldest son, Antyllus, as possible rivals, he executed both of them, Caesarion being lured back from India for this purpose. However, Octavia succeeded in persuading her brother to spare Antony and Cleopatra's three surviving children, whom she raised as her own. Herod won back the whole kingdom of Judaea and also lived to a ripe old age, surviving long enough to execute his mother-in-law, Alexandra, his wife, Mariamme, two of his sons and, if legend is to be believed, to perpetrate the Massacre of the Innocents just before the birth of Christ.

Cleopatra continued to be worshipped as a goddess long after her death and many of Alexandria's greatest monuments and architectural masterpieces, such as the famous lighthouse, were believed to have been her work. Like Alexander the Great, she exerted an enduring fascination over her followers in life and became a legend after her death.

SIGNET

Published or forthcoming

Sherry Ashworth

While her husband Richard is away, Stella embarks on a dazzling new career...

Having ostensibly conquered her own personal problems, Stella Martin – once the high priestess of Slim-Plicity – is now preparing to liberate other people from theirs.

Undergoing therapy with the slim-hipped Roland Temple after the departure of her previous therapist Gill, Stella decides that an absentee husband is no bad thing, and in a positive frame of mind she starts up her own therapy group.

Stella visualized the group; now it has formed with the terminally indecisive Sandra and her 'victim' friend Zoë, with Carol the professional patient and Jim the compulsive liar. Stella is their guru. But who will guide Stella through the storm when she finds out the bitter truth about the people she trusts most in the world: Richard and the delicately vulnerable Roland?

Published or forthcoming

LONDON LODGINGS

Claire Rayner

It was 15 September 1855: her wedding day, the day Tilly had dreamed of. All her life she had been bullied: by her father, by the housekeeper and, worst of all, by Dorcas, Tilly's maid. But soon she would be Mrs Frank Quentin.

However, married life, as Tilly quickly learns, is just as full of pitfalls and pain. And when her husband's tragic death is followed by her father's she finds herself in financial straits.

The sparkling first episode in Claire Rayner's new series, The Quentin Quartet, opens its doors on the bustling streets of Victorian London, where grocers vie with haberdashers, trade is on the up … and, in the shadows, jealousy, revenge and greed lie waiting.

SIGNET

Published or forthcoming

BORN IN FIRE

Sarah Hardesty

A child of the wild, unspoilt Clare country-side, Margaret Mary Concannon is as tough, beautiful – and vulnerable – as the exquisite glass sculptures she creates from sand and flame.

Rogan Sweeney, a wealthy and sophisticated Dubliner, is the owner of the Worldwide top international art gallery, who can bring fame and fortune to Maggie: if she will submit to his terms.

But Maggie is not given to submission. Wilful, solitary and determined to be beholden to no one, she is drawn into a tempestuous battle with Rogan over which of them has control of her work, her money, her life – and her heart.

SIGNET

Published or forthcoming

IT TAKES TWO

Maeve Haran

Hotshot lawyer Tess Brien and her ad-man husband Stephen know that a good marriage is hard to keep. They should. Enough of their friends' relationships are crumbling around them. But theirs is a happy home, a secure base for their two lively teenagers.

But when Stephen suddenly gives up his job, leaving a stressed and angry Tess to pick up the bills, and another woman seems determined to have Stephen at any cost, distrust and disruption threaten to destroy their idyllic home …

'Maeve Haran has a feel for the substantial concerns of her readers … which is why she has become required reading for modern romantics' – *The Times*

SIGNET

Published or forthcoming

FIRST BLOOD

Claire Rayner

An American in exile, Dr George Barnabas, forensic pathologist, never imagined that she would exercise anything more than routine professional skills in her new post at the Royal Eastern Hospital, London. Events prove otherwise. Not that the death of a rich, indulged man in late middle age – or a second on a dangerous building site – should necessarily indicate foul play.

But George has learnt not to take events at face value. Launched on a murder investigation, she finds bloody-minded feminine intuition an excellent weapon with which to play the police at their own game. And, of course, the murderer.

SIGNET

Published or forthcoming

Hidden Riches

Nora Roberts

An actress turned antique dealer, Dora Conway believes in living life to the full.

When Dora rents out the empty apartment above her thriving antiques shop to Jed Skimmerhorn, she gets more than she bargained for. An ex-cop with an aching secret buried in his past, Jed will push the world away rather than risk more pain.

Her curiosity aroused by Jed, Dora suddenly finds herself swept into another dangerous mystery – and one that has at its heart the powerful forces of money and obsession. But when she realizes that she has become someone's prey, the danger has already come too close to home …